MIDNIGHT
WOLF

MIDNIGHT WOLF

PROPHECY UNFOLDS

J. LYN JACKSON

CITIOFBOOKS, INC.
3736 Eubank NE Suite A1
Albuquerque, NM 87111-3579
www.citiofbooks.com
Hotline: 1 (877) 389-2759
Fax: 1 (505) 930-7244

Ordering Information:
Quantity sales. Special discounts are available on quantity purchases by corporations, associations, and others. For details, contact the publisher at the address above.

Printed in the United States of America.

ISBN-13:   Softcover   979-8-89391-994-3
                eBook   979-8-89391-995-0

Table of Contents

Hello Lovely Readers,

Every work of fiction holds pieces of truth to it. In this book, the foreign language you will read is not fictional.

It is the Takelma language, use by my native people, The Cow Creek Band of the Umpqua Tribe of Indians. The language technically died in 1934 with the last known native speaker.

There was work done between this speaker, Frances Johnson and linguist Edward Sapir in the early 1900's to document the oral language. Due to this collaboration, work is currently taking place to revive this lost language amongst the people.

The Takelma language was an oral dialect and passed along through generations that way, because of this, it is a language that has a sound chart and not an alphabet. The written form is based on Mr. Sapir's translations as a linguist.

Below I will give the best way to sound out the characters' names that use this language.

Thank you,

J. Lyn

Takelma- Da-gel-ma

Nóox- Rain- NOH-x

Wiláu- Arrow- who-LAH-oo

Yulúm- Eagle- yoo-LOOM

Lóom-Cedar- LOHM

Tiiyú- Waterfall- dee-YOO

Haayí- Cloud- hah-YEE

Yáakhw-Bobcat- YahKW

Wúlx- Enemy- WOOL-x

Chapter 1:

The Start of It All

(Jasmine's POV)

Average.

What a wonderfully unassuming word. Average. What I have wanted to be for as long as I can remember. I just want to fit in with my peers, not stand out and have all these overwhelming expectations. Average—a life never meant for me.

I give a heavy sigh from deep down in my core and flop myself onto my bed. Nothing in my life has ever been average. Not my birth or childhood, and now I am starting my teen years off the same. I rest my head on my pillow, cross my arms over my chest and glare up at my ceiling. I stare at the clouds painted there and wish myself away, while reflecting on my life.

Don't get me wrong, my life is not bad, just highly demanding. I am the only child in my family. My father, Alexander, is Alpha to the Whispering Winds Pack, again not average, nope, largest, wealthiest, and most powerful werewolf pack on the American continent. A pack I am expected to take over when my father decides to retire.

My mother, Abigail, is a witch, her family line is made up of elemental, green and hereditary witches. This gives her a long history of being able to perform magic, passed down through the family and her connection to earth and the elements is intense. She can control all four elements of earth, wind, fire, and water, which is almost unheard of. My mother sits as the head council member for the Witches' Council. The expectation is that one day I will take her place.

That makes me a hybrid. A hybrid child of two immensely powerful beings, with significant and overwhelming expectations of what my life is going to be. A direction has already been set out for me and I am to blindly follow and do great and amazing things in this life. I sigh again, and roll over to my side, bringing my knees up into a fetal position and let a tear slip from my eye.

Today was a disaster. I was working with my mother on a wind-harnessing spell. I memorized and practiced the spell for the last two weeks. I had it down perfectly, I don't know what happened. I was standing in the middle of the training grounds, concentrating on the power of the wind, and I must have missed a word, or uttered it incorrectly. Next thing I know I sent a tornado into the main dining hall.

Luckily, nobody was in the dining hall, but we are going to have to construct an entire new building and find a way to feed all the warriors while it is being built. My dad's warriors flooded to the area, some shifted and some in human form, ready to defend the pack. There was confusion on their faces when they arrived and there was no threat, then there was laughter when they realized my magic had gone awry.

Mortified, all I could do was flee from the area, run to the sanctuary of my room. Run from the mistake I made and disaster I caused. Here I am now, wishing to just be average. No excess powers, no high-profile family and no demands and great expectations weighing on my shoulders. Grabbing my pillow, I cuddle it to my chest, squeezing my eyes shut, wishing I could portal somewhere away from my mistakes.

There is a knock on my door. I can tell by its softness that my mother is on the other side. The thought of seeing anyone at the moment is too much for me, so the knock goes unanswered, my self-pity winning out over etiquette.

Soon after her gentle, caring voice calls out to me. "Jasmine, honey, are you okay? Can I come in, sweetheart?"

Realizing Mom will not go away, I raise my head from the pillow and call for her to come in. Mom slowly opens the door and peeks around the edge. She has a slight smile on her face and her green eyes shine warmly.

Mom comes over and sits on the edge of my bed and runs her fingers through my hair. She giggles softly and says, "I remember the first time I did that spell. While I didn't take down a whole building, I did dump your grandfather into the lake. I will never forget the surprised look on his face. I really thought I was in for it, but your grandfather came out of the lake, took me by the hands and let me know I gave it a great try and we were going to continue working on it. I am here to tell you the same thing, love, we are going to continue working on it. You can never perfect something unless you practice. Besides," she laughs, "it was time for a new dining hall anyway, the one we had was getting too small."

I look at my mother, tears shining in my identical green eyes. I sit up, throw my arms around her shoulders. She tightens her arms around me. I bury my face in her neck, breathe in deeply of her comforting scent, and mumble, "I love you so much, Mom."

"I love you too, honey," she says. "Now let's get some lunch and begin planning a new dining hall."

Nodding in agreement, we stand together, Mom helps me wipe the tears from my eyes and waits while I finish composing myself with a few deep breaths. Arm in arm we head to my door, reaching out for the door handle a flame bursts out from my palm, charring the wood of the door. Surprised, we look at each other.

"Well, it appears you will have at least two powers. We better start training you to control all of the elements just in case you have the same gift as me. Otherwise, we may not have a house to live in for long." Mom laughs gently, wrapping her arm around my shoulders and giving me a side hug.

It is beginning to look like average is a dream that will have to be given up.

Chapter 2:

Birthday

(Jasmine's POV)

I stand, looking at myself in my mirror. My raven hair falls, straight and flat to the middle of my back. This hair holds no curl, no matter how hard I try. It limits me in what I can do for hairstyles, down, partially up or up.

My green eyes look back at me from my heart-shaped face as I look at myself critically in the mirror. I have always thought my nose looked like a bubble, but as I get older it has narrowed out. My lips, I think, are my best feature, full and pouty, with a natural pink color to them, rarely do I have to add any gloss or stain to them. I am blessed with naturally tanned skin, inherited from my father.

If I could change one thing about myself, though, I think it would be my height. I stand 5 foot 11 inches, putting me on average with most males my age, well, most males in general.

I look at my outfit for the day and sigh. I am wearing a dusty pink coldshoulder shirt and jean shorts that sit about mid-thigh, finishing off the look is my favorite pair of beige sandals. My hair is pulled up into a high ponytail. I decided not to do my make-up, feeling in the natural kind of mood. My outfit looks good on my lithe and toned frame, but I just feel like there is something missing. Like there is something else I need. I shrug my shoulders, yep, this is me, Jasmine Rose Oscuro, daughter of Alpha Alexander and Luna Abigail Oscuro, soon-to-be Alpha of the Whispering Winds Pack and counselor on the Witches' Council.

My father decided today the pack would all be having breakfast in the main dining hall together. I can't believe five years ago today, I knocked down the old one by sending a tornado through it. I shake my head and smile to myself at the memory, while some of the awkwardness of that age is gone, there is still plenty looming in this body.

Although, with training and the help of my mother, I am a master of my powers, well, somewhat. No longer are the pack buildings in jeopardy of being destroyed at my hand. The time on my bedside clock catches my eye as my reminiscing comes to an end, guess I better get going to the dining hall, time to get this birthday celebration started.

Today is my 18th birthday. I graduated a couple months ago from high school and have been splitting my time between training with my dad to take over the Alpha position, training with my mom for the Witches' Council, and volunteering in the clinic.

I know I am taking over as Alpha, but medicine is my passion. I really enjoy being able to help folks and being as I am part witch, I have the ability to help wolves heal quicker than we already do. Werewolves have the special ability to heal significantly faster than humans. My powers allow me to decrease that healing time even more.

Turns out I have all the same powers as my mother and a few others, such as the ability to heal. Yay for being average. I still hold on to the dream from five years ago but am slowly accepting it will not happen.

Excitement flows through my veins as I make my way down the stairs from my family's floor, and I can hardly contain my giddiness. Today I may get to meet my wolf. Normally a hybrid child only gets one of their parents' powers and since we already know I have my mother's powers I may not get a wolf. A conscious effort has been made on my part to not get my hopes up, but with the day being here, my emotions are running my thought process.

Maybe that is what I feel is missing. My wolf and I will share a body, but have two minds, a being who is always with me and knows me. My other half.

My, hopefully, partner in crime. Of course, if I do have both of my parents powers my entire life of attempting to blend in and stay under the radar will have been in vain. I will essentially become an anomaly. Signing at the split feelings on the subject, my thoughts bring up the only response that can be given, we will get our answers at midnight.

I exit through the front door and begin to descend the marble staircase, my mother had it redone the same time as the new dining hall. She wanted a more elegant look, since we are a bunch of animals. My mom has a wonderful sense of humor, but every now and then she misses on the joke.

As I get to the last step, I catch movement out of the corner of my left eye, right before somebody flings their arms around me, wrapping me in a tight hug. It's my best friend Ashley. Five foot 8 inches of fire and spunk. She's a sassy redhead with bright blue eyes and a smile that can brighten the darkest night and is also the daughter of my father's Beta.

Her brother Ezekiel is thought to be next in line as my Beta. I would not mind having him. That boy is a computer genius, outstanding warrior and so levelheaded. Plus, I am already like a little sister to him so that just makes things even better.

"Happy birthday to my sister from another mother and father! I am so excited to see if you have a wolf! I wonder what they will look like! I hope mine is red, yours can be gray! A dark gray! That would look amazing with your green eyes! We can go on runs and hunt! Oh, we can even start our wolf training together. Who do you think will shift first tonight me or you? I am going with me, because, as we all know, I am the wolf who can't be beat!" Ashley finishes her torrent of questions and ramblings with an infectious laugh.

Wrapping my arms around her, returning the hug, we laugh together. There is no way to have melancholy thoughts when Ashley is around. Besides being best friends, we also share a birthday. There is no one else I would rather share my day with. Arms linked, we head off towards the dining hall.

Ashley looks at me with dreamy eyes and giggles excitedly. "Do you think we'll find our mates today, Jazz?"

The Moon Goddess pairs each wolf with a mate. A wolf's mate is the other half of their soul. When we first find our mate, there is an amazing scent only a mate can smell, tingles when touching skin to skin, and once eye contact is made, the eyes pull you in and a wolf can get lost in the depths of the window to the soul. A bond develops and instantly your lives are intertwined, and you live for each other. A mate can reject the other, but this causes great pain and in some instances death. Death depends on where you are in the marking and mating process when rejected.

"I am not overly worried about a mate right now. I have enough on my hands learning the position of Alpha and getting prepared for the Witches' Counsil." I sigh.

Chatting excitedly with each other, in no time at all we arrive at the large dining hall. We enter in through the double doors, and a chorus of…

"Happy Birthday!"

"Look, it's the birthday girls!"

"Congrats on shifting tonight!"

"Who is going to be the lucky mate?"

"Finally, adults."

The remarks fill the air and space around us. The pack members surround us, giving us hugs, pats on the back and well wishes. Happiness flows over me accepting the affection and attention of my packmates. This is what pack is about, family, caring, loyalty and love.

Afterwards we sit down to an amazing breakfast, all of mine and Ashley's favorite morning foods: waffles, eggs, bacon, fresh fruit, juice, and coffee, lots of coffee. I may or may not have an addiction to the roasted bean, especially with creamer in it, vanilla is my favorite flavor bringing out the creaminess and giving a warm internal hug as it flows into the stomach.

My dad looks over at me and asks, "So, what are your plans today, my dear?" I look up into his dark brown eyes and smile. For being in his forties he looks amazing. He has raven-black hair like me, a square, strong jawline, eyes that can be hard as stone or as gentle as a doe's depending on mood. He is 6 feet 8 inches tall and as broad as a barn, alright, not that broad, but still a big guy. I don't think my dad has an ounce of fat on him. Not a figure I would want to meet unexpectedly on a dark street.

I swallow a mouthful of bacon and eggs before speaking. "Ashley and I discussed going into Lookingglass to the mall and spa, if that is alright? We can take my car and we'll be back by five o'clock since the party is going to start at 7 P.M.," I replied.

My father takes a moment and pretends to be thinking it over. He turns and looks at my mother, with mischief in his eyes. "I just don't know, Jazz. What do you think, Abby?" he asks, turning to my mother.

My mother looks back at him with the same amount of mischief in her green eyes.

My mom is absolutely stunning. She is 5 foot 9 inches tall. We share the same facial and body structures, but her hair is auburn. She and my dad together make quite the feisty pair, but there is no doubt they are the absolute best Alpha and Luna.

"Well, I do have some chores that need done around the packhouse. The dining hall needs cleaned, decorated, and tonight's menu finalized...," Mom says.

Ashley and I look at each other, dismayed. It sounds like Mom has already planned out the day for us and our plans of a girls' day has just gone down the drain.

"But I guess, maybe, just this once is alright, can't have the girls accusing us of treating them like Cinderella," Mom quips, causing Ashley and I to look up, understanding dawning on us we have been being teased. "My only condition is you take Claire with you," Mom finishes, putting a slight damper on my festive mood.

I look at Ashley and roll my eyes. Claire is more brawn than most of our male fighters, I doubt a feminine outing is her style. Recently Mom and Dad have not been letting me leave pack lands without a guard. At least this time they are choosing to send a female, well, sort of. Ashley just shrugs her shoulders and nods.

I look back at my mother and say, "That sounds fine to us. May we go as soon as we are done with breakfast?" My father's voice reenters the conversation, "That sounds fine. Let's make sure Claire is ready to go."

His eyes go hazy as he mind-links Claire. Once his eyes are back to normal, he reaches into his shirt pocket and pulls out a card for me and one for Ashley.

"I guess you ladies should open your cards before running off to town, though."

He hands them over to us and we eagerly grab them. Ashley delicately opens hers and I slip a finger into an opening and rip it apart—who keeps the envelope anyway?

The message inside from Mom and Dad is very endearing. Reading through tears spring to my eyes and I feel emotions of love and gratitude well up inside me. My parents have always been amazingly supportive and patient with me; my hope is that I grow into a daughter and leader they will be proud of.

Accompanying the birthday card is a credit card with my name on it and a gift certificate to my and Ashley's favorite spa. I cannot wait to break in the credit card and spend a day at the spa.

Ashley has been viewing her card at the same time, she appears to be as emotional as me. My parents have always treated Ashley and her brother like their own children. Ashley's parents have been the same with me. Not knowing the message written for her, it appears to be heartfelt and touching. She also has a gift certificate to the same spa, and they have given her a gift card for use at the mall today.

I get out of my seat and run over to my parents, wrapping them both into a tight hug. "Thank you so much. I love you both more than you will ever know."

My dad squeezes me back and says, "You girls have an amazing day. Pamper yourselves as much as possible." Dad turns away from me for a moment, clears his throat and turns back, "After today the real work is going to begin." Dad follows that with a wink and smile.

Mom also squeezes me back and sniffs a little. "You girls call when you get into town and again when you are getting ready to come home. I love you so much."

Ashley and I turn to each other and squeal in excitement. We run out of the dining hall towards my car.

"Don't forget Claire!" my dad yells after us.

Chapter 3:

Girls' Day

(Jasmine's POV)

Ashley, Claire, and I pull into the parking lot at the Lookingglass Mall, find a parking place, then walk into the mall through their grand entryway, bypassing vendors selling the newest phone cases and sunglasses. We have come into the human city for shopping. Our pack grounds have small shops, restaurants and a bookstore, it is more of a small town, so there are no places for actual shopping.

"Alright, ladies, we have arrived. Shall we try out this new credit card my dad and mom have given me?" I ask with a smile.

Ashley lets out a squeal and Claire takes in a deep breath, steeling herself for what is to come.

I don't mind the fact Claire is with us. She is five years older than Ashley and me, and at times it seems Claire can barely tolerate us. She is very dedicated to her role as lead female warrior and is highly serious about it. I doubt she will be interacting with Ashley and me today on a personal level. That is alright. I still plan on springing on a manicure for her at the spa.

The three of us make our way farther into the mall. It is just reaching 11 o'clock, so we have a few hours prior to our spa appointments. Ashley wants to look for dresses for tonight's party. Claire looks like she is going die of boredom at a moment's notice, the mischief maker in me decides to make her pay a little.

"I think starting off with dress shopping is perfect, Ash. Then we can go and buy our shoes and accessories, ooh, new make-up should be in order too. We will be the belles of the ball tonight," I say enthusiastically.

I see Claire pale at the thought of shoe shopping. Inside I have a huge smile on my face. I am by no means a girly girl, but there are times I am surprised Claire knows what a dress is. She has always been all about clothing for training and patrolling.

We go inside and find our favorite shop. It is a quaint place but carries amazing styles and the staff is always extremely helpful. We head directly to the dress section. Our favorite assistant, Susan, notices us, raises a hand in welcome and comes over.

"How can I assist you lovely ladies today?" she asks, a smile spreading across her features.

"Today is our birthdays and we need new outfits for our party this evening," Ashley informs her, excitement clear in her voice and body language.

"I have the perfect selection for you girls! They just came in today and I haven't been able to get them out on the racks yet. Follow me," Susan states, matching Ashley's excitement level.

At this Claire raises her eyebrows and looks around suspiciously. Checking to see if there are any hidden areas or threats. She tilts her head slightly up, sniffing the air subtly.

"Oh, Claire, Susan helps us all the time, she is not a threat. Come on already," I say, slightly annoyed at her demeanor.

We follow Susan to the back of the store, and she begins pulling out dozens of new dresses. Ashley and I are excited to be the first ones to get to see them and choose. An amazing creation catches my eye. It is a simple halter top summer dress; the top starts out as dusty pink and the farther down it gradually turns into a burgundy. There are white jasmine flowers imprinted over it. I grab the dress and rush to try it on. Ashley is right behind me with a choice she managed to find.

We decide to share a changing room, since we know Claire has no interest in seeing what our selections look like. I try on my dress; it fits like a dream and the fabric is so soft on my skin. Ashley is gushing over the way it fits and how I look in it.

"You are amazingly beautiful. This dress is a must. Perfect for our party," Ashley squeals excitedly.

Ashley tries on a great mint green and silver dress. It complements her red hair beautifully. It has capped sleeves and hugs her figure falling just above her knee. She giggles in delight, and I encourage her to take the dress. It is perfect. Lucky for Claire, the first shop we came to had what we wanted; she is getting off easy. We may need to spend extra time in the make-up department, a mischievous smile crosses my face.

We make our purchases, thanking Susan for her time and assistance.

Promising to have a splendid day and let her know how our party goes.

"See, Claire, no danger at all," I remark as we leave the shop.

Claire just grunts at me and continues to follow us.

Our next stop is for shoes to match perfectly with our clothing choices. I have to suppress a giggle when Claire snaps at Ashley to hurry up and decide between three pairs of shoes. Being rushed, Ashley opts to buy all three pair, stating it is her birthday and it can be a present from her brother, who probably forgot a present anyway. Once finished with shoes we found our make-up and accessories, keeping that part quick.

Our time was getting short, and we still needed to get lunch. At the mention of food Claire's eyes light up. Finally, a part of our trip she likes.

As we sit eating our pizza and drinking our Cokes, Claire sits straight up and starts looking around. Ashley and I look up from our meals confused. I take a moment and sniff the air. There is a sour smell, mixed with dirt and decay.

I scrunch my nose up, "What is that smell?" I ask in disgust.

"Rogues" is the single word reply from Claire. "Girls, get your things. We are done here," Claire states.

Rogues are wolves that either choose to live outside of a pack or have been kicked out of their pack for some crime. Generally, if they have been kicked out due to crimes, their wolves become more feral, and they end up with a particular scent, they also tend to be more aggressive and vicious. That is what we are smelling now.

We grab our bags and make our way out to my car. Claire is on high alert the entire time, scoping the area for any imminent threat. We get to the car, pile in our things, and leave the mall without incident. I start heading towards the spa.

"I think we should head back home. With rogues being in the area it is safer for you to be on pack lands. Since it is your birthday today and you may end up with a wolf, there are many dangers out there to you," Claire says from the passenger seat.

"Oh, Claire, no one followed us out of the mall, you saw that. Rogues can go shopping too, you know. I appreciate you are taking this task seriously, but there really is no danger," I snap back.

"I really think it is better if we return home. You and Ashley can pamper yourselves in the packhouse and do your girl day there" comes Claire's terse remark.

"Well, too bad. I am the one driving and I am driving to the spa. Feel free to mind-link my father if you must, but I am going to the spa and enjoying my day," I retort.

Perhaps my behavior is petulant and childish, but Claire's reaction to the rogues grates on my nerves. Being cautious is important, but currently, I think she is being excessive.

Claire grits her teeth and sets her jaw but discontinues the conversation with me. Soon we pull up in front of the spa. Ashley and I jump out of the car, excitement oozing off us. Claire dutifully follows us in. Ashley and I have a full treatment planned, massage, facial, manicure and pedicure. Perfect pampering for a birthday. We quickly get started, very happy to begin with a massage.

During my facial I am leaned back in my chair, I have on a clay mask with a gel pack on my eyes. In an instant the entire room has a sour smell, overriding the floral scent the spa had moments before, the same sour smell from the mall. I am momentarily confused and then I hear a thud. I call out to the attendant in the room but receive no answer. I start to sit up but am roughly pushed back into the chair. A hand comes around my throat and begins to squeeze, closing off some of my air, but not completely.

"You are coming with us, little Alpha," a rough sandpapery voice rasps out. "If you choose to fight, the people in here die. You don't want to be the cause of unnecessary death, do you?" questions the voice.

I try to squeak out an answer but can only manage a high-pitched sound. Without warning the hand is torn away from my throat and a raspy grunt is heard as there is another thud in the room. Jumping up, I yank the gel pack from my eyes and see Claire engaged in a fight with the man who tried to take me. "Get Ashley and run!" yells Claire.

I run out of the room to find Ashley, I am quickly filling her in on what is happening as we race through the establishment, making our way to the car, we see three large bodies blocking the door and our path to safety. I push Ashley behind me.

"Go lock yourself in the bathroom and call my dad," I direct.

She breaks away and does as I ask her; without our wolves we are unable to mind-link and Claire is busy with a rogue in the other room to be certain she has been able to reach out.

I look around me to see what I have to work with. There is not much to use in the way of self-defense in a spa. I back into the room, where Claire has managed to put the first rogue down. I do not know if he is unconscious or dead.

"I thought I told you to get Ashley and run," snarls Claire.

"I tried to, but three large bodies thought we needed to stay here. Ashley is locked in the bathroom calling my dad," I reply.

Just then we hear a terrified scream. Claire and I jump out of the room we are in.

Chapter 4:

First Fight

(Jasmine's POV)

Bursting into the main room, Claire and I notice one of the men has Ashley pinned against the wall.

"Who do you think you were calling?" snarls the evil-looking man.

"No one. I was just calling my boyfriend to see if he was ready for our party," Ashley lied.

"Nice try," he snarls. He looks over in our direction and the yellow of his eyes pierces into me. They have the same sour, dirt, and decay smell as the other man. "Get the black-haired girl and kill the other one," the evil man directs the other two men.

Claire is already in a defensive pose from the moment we left the room. She is ready and begging to continue the fight from earlier. She almost looks excited.

"Just stay behind me and let me take care of them. The moment you can, get out of here and run," Claire states with steely resolve.

There is no way I am going to leave Claire to fight alone. I may not have my wolf, but I have been training in human form for fifteen years. My dad started me early and I do know how to fight; I just never had to outside the training ring.

Lowering down into a defensive pose next to Claire, she looks at me sideways letting out a huff. She can't really argue since I have nowhere to run to and Ashley is still being held captive.

The two men cautiously approach us with smirks on their faces.

"These two really think they are going to challenge us. This should be entertaining and short lived," the short, squat one chuckles.

His buddy with dark hair and a beard just snorts back with mirth.

The short one lunges forward, and Claire catches him under the jaw with an upper cut, setting him back on his heels.

He shakes his head and glares at her, "Fine, you want to play rough, we will play rough, little wolfy, your death will be a delight," he snarls maliciously. He lunges again and this time his buddy lunges with him. The short one kicks Claire in the hip, but she recovers and counters with a leg sweep knock-

ing him off his feet.

The bearded man lunges at me aiming a punch to my stomach. I am able to sidestep him and use his momentum to push him headfirst into a wall. His head makes a dent, but he pulls away and reengages with me. He throws a naildrying lamp at me and while I dodge it he delivers a punch to my left cheek. My head explodes into stars, but I refuse to give in.

While I am getting my senses back, he grabs me by my throat and pushes me against the wall squeezing off my air. At this point I have lost sight of Claire and Ashley. I know I must continue to fight; I don't know if Ashley has managed to get ahold of my dad.

As my vision starts to dim, I frantically feel around me for anything I can use as a weapon. My hand lands into something hot and sticky. I scoop some of the hot sticky stuff onto my fingers and bring up my hand rubbing it into the bearded man's eyes. He lets out an agonizing scream and lets loose of my throat, tearing at his eyes with his fingers attempting to dislodge the goo.

I fall to the ground, roll out of the way of the thrashing man, and recover my breath. I see Claire fighting with the short man and making headway. She is more powerful than her opponent and is quickly dominating the fight with him. She is pounding his face at the moment, but he refuses to go down. She picks him up and hurls him into a wall and then leaps on him. She is like a cat playing with her prey.

I search around the room for Ashley and see she is engaging with the evil guy. He definitely has the upper hand in this battle, and I jump in to assist her. As I am running to her aid I stop and get more wax on my fingers. I jump on the evil guy's back and smear the wax into his eyes too. This time it is not as effective. I don't know if it has cooled down, but it is making it difficult for him to see. As I hang on his back distracting him, Ashley kicks him in the manly parts. He lets out a deep breath and falls to his knees. I jump off his back, grab a chair and bring it down over his head. He slumps to floor, oblivious to the world around him.

I turn around to see Claire has managed to subdue the short guy. We look around for rope but cannot find any in the salon. We decide to use wires from the computers to tie them up while they are still unconscious. Once done we set them up against the wall, keeping them in our sites while Claire grabs her phone to call back to the pack.

Just as she starts to dial, the front door of the spa bursts open and through it comes a very angry man, letting out a monstrous growl, eyes black as night, canines and claws extended, followed by ten others at the ready as the first man. Their wolves are in control. My father has arrived with his Beta, Gamma and eight of his best warriors. I guess Ashley managed the call, after all.

My father looks around the room, searching for the threat and sees the three men tied up and unconscious. "You did some nice work here, Claire. Thank you for taking such good care of my daughter and Ashley," my father says to Claire.

"Well, sir, I cannot take credit for all of this. Both Jasmine and Ashley fought beside me," Claire responds back.

My father looks at me with a mixture of pride, fear, and anger. He walks over, wraps me in his arms and hugs me tightly. "You will be an amazing Alpha; I am so proud of you. I love you so much," he whispers into my ear.

I just hang on to him, the moment catching up with me. Ashley is wrapped in her father's embrace as well.

"Get these rogues to our cells. We will interrogate them later. Young lady, let's get you three home," my father says with authority.

The warriors come and grab the rogues, forcing them into one of the vehicles they brought. My father insists on driving my car back with us. Claire gladly jumps into one of the SUVs, switching places with Ashley's dad, Mark. On the way home we tell my dad the entire story. He is quiet and thinking.

"We will get to the bottom of it, once we question them," my father says quietly. "I am so glad we sent Claire, also that you and Ashley have been trained from a young age. Today could have had a terrible ending. Maybe we should delay the party," my father says.

"Oh, Daddy, please, no. You have trained me and Ashley for circumstances like this. Yes, it was scary and I am so glad you came to save us, but Daddy, Ashley and I will only have this celebration once in our lives. We are stronger than you think we are. Please don't take this from us," I plead with him, giving him my best puppy-dog eyes and pout.

He quickly glances my way and gives a chuckle. Looking in the rearview mirror he sees Ashley nodding her head in agreement to what I have said, Dad says, "What do you think, Mark? Should we have the party?"

"Well, Alpha, we will be on pack lands, we can increase border security and we know the girls can fight effectively. All three took down those rogues in human form so we know they can handle themselves. I think maybe we do forget how strong our baby girls are. I think a little happiness is in order after their day," Mark replies.

My father graciously gives in. He is looking at my face and neck, storm clouds cover his eyes. I know things will not go well for the rogues being brought back to the cells.

Once we arrive back at the packhouse Ashley and I are wrapped in our mothers' arms. They are fretting over us and quickly escort us into the house. We end up in the kitchen with hot cups of tea in front of us. Mom says it is to help calm our nerves, but I think it is more for her and Patricia's nerves. Patricia is our Beta female, Ashley's mother. They insist we tell them all that happened.

We recount the story, leaving nothing out. Our mothers look livid and proud. I think it is best for those rogues they are in the cells with guards; otherwise, they may lose their lives to these pack mamas.

I look at my mother and say, "Mom, I think we need to work on me using my magical powers in a fight. Today I didn't even think to use them, and I am not even sure I would know how. I think it is time we added in this new training."

My mother looks at me and nods in agreement. "I think you are correct. I was thinking of the same thing. We can start tomorrow, but tonight is about you girls and your next steps in life."

Chapter 5:

Party Time

(Jasmine's POV)

Ashley and I have been up in my room since our mothers allowed us to leave their presence, ensuring we had come to no actual harm. Due to the attack security has been increased, we of course have guards at the door and for the foreseeable future I will have a team of five guards headed by none other than Claire.

Honestly, I am alright with this. Since our ordeal today I have developed a new respect for her. A respect I should have had from the start. Claire was willing to take on all the rogues so me and Ashley could escape unharmed, selfless, and loyal, she deserves recognition, I am thinking about making her my Gamma in the future.

Ashley is spread across my Queen-sized bed, looking up at the ceiling and moving her arms back and forth over my teal velvet comforter. "I love the feel of this fabric on my skin," she sighs. "I should get one too, but in pink, pastel pink, with flowers. That would be perfect," she states, drawing my mind back to the present.

I laugh at her comment and flop down next to her. My ceiling still has the clouds painted on it as it did five years ago. That is the one thing in my room that never changed, my little private escape, a small smile graces my lips at the memory of that day. Looking back one can see the humor of the situation, one that brought my mother and I closer.

I turn my head to the right and look at Ashley, "Well, should we begin to prepare for our party, birthday girl? It has been a birthday we won't forget so far, so we may as well end the night strong, hopefully with no more violence. Maybe a little harmless flirting and dancing, lots of dancing," I say with more energy than I actually have.

Ashley turns to look at me, this is when I notice she has tears brimming on her lashes. "I am so glad you were with me today. I am so glad we managed to fight them off. We have trained for years, but none of that training came close to what an actual fight of life and death is like. I was so scared. Scared to die, scared to lose you, scared of so much. I love you," she sobbed.

I roll over and wrap her in a hug, letting her tears soak the fabric covering my shoulder, this is the first time she has broken down. I let her have this moment, Goddess knows we earned it. I continue to hold her and rub her back.

After a few minutes she pulls herself together, wipes her eyes, gives a little hiccup and a laugh. Looking me in the eyes she says, "Let's get this mess cleaned up," gesturing towards her body and face, "and show this pack how to throw a real birthday party, my sister."

I laugh and nod my head. I get up from the bed, turn to Ashley holding out my hands and help her get up. Ashley runs and calls dibs on the first shower. While she is the bathroom, I take that opportunity to lay out our dresses. I am excited for what the evening will bring.

Ashley comes out of the shower wrapped in a towel, makes a mock bow and says, "The bathroom is all yours, milady."

I giggle at her and go in to take my shower. Shortly I am back out in my room wrapped in a towel. We get dressed and do each other's hair. I have decided to wear mine down but have French braids crossed over the top. Ashley is going for the cascading waterfall curls down her back, a smidge of jealousy hits me looking at her hair, oh, to have curls! With this hair of mine curls will always be a dream.

I decide on a light natural look for my make-up and Ashley follows in my footsteps. We finally feel like we are ready to go to our party. Looking at the clock we have five minutes until it starts, but who really expects the birthday duo to be on time.

Ashley and I link arms, walk out of my bedroom, and begin to descend the stairs. The Alpha quarters are on the eighth floor of the packhouse so we have a few flights to get down before walking to the main dining hall. We get to the main floor, where we see our families waiting for us. Surrounded by guards and loved ones, we make our way to our birthday celebration.

We enter the main dining hall and all the tables have been moved to the sides up against the walls, making an amazing buffet. There are so many wonderful foods spread out over the tables. I think back with a little guilt, we never did help finalize the menu.

Mom sees the look on my face and whispers in my ear, "We just decided to have everything with the day you girls had. Happy birthday, my love."

I look at her, smiling, she always knows when I need reassurance.

The room looks amazing, balloons and streamers done in my and Ashley's favorite colors, teal and pastel pink. Flower bouquets of lilies, daisies and sunflowers are set in the center of tables scattered around the room. Near the back wall is a dance floor and DJ booth, music is pumping through the entire building. It is a great start.

"This looks amazing! Thank you so much," I say to my parents, Mark and Patricia.

Ashley echoes my gratitude. We have gigantic smiles across our faces, and we begin mixing with the crowd.

Ashley links arms with me to my right side, but I notice a presence directly to my left. None of my guards dare to stand this close to me, I look over and see a very protective Ezekiel next to me, keeping an eye over his little sisters.

Ezekiel looks at Ashley and me. "Happy birthday, My Sun and My Moon. I cannot wait to meet your wolves. I know you have one, Jazz; I can feel it. You and Ash are meant to be special and accomplish great things together."

Ezekiel has always called me My Moon, and Ashley, My Sun. Zeke says we complement each other, and we are not whole without the other and he is not whole without both of us. It is rather sweet.

The time flies by as we dance, eat, and visit with pack members. People get up and tell embarrassing stories about the mischief Ashley and I got into as young pups. The shared memories bring tears of delight to my eyes as the laughter is abundant and my sides are beginning to ache from it. A better party could not have been planned.

There is a consensus the pack hopes it won't continue into our adult years. Ashley and I just share a knowing smirk.

In what seems like no time at all my dad takes the stage, the music stops, and the pack is called to attention. My father starts his speech.

"Welcome, pack. We are here this evening to celebrate a very special birthday for Jasmine and Ashley. Today these amazing young ladies turn 18. They enter with us into adulthood and the next stage of their lives. Tonight, we hope to see both gain their wolves. As we know Jasmine has been blessed with her mother's powers so it is possible she may be without a wolf. Ashley, though, will turn and let us all enjoy greeting this new wolf and taking their first runs with them."

At this the pack breaks out into cheers and well wishes.

It is nearing midnight so we all head outside. Ashley and I disrobe behind a tree and come out covered in blankets. We kneel on the ground next to each other and clasp hands. We have watched many first-time shifts, we know it will not be a comfortable ordeal, there is some apprehension regarding the pain we will endure, at least that Ashley will endure. I will do everything I can to make sure her transition is as smooth as possible.

I am hoping beyond hope I have a wolf. I want nothing more than to share this moment with my best friend. How could I be an Alpha without a wolf? I am sure multiple people have thought this but were waiting to bring it up as an issue. Tonight will tell my future. Oh, please, Moon Goddess, bless me with a wolf.

As midnight draws near Ashley lets go of the hold she has on my hand and drops down on all fours letting out an agonizing scream of pain, once the scream stops, she pants trying to fill her lungs with air. Soon her back hunches up and hair begins to sprout out over her body. Snaps and cracks of breaking bones can be heard as her skeletal system rearranges. The first shift is always the most painful, we have been told, and from watching her I see it is not a lie. I reach out and lay a comforting hand on my friend. Tears form in my eyes and I wish there is something I can do to help with this pain she is in. I have healing powers as half-witch, but they do not reduce pain. I wish so badly they did.

Chapter 6:

Meeting the Wolves

(Jasmine's POV)

Ashley's breath is coming in short gasps between her screams of pain and agony. Tears are streaming from her eyes. As the shift is progressing, she forms a snout. Next come her paws. After about twenty minutes the transformation is complete and before me stands a deep red wolf with three white socks, two on the front and one on the back. She also has a white moon, crown in the center with a sword through it in the middle of her forehead. She is stunning. I am so incredibly happy for my friend, my sister. I slowly reach my hand out to her, and she places her head under it.

"You are the most beautiful wolf ever, Ashley. Looks like you didn't get the red you wanted, but this deep red is close and gorgeous. You did an amazing job."

Ashley gently licks my hand, turns her head to the side and looks at me expectantly.

I look down at the ground slightly disappointed and sad. "I don't think I am going to be blessed with a wolf. We knew this was a possibility. It is alright, Ashley. You enjoy your—"

I don't get to finish my sentence. An intense pain sweeps over my body, taking my breath away as if my lungs have been punctured by a knife. I suddenly feel like I am burning up in flames. Thousands of spears are piercing my body all at once. I try to breathe through the sensations, I try to hold back from screaming, but eventually a guttural sound leaves my lips. Soon I hunch over the same as Ashley had done and the snapping and cracking of bone can be heard again, only this time, it is my body. After thirty minutes of torture my transformation is complete. I am so thankful the pain is only the first time through.

I stand on shaky legs and take in a few deep breaths. I hear the crowd gasping and staring at me. I am sure they are all as surprised as I am that I have a wolf. I have become the anomaly I was worried about. I am a product of two opposing worlds, who possesses the power of both parents. Life has just become even more complicated and dangerous for me. There are people who will see me as a threat because of all the power I hold. I am so deep in thought and concern; it doesn't even occur to me to see what my wolf looks like. I hear my father through our mind-link.

"Jasmine, your wolf is the most splendid wolf I have ever seen. What is your wolf's name?"

Her name? I haven't even thought to ask my wolf her name. I have been so deep in thought and surprised to be blessed with a wolf, I had hoped, but didn't expect it.

I search around in my mind for my wolf's presence, I feel her. "Hello?" I say tentatively. "Are you there? Are you alright? What is your name? I am so excited to get to know you, to share our lives."

There is silence for a moment and then a voice that sounds like a bubbling stream says, "My name is Brooke, I am so happy to finally meet you. We are going to grow strong together and face many challenges. We will accomplish many great things."

I giggle and respond back. "Did you speak to Zeke before our birthday party? He said almost the same thing to me."

My wolf is softspoken and calm, this is not what I expected for a new wolf, but to be honest, I really don't have any comparisons to go from. Many people don't speak to me about their wolves knowing I have my mother's powers. It seems they were being gentle with my feelings.

"No, Young One, you are the first I have spoken to."

The breeze begins blowing through my fur and I hear a gentle whisper brushing by me.

"Run, young one, run and feel your new being. Run and look at yourself in the lake." As soon as the sentence is done the wind stops and all is still.

I look around in amazement. It doesn't seem anyone else has heard the whispers. "Did you hear the whispers, Brooke?"

"I did. Only the two of us can hear them. Listen to them, they will guide you."

I am beginning to think my wolf is an old soul, she is perfect.

I look at Ashley while prancing around, she looks up catching my eye as if reading each other's thoughts, we turn around and take off. I mind-link Ashley, "Let's go see what we look like in the lake."

Ashley and the rest of the pack are right behind me.

Running through the trees and the grass is a new sensation. I have never felt this kind of speed before. I can hear all the small sounds of the forest as we run through, I can smell the leaves, dirt, trees, and nature all around us. I can feel the moonlight giving me energy. This is the most amazing feeling ever.

As we get to the far northern edge of the forest we are running through, I can smell the lake. The lake is in neutral territory between three pack lands. Luckily, we are allies with both packs, Midnight Moon and Red Crescent, so we are safe here. The three packs get together a few times a year and have a bonfire and party, we are all close and it has helped wolves find their mates.

I come to a skidding stop before I reach the bank of the lake and wait for Ashley. I am going to need to go on more runs to get accustomed to this new form, I almost put myself in the lake. Ashley comes up beside me with her tongue lolling out of her mouth. I mind-link her.

"This is such an amazing night, and we get to share it, I am so happy right now. Ashley, what is your wolf's name? Mine is Brooke."

Ashley replies, "Her name is Grace. She is amazingly strong. I am so excited, but Jazz, we need to talk in private."

Ashley sounds so concerned and slightly scared. This is not normal for my bestie.

"Alright, we will, first I want to look in the lake and see Brooke. I see you are concerned, and we will talk about anything you need. Are you ready to see our wolves?" I ask with excitement and a little trepidation.

Ashley, or Grace, nods her head. We slowly make our way into the water.

Chapter 7:

Grace and Brooke

(Ashley's POV)

I slowly walk up to the bank of the river with Jasmine by my side. I am so excited to see my wolf. It is a blessing Jasmine has Brooke with her this evening. A blessing, but this also means great danger to her and the pack, though. Jasmine and her wolf will be sought after because of all the power they have, they are the only hybrid on Earth to possess the powers of both parents. I am worried for my friend and my pack.

I am anxious to see what Grace looks like. I push all my foreboding to the back of my mind; plans will be made once I can speak to Jasmine. I want to enjoy this moment, this connection to my other half. The entire pack was slackjawed when Jasmine and I shifted, causing me excitement and anxiousness.

"Ashley, look into the water and see me, see your other half," Grace encourages me.

I look down and I see my deep red fur, I see the white moon, crown in the center of the moon, with the sword through it on my forehead and my white socks.

"Grace! You are so amazingly beautiful; I love the way we look. You are everything I have ever dreamt of. I have been blessed to have you, but Grace, what does the symbol mean?" I ask nervously.

"The color of your fur represents the blood that will flow from the enemy, for fighting the Queen. The mark is the sign of a Moon Goddess warrior. You have been chosen to protect the person who will be the leader of all wolves, for all supernatural. The one to rule and take our packs into the new era and bring peace between all supernatural beings. You are to be the guardian of our Queen and lead her warriors," Grace tells me.

"How am I supposed to do that when I am not sure who the Queen is, when I am not yet trained in my wolf form? How am I supposed to do this and why was I chosen? I am not special, I do not stand out in anything," I whisper back, ashamed and scared.

"Before you did not have me. We are stronger than you can even imagine. Soon trainers will come to us. We will learn all that is necessary to protect our Queen. She is closer than you know. You have a bond that will not be broken," Grace assures me.

I lay down on my stomach at the lake's edge and rest my head on my paws. I have a lot to think about. I have more to share with Jasmine.

I look over at Jasmine, really seeing her wolf for the first time and my heart skips a beat, my mouth goes dry, and fear runs through my body.

(Jasmine's POV)

The moonlight shining over the lake takes my breath away. I put my nose up and take in all the scents around me. I feel more connected than before. I feel so blessed. I do not know why Moon Goddess has granted me the powers of both parents, but I am thankful for this experience. I thought I would hate it, that this power making me an anomaly would be instant regret. That just is not the case. I am so excited.

I feel the cool water lap at my paws. I walk further in and look down. I am taken aback. Brooke has silvery blue fur and black socks that come up to, what would pass for knees. I look like the night sky turning from soft blue into dark black. On my right shoulder is a full moon with a crown on top in white, inside the moon is a wolf head. Underneath the moon is a wand with three small stars at the end. I take a deep breath and swallow hard.

I am not sure what the mark means, but my wolf is splendid. "Brooke, you are the most amazing wolf I have ever seen. You are so beautiful," I whisper to my wolf.

"Young one, we have much to prepare for. Our training must start immediately. We do not have any time to waste. Our future has been set for us, there will be many trials and tribulations, but Moon Goddess has sent you protectors. We are on a mission to unite the supernatural world. You are to be the Queen that unites us," Brooke tells me with urgency.

I absentmindedly nod my head to her, only half hearing what she has told me, still lost in how splendid her coloring is.

The wind picks up again and I hear a faint whisper, "Welcome, Queen, your time has come. A war is looming. You must prepare." Then the wind goes away.

The air is still, and I feel trepidation come into my being, Brooke's words finally break through the fog of my amazement.

I am to be the Queen that unites the supernatural world. Me? What is going on? There is no way I can be the right person for this! All I want is to fit in with everyday life. I want to study medicine. I am not sure the Moon Goddess got this one correct. I am fine with just finding my mate, becoming Alpha and Luna of the pack and taking my seat on the Witches' Counsil, but Queen? War? A war is coming, and I am supposed to fight it? How am I supposed to fight a war? Who are these protectors? This just can't be correct! I feel nauseous. My heartbeat is increasing, and I feel like I want to run. My feet, however, are planted and my body is still as I have all these doubts and questions.

I am still looking down into the lake, not seeing anything, lost in my mind when I feel a snout push into my neck. I look to my right and my father is standing next to me, concern glows from his eyes.

"Jasmine, we need to go back now. We need to talk about what has happened this evening. We need to protect you. It is no longer safe for you out here," he tells me.

I look over to my left and I see Ashley lying by the bank with anxiety and fear in her eyes. She looks like she is fighting an internal battle and has some doubts, just as I do. I need to speak with her soon, as she requested. I think maybe it is best if Ashley, Mark, Ezekiel, Claire, Simon, my father's Gamma, Mom, my father, and I all meet together.

I look back to my father and nod my head, then walk over to Ashley and gently nudge her with my snout and lick her muzzle. She picks her head up, glaring at me for licking her. I gently bat her with my paw on her shoulder and turn to run. I look back over my shoulder to see if she is following.

Ashley gets up and begins to trot after me. The run back to the packhouse is not filled with the same excitement and joy that the run to the lake was filled with. Even though I have tried to lighten the mood with playful actions, many of us are lost in our thoughts as we run back. I notice this time guards are circled around us. I did not pay attention if this was the case on the run to the lake.

I guess Dad was right; after today the real work does begin.

Chapter 8:

Realization

(Jasmine's POV)

We return to the main grounds with Ashley and I leading the pack, the jovial mood from earlier gone. It is beginning to dawn on me the jovial mood was mine and the pack was anxious since I turned, filled with questions and worries. Finally, we are back to the area of our shift. Dad and the Betas change back to human form and Mom brings blankets to cover our wolves.

"Picture yourselves in your human forms, concentrate on your different body parts and you will shift back. The transformation will be painful, but it shouldn't be as bad as when you changed into your wolf," my dad tells us.

I close my eyes and picture my hair, hands, and legs, I feel needles throughout my body. I do not hear the cracks and snaps as before, but it feels like my muscles are going to pull apart. After about fifteen minutes I look down and see I am on my hands and knees, breathing hard. I wrap the blanket around my naked body, I look over to Ashley.

She is standing a few feet away, wrapped in her blanket and parents' arms, she has a faraway look in her eyes. Her normal bubbly personality has abandoned her.

I walk over to her, I put my forehead on hers and whisper into her ear, "I do not know what is on your mind and in your heart, but whatever it is, we will get through this together. We are family, one. I love you, sister."

"I love you too, Jazz. There is so much before us. We have a destiny I don't know I am made for. I am so worried I will fail you, and that my failure could mean your death. I promise to defend you with all I have. I will always be by your side and have your back. You can count on me," Ashley says quietly. Her entire body is shaking, but the promise in her eyes cannot be doubted.

I am not sure exactly what she is talking about. I think the time for us to have the meeting is now, though.

I look at the rest of the pack and everyone has shifted back to human form. "Thank you all for sharing our transformation and first run," I say to the crowd. "You all have made our day and evening special and reminded us of the love we all share in our pack. I would like to stay with you all for a bit longer, but it is important I meet with my father now. Tonight has been a surprise for us all and I am sure I am not the only one with questions and concerns."

The group quietly nods, it seems they all are wondering what this means for the pack.

"Abby, Jasmine, Ashley, Ezekiel, Claire, Mark, and Simon, please get dressed and meet me in my office. There is much to discuss. Time is imperative," my father says. "Whispering Winds pack, there are things in motion I do not quite understand yet, a change has come to us and our way of life. There is not much I can go into at this time, but I ask you all to keep quiet about Jasmine's and Ashley's wolves for the time being. I will address everyone tomorrow and give more detail then. Have a good night," my father finishes.

The pack members wander off to their homes, or the packhouse, softly talking amongst themselves.

I run to my room and throw on some sweatpants, t-shirt, and tennis shoes. I put my hair up in a ponytail and head to my father's office. Luckily it is located on the eighth floor also.

Our packhouse is shaped in a three-quarter square. The center is a courtyard with the forest behind us. The left side of the eighth floor is the living quarters for the Alpha family, the other side is the Alphas' and Lunas' offices, secure meeting room, small kitchen, and a couple restrooms. In the center we have a few guestrooms for visiting dignitaries.

I walk to my father's office and knock on the door. My father calls for me to come in. I open the door and walk in, against the far end of the room is my father's desk. His back sits against a wall, there are windows on both sides of him, high up the wall and tinted. This allows for natural light, without giving an enemy site of him. In front of his desk are two armchairs. They have very straight backs, and they are designed to be the most uncomfortable chairs imaginable. If you are called up here to meet the Alpha and are required to sit in front of his desk, comfort is the last thing you are granted. To the left of his desk are two couches facing each other with a table in between, at each end of the table are more comfortable armchairs. This is where we will be sitting for the meeting. The walls around Dad's desk hold bookshelves holding scripts about pack history, law, treaty agreements, and so many others, all works for pleasure reading are on bookshelves next to the couches. The right side of the office has a massive table that holds maps; Ezekiel automated the table so the maps can be pulled up as needed. At the moment a detailed map of our pack lands is ready for view.

"Hi, Daddy," I call out as I enter the room, uncertainty is laced through my voice, the importance of what is happening is not lost on me and I fight the butterflies trying to escape my stomach.

"Hi, honey," he replies, running his fingers back through his hair. He is sitting at his desk, looking at the computer screen. His face is emotionless sitting there and the only clue to his nervousness is his habit of messing with his hair. On his desk are multiple books, all open to various positions.

I walk up to his desk and look at the spine on some of the books, making sure not to lose the place. Legends of the Werewolf, History of Werewolves, Werewolf Lore, Werewolf Symbols.

"What are you looking for, Dad?" I ask, interested in all the books lying there.

"Well, sweetheart, there is a prophesy that closely follows what is happening. Your great-grandfather told me the story when I was young, but I did not pay much attention to it. Now it looks like I should have. I am trying to find the meaning of the symbols on your shoulder and Ashley's forehead," he explains to me in a tired voice.

"According to my wolf, Brooke, I am to be the Queen that unites the supernatural world. I will have protectors that come to be trained and will help us train," I say in a low voice.

My father looks up at me with wide eyes. He is about to say something when there is another knock on the door.

Dad turns his attention to the door and beckons for the rest of the group to come in.

"Please, everyone, come in, have a seat on the couches and chairs. Let me grab my laptop and these books. There is a lot to discuss. Jasmine has something to tell everyone about a message her wolf gave her. She is aware of what her symbol means. Ashley, did your wolf speak to you about your symbol?" Dad asked, getting straight to business.

"Grace did speak with me about my symbol. I can explain after Jasmine tells us her story."

Chapter 9:

Understanding

(Jasmine's POV)

The dark-chocolate-colored suede couch is my favorite one, and I choose that as my preferred seat, since it is up against the wall it doesn't move around like the other couch. I sit near the edge with my feet on the floor and lean slightly forward. My deep desire is to cuddle up under a blanket and pretend this is all a dream; unfortunately, I am not able to do that. Getting my nerves in check and thinking through the best way to share my knowledge, I clear my throat and begin.

"When we got to the lake and I was able to view my wolf, Brooke, I asked her what the symbol on my shoulder meant. Brooke told me I am meant to be a Queen. A Queen that is going to unite the supernatural world. After she told me this, the wind blew and voices in the wind welcomed me and told me a war is coming and we must prepare. Brooke said protectors will be sent to me, also that training needs to start immediately. Something about many trials and tribulations, but we will accomplish many great things, that is all I know. It sounds crazy, especially the voices in the wind. Maybe someone is playing a joke?" I say hopefully, but without much conviction.

I look around the room to gage expressions, my father, Mark, and Simon look concerned, my mother is also concerned, but also has a look of determination and pride. Ezekiel and Claire share looks of amazement and shock, Ashley is shaking her head at me and looks fearful. I do not understand the fear. I really want to have our talk, but we need to get through this first.

"Is there anything else you can think of, Jazz?" Dad inquires quietly. After I shake my head no in response, he turns his attention towards Ashley. "Could you please inform us on the information your wolf gave you?"

This is a direction versus a question, the time for etiquette has passed.

Ashley takes a deep breath, looks up at the group and starts, "My wolf, Grace, said my mark is the mark of a Moon Goddess warrior. I was told I am destined to be Jasmine's guardian and lead the Moon Goddess' warriors. There will be other protectors coming to train us. Train us and the other protectors who will be called here. I am not sure why we were chosen. Grace did not go into detail as to why, just what is expected of me."

I look over to see how Claire is reacting, since she is head of my personal guards. Claire is just staring at Ashley and blinking. No reaction. I am not sure how to take it. I am sure this is a shock to everyone; it is a shock to me and my system. I am still fighting this is true. At least now I know why Ashley has been behaving as she has been.

"Thank you, girls," my father says, he continues, "I have been doing some initial research, while waiting for everyone. I need to do more, but there is a prophecy my great-grandfather used to tell me. The prophecy says that when all the species are at war, when there is strife and discontent among the supernatural, a being of two worlds will rise and unite the species. This being will encounter a war against the dark forces of each species, who have united, and they will combine as an army to overthrow the Queen, to continue the decline of the supernatural world.

"Jasmine is the only supernatural of two worlds who has the power of both parents, so truly she lives a split life. She has no allegiance to one species or another, an unbiased leader of all. That along with her wolf's declaration makes me believe all that is being said by her and Ashley. I think we need to start to plan and prepare. Claire, you will start to train Jasmine and Ashley in wolf form, until this trainer arrives. Abby, I think it is important we increase her witches' combat training and spell use. We will need to find a way to validate whoever it is that comes, regardless of how many come, no imposters will be allowed in to harm our pack," says my father.

"A protection barrier can be placed around pack lands. We will have to grant passage to anyone wanting to come onto our grounds who is not a pack member. If they are a protector, it is safe to assume they will have the same mark as Ashley. I don't know about trainers; I could meet them at the border and do a truth spell. Members will be able to come and go as they wish. Jazz, you will accompany me while I do these spells, it gives you the opportunity to assist me and learn," Mom informs us.

My father nods at her in approval of her plan.

Claire looks up at my father, "I will be happy to start their training in the morning, Alpha. My question is, if Ashley is to be Jasmine's protector what is my future role going to be?"

The room is silent for a moment, clearing my throat all attention reverts back to me.

"Claire, I would like for you to be my Gamma. As my Gamma you will still be a significant part of training and protection plans, only it will be at pack level versus just for me."

Claire looks at me with an open mouth, eyes wide, but nods her head. "I accept," she says firmly.

"First thing in the morning, Mark, Simon and I will go down and interrogate the rogues we brought back. I need to know who was behind the attack and why. Jasmine, if you would like to come with us that will be fine. The interrogation will help with training on how to get information from prisoners for when you are Alpha... or Queen," my father says.

Quickly, I acknowledge him with a nod of my head.

"Claire, please increase security around Jasmine. Ezekiel, please do the same for your sister. Simon, I need you to get with the head warrior and increase security around the pack borders. Mark, you and I are going to continue to research and reach out to our allies. Once we have more information, we will call an Alpha meeting here with our ally packs."

My father has a plan in place, and I am amazed by him. My hope is to run this pack as well as he and my mother have. They have been amazing influences and role models, my heart swells with pride and love for them.

"Let's call it a night and start putting everything into place in the morning," Dad dismisses us.

With an initial plan in place, we all head off to bed. It is already past one in the morning, and we all have an early start.

CHAPTER 10:

Interrogation

(Jasmine's POV)

My alarm blares at me at six in the morning. I reach over and smack the offensive sound off, letting out a groan. Dragging my body slowly out of bed, my legs feel like hundred-pound weights and my eyelids have been stapled shut. I make my way to my bathroom, hopefully a quick shower will help wake me up. Normally I am a morning person, but sleep did not grace me with its presence after the meeting. My night was full of dreams, or more accurately nightmares, brought on by the discoveries of the night before.

I get out of my shower feeling a little more prepared to face the day and maybe my new reality. What I really need is some strong coffee and that is my next goal, well, once clothing is on my body. Today is the perfect day for yoga pants, a sports bra, t-shirt and some cross trainers, comfort all the way. I put my hair up in a bun. Training will begin as soon as the interrogation has been completed, or at least the initial phase of interrogation. I wonder what Claire has planned for us today, most likely it will be intense, just like our trainer, although I am thinking training with Claire will be a walk in the park compared to what my mom has planned for me, and I am all hers after Claire finishes with me. Life as I knew it no longer exists, my carefree days are done and now the weight of the supernatural world is on my shoulders. Thank Moon Goddess my friends and family are by my side supporting me.

"Alright, Brooke, we are headed into our first interrogation. Are we ready for this?" I ask my wolf.

"Absolutely, so ready to put eyes on the men who dared to attack us. I want to see them squirm under my claws," Brooke growls.

"Easy, girl, we are learning this time around, Dad is going to be doing the interrogation and we are learning from him," I remind her gently.

Brooke rolls her eyes at me, in my head. There is so much more to learn about my wolf, but I am thinking she is going to be a handful.

Breakfast is calling me, or more accurately, coffee is calling me; I make my way downstairs to the first floor and go into the kitchen. My eyes are still semi-closed, and I ignore all in the room and stumble my way straight to the coffee pot. Once my coffee is in hand, I breath in the steamy aroma of freshbrewed goodness and make my way over to the table and mumble a "Good morning." My dad, mom, Mark, and Simon all smile at me.

I look at my mom with a questioning glance, a little surprised to see her there with us. Mom looks at me and sees my expression.

"Good to see the zombie has regained her life." Mom laughs at me and my morning antics. "I am going with the group to place a truth spell on the prisoners. You can count this as some of your training," she says.

I nod my head and drink down my coffee. Dad stands up from the table and the rest of us follow his lead. We clean our dirty dishes and head out to the prison.

Our prison is located underground and is not obvious to those outside our pack. The entryway looks like one of the supply buildings next to the training grounds, behind the training grounds is our garden. The garden sits on top of the prison. The prison's support walls and ceiling are heavily reinforced to hold the six feet of dirt piled on top. There are three levels to our cells and the farther down your cell level, the worse your crime. Since I was the one attacked, the rouges are going to be on the lowest level.

We go in through the entry and the guards on duty nod to our group in respect. We acknowledge them back with nods of our own and tell them good morning. We head down to the third level of cells. The air down here is thick and smells like mold and must. There is a ventilation system, but it doesn't work as effectively at this lower level. We come to the cells holding the rogues. Each rogue is chained in the center of their cell with silver shackles on their wrists, ankles, and necks. Their skin is red and burned where the restraints are placed. My mother walks to the cell in the center and places her hands out to her sides. Her eyes begin to glow blue, and she chants lowly. I step closer to hear the spell she is using; it isn't recognizable, so I make a mental note to ask her about this spell later. There are only three rogues in the prison, so I am assuming the rogue who initially attacked me did not survive Claire's attack, it doesn't sadden me to think he lost his life, honestly. I would think a loss of life would bother me, but it must be the werewolf instincts I have, or the fact it was his life or ours.

"What the hell!" sneers the evil-looking rogue. "A damn witch."

"Watch how you talk to my Luna," growls my father, sending a chill through all present with his aura and power. He is a very strong Alpha, the strongest in the United States, and does not tolerate anyone talking down to my mother.

"A witch is a Luna? That can't be, species don't mix. Once I am out her life will end at my hands," evil rogue remarks.

He is not a very smart beast to be making such remarks, everyone knows to disrespect a Luna in front of her mate, her Alpha, is a death sentence, especially since the rogue is confined by silver. Silver weakens werewolves, slows the healing process and at high enough doses can kill us. That is why we use it in our restraints.

My father steps towards the cell, his claws coming out, and teeth elongating, before he can get to the cell door my mother places her hand on his chest. My parents have fought these views since they felt their mate bond, they are confident in each other and refuse to acknowledge those who look down on them.

Mom looks at Dad and says quietly for only our ears, "I placed the spell on them. They can only speak the truth; therefore, he is being bold, he is unable to filter."

Dad nods at her in understanding, regains his composure, and approaches the cell.

"I have some questions for you three. Any of you can answer, it seems, though, as if you are the leader," Dad says to the evil-looking rogue.

The rogue nods his head.

"One of your friends didn't make it through the initial attack, I would like to say that is a pity, but it would be an outright lie. How about I am truthful with you, and in turn you are truthful with me," Dad states.

The rogue just glares at him.

"I want to know who sent you to kidnap my daughter," Dad starts.

Evil rogue looks at him, refusing to give him an answer.

"That is fine, don't answer. Just know I am going to make sure you have a good reason for not answering," my dad says with a smirk on his face.

Mark opens the cell door and walks up to the rogue, punching him in the jaw. There is the sound of breaking bone, the rogue lets out a howl and spits blood and teeth onto the floor. A small trail of blood drains from the corner of his mouth, a bruise is starting to form on his jaw. He will be a long-time healing because of the silver he is chained up with.

Mark steps back from his prisoner and closes the cell door after he exits, a look of satisfaction on his hard face. The desired outcome was met in one hit from our Beta's hands. We have to remember his daughter was also attacked and injured by this very rogue, Mark is out for retaliation as well.

"Since your friend can no longer speak with a broken jaw, I will ask the two of you. Who sent you to kidnap my daughter?" Dad repeats.

This time the short rogue speaks up, "We don't know. We received a call from an anonymous person. The price was right, and we needed the money. At the time, we didn't know she was an Alpha's daughter. Once there we had come too far to turn back. We went with the original plan."

This rogue's eyes dart back and forth between my father and Mark. His shirt is already damp at the armpits and through the chest, becoming increasingly soaked as Dad and Mark glare at him, it does not do any favors for his already nauseating scent. His eyes are barely open slits, he sticks out his snakelike tongue to attempt to moisten his cracked lips and offers us a half-smile, but fear still sits behind his eyes.

"How were you supposed to turn my daughter over to the person who hired you?" Dad growls at the rogue.

"We have a burner cellphone they sent to us. We were to take her to a cabin and then send them a message. No calls. They are supposed to pick her up at five o'clock this evening. We were just to leave her tied up to a chair in the middle of the room" came the rogue's nervous reply.

"Who was the one holding on to the cellphone?" questions my father.

The rogue points over to his evil-looking cohort. I look at my dad and his eyes have clouded over. I am not sure who he is mind-linking. Soon a guard comes down and hands Dad a cellphone. Dad is pushing different buttons on the cellphone and then looks at the evil rogue.

"What is the passcode to unlock the phone?"

The rogue glares at him but uses his left hand to hold up fingers. 2. 4. 1. 2. Dad puts in the code. Looking over his shoulder, I see the phone only has one contact. This is our first step to finding out who was behind the attack and if there is a connection to the prophecy. I am not sure there is because I had not discovered my wolf when they attacked us. Mom says it could be they wanted me prior to my shift to see if the change would come and then I would already be in their control, guess it is possible.

"Is there any other information you can give us?"

The question from Dad is directed to all of them, but his eyes land on the short rogue, who has been too willing to give us information. All three shake their heads in a negative response.

Giving them hard stares, Dad nods to them then mind-links again, two more guards come down. My dad nods to the guards, one guard enters each cell. The rogues look up at us with terror and defeat in their eyes. Before I can blink again the guards have snapped the necks of the rogues. Their bodies have gone limp against the restraints and all light has left their eyes.

"They were a threat, willing to do anything for a price, and we cannot have that," Dad tells me.

Shock is evident on my face, unsure how to feel about this. I do not feel pity for them, but I have never taken a life either. They were willing to kill Claire and Ashley just to get me, so I guess it was a "kill or be killed" situation. As they said, they do have their price and what is to stop them from another attempt if they are set free?

"Looks like we are done here. Guards, clean up this mess and dispose of the rogues over our border lines. Jasmine, you are due up on the training field. I am going to take this phone to my office and see if Ezekiel can help me trace the other party. Jasmine, before you start training with your mother come to my office," Dad directs.

I nod my head, straighten my shoulders, and start up the prison levels, can't keep Claire and Ashley waiting too long.

Chapter 11:

First Lead

(Alexander's POV)

The interrogation does not get us the results we had been hoping for, at least we are able to get the cellphone given to the rogues, hopefully there is something on it of use to us. On the way to my office, I mind-link Ezekiel and let him know I need to see him immediately.

Ezekiel is a master at communications, computers, and all things technology oriented. He has his degree in programming, and another field I am unable to recall, in which he excels. He is also the best at hacking, but we aren't going to go into that. It is nice in instances like this when we need information to protect others.

On top of being a genius, Ezekiel is one of our top warriors, not only strong, but with a gift to plan and strategize. He is the all-around package. Luckily my daughter has agreed to have him as her Beta, since he isn't her mate as we, the parents, had been hoping, this makes me feel more at peace. Add Claire into the mix as the Gamma and they will be an unstoppable team.

I look at the phone in my hands, as I enter through my office door. So much hope sits with one little device, I stride over to the desk and toss the phone down, letting out a heavy sigh.

Reading through the messages gives no indication who was behind the attack. I have been racking my mind attempting to think of who could possibly want to kidnap Jasmine and kill my pack members. The prophecy is heavily weighing on my mind, causing me to go through my mind to recall those who have aggressions with us, to come up with who could be working towards the dark end, no one specifically comes to mind.

Whispering Winds has enemies, none of them are that deep seated in hate, though. Those who oppose us are generally against the way we choose to run the pack. Are against the fact my Luna and I are a mixed-species relationship.

Perhaps I should be looking at those who oppose us due to the mate bond we have. Those who want to keep the species in their own sectors and fighting each other. Not all members of the Supernatural world think species should be separated, but there is a growing number, and they are pushing their agenda hard. The prophecy does state this war is about bringing the supernatural world together.

I sit at my desk and open a new file on my laptop, lists need to be made of those who oppose us, the list only contains four individuals I know of.

The other area we need to look at, and that makes me uncomfortable to believe, is our pack. The rouges were first scented at the mall, and then the spa. The girls said no one was noticed following them. I hope against hope we do not have a traitor in our pack. The very thought causes me to feel nauseous and a deep-seated rage. This person will be found and then we will make them pay.

While I am sitting deep in thought, there is a knock at my door. By the scent I know it is Ezekiel.

"Come on in, Ezekiel," I call out.

The door opens and Ezekiel walks up to my desk. He gives me a nod of respect.

"What can I do for you today, Alpha?"

"I need you to take this cellphone and work your magic. This is the phone we got off the rogues. They said the person who hired them to kidnap Jasmine gave it to them as a burner phone. There is nothing in the messages to indicate who is behind the attack. I need to know as soon as possible. If you are unable to get the information we will need to move to a different plan."

"No problem, Alpha. I will get back to you in the next couple hours. The process can take a bit, but I should know by then if I can get any information or not."

"Thank you."

Ezekiel takes the phone and leaves.

Based off what Ezekiel has said, there is two hours to work with, wasting no time a mind-link is sent out to Mark and Simon. We are going to need to have an additional plan in place just in case this does not work out. I am dreading the option that is left to us. As a father, it is not an acceptable choice, as an Alpha protecting his pack it is the only way to go, prayers are sent to the Goddess for guidance, hopefully Ezekiel manages to find something.

Mark and Simon come into my office, after giving a cursory knock at the door. They have questioning looks on their faces. They do not doubt me but are curious as to the summons.

"Gentlemen, I gave the cellphone to Ezekiel to see if he can get any information from it. He said it will be a couple hours before he will have any type of information for me. Just in case this is a dead end we need to have another plan in place. Also, I have compiled a list of known packs who have issues with Whispering Winds based off the mixed-species relationship of the Luna and me. These individuals need to be watched and all information possible collected on them."

The men nod to me. Handing them the compiled list, they look up to me with questioning eyes.

"Alpha, this list only has four packs on it," Mark clarifies gently.

"Those are the only packs that have vocally opposed the union between Abby and me. If there are others to add, let's update the list now." It would be arrogant of me to think this is a complete list, the input of my Beta and Gamma is crucial and appreciated.

They nod their heads, but do not offer any additional names.

"There is an initial plan. I am not thrilled with it, and it will need to be absolutely fine-tuned. My plan is to contact the person on the phone. Unless this is an inside job, or the person was watching, they will not know the rogues failed. We can tell them Jasmine is captured and, in the cabin, waiting for pickup. I thought about only placing something with her scent in the cabin, but I do not know what type of Supernatural we are dealing with. I think Jasmine would have to physically be present in the cabin. We would have our elite warriors strategically placed around the perimeter and Abby could place a scentblocking spell on us... or Jasmine could place the spell too."

"Alpha, you said something about an inside job. Do you think a pack member planned this?" asked Mark in a deadly tone.

"I am not sure, Mark. Thinking it over, it is possible. The rogues were at the mall and then the spa. How did they know the girls were going to be at those places unless they were tracking them? We all know Claire would know everything happening around them, they do not recall being followed and they were watching more carefully after leaving the mall."

Simon let out a growl and Mark's eyes turned black, clear indicators they were not happy with the thought either.

"Let's make sure only the individuals involved in this plan are aware, keep it under wraps, just in case. I need to get to the main dining hall now for the pack meeting I promised last night."

They nod and make their way out of my office to begin preparations. We will be ready to move as soon as we need to if Ezekiel isn't able to get what we need.

Chapter 12:

Technology

(Ezekiel's POV)

The Alpha has given me a significant task, it is a confidence boost to know he has such faith in me. It could also be he knows I am as involved in this as the next person. It was my little sister they threatened to kill and my other "little sister" they planned to kidnap, there is no doubt I am completely and totally invested in discovering who orchestrated this.

Taking a seat at my desk I bring up my computer systems, and flick on my screen. This is what gets my blood moving, the excitement of tracking down the wrong doers via technology—yeah, super nerdy, but it gets my adrenaline pumping. It is a game of smarts, logic, and the feeling of coming out on top consistently is amazing. I just hope I can make it happen again.

My computer finishes booting up and I make sure to go into a protected mode. Most of the programs used on my system are not known, I have developed them myself, keeping them quiet not wanting to share them with the general population. It is always a good idea to have a few secrets or tricks up your sleeve in the ever-changing cyber world.

I plug the phone in and run an initial security scan; it is important to make sure there isn't anything loaded on the phone that will attack my computer and abort all the information on the phone. It is a burner phone, so I don't think anything like that will be loaded on it, but it is always better to be safe than sorry. Especially since we have no idea who we are dealing with.

The security scan comes back clean, time to start running some of my special programs. Leaning back in my chair, I make a show of stretching my arms over my head, intertwining my fingers, then popping my knuckles, shrug my shoulders a couple times and move my head side to side to make sure my spine is relaxed, the last part of putting on my game face.

The phone itself is not able to be traced, I am hoping the person texting with the rogues did not use a burner phone themselves. If they did that will just make my job even more difficult. With the programs running it is time to kick my feet up on the desk, sit back in my chair and wait.

While waiting for results, my eyes scan my little lair. I put a false wall in my room, not so big it is obvious. The false wall only creates a room that is big enough to place a couple long tables for all my equipment and a chair. Maybe six feet in width. There are self-installed vents so there is some air and cooling abilities, also the entire space is soundproof, not just this room but my entire bedroom too. Because of being hyper-security conscious, I also made the vents escape routes. There is not a concern about someone sneaking in through the vents, my room is on the seventh floor and the outside wall to my room is flat faced. I know, genius. Another part of my security package is a monitor next to my computer screen and a surveillance camera in my room.

There is a row of bookshelves across the false wall in my room proper, so it looks natural, and no one questions why my room may appear smaller. I thought this was the best idea in hiding my secret entrance. There is a code box, set into the false wall behind a panel that matches the wall, all located behind a set of books that have a sensor set into them alerting to my watch if a specific area of the books is not triggered quickly.

A code must be put in to enter my lair, if you don't enter the code and break in, there is a failsafe in place. My computers will catch fire and the hard drives wiped, no one will be getting my data. I know what you are thinking, if my computers catch fire the building will burn down.

Nope, my entire bedroom, to include the little room, is fire safe. Nothing will burn outside this room. I am excited for when I become Beta and can show this to Jasmine. It would be nice to implement some of this into our security protocols and data technology sector. At the moment, this is only my little secret.

Jasmine... thinking of what happened on the girl's birthday sets my blood boiling. How dare someone attempt to harm My Sun and Moon. I have been protective of them since they were born. I have a picture on my desk of me holding them when they were just minutes old, Jazz was 50 minutes old, and Ash was 47 minutes old. They don't know about the picture; it is in my secure office and its existence will not pass my lips. I know our parents have always hoped Jasmine and I would be mates, but that would be awkward, relief flowed through my body and mind when Jasmine did not recognize me as such.

I move over to another screen; the dark web is another good place to run a search on an alternate computer while the scans run on my main setup. Maybe there is something there. Once in the web I do a search to see if I can find anything, one option is to put myself out in the classifieds, pretending to be a mercenary for hire, my ad gets completed. According to my profile I specialize in kidnapping, torture, and surveillance. Now it is a waiting game on all fronts.

With everything completed on my end the waiting commences, it is during these times my Switch saves me from boredom, locating it in one of the desk cubbies, behind some presumably stale chips, I grab it and begin playing. I want to be here to see the information as soon as it comes through so I can inform the Alpha. What better way to not watch the clock than to play a game or two?

About an hour into my game an alarm sounds on one of my servers, I look to the screen and gulp. The number being tracked does not give me a specific name, but it does give a location. I cannot believe my eyes, what could they possibly want with Jasmine? I print out all the information and place it in a privacy envelope. No need for anyone to chance seeing what has been discovered.

Mind-linking the Alpha, I let him know my search has resulted in some information and it is imperative we meet as soon as he is able.

He asks me to meet him in his office, before leaving I quickly check the dark web to see if there have been any hits on my profile, so far nothing. The envelope of information is in my hand, and I am ready to leave, making sure to secure my office, then rushing through the hallway, heading for my meeting with the Alpha.

Chapter 13:

Training

(Jasmine's POV)

I run to the training field, Claire and Ashley are waiting for me impatiently. Jogging up to them, my best apology face is on.

"Sorry, guys. I just finished at the interrogation."

"Understand," states Claire.

"Let's get to our first day of training. I have designed a specific training regimen for you and Ashley. It is important you two train together since Ashley has been chosen by the Moon Goddess to be your protector. This will allow you two to know each other's, style, strengths and weaknesses. It gives you the ability to fight seamlessly and only need to have limited communication. Muscle memory is what it is all about, ladies. Eventually we will add in fighting together with Jasmine using magic, but for now non-magic combat only," Claire gets right down to business.

"Sounds like a solid plan to me. Where do we start, Claire?" I ask with anticipation dripping from my voice. I love training and am excited for this new plan.

Ashley and me very rarely trained together. We were in the same training, but never partners. There were a few incidents that occurred, causing the trainers to keep us separated and them to wear extra protective gear when we were on the training fields.

"I want to start with the two of you sparring so I can get a sense of where your skills are. It was brought to my attention the fight we had with the rogues was the first actual fight either of you has had off the training field, so, there is a vague idea of your skills, but I want a more in-depth look," Claire tells us.

Ashley and I nod to Claire. We step into the sparring ring. We have been training since a young age in different fighting styles, but never used any of it once we left the training area, unless it was involved in a prank on Zeke and his friends. This promises to be fun. There is an excited glint in Ashley's eyes as well.

We circle each other, sizing the other one up. Trying to find each other's weaknesses. Ashley lunges at me, faking a left jab and following through with a roundhouse kick. I manage to crouch down, causing her to miss, and sweep my leg out, taking her feet out from under her. Ashley jumps right back onto her feet and reengages, she runs at me, but at the last minute springs into a handstand and wraps her legs around my neck, flipping me over her body, she then jumps on top of me, putting an arm bar on my throat, trying to make me submit. I flip her off and spring to my feet. She recovers and comes at me again. I land an upper cut to her jaw. We continue this way for an hour before Claire calls us to stop. Neither one of us submitted to the other. Ashley is much stronger than she was before and she has never been a delicate flower, her wolf has enhanced her power.

Looking over at Ash she is a sight, bent over sucking in air, most likely people get the same sight from me. We fought hard for over an hour. There is some bruising on her cheek and arms, a deep cut on her chin, plus multiple scratches, and scrapes all over her body. She has dirt, mixed with sweat and blood matted in her hair. She is a sight, but I assume I am no better to look at. Catching each other's eye, we begin to laugh, coming together for a hug as a congratulatory "You've done well."

"Amazing job, sis. You almost beat my booty that time. Guess I need to up my game now that you are a Moon Goddess warrior." I smile down at her.

"Thank you. It felt great to get out there. There is so much more power and strength with Grace. Just think what we will be able to do with more training. I feel better about my destiny, I no longer feel like I will fail you."

"Great job, ladies, very impressive. I enjoyed watching you two. Tomorrow you will spar in wolf form. I know you ladies just got your wolves, but I need an idea of where to begin our training. To finish out our training today you two will spar together against a couple of our warriors. I am very happy with your form and fighting styles as humans, so we can progress to the next step after today," Claire explains to us.

As she is telling us our next steps two of the pack's top elite warriors, Jacob and Sean, come to the training field. Claire must have mind-linked them while Ashley and I were sparring. Claire is not messing around when it comes to our training. She is starting us out against the best. I look over at Ashley, and she gives me a wide grin, the sparkle and mischief has returned to her eyes, this sparring match is going to be fun.

We step into the sparring ring with the warriors. We have males and females train with and against each other regularly in our pack, there is no concern these two will hold back with us because of our gender.

"Here are the rules. This is a fight to submission, both members of a team must give in. Fighting will be done in human form only and no partial shifting. Jasmine, no magic. Let's get to it," Claire instructs us in her no-nonsense style. Jacob and Sean are used to working and training as a team, while Ashley and

I have been separated because of our antics. We have been known to be a couple of pranksters. All in good fun, but still. I think now, the mischief has worked against us. Luckily, we have a strong and solid bond due to our sisterhood.

Ashley and I stand back to back, crouched down into a fighting stance. Jacob and Sean move around us and size us up. They are looking for any weakness and an opening to start. We are turning with them, so they are never out of our line of sight. Suddenly Sean moves forward, attempting to kick Ashley in the hip. Instead of moving, so the kick misses, Ashley blocks it; this is so I do not inadvertently get kicked when she moves. Since Sean is still close, Ashley counters with her own kick to the side of the knee. Sean goes down momentarily but is quickly back up.

We have been sparring for almost an hour when I notice Jacob is leaving his stomach open, it is not obvious if this is on purpose or not. I mind-link Ashley.

"Opening on Jacob. Taking it. Moving away. NOW."

I keep the communication short; Claire had told us earlier we needed to have limited communication. We want to stay on Claire's good side, so we are doing our best to listen to all her directions and abide by them.

I leap forward and place a kick to Jacob's midsection; we hear a crack and I am pretty sure there is a fractured rib or two. Jacob bends slightly forward after the kick and I follow through with a jab to the nose, causing it to break and blood flow down Jacob's face, while he falls to his knees. He quickly gets back on his feet and blocks my next punch, landing one of his own into my side. The air is forced out of me, but I remain on my feet and quickly recover. He throws another punch and I block it, keeping hold of his arm.

I mind-link Ashley, who has Sean in a head lock punching him.

"Jacob, coming your way."

Using the momentum of Jacob's punch to send him towards Ashley, she lets go of Sean and delivers a roundhouse kick to Jacob's face. He goes down, unconscious. When Ashley moved away from Sean, I move forward and do a leg sweep on him. He goes down. Leaping on top of him, making sure his face is to the ground, I grab his arm and twist it up behind him, while with my other arm I wrap it around his neck and pull up. Ashley comes and stands in from of him. She places her heel on his chin. Sean looks at us and since he cannot tap out, says he submits.

We help Sean up to his feet and make our way over to Jacob to see how he is. Jacob is starting to come around; he will be fine. His wolf will heal him in a couple hours.

"Nice job, ladies. You two work well together, though I noticed the couple of mind-links that happened, and we will work on how to use specific sounds and motions to alert the other to what is happening. I did like that the mindlinks were kept short. Super excited to see what you can do in wolf form. Jasmine, the Alpha is waiting for you, so I am going to let you guys go for the day. Let's start training at 6 A.M. tomorrow," Claire updates us.

Ashley and I walk away from the training field after shaking hands with Jacob and Sean. We thanked them for working with us. I offered to heal Jacob's ribs, but he declined, most likely it was an ego thing.

Walking back to the packhouse, this is a good time to check in on Ash. "How are you feeling? I noticed some of the spark back in your eyes. I was worried about you after we got our wolves."

"I am doing great. Grace and I had a long talk last night. Feeling more prepared and excited to accept this honor granted to me. It was just a lot to take in and process last night. I am ready to defend you and the supernatural realm with all there is in me."

I hug Ashley tight. She wraps her arms around me in return and squeezes. If I have to go through this with anyone, I am glad it is this little spitfire. "We definitely dominated the training field today, didn't we?" Ashley giggled.

There is a wide smile on my face. "We didn't do too bad. We have areas to fix, but, yeah, we totally rocked it. I am ready to learn to fight with Brooke. I think we will be unstoppable when we pair with our wolves. It is exciting to see what Claire has planned, she is an amazing trainer. We should have spent more time with her in the past."

We have reached the packhouse. I head up to my room and take a quick shower, Dad probably wouldn't like me to show up in his office sweaty and smelly getting my funk all over his upholstery.

Chapter 14:

Meeting

(Jasmine's POV)

Getting to Dad's office, I stretch to work out a few muscle kinks, prior to lifting my hand and knocking on the door. He calls out for me to enter. Opening the door and entering the room, conversation is already happening, there is surprise seeing everyone in the room, initially my impression was this meeting was just between Dad and me. Sitting on the couch against the wall is Mom and Dad, the couch opposite is Mark, Simon and Claire, Ashley is in one of the chairs, while Ezekiel is in the other chair, being left with no other options, I snuggle in between Mom and Dad.

Looking around the room, there are grim expressions on everyone's faces.

"Does someone want to catch me up?" I inquire while raising my eyebrows in question.

Dad places an arm around my shoulders, then begins. "Ezekiel ran a scan on the phone we got from the rogues. We weren't able to find a specific person, but it did give us a location to start looking into. The issue is their security is very advanced and we would take great risks asking Ezekiel to hack it. There is a large population there too, so it would be very difficult and time-consuming to narrow down suspects."

"Where exactly are we talking about, Dad?" Trepidation begins to fill me between the looks on their faces and how cryptic Dad is being.

Dad looks at me. He is hesitating to come forward with the answer, my eyes meet his and we stare each other down, this is my life we are talking about. I think I have the right to know all the information, the danger I am facing.

Dad lets out a long sigh, rubbing the back of his neck. "I want you to remember we do not have anyone specific in mind. We are still looking at a possible inside job, and at individuals and packs that have issues with Whispering Winds due to the mate bond between your mother and I."

Slowly my head nods up and down at him in understanding, while my eyes encourage him to continue.

"The location Ezekiel managed to find is the High Wolf Council city. Again, there is no one specific, we just know it came from the area," Dad quickly reminds me.

My heart skips a beat and begins pounding in my ears. My breath catches a little and I feel nauseous. I would think if it was someone specific on the council they would just come to the pack and speak with us or summon me to the Great Hall. I am trying to wrap my mind around this information.

Uncertain, fearful eyes look over to my dad, managing to take a deep, calming breath I ask, "What does this mean for us? Where do we go from here?"

Dad clears his throat. "We do have a plan in place. None of us agree to it and we were discussing it when you came in. The plan is to text the person who hired the rogues and let them know you are secured in the cabin. We would have our elite warriors surrounding the area, along with myself, Mark, Simon, Claire, Ezekiel, and Ashley. You would place a spell on us to hide our scent. It is a risky plan. I am sure you can see why we are not in agreement."

I take in the information and look around the room. My eyes settle on Ezekiel. "Zeke, there is no way for you to get any more information from the phone?" A small glimmer of hope holds on.

"I ran every scan I had available, Jazz. This is the best I could do. I really wish there was more I could pull off it. The idea of risking you, My Moon, is not optimal or even justifiable in my opinion," Ezekiel says, looking down at the floor.

Taking a moment to process all the information given to me, I swallow hard and look at the group. "Well, I guess we need to start preparing, and make sure we each know our role. Mom, I would like to go over the spell I will use with you, just to double check I have it correct since the lives of everyone could depend on it."

"Honey, you know that spell inside out. You and Ashley have used it so many times to pull your pranks, but I will be happy to go over it with you. There is no doubt in my mind you can do this. I have faith in you and the group," Mom says comfortingly.

There are no words to express the appreciation in my heart for my mom. She is always so supportive and knows just what to say when it is needed most. I hope I am as good of a person and leader as she is, I try my best to be.

Shaking my head slightly to clear it of side thoughts, it is time to focus, I need to concentrate on this plan and on this spell. There is so much riding on this for all of us. It must be done correctly, a flash of five years ago sweeps through my mind, no mistakes.

Apprehension runs rampant through my system; I know Dad has thought this plan through as much as possible and worked out all the details he can. There is so much room for error, though. What if we are dealing with a vampire or demon, or something that can teleport in and out? With them being outside no one would know I was gone until well after. My mind is instantly going to worse-case scenarios. Time to calm down and take deep breaths, slowing my respirations. This is for the safety and wellbeing of the supernatural realm; I will do whatever it takes to keep us all safe.

"Young one, we will be fine. Have faith in the people around you and yourself. With them we will gain valuable information. Remember, I will not leave you; we are a team and will work through this together," Brooke pops into my head.

"You are right, Brooke; I have to get used to having you with me. For so long the thought was, I would be wolfless, I didn't anticipate you being with me. I hoped for it, but never thought it a reality. We will be the strongest team imaginable."

"That is a good pup. Let's get this planned and prepped. We have much work to do and many things to learn." With that Brooke retreats to the back of my mind and I refocused on the business at hand.

Tuning back into the room and people around me, a weak smile spreads across my face. "Let's make sure we are all on the same page."

With that we get up and meet around the map table, hashing out all the details.

Chapter 15:

Plan in Action

(Jasmine's POV)

All members of the plan received a detailed map of the area the cabin is located from Ezekiel. Unfortunately, the cabin is in neutral territory and has been abandoned for years, plus there is no owner on record, allowing us no clues to who is behind the kidnapping attempt.

Luckily the area is heavily wooded offering many places for our warriors and other members to hide. After doing a complete walkthrough of the area, we decided some of the warriors would be up in the trees to be lookouts, one in each direction, and some would be on the ground for quick entry into the cabin if needed. We have identified a couple different points of egress if our plans do not go smoothly. This does a lot to calm my nerves, there is still more to do before settling in and waiting.

Mom and I worked on the spell to hide scents, as well as a couple spells to use, if needed, in battle. Since that day at the spa, we haven't been able to do any training for use of my magic in aggressive situations, so we spent our first training covering these specific spells for this plan. It is nice to have some options versus none, that fight opened my eyes to many places I am lacking to be able to protect myself and my pack.

Our group walks up to the cabin. It is small, and most likely built to be off the grid, which explains why there is no owner information. The wood is a washed-out brown, from exposure to the elements, and the entire building is slightly leaning to the left. Oddly enough, there are no windows in the cabin and the thick door is held on only by the bottom hinge. From the outside this place looks more like a storage area to me than a living space.

Casting my eyes around as we walk inside, dirt covers every surface and crevice, my nose begins to twitch, indicating my need to sneeze from the dust. It is very dark from the lack of windows, allowing some apprehension to enter back into my being. We walk through the two-room cabin and do not find any other entry point, or hidden access points, then Dad decides the best place to put me is a little off to the side of the main door. This way when the person opens the door, there won't be an issue of the sun possibly blinding me and making it difficult to see what the person is doing or looks like. I think this is a smart move.

We head back outdoors, and the group gathers around me, it is time to place the cloaking spell, I take a deep breath in and close my eyes, concentrating. I can smell the earth, feel the light breeze through the trees and the sun warming my skin. Energy begins to run through my body, I open my eyes and begin to chant, unlike my mother's eyes, mine glow white, outlined with blue. The chanting continues for a couple minutes and then finishes. A smile graces my features, there is no smell on any of the wolves around me. Mom was right, I have used this spell so much, it is second nature to me. My and Ashley's mischief was good training, who would have guessed it.

With the spell in place the warriors designated as lookouts take to the trees. Everyone else finds a hiding spot. Dad, Zeke, and I go back into the cabin. We pull a chair out of the other room and set it in the preferred spot. Dad and Zeke have brought silver chains to tie me to the chair. What the person will be unable to see is the thin strips of fabric placed on the underside of the silver, so it is not touching my skin, therefore not weakening my wolf. The chains are loose, allowing me to slip out of them, if need be, but giving the appearance of being tight. Even though escape is easy, if need be, nerves begin to get the best of me being tied to the chair, taking deep breaths my body begins to center and relax. While taking this time a thought comes to me, I need to ask my mom if silver has any effect on my magical powers.

"I will be in the back room watching over you, My Moon," Zeke assures me. "We will find who planned against us, you will be safe."

His use of my nickname and the thought of someone I trust being close by does comfort me. We decided to have Zeke instead of Ash in the cabin with me, since Ash and I are still in the early phase of our training and have a long way to go.

Dad looks down at his watch. "We have thirty minutes until the designated pick-up time. I am going to go get in position. You have this, honey; you are doing a great job and I am so proud of you."

I smile at him. "I love you, Daddy. Let's get this person."

Dad walks out the door and Zeke heads into the back room. Thirty minutes to sit and think, this could be bad or good, depending on where my mind travels. We are not mind-linking unless something is happening, we all want to be on guard and not distracted.

"Young one. This is very brave of you to do. I am here and will give you strength. I will always be with you. Trust in us and our power,"

Brooke says to me. Brooke and I have not had much time to get to know each other, her presence is always felt, and she made it known she was with me while training today. Once this plan is done, there will be more time for bonding with her and it will be a priority, there are so many questions in my mind to ask her.

I close my eyes and connect with my surroundings. It is one of the great things about my witch ancestry, the ability to connect with the environment around me. Taking in the scents around me, smells of earth, fir, pine, deer, rabbit, squirrel, birds, and water invade my senses. I take in the sounds, breeze through the trees, bird song, the babbling of the stream. I feel the slight sway of the building below me and the calm of the woods around me. I am amazed I do not feel our team, they are impressive.

After what feels to be is twenty minutes later, I hear a faint voice in the wind. "They are coming, young one. Be prepared."

Refocusing on my surroundings again, the bird song has gone away, footsteps are vibrating through the wood below my feet and the sour, dirt, decay scent from the mall permeates the air. I am surprised there are more rogues coming, there is another scent mixed in with theirs, but I cannot place it. Based off the vibrations my guess is there are at least five wolves. There is no scent of any other supernatural apparent, so all we are dealing with are wolves. That is a slight relief, our training so far has only been to combat wolves, while we wait for the other trainers and protectors to arrive.

In a matter of minutes, the door creaks open. I look up and see a tall wolf in front of me. He is not a rogue, he is the one with the unrecognizable smell. Squinting at the little bit of light let into the room, his face comes into view, he is a foreign wolf to me, there is no recognition on my part. Feeling frustrated, who better to take it out on than this wolf in front of me.

"Well, it is about time you showed up," I sneer. "Leaving a young girl tied up in a cabin with no food, water, or ability to use the facilities. Do you mind letting me go, my bladder is full and I would like to take care of it?"

The man lets out a harsh laugh, then speaks to me in an unamused and impatient tone. "There is no way I am letting you go. You are just going to have to hold it in longer or just wet yourself. Your choice, I don't really care what you think or how you feel. I am here to do a job. As long as you show up alive, that is all that matters."

"You aren't even the one behind me being taken away from my family? You are just some paid goon?" I mock him.

"Watch your tone! The only thing I must do is make sure I deliver you alive, other than that what condition you are in does not matter. I would love nothing more than to shut that mouth for you," he snaps at me.

I lower my head, hopeful he thinks it is in submission, but I am doing it so I can mind-link the group.

"Do not move in. They are not the ones who initiated this. They are taking me to the person who is responsible. Follow us, the spell to remove your scent is good for 72 hours. Mom put a tracking spell on me before we left just in case something went amok." My message goes out to the group.

"Elite warriors and Ezekiel, follow at a distance, give detailed reports about where you are heading. I want back up to the tracking spell and terrain descriptions for the area. We will send in an army if needed," Dad links out.

I lift my head up and glare daggers into the man in front of me. "The least you can do is give me your name for this journey, so I don't have to call you 'Hey, guy,'" I spit back at him.

"You are spunky, not too smart, but spunky," he says while giving me an irritated look. "My name is Saul. Speak to me again with such attitude and tone, I will be forced to teach you a lesson. I do not tolerate insolence, especially from a mixed breed," he says to me condescendingly.

Saul steps out the door and comes back immediately followed by two rogues. The rogues walk up to me, one stays in front and the other goes behind, next thing I know there is a sharp needlelike feeling in my bicep, looking to the area of discomfort the rogue behind me has injected me, the needle still in my arm, as the syringe is drained.

I look over to Saul with questioning eyes.

"Just a little wolfsbane to keep you docile. We have a little way to go and don't want to deal with any escape attempts. Since we don't want to draw attention to ourselves, we can't have you tied up," Saul explains.

"Oh, man! Wolfsbane is just as bad as silver to a werewolf, please don't let the dose be too large" is the prayer sent up to the Goddess. Knowing my wolf powers will be decreased soon, I hope my mom can still use the tracking spell, we really need to have a talk when this is over, it is imperative to know what silver and wolfsbane does to my magical powers. This circumstance is making my lack of knowledge in areas painfully obvious.

While I have been lost in thought the rogues have undone the silver chains and yanked me out of my chair. Luckily it is so dark in this room they are not able to see the lining on them, plus their hands are covered in gloves, as not to be burned by the silver. I am feeling a little weak and end up needing to use one of the rogues for support, this is not preferred because as soon as his smell hits my nose, vomit wants to come up from his stench.

"Let's get this hybrid to the Alpha," Saul calls out to his minions, without pause they grab hold of me and pull me along, beginning our journey to getting answers.

Chapter 16:

On the Move

(Jasmine's POV)

We have been walking through the forest for two and a half hours. Saul got tired of me slowing down the group, so he had one of the rogues carry me. Saul is assuming I am unable to shift into my wolf due to the wolfsbane. He is at the head of the group and does not appear aware what is happening with me, my plan was to slow the group down, so Whispering Winds warriors could keep up and get all the details of the area necessary. He is happy as long as it is quiet and there is no fuss, but him having me carried just ruined my plans.

"Young one. Be strong. The wolfsbane in our system is not enough to block me or weaken me. It was important to wait until now to let you know, so you wouldn't attempt to fight them, luckily, they did not give us a higher dose. It is not clear if they know about me; if they did, I think they would have given you more. Whatever you do, try not to shift, we want to keep me a secret as long as possible," Brooke whispers in my head.

"Brooke, I am so glad you are alright. So, we are resistant to small doses of wolfsbane? That is good to know, my plan was not to shift anyway, I am wanting to gather as much information as possible on who is behind this, then use magic to fight if needed. I need to find out if this is part of the prophecy or just bad luck," I reply, relieved to know Brooke is alright.

"This is the start of the prophecy. We are going to experience much pain soon. Believe in us and our power. We are stronger than you know. Learn and grow from the pain you will experience, lean on me, and let me help you when the time is right. I will never leave you," Brooke finishes and goes to the back of my mind.

As our conversation finishes, the group of kidnappers break through a clearing, sitting about half a mile away are three SUVs, this is unexpected, the thought our aggressor was not within running distance in wolf form did not cross our minds, we focused on groups close to our pack with hostilities. This is getting more difficult as we progress.

I pretend to be asleep on the rogue's back and try to mind-link Zeke. "Zeke, are you there?"

"I am here, My Moon" comes Zeke's reply.

"Zeke, we just came through a clearing and there are three SUVs waiting for us. We are about half a mile out from them. There has been no talk of where we are going or who we are going to. Once in the car, I will continue to pretend to be asleep and give updates as possible. The group should head back to the pack now, you will not be able to keep up with the vehicles. Remember, Mom put a tracking spell on me. Oh, yeah, the dose of wolfsbane they gave me was not enough to affect my wolf; Brooke says we have a higher tolerance for it. See you soon, Zeke."

I cut off the mind-link and put up a wall for now, it would be detrimental if someone linked me at a bad time. I can't let my captors know I have control of my wolf or that I even have a wolf.

A rogue pulls me off the back of the vile creature I have been riding on, and roughly throws me into the back seat of one of the cars. My head smacks on the car window when the rogue slams the door shut. No pretending to be asleep now, I think to myself as I rub my forehead and feel a knot forming. Looking to my left, displeasure courses through me to see Saul is my car mate for the drive to who knows where.

I make sure I continue to act as though the wolfsbane is affecting my system. I drop my arm limply down to my side and lean back into the seat. Making it seem as though the act of rubbing my forehead took all my energy. Saul just smirks at me and tells the driver to go. My acting skills must be believable, thank Goddess.

No one puts a hood over my head to block my sight of our travels, this amazes me. Even though there is wolfsbane in my system it is surprising they are this lax on security measures. I am taking full advantage of it, though. Looking at the road signs to notice which direction we are headed, it becomes clear we are headed north, I am trying to think of what packs are north of us, who we have aggressions with. None come to mind at the moment. I honestly thought we would be traveling to the west because that is the direction of the High Wolf Council city.

It is time to try to update my dad on where we are, how can this be inconspicuous? A thought comes to me, I yawn and curl up with my face towards my window, shutting my eyes, the plan is for Saul to think I am asleep. Hopefully I am not so far away that I cannot mind-link. Bringing down my wall, Brooke helps me to attempt contact.

"Daddy, are you there?"

"I am here, sweetheart. How are you?"

"I am fine, Dad. We have been traveling north, by car for about an hour and a half. We passed Marionville about ten minutes ago. We seem to be staying on the main roadway. Saul is the name of the guy who took me, no last name right now. He isn't speaking with the driver so I have no idea where the end destination is, and I cannot get a look at the GPS unit."

"You're doing great, honey. That was a good update. We can map where you are and try to figure out where you are going."

"Is Mom there?"

"She is right here next to me."

"Ask her if my magic is affected by wolfsbane and silver. They gave me a small dose of wolfsbane, but Brooke says we are resistant to small doses."

Everything goes quiet for a bit.

"Abby says neither one will affect your magic. You still have full use of it. Use it wisely, though, because it can drain you. We love you and we are coming to get you back."

"Love you too. I will get as much information as possible until you get here."

I cut the mind-link and set the wall back up, my plan was to keep the link short, but I am unsure how much time elapsed.

I open my eyes slightly looking out the window, hoping to see a landmark or something. The area this far north is not very familiar to me, we have only traveled this way a few times. I am still looking for road signs, counting on my wolf vision to see in the dark. We take an exit, but I can only see the exit number, no name of a town. We take a right from the offramp and drive for another hour. We are heading in the opposite direction of the High Wolf Council city, so I move any thought of them from my mind. Soon there is a right turn onto a gravel road.

Based off the minimal chatter from the other members in the car, it seems we are getting close to our end destination. I take down my wall again and mind-link my dad.

"Dad, we are close to our destination, so there isn't much time. We took Exit 271, took a right from the off ramp, traveled about one hour fifteen minutes, and made a right onto a gravel road. We are in the complete opposite direction of the High Wolf Council city so it seems safe to say, we can forget about them for now."

"Got it, honey. Looking at the map, it appears you are heading into Broken Moon territory. They are a dangerous pack, be careful and we will be there soon."

Broken Moon, my heart goes cold. I feel fear creeping in. This pack is rumored to be cruel. They are elitists, looking down on all those they consider inferior. They are known for torture and abuse. What could this pack possibly want with me? As far as I know Whispering Winds has no communication with this pack. We are not allies, but we are not enemies either.

I yawn and stretch, sitting up in my seat. Saul gives me an irritated look for disturbing his peace, a smile is my response to his glare. I am about to make a comment, when we pull up in front of a large packhouse, too much detail cannot be seen of the area due to the darkness, but a sense of foreboding rushes over my body being here. I take a deep breath and gulp down my fear. This pack will not be allowed to intimidate me, I am an Alpha!

Chapter 17:

Broken Moon

(Jasmine's POV)

The SUV stops in front of what appears to be the main house. There is a massive staircase leading to the main door, it is rather ostentatious, like they use it to look down on all those who dare make an appearance in their pack lands. There is someone standing at the top, but they are covered in shadow, and it is impossible to make out any features. Time to prepare to meet the Alpha.

Without warning my door is flung open, Saul grabs me by my hair, dragging me out of the car. Apparently, he can move quickly and quietly, I never noticed he had gotten out of his seat, he does not release my hair as he hauls me to the top of the stairs, throwing me on the ground at the feet of the person waiting for us.

I look up into the cold amber eyes of a wolf my age, we are about the same height, but he has a very sturdy build. Based off the power and authority flowing from him, he is not the Alpha, but a wolf of high ranking. There is not an ounce of friendliness in the wolf before me, his gaze causes my breath to stop. I have no idea what is in store for me here, he gives nothing away.

This man does not make a move to help me up, still playing weak from the wolfsbane and not wanting to ruin my cover, I make a couple feeble attempts to stand and then give up.

The man looks at me mockingly, before giving a contemptuous sigh and relegating himself to address me. "I am Beta Clark. It is unbelievable you are supposed to be the next Alpha to Whispering Winds. Perfect example of why women should not be in charge, not just women, but mixed wolves in general. You have two strikes against you already," he sneers derisively and spits on me.

How dare he spit on me! How dare he mock me! It takes everything in me to keep from attacking this wolf, his blatant disrespect is beyond acceptable and only gives me an idea of what is to come at the hands of this pack. It is imperative my temper does not control my actions, there is still more to be learned here before my pack arrives.

"Take her to the dungeons. Alpha Blaine is out at the moment but will deal with her on his arrival." Beta Clark turns and walks away, dismissing all of us and leaving me sitting on the top stair.

Still sitting in shock, surprise hits me when hands grasp me, pulling me up by my hair, clothing, and arms, dragging me down to the dungeon.

"Keep up, hybrid, we have spent more than enough time with you already," growls one of the guards when my pace does not match theirs.

As we make our way to the holding area, fury runs rampant in my mind. Who the hell does he think he is? The condescending tone and disrespect that is being shown to me here by all member is disgusting, these jerks need to be taught a lesson. Soon I am thrown into a cell, the gate slams shut, and the guards leave without a backward glance. Hopefully the Alpha will arrive soon, and I can gather more information before my dad arrives. A battle with this pack just looks better and better the more time is spent here.

My eyes take in the cell, that is now my home for a bit, I assume the bars are made of silver since the guards didn't touch them. Reaching out to barely touch one with my finger, a sizzling sound hits my ears. Gasping in pain, I pull my hand back quickly and view the damage, there is a small burn on my finger from the silver. Good to know my wolf and I have no resistance to silver.

The stench down here is overpowering now that my mind is calm enough to take in other details. The mixture of blood, fear, urine, feces, rotting food, rats, dirt, and death all combine in a repugnant smell. It takes all my self-will and power not to retch. How many have been left here to die on their own, their family never knowing what has happened to them? These smells only come from complete and utter despair.

I walk over to what looks to be a bed against the back wall. On closer examination it is a stone slab with a filthy blanket that is slowly falling apart. It appears the rats have been taking small bits of it to add to their nests, they can have it. A shiver runs through me. If this is the welcome I receive upon arrival, nothing good is meant to come of my time here. The back wall of the cell and the side are made of stone, reinforced with silver, the stone looks damp, mold covers patches of it, my only thought here is that mold needed a warm, moist environment to thrive, and this place is not warm.

Sitting in my cold, damp cell, on this hard bench, for over an hour, the decision has been made, I have had enough playing meek-and-weak. When Alpha Blaine finally decides to grace me with his presence I will demand some answers, he is not the only Alpha here, well, soon-to-be Alpha for me anyway, and this is not acceptable. This is an act of war against my pack. I just need to play it smart, though, my temper cannot take over.

"Brooke, I really need your guidance and calm right now. Help me through this, please," I say to my wolf, while sitting with my head in my hands.

Despair is not why I am seated like this, there is no way my back or head is going to make contact with the stone slab, and the walls are not an option to lean on since they have silver embedded in them. This is currently the position of most comfort for me.

"I am here, watching and listening. We are about to deal with a significant amount of pain. When you start to feel the pain, accept it, and everything that comes with it. Once you have accepted it, let me take control. Alpha Blaine is on his way. Stay strong, Jasmine, you are a Queen," Brooke says in a sad tone.

Before there is an opportunity for me to question Brooke further, the sound of squeaking comes from above me. The door to the dungeon is opened. I hear one set of footsteps enter, with the footsteps comes an amazing scent that pushes out all the other smells. The smell is of pine and pecans. My breath catches, my pulse races and I feel giddy. What in the world is happening? Then it dawns on me. Oh, no! It can't be.

A man stops in front of my cell and looks me over. He is 6 foot 4 inches easily, black hair, athletic build. He is amazingly handsome, needs to learn some manners, but handsome nonetheless. He possesses a heavily muscled frame, square-cut jaw, but his lips are pulled into a snarl, I look into his stormy eyes and see…hatred? That is odd, I am swooning over this man before me, and he hates me? I thought we were supposed to have a connection. His face holds no emotion, and his posture is tense. After a few minutes of "viewing me," he finally speaks.

"I am Alpha Blaine, it appears you are my mate, hybrid. I find that vile and repulsive. There is no way I would ever accept you as mine. I, Alpha Blaine Michael Slape of the Broken Moon pack, reject you, Jasmine Rose Oscuro, future Alpha of the Whispering Winds pack, as my mate and Luna," he says in a cruel voice, with no remorse.

I gasp, a painful squeezing sensation tightens around my heart. The urge to scream and cry sweeps over my body. My legs feel weak, and all my muscles have lost their strength, my body begs to fall to the floor and curl into the fetal position, protecting my body and heart from what this man has inflicted. The pain is beyond any I have ever felt. The need to beg for him to reconsider is strong. I will not. Brooke's words come back to me; she is sending her strength to me.

I breathe through the pain, stay on my feet, straighten my spine, raise my head proudly and look directly into the icy, soulless blue eyes of Alpha Blaine and say, "I, Jasmine Rose Oscuro, future Alpha of Whispering Winds pack, accept your rejection, Alpha Blaine Michael Slape of Broken Moon pack. You are not now, nor will you ever be, good enough for me, my family, or my pack. May you rot in hell."

A glimmer of pain flashes in his eyes but is gone as soon as it appears. He lets out a loud snort and says, "The only one who will be rotting around here is you, in this cell, until I decide how to dispose of you. Consider yourself my prisoner. I will be back when I decide the most entertaining way to take your life. It is important to me that you enjoy the pain of rejection before I take everything from you."

With that he stomps off, the dungeon door squeaks open, and slams shut, throwing me into darkness and silence. I sink down to the ground now that he is gone, not caring about the grime and dirt beneath me. I let Brooke take over to heal the pain, slowly the pain and ache of rejection reduces.

Even though I am glad I was rejected there is a sense of loss. To think I was rejected because my blood comes from two species. To look down on me because my family is accepting of all creatures. I will see the end of this pack and all those who support the segregation of the supernatural species, my mission is to find the real threat, Alpha Blaine is not it, and terminate it. I will rise to Queen and have peace in this land. My resolve and strength have returned, my path in this world has become clear.

It is time to mind-link my dad, there is no more information for me to learn from Alpha Blaine. "Dad, you were correct, the Broken Moon pack was the end destination. I do not know what the security looks like here, I was placed in the dungeon almost immediately after my arrival. The displeasure of meeting the Alpha and Beta of this pack has been mine, after our interactions, there is no more information for me to gather from them."

"The dungeon?! How dare they. We will be there in the next hour. There is already a plan in place to deal with their fighters. Ezekiel pulled all their information for me; we have enough warriors with us to subdue them. We will get you out and bring you home."

"Dad, their plan is to kill me, they will be hostile the moment you come to the main gate and attack you, there is no need to put our pack in danger of an ambush. Wait for me at the end of the gravel road. Keep the mind-link open. I am breaking out of this dungeon and will contact you if I need help."

Cutting the mind-link with Dad, a plan begins to form in my mind.

Chapter 18:

The Escape

(Jasmine's POV)

"Brooke, we are getting out of here, there is no way we are going to give these jerks the opportunity to kill us. Everything in my power will be done to not shift, but I will need you to give me some of your strength. My magic is going to be the first line of defense to get us out, and we will rely heavily on it, but I may need to fall back on pure power and muscle at some point," I alert my wolf.

"My strength is yours as well as enhanced hearing and smell too. We need to be able to sense a threat before it is on top of us. Your strategy of using your magic and having your senses as back-up is solid, we will be fine, Young One. Let's get back home."

Before doing anything else my scent needs to be hidden, my best bet is to sneak out of here instead of forcing my way out. One wolf, regardless of power, is not much against an entire pack, plus Dad is still an hour out. The spell goes smoothly, plus it goes much quicker when it is done to hide just my scent.

First things first, time to get out of this cell, checking out the lock on the door it does not appear to be reenforced. Placing my hands as close as I can to the lock, without touching the silver bars, I close my eyes and concentrate. Slowly a warmth builds up in my hands, it reminds me of a hand warmer in a mitten, looking down, the lock is melted allowing the cell door to open a bit, a smile graces my lips, and we leave the cell. First part of my plan is complete, if only the entire process goes so well.

Carefully placing my feet on the stairs, ascending to the top floor we pause at the dungeon door and listen; there are two heartbeats on the other side. Sniffing the air, there is no scent to give any indication of who is on the other side. Due to Blaine's visit earlier, we know the dungeon door squeaks, so I need to be ready to act once I dedicate to opening the door. Taking a deep breath, I take a moment to prepare and steady myself. My plans have to quickly change as the door begins to open under someone else's power.

Quickly and silently standing off to the side, so the door will hide me, anticipation washes over me to see who will be making an appearance. Thankfully, having no detectable scent will make hiding easier, plus they do not see me as a flight risk, I should have the element of surprise unless my heartbeat gives me away. The door continues to squeak open, luckily, the figure walking through is one of the guards doing a check.

Whispering a sleeping spell before the guard has a chance to discover me, he slides to the floor soundlessly, I put my foot out to keep the door ajar, and step into the open where the other guard is sitting, placing the same spell on him he slumps over his desk. No one has been alerted to my escape attempt yet. Grabbing the guard from inside the door, I let the door shut behind me and position the guards, so it looks like they fell asleep on duty. Most likely they will be punished for this, but that is not my concern, and no empathy finds its way to my heart for them.

Since everyone misjudged me when I got here, and took no security measures, I know where the main gate is located and what is available for cover to get there. Act like a weak, feeble girl and they will assume you are no threat every time. There is no remorse felt by me using their ignorance against them, never would my pack be so lax with prisoners.

Staying in the shadows the forest line is just ahead, my progress so far has been unimpeded. There is better luck being in the trees, but the same camouflage and protection it offers to me is also offered to the guards on duty. After dealing with the Alpha and the Beta, I do not have much hope the guards are going to be any nicer.

Using the heightened senses Brooke has leant me, we move along slowly, staying aware of our surroundings. I stop behind a tree, to my left comes the scent of wolves. Darn my luck, this must be one of the patrols, curse my thoughts of them earlier, it is like they were summoned. Listening closely there are three heartbeats, the number seems correct for a patrol number. Waiting for them to come further into the trees, I again use the sleeping spell, this keeps them from mind-linking anyone and notifying them of my escape.

I continue through the trees, soon the fence line is a few feet in front of me. The main gate is close to half a mile away to my right. I pause and listen around me. There are no sounds or movements that are abnormal for the night, sniffing the air gives no scent of wolves close to me, this is a good holding spot for now, while I take in my area.

The Broken Moon pack made sure there were no trees close to the fence line on the neutral territory side of the fence but did not take the same precautions on the pack side. Now to scout out a tree that is close enough for me to climb, then jump onto the top of the fence and drop down to the other side, the perfect tree soon shows itself to me.

Halfway up the tree I hear a commotion at the front gate.

"The prisoner has escaped. The Alpha wants us to be on the lookout for her. Link him if you catch site or smell of her; he wants to deal with her personally. Brian, Mike and Pete, go to the west; Darrin, Paul, and Scott, go to the east. I want full perimeter checks. Link in every half-mile, it appears she is using a sleeping spell on us. Move out!" an unknown voice commands them. It is best to pause my climb for now, it would be problematic to make a sound and give away my position. I am far enough up I am blocked from sight by branches and leaves. Now to work on calming my heartbeat, they would pick up on a racing heartbeat in no time, especially since there shouldn't be one in this area this late at night. Making out three figures, who I assume is Brian, Mike and Pete, approaching my tree, their noses turned up sniffing the air, trying to pick up a scent. It seems they are heavily relying on sense of smell and no other senses. Yet another weakness in their training to use against them.

Breathing a quiet sigh of relief, the wolves do not pick up my heartbeat and continue on their way, still it is best to wait another thirty minutes before continuing up the tree, to ensure they don't backtrack. Finally making my way to the necessary height to get me onto the perimeter wall, I walk out on a limb as far as I dare and leap to the top of the wall.

Keeping my body flat on the wall and listening for any sounds or movements, or if my jump caught any unwanted attention, a few minutes pass and there is no response to my jump. I roll my body over the side of the wall, holding on to the top until I am stretched out as far as possible, then let go and drop soundlessly to the ground.

Instantly, I press my back against the fence and listen again to see if there is any indication the wolves have been alerted to my presence. Again, all is quiet. Staying in the shadows I begin my trek south, mind-linking on my way.

"Dad, I am out of the pack territory, heading to the vehicles now. Make sure the engines are running and ready for a quick getaway. They know I have escaped, but do not know my location presently, patrols are looking for me now. Once they find the sleeping patrol in the trees, they will know I have made my way to the fence."

"Good job, honey. The cars are waiting and ready. We are on heightened alert. See you soon." Then Dad cuts the mind-link.

Being far enough away from the fence now no one will see me, I take off at a run towards the cars. About thirty minutes has passed by, with me at a steady run, when I see the cars ahead of me, there is an enormous amount of relief felt seeing my pack members. I am not about to drop my guard yet, though. Not until these people and network have been taken down will I rest.

Closing in on the vehicles and my dad, I hear a loud, angry howl behind me. My blood runs cold in my veins, that growl could only belong to an Alpha. The howl was still a way off, but if the Alpha and Beta are in wolf form they will be here in no time. I increase to a faster pace to get to the SUVs Dad brought, some of our fighters are shifting into their wolves, making their way to me, not willing to let me face the threat on my own. The arrogance of this pack, they should not be pursuing me in neutral territory, but they are. Apparently, they believe rules don't apply to them.

There is a growl behind me, and I turn as a massive body collides into me, tackling me to the ground. I bring my knees up as I am going down and use the momentum to flip the wolf off me. I jump up quickly glancing around me, noticing I am surrounded by wolves and my pack is currently in the middle of a battle, it is time to use some of the spells in my limited arsenal, I mumble one under my breath and tree roots come up from the ground, I use my hands to direct the roots, and they wrap around the wolves encircling me, from the feet up. The wolves all shift back to human form, but that is no use, the roots clench down, allowing no movement.

Rushing to assist my pack still engaged in the battle, I notice three wolves teaming up on my dad. Using my magic to throw one into a tree, I run in and jump on the back of a second wolf, wrapping my arms around his neck and cutting off his air supply. He reaches up and scratches my arm, attempting to dislodge me but I continue to hold on.

The wolf reaches around with his paw and sinks his claws deep into my shoulder. A furious growl leaves my lips, as I twist his head, snapping his neck. He falls to the ground lifeless, sightless eyes staring right into mine, I stand there looking at him in shock, nausea spreading through my belly and bile rising in my throat.

I have never taken a life.

Chapter 19:

Post Escape

(Jasmine's POV)

The battle continues to rage on around me, but my attention is not on the battle, lost in my thoughts and the fact I took a life my system seems to have shut itself down. My entire body shakes as my eyes continue to bore into the wolf on the ground in front of me, it does not matter the wolf would have killed me, had I not broken his neck, I am still sickened by my actions, balking at the image in my mind.

A gentle hand is placed on my shoulder, turning, my dad is standing there. He opens his arms and I fall into them, burying my head in his chest, taking deep breaths of his scent.

His smell is calming and safe, has been for as long as I am able to recall, there is no doubt I am protected with him near. After a few minutes of him holding me, stroking my hair, and whispering comforting words my eyes raise to him, tears lay at the edges of my eyes threatening to stream down my face. Dad gently takes hold of my chin and looks in my eyes. "Jasmine, it is never easy when you take a life, it never gets easier, you just learn to put it aside while you are on the battlefield and think about it after. You didn't take a life the entire time you were escaping, instead you used magic, you only took a life when it came down to him or you. You did everything you needed to do to protect yourself and your pack. You behaved as a true Alpha, and I couldn't be prouder of you than I am now." His voice is gentle and soothing.

"Thank you, Dad." My voice is shaky as it leaves my mouth. I take a deep breath and a step back from him, resolve running through my being. "There is something I need to take care of before we leave."

Dad nods at me. "Just let me know if there is anything you need my help with. Now that the battle is over a group of us will be with you at all times."

Nodding my understanding, I turn and walk towards the wolves still confined by the tree roots. Dad and Zeke are behind me. The rest of our fighters are policing the area and doing basic clean-up, pride surges through me when it dawns on me we lost no pack members during the battle.

Beta Clark is the first wolf my path takes me to whom I recognize. I step up to him and look him in the eyes.

"Recognize, Beta," I spit out vehemently, "it is the female half-breed who kicked your sorry ass. Your entire pack was unable to capture me while I escaped. Understand, I will be the nightmare that becomes your reality," I finish coldly.

Beta Clark's eyes widen in shock, there may be a hint of fear there as well.

Next to feel my wrath is Alpha Blaine. "Alpha Blaine, I am not so easy to kill, am I? Guess you lost your entertainment for the evening. You will perish and rot in hell caused by my hand but first I want you to let everyone in your network know I am coming for them. We will meet again, and it will be a fight to the death. Your death." I am directly in his face and leave no room for doubt. "Another thing, Alpha," I say, Alpha dripping in disdain, "you should look at training your goons and pack better. I have never seen such horrible security practices in all my life. Perhaps all they need is a real leader," I taunt.

I spin on my heel and start to walk away, when another wolf catches my attention from the corner of my eye. Saul.

"Zeke!" I call.

"Yes, Jasmine?"

"Take this wolf with us. I want him placed in the dungeon and interrogated. He is the one who had me injected with wolfsbane in the cabin. He comes with us. Also make sure the rest of these loathsome creatures know what it looks like when real security measures are taken."

"Yes, ma'am. We will get him secured now," Zeke responds.

I give Saul a cold smile and lean in, whispering into his ear, "You are mine now."

He gives me a look of loathing, but it does nothing to phase me, I shake my head at him, give a smirk and walk off. There is nothing left for me to do here, they will not be released by my hand from the tree roots—no, their pack members can have fun with that—however, there is a protection spell on the trees so they will not be harmed when their roots, acting as bindings, are cut. Thinking back on what had just occurred, it is unclear where my aggression came from while dealing with the Alpha and Beta, but it must be the influence of Brooke and the support of my dad. I like the confidence I feel, the slight change. Once back home, it will be time to speak with my wolf, Brooke will hold the answers for me about this and where it came from.

I climb into the back seat of an SUV with my dad and Ezekiel, instantly my head is on my dad's shoulder. It has been an exhausting and emotional few hours for me. Seems like it should have been days versus hours, but this is the reality of it. At this moment, basking in the love and protection of my loved ones is enough, letting the feelings calm and sooth me. I know I am going to have to go into detail and tell them everything when we get home. Dread sends a shiver through me at the thought of having to relive the rejection, I only want to tell the story once.

Now that Brooke has taken her strength back, and the adrenaline is gone, the pain is creeping back from the rejection. I refuse to cry, but the pain in my heart is agonizing. The breaking of a bond is painful, and I will have to suffer through. At least this pain is not as bad as the initial rejection pain, perhaps Brooke didn't pull back all her strength.

I give a deep sigh and cuddle more securely into my dad's side, silent tears streaming down my face. I just need his warmth, strength, and love. In no time I fall asleep, and Dad lets me sleep undisturbed the entire ride back to our pack.

CHAPTER 20:

New Day

(Jasmine's POV)

Slowly my eyelids begin to flutter open as my being begins to awaken, my body is snuggled deep into my comforter, sunlight, shining in brightly through my window. I blink a few times trying to gauge the time of day. Was the past day a figment of my imagination, was it all a bad nightmare plaguing my dreams?

Yawning deeply, my arms stretch above my head while my body remains in the prone position. I grab my pillow, fluff it up a bit and snuggle back into it, not ready to face the day or my loved ones.

The pain making its presence known in my heart reminds me what occurred is no nightmare, it is the reality of being an anomaly. Who knew the impact a rejection could have on one's body and mind? Thankfully we did not have a stronger connection when this happened, and Brooke assisted me with the fallout, or I would be worse than I am now.

There is no desire or energy running through my body to do anything other than sleep away the day, maybe lay here and stare out my window, but nothing that is even remotely productive. This is even worse than the time my spell went wrong, and the main dining hall was wrecked, at least Mom was able to pull me out of that funk in less than an hour.

Now awake, but not willing to get out of bed, my mind is replaying all the events that have recently occurred, good and bad. My life has taken an unexpected turn and my acceptance of it is amazing me, at least it wasn't all quiet acceptance. My mind wraps around the fact that in 18 years I never experienced an actual fight or battle, in the last few days there have been two added to my fighting resume. Letting out a heavy sigh as I continue to lay in bed, staring at the clouds on my ceiling, my thoughts go back to those of five years ago, wouldn't it be nice to just be able to teleport away somewhere?

"Brooke, how are you doing?" I ask groggily, feeling slightly guilty it has taken me this long to check on her, while wallowing in self-pity.

"I am doing alright, Young One. It is best we were not forced to stay with him, he does not know the blessing he gave us. It is painful but will soon pass. It saddens me to not be able to take away all your pain, but it is lessened a little. We have a lot to prepare for, enough to take your mind off this. Be warned, though, we will meet him again. He plays a significant role in what we face. I am glad he does not know you have me."

"There is no dispute there is a lot to prepare for, the events since my birthday have shown me there is a plethora for me to improve on and begin taking seriously. Brooke, when will the trainers Ashley was speaking of arrive? How will we know they are actual trainers, and not impersonators?"

"I will recognize them. They have been my warriors and trainers for generations. I am not a new wolf, Young One. Moon Goddess has made sure to pair me with a strong person, a person who will not back down and will fight for this just cause. There are no doubts in our abilities, I will admit, having a person who can also do magic is new for me, we are a strong team. Grace will also recognize them; she has been by my side since the start. That may be why you and Ashley have always shared such a bond and were born so close together."

"Thank you, Brooke."

"It is time to get up now, Young One. There is much to accomplish today. Speak with your family, give them all the details. Research Alpha Blaine and the Broken Moon pack. They have a dark history, but you must learn more of it for yourself. Get yourself together, you will have a visitor soon. Do not hesitate to reach out to me, I am always with you."

Groaning my disapproval of Brooke's direction to get up, my legs swing over the side of my bed. Rubbing my hands over my face and through my hair it occurs to me, there is really nothing to keep me from lying back down, except Brooke is correct, it is time to get up and put this melancholy mood aside. Shaking my head in the last ounce of denial left to me, it is clear, it is time to face reality. There is a storm coming our way and we need to be strong enough to face it.

First things first, a shower is much needed, looking at my exposed skin there is evidence someone assisted me to bed, without cleaning me up. That means dungeon gunk is still lurking on my body, a shiver of disgust runs over my body, the water cannot warm up quickly enough for me. All I need is to wash away the dirt, grime, and dejection of yesterday, then hopefully the warm, caressing water will slightly invigorate me and my motivation will kick in.

Once out of the shower, the clothing from yesterday finds its way into a trash receptacle, never again will they grace my body. Finding a clean outfit for the day I finished dressing and grooming, feeling presentable it is time to get some breakfast and coffee. Reaching out to grab the handle of my door a knock sounds from the other side. I jump a little at this unexpected sound and laugh quietly to myself at my overreaction, putting a smile on my face and opening the door. Zeke and Ash stand in front of me, perfect company to begin my day.

Ashley barges through the door and jumps on me, "I am so glad you are awake! Your mother, I mean Luna, would not let me come up and check on you. She said you needed to sleep and heal from your ordeal yesterday. I understand where she is coming from, but I am you defender and I need to know you are alright. I am your sister and I need to give you a big hug," Ash blurts out, her arms still wrapped around me.

Returning the hug, a light giggle fills me, "Everything is fine, Ash, just needed some sleep after all that has occurred. I was exhausted physically and mentally but feel a lot better now. All the details will be explained to everyone after breakfast, well, assuming it is still breakfast time."

"You are in time for breakfast, but I thought I would jumpstart it for you and bring you a nice hot cup o' joe. Made just the way you like it."

I smile gratefully at Zeke and wrap my hands around the steaming cup of goodness, tipping the cup up a big gulp slides down my throat, a small groan of happiness escapes my lips. My cup of coffee is finished before we make it to the dining room. We are eating in the packhouse today, so we only had to go down to the first floor, which I am thankful for because I am starving.

It is just the three of us in the dining room enjoying breakfast, we have almost finished when we get a mind-link from Dad asking us to come to the private meeting room on the Alpha floor. We put away our dirty dishes and hurry to the meeting room, the time has come for the moment that has been causing me dread.

Brooke has advised it is best to tell them everything, the entire story, leaving nothing out. She stressed this point multiple times, but I don't want my parents to be hurt by the fact I was rejected because of my lineage. There is no doubt we are a more cohesive team if everyone is on the same page, though does the reason for my rejection really matter? Based off the prophecy the only true answer available to me is yes, it does matter, with that in mind I take in a deep breath and square my shoulders. It is time to behave like the Queen I am destined to be.

We get to the office door and knock; my dad calls for us to come in. Zeke opens the door for us, and we enter. This room has never appealed to me much, it is so impersonal. A huge rectangle table takes up most of the space, it has twelve brown leather chairs surrounding it. Around the edges of the room is counter space with cupboards underneath. The area closest to the door has all the office items you would need. Next to that is beverages and snacks. There is an open chair next to my dad and he motions towards it, giving me my cue to take that seat. Zeke and Ash sit on the other side of me then all eyes land on me expectantly. Clearing my throat, it is time to begin the briefing.

"After Saul had me injected with wolfbane and took me from the cabin, his group walked for a long time through the forest until we came to some cars they had planted for us to escape in, from there we headed to the Broken

Moon pack. They were very lax on security measures with me, probably because they had injected me with wolfsbane, but I have a tolerance to small doses. They never did place anything over my head to keep me from knowing our route, which is how I was able to update Dad. The first wolf I encountered after arriving at Broken Moon was Beta Clark. He mocked me for being a woman and a mixed-blood, then had me thrown into the dungeon to await Alpha Blaine's arrival. Clark must have been under orders not to do anything to me, besides spitting on me and having me thrown into a cell, he did not land a hand on me. After hours of being there, Alpha Blaine arrived and—"

I stop for a moment, there is pain and a squeezing sensation around my heart, a tear slides down my face. Gasps sound in the room at my emotional distress. Ashley wraps an arm around my shoulder and pats my knee with her other hand. I give her a thankful smile, then continue.

"It turns out we were mates, Alpha Blaine and me. He rejected me because he cannot have a Luna, who is not a pure blood. He sees me as a disgrace. I accepted the rejection. He left me in the dungeon until he could figure out an entertaining way to kill me. That is when the urgency hit for me to escape and waiting for Dad and our warriors was no longer an option. Brooke remained hidden the entire time, pushing forward her strength and heightened senses, magic was the only thing used to break me out. As far as I know, they do not know I have a wolf."

Looking around the room at the shocked faces has me feeling slightly selfconscious. Zeke has his hands balled into fists in his lap, my mother's eyes are starting to shine blue. My father jumps to his feet with a loud growl, knocking his chair over backwards.

"Alpha Blaine has committed acts of war against this pack! If it is a war he wants, it is a war I will give him! It will be my pleasure to tear his treacherous heart from his body and burn it. How dare he hurt my daughter." My father's voice is low and threatening. There is a consensus in the room to end Alpha Blaine and his pack.

"I agree the Broken Moon pack needs to be dealt with, Dad. Brooke has asked me to do some research into their background. There is more than we see on first glance; it may be wise to step back from an immediate response, gather our knowledge and formulate a plan. I escaped, accepted the rejection, and believe he is the first clue to figuring out who is the main person or group behind this."

Others around the room are nodding in agreement, they are not happy, but they understand the logic.

"Alright, Jazz, if that is the way you want to move forward with this. Zeke, assist Jasmine in her research, one of the positives is we know who we are dealing with; the other is my daughter put a hurt on Alpha Blaine and showed him her strength. Regardless of that, I want her protection detail doubled. Claire and Ashley, get together and make sure this happens immediately," Dad directs us.

"One other thing, when the trainers and other protectors arrive, we will not need to do truth spells on them. Brooke told me she and Grace will know them, they are old wolves and the people coming to us have been with them for generations. More research needs to be done on our wolves too. Brooke said she and Grace have been together for a long time and she believes that is why the Goddess had Ashley and me born so close together," I inform the group.

Ashley's eyes light up at the new information. "Let me help you with that research, Jazz. I am excited to learn more about Grace. She has been a little tight-lipped recently about the prophecy, only telling me to train and prepare."

"Of course, it will be fun to learn more information together on them. It seems their bond is as strong, if not stronger than ours." Excitement courses through my system to find these discoveries together.

"We all know what we need to be doing. Let's get on with our plans and once we have more information, call another meeting. Let's go, folks," my dad directs everyone.

Zeke, Ashley, and I exit the office.

"Ashley, go with Claire first and make the arrangements my dad has asked for, please. I will mind-link you when we start the research on our wolves."

Ashley nods and walks off with Claire while Zeke and I make our way to his office in the technology center.

CHAPTER 21:

ALPHA BLAINE

(Alpha Blaine's POV)

Pacing back and forth in my office, I am raging inside, the current situation before me is unbelievable. How? How did this happen? I know physically how, but why were my men so neglectful with that vile beast? We had her in our dungeons, drugged with wolfsbane, in a cell, embedded with silver on all sides. Who just walks out of that? No, not walks, blatantly saunters through the damn doors, placing sleeping spells on my guards and evading my men as if they have no training!

To make everything even worse, I just received a call from my grandfather, he will be here in the next hour, to discuss our failure. This is not a meeting I am looking forward to, and there will be fall-out, mass amounts of fall-out for everyone, including myself.

There is an unexpected knock at my door. "Who's there!" I bellow out, irritated at being bothered.

"Beta Clark, Alpha."

"Come in," I growl.

The door opens and in walks my Beta. He looks at me with his emotionless eyes and informs me with a voice also devoid of emotion.

"The guards on duty at the dungeon have been dealt with. They will never have the opportunity to fail you again."

"That is good, I cannot abide what happened. Tell me everything that occurred from her arrival. I need to have this all figured out before my grandfather arrives. Did you manage to talk to the rogues Saul used to bring her here?"

"The rogues assisting Saul have been located, as a matter of fact, I have the leader of the group standing outside the door. I did not want to bring him into your office without permission, Alpha."

"Very good. Bring him in, we will get his story then kill him and the others. We do not need anyone slipping out information. I am counting on Saul to keep quiet. Use the rogues as training for the junior warriors. It is time they start to learn how to kill. Since I didn't get to kill the half-breed, someone must die," I direct Clark.

A slow smile crosses Clark's face at my direction. "I am happy to make it work, Alpha. I will get the rogue now for you."

Clark opens the door, and the rogue enters. His eyes are downcast, there is noticeable sweat on his brow. This especially pleases me, to have a wolf in my presence and know they fear me. I look the rogue up and down. He will make great training for my youth warriors. He doesn't even know his fate yet.

"Tell me what you know about Saul taking the girl from Whispering Winds," I demand in a hard voice.

The rogue jumps a little, making me smile. He keeps his eyes averted.

"S-she was tied to the ch-chair with silver as directed. We injected her with the wolfsbane as t-told. She did not put up any f-fight. The entire p-process was smooth. Th-there was no s-scent of other w-wolves in...in the area. S-She was w-weak and s-slept most of the d-drive."

This rogue is very nervous, and his body language screams to me how weak he is. I curl my lip up and glare at him in disgust, not that he notices, coward won't even look in my direction.

"Did she attempt to shift? Did you notice any signs of a wolf in her?"

"N-none. T-the s-s-silver did not b-burn her s-skin either."

"Take him out. I have no further use for him."

Clark grabs the rogue by the back of the neck and throws him to the waiting guards, who bound his wrists. Terror crosses through the rogue's eyes when he realizes he is not leaving. I chuckle at his realization. The guard drags the rogue out of the room, while he pleads for his release.

Turning a deaf ear to him, my attention sways back to my Beta. "Clark, tell me about your interactions with her."

"Saul hauled her out of the car by her hair and threw her on the stairs in front of me. She made a couple weak attempts to stand, but gave up, such a pathetic creature. I directed her to be placed in the cells to wait for your return. The guards dragged her there since she was unable to walk. She did not cause any issues while waiting in the cells. There was no sign of a wolf in her, I couldn't smell one or sense one. I even made it a point to mock and spit on her. No reaction, an Alpha wolf would have responded regardless."

Interesting facts indeed, running them over and over in my mind, there is only a single conclusion that can be made. A knock sounds at my door while I am still reflecting.

"Come in." My wolf is quickly losing patience at the constant interruptions.

In walks the imposing figure of my grandfather. I swallow hard and feel my stomach begin to clench, my wolf cowers slightly in my mind. It takes a momentous effort to show no signs of my distress outwardly, especially with Clark in the room.

"You may go, Clark. Make sure the rogues are taken care of as directed."

Clark nods to me, then to my grandfather and leaves. My eyes have not left my grandfather since he entered the room. I wait to hear the door shut behind Clark before addressing my grandfather.

"Hello, Grandfather. It is unfortunate to have to call you here for this meeting."

"I agree," sneers my grandfather. "I give you and your pack one simple job, and you manage to ruin it. All my plans require us having this girl in our possession, Blaine. I thought I made that very clear to you."

"Yes, Grandfather, you did. I spoke with the lead rogue who was with Saul and—"

"Where is Saul?" my grandfather interrupts me. He stares me down with hard, angry eyes.

"Saul was taken by the Whispering Winds pack."

"HE WAS TAKEN!" bellows my grandfather.

Before I know it, he is in front of me and lands a punch to my left jaw, dropping me to my knees on the ground. Blood is dripping from the corner of my mouth, down my jaw, then onto the floor, but I keep my eyes averted from the man who caused the bleeding.

"You were raised better than this. You were raised to be a competent Alpha. It appears there was a flaw in how you processed my training and teachings, apparently, I was not hard enough in my training of you. You continue to be a failure at every turn, needing me to come in and clean up the mess," Grandfather spits at me.

"We do not think she has a wolf, Grandfather. She never attempted to shift during the entire ordeal. She was chained with silver in the cabin but had no burn marks on her. There was no smell of other wolves in the area when she was taken from the cabin. Beta Clark could not smell or sense a wolf in her. When she managed to escape, she only used magic, she did not have a wolf that came forward. Is it possible this is not the girl?" I dare to ask.

"Of course, she is the girl! If you did not smell any wolves at the cabin, how did her pack manage to find her location?"

My eyes widen at this realization. If she had been taken by the rogues as initially planned her pack would not have known she was at the cabin or being brought to Broken Moon. She had to have mind-linked them. She couldn't mind-link without a wolf. I am such a fool, but on the other hand her mother is a witch, which leaves other avenues.

"Her mother is a witch, Grandfather, she may have put a spell on her to find her if taken, since she left pack territory and was unable to use mind-link. Also, she didn't show any emotion or pain when I rejected her. If there was a wolf in her, there would have been some sort of a reaction. She just accepted the rejection, no begging, crying or anything," I say lowly.

"When you what?" Grandfather asks incredulously.

"When I rejected her, Grandfather."

"That girl was your mate? You rejected her? You fool! That was the ticket to keeping her with us and you screwed that up too. We could have used the bond to our advantage and then killed her once the plan was complete," Grandfather screams at me, losing control, he kicks me in the head, followed by a few blows to my ribs and back.

I fall the rest of the way to the wooden floor, barely able to keep my eyes open. Grandfather bends over me and snarls.

"My influence only goes so far. I cannot lose the respect and faith of the Collaborative. Fix this or I will kill you and find a more suitable replacement. Your Beta seems to be a decent replacement choice for you, at least he has a few firing neurons in his head."

With one final kick to my stomach, he turns and walks out the door, then darkness takes over.

Chapter 22:

Preparation

(Jasmine's POV)

Fall is here, we are beginning to have shorter days and longer nights, a cool wind has begun blowing across our lands, the hillsides are ablaze with color. The forest sounds are beginning to quiet, especially with the birds making their migration South. The change of seasons and climate shouldn't affect my warriors, but it does need to be taken into consideration for a looming war.

It has been three months since the meeting in the office. Three months since I decided to dedicate myself wholly to my destiny.

The few hours I spent in the Broken Moon pack changed the way I view life, mates and my future. Knowing my life was so close to being ended by a psychopath, without being able to see my loved ones or tell them goodbye, has brought more appreciation of my time with them, but also forces me to recognize we are not invincible.

Having a mate was not a priority for me, but it was something I was looking forward to in the future, after settling into my role. It was arrogant of me to think destiny can be made to fit in the picture you have set for yourself. Destiny slapped me in the face with the mate chosen for me, now my focus is purely on the prophecy and the supernatural world, protecting them from the bigotry and hatred growing in our society. It does sadden me some to think I will never experience the connection and love my parents have. Being a Queen, I will have many to love, and that is what consoles my heart.

Some people in the pack are happy to see I have grown up. My parents and friends seem concerned about my new attitude. I am not going to lie, revenge against Alpha Blaine is high on my priority list and knowing he is connected to the prophecy only encourages my desire to make him and his pack pay.

Brooke has been cautioning me against revenge, she says it a self-serving desire and my focus needs to be on bigger things, Blaine is a pawn, a pawn that needs to be dealt with but a pawn, nonetheless. Spending too much time planning against him allows the others responsible for the strife-facing the world to gain stronger ground. It is irritating sometimes how logical and correct she is but there is no other wolf I would rather have with me.

Speaking of Blaine, our research found multiple businesses the Broken Moon pack is involved in. It is unfortunate most of them are illegal fronts and the pack is paid handsomely to be mercenaries and assassins. Their specialty is hunting down and eliminating mixed species. There is one benefactor, who uses them frequently, but we are unable to trace this person or group. It is frustrating to have your next clue right in front of you, and then just taken away. Zeke refuses to give up on this search and he continues to work his magic in the technology sector, his talents amaze me, and I know if there is information out there to be had, he will discover it.

Claire and Mom have combined the training for Ashley and me. We now spar against my dad and Mark; every now and then Mom joins in on the sparring so we can learn to battle multiple species at once, there is no one left in the pack who can remotely challenge Ash and me; we are too strong, can communicate without mind-link on the field of battle, add in my magic, we are unstoppable. Well, to the folks we have to mock battle with. I hope the Moon Goddess' trainers and protectors begin to arrive soon, I do not want to be stagnant, I want to continue to progress.

When training is finished with Claire and Mom, Brooke and I go for a long run and personal training. We set up our own area to the Northwest border of the pack territory, near the boundary with the Midnight Moon Pack. I don't want everyone to know we continue practicing for another couple hours after. There is a driving need in me to better my magic and wolf skills, Brooke is an amazing teacher, she has helped me to grow, and we are bonding closer every day; Brooke is amazing and I am thankful to have such a patient and worldly wolf to help guide me.

When we finish our secret training, I spend a couple hours assisting in the pack hospital. Even though I am not able to pursue medicine for my career, it is important to me to be as involved as possible. Our pack doctors are a wealth of information and they have adopted me into their routine seamlessly, I mainly volunteer my time in the emergency room since my skills will most likely be used on the battlefield. The doctors have made it a mission for themselves to teach me treatment techniques for all supernatural species, what I have learned in the hospital, along with my ability to heal will be very beneficial.

When finished at the hospital I spend the rest of the day with my dad, learning how to run the pack, what businesses we have and who assists in managing them. It has never been a secret to me the pack owned businesses, it helps to keep our pack functioning, what I failed to realize was how many we own and the diverseness of the companies. Our pack has a strong financial future, due to the foresight of my ancestors, pride wells inside of me to see how they have cared for this pack, well into the future, I hope my legacy and reign as Alpha is as beneficial.

Once the day is over, and there is time to concentrate fully, Brooke and I strategize on how to move forward regarding the prophecy. The busier I am, the more I can keep my mind off being rejected, it is a sore subject for me, and even though most of the pain is gone, I do feel twinges in my chest, plus once my mind is not engaged with something, my thoughts return there, causing sleep to evade me. Hopefully the effects will go away soon.

Bringing my thoughts back to the present, excitement runs through my system, today Brooke and I plan to practice magic while in wolf form. There is no one to assist us in this area so we are learning through trial and error in our special area. It helps to know nobody is watching and judging.

We accidently discovered, while in wolf form, Brooke can use my magic. While doing our private training we set a few bushes on fire, thankfully water is also an element we control and were able to extinguish the fire quickly. We are keeping this information to ourselves for the time being, we want to know more about what we are able to do.

Our private training grounds are just in front of me, we run into the grove of trees that has become an oasis for us, a place we discover new talents but also have deeper discussions on life and the future. To ensure this area remains private, I have made it habit to hide my scent the moment I leave the training field so no one can follow me. Quickly shifting back to human form, it is time to set up the area.

"Young one, today I think we should see if I can control earth. It could be beneficial in battle."

I nod my head to Brooke, even though she is unable to see me nod, it is a habit that is difficult to break. Looking around the area to see what we have to work with, a few fallen logs catch my eye, they will be perfect to practice on; in a short time, they are set up, let the magic begin.

"Okay, Brooke, we will do this the same as we have been, I will say the spell and push it through you, just ensure you are facing in the direction where you want the spell to perform. We will work on having roots come from the ground and ensnare the enemy."

"Sounds good, Young One. Let's begin."

Shifting back into my wolf doesn't hurt as badly as the first time, but it is still not comfortable. Luckily it takes only a few seconds now. Turning my control over to Brooke, she turns and faces the logs I have placed around, she takes a defensive stance like she would in a battle. We take in a deep breath and begin the spell, I feel the energy traveling through me and push it on to Brooke, anticipation is high as I watch through her eyes.

Nothing... the spell did not work.

I furrow my brow and frown slightly, let's think this over for a moment. When I am doing the spell, my hands are used to direct and transfer the energy in the area I want it to go. Maybe this is not the correct spell to use with her. Our paws will be on the ground and unable to direct the roots.

"Brooke, I am going to change the type of spell we are doing. The other one requires the use of hands to direct it, this new spell will have the energy go from your paws into the earth. We are going to make a rolling earthquake, kind of a wave, small for now, just to test it, not sure if the wave will go clear around us or just to the front."

"I am ready to try, Young One."

Brooke resumes her defensive stance, I begin the spell, the energy is again flowing in my body, and I push it on to Brooke. Watching through her eyes, our markers in the distance begin to move up and down, Brooke looks to her left and right, we see no movement from the markers on either side, she turns a 180 and again no markers are moving. The energy force moved to the front only. This is good news; this means we will not affect our own warriors using this spell.

"Brooke! We did it. We have found an earth spell we can use." This is an amazing discovery and happiness is washing over us.

"This is very exciting, Young One. I have never done magic before, it is exhilarating. You have brought a new strength to us. I am so proud of you for thinking of attempting this."

"Well, we happened upon it, but decided to continue experimenting, regardless, we need to practice more and at varying strengths. We need to know if it will continue a forward-only movement if we increase the strength."

"Very wise, Young One. I like your plan."

I shift back to my human form and grab various supplies, then begin placing markers at further distances, making it so the markers will fall if hit with the wave. Markers are placed in all directions so we can tell if the increased energy broadens the width of the path, once everything has been set up, we scan to ensure Brooke and I are still the only ones around. I sniff the air and listen in for heartbeats, all is clear, and I feel confident to continue with our training. Brooke takes control again and we get back to our starting point and resume our stance.

"Brooke, I am going to increase the energy this time, not by much. We will be able to see the markers from here. As the energy increases and the wave hits farther out, we will need to shift back and forth to check on them, it is still not time for anyone to inadvertently see you yet."

"I agree, it is best to keep me hidden for as long as possible. Let's start. I am eager to see what will happen."

Her infectious attitude makes me smile; if a wolf could be giddy, I would say Brooke is giddy. Reigning myself in, it is time to concentrate and do the spell again, the energy is building up in me and then it is pushed forward.

Looking through Brooke's eyes I see we have sent the wave farther than before and only to the front again. Brooke lets out a yip of joy.

We continue for another hour, increasing our energy level little by little.

"Brooke, this will be the last one, then we will need to head back to the packhouse."

"Alright, Young One. We will need to practice this one again. Tomorrow let's see what we can do with air."

I let out a small groan as my mind goes back five years, we will not start with that spell. I focus my mind; the energy builds up and we send out our biggest wave yet. Brooke is prancing around the grove with her tail up and her head held high. This is the first time I have seen her this happy with training. Maybe it is because she is learning something new. Having lived for generations I am sure fighting in wolf form is a little boring. Once she has stopped prancing about, we shift back to human form, time to see how far this wave went.

Chapter 23:

Inadvertent Meeting

(Jasmine's POV)

Setting out to check the markers and see how far this last wave of energy advanced, I am close to our third marker, when I hear a loud yelp. My head snaps up in the direction the sound came from, there was no one in this area, is someone spying on me? That is ludicrous, the sound came from the other side of the boarder on Midnight Moon's side, no one from that pack knows about my wolf, I sniff the air and pick up the scent of Alpha Keith, for a moment, then it is gone. That is odd, better head over to see if everything is copasetic.

Keith is a couple years older than I am, he and Zeke attended school together and were close friends, during their younger years, Keith spent a lot of time at our pack. Rushing to the border, I am just in time to see Alpha Keith picking himself up off the ground.

"Are you alright? I heard you yelp," I ask.

Alpha Keith's head snaps in my direction, irritation written all over his perfectly chiseled features. His eyes are dark and dangerous, letting me know his wolf, Aspen, is near the front. It is best for me to remain here, since we surprised him with our presence, it would be bad if he saw me as a threat, making sure not to move or have any aggressive movement we give him time. As he looks at me his facial expression softens, and his eyes go back to soft brown.

"Hello, Jasmine. I didn't know you were around. I am not sure what happened, it was like a wave went through this area, causing me to lose my balance. Silly, right?"

I just nod my head looking down at the ground, a slight redness has found its way to my cheeks.

"Yeah, super silly," I mumble guiltily, keeping my eyes adverted, checking out the grass around my feet.

"Jasmine, are you the cause of the wave?" Alpha Keith asks, looking at my expression and blush, he is very familiar with some of the pranks we used to pull.

"Umm, yeah. I was practicing my spells and thought I was the only one in the area. Although to be honest, it didn't occur to me to check on your side of the border and didn't think the energy would travel that far. I am sorry, Alpha Keith."

"It is fine. I am unharmed. Maybe next time a forewarning call would be nice so we can avoid the area. Also, please just call me Keith, we have known each other too long for such formalities." He chuckles at me.

I raise my head and look into his eyes, I see nothing but genuineness in them, a large grin breaks out on my face. It is nice to see, he did not take this poorly.

"Looks like you are still working on your control, huh. Why am I always the one on the receiving end of your wayward spells?" He laughs.

Brooke starts stirring inside my head. "He is one of our protectors, Young One. This Alpha is to be by our side, we can trust him. He does not know yet, but soon Moon Goddess will let him know. It is good you have a connection with him already."

Yes, a connection, also a few pranks Ash and I pulled on him and Zeke growing up. Keith hasn't spent as much time around our pack since he started training to take over as Alpha for his pack, just the regular visits of a dignitary. Fond memories make their way to the forefront of my mind.

I have missed him being around. He always brought happiness and laughter with him, he was, is, like another brother, who took the pranks of his sisters well, even when I ended up catching him on fire, while he was flirting with a girl at school. The flame had shot out as Ash and me were arguing with

Zeke about an after school gathering. Thank Goddess I can control water as well.

He had just ruffled my hair, much to my dismay, and said I needed to work a little harder on control.

"It is good to see you again, Keith. You should come to dinner soon. I know everyone would be happy to see you. How are things now that you are Alpha?"

"Going well. I was stressed when I first took the reins, but I am getting into a groove."

A thought crosses my mind, I sniff the air and notice there is no scent. Keith has masked his scent and I am curious why.

"Keith, I cannot smell your scent, is everything alright?" I ask, raising my eyebrows and frowning just a little.

"We have had some trouble in the pack recently, not pack members causing problems, but someone coming over one of the borders and kidnapping or killing she-wolves, I masked my scent and am walking my borders to see if I can find anything; so far nothing except your magical wave," he teases me, attempting to lessen the seriousness of the situation.

A shiver runs down my spine at the information he has given, especially since an attempted kidnapping happened in our pack too. "You really need to come to dinner so we can discuss this in depth. Our pack may be able to assist you. Let me mind-link Dad. Are you available this evening?"

"Yeah, I cleared my schedule for the day so I could do a thorough check."

My eyes glaze over as I link my dad. "Dad, while on a run I came up to the boundary with Midnight Moon. Alpha Keith is here so we stopped and had a chat. He has been having issues with someone crossing his borders and kidnapping or killing she-wolves. I asked him to dinner this evening to discuss his troubles. Will this work with our schedules and dinner preparation?"

"We can make it work. Tell him dinner will be at 6 o'clock. He is always welcome to arrive earlier if he wishes. We will plan for him and a couple extra in case he wants to bring his Beta and Gamma."

I look back to Keith.

"Dinner is a go. Dad says service will be at 6 o'clock, but you are welcome to come earlier if you want, also your Beta and Gamma are welcome to attend as well."

"Thank you, Jasmine. I look forward to seeing everyone tonight, even if it is for abhorrent reasons. Time to get back to the border check so I will be done in time, don't want to keep your father waiting."

"I understand, Keith. It is time for me to get home and work with Dad too. See you this evening. Oh, could you keep this a secret between us, no one knows about this experimenting with magic thing happening." A blush returns to my cheeks as I am forced to admit he caught me.

A deep laugh escapes him. "Oh, little Jazz, always keeping people on their toes. It is time we shared a secret and this one is not so bad to have, it is safe with me." He gives me a small bow, mischief sparkling in his eyes, sending him a nod of thanks and my own smile, I wave goodbye.

We part ways and I return to the packhouse, my mind full of questions for Keith when he arrives for dinner.

Chapter 24:

Alpha Keith

(Alpha Keith's POV)

My run of the borders finally finished around two o'clock in the afternoon. Fatigue is beginning to settle in my body and mind, my alarm sounded off at four in the morning, waking me to begin my task.

There are no signs of where the intruder or intruders have been coming through, absolutely nothing disturbed, no broken branches, no footprints, it is like this threat is a ghost. I am frustrated and feel as if I am letting down my pack. As an Alpha I should be able to locate the threat and take care of it, I should be able to keep my she-wolves safe from this predator.

Anger overcomes me and my fist contacts the oak desk, pain wells up inside me, not just from my hand, but from the loss of pack members. I turn towards the map of my pack lands, there is not a single inch of my territory that has not been scoured and searched, at the moment, it is beyond me what my next move should be.

Running into Jasmine today has given me a bit of hope, perhaps Whispering Winds can assist us, come up with a plan of attack. Maybe Jasmine or Luna Abigail can place a protection spell around my pack, ideas and options are becoming less and less as this progresses. Whatever is happening or is the cause needs to be identified and stopped.

I mind-link my Beta and Gamma to come to my office. They have been doing their own investigation in other areas while I checked the physical land, maybe Beta Andrew was able to find something in the cyber sector. Gamma

Daniel is looking into known enemies of our pack, he is checking out our alliance members as well, just in case one of them is changing sides and tactics.

Recently there have been more attacks in the area against those of mixed species. Rumors of a collaboration being built to ensure the separation and purity of the species have been going around, although no one seems to have had any personal dealings with this collaboration, even though I cannot validate their existence, this rumor is something to keep in mind.

As this dilemma continues to circulate through my mind, there is a knock at my door "Come in," I command.

Andrew (Drew) and Daniel (Dan) come walking in and sit down in the chairs across from me. I have known these wolves since we were pups. Growing up together has created a strong bond. I trust them with my life. Andrew is as close to a brother as I will ever have. My parents raised him, after the death of his parents seven years ago. We are not sure what happened to them, every investigation ended in no answers, every lead was cold.

Both men have serious looks on their faces, and know this situation is grimmer than originally thought.

"Thanks for coming in, the entire border has been searched by me personally and there is no sign of an entry point, or any abnormal scents. I did run into Jasmine Oscuro on the North border. We spoke a bit about the goings-on and she invited us to dinner this evening so we can discuss everything we have found, Alpha Alexander said we eat at six o'clock. I would like for the both of you to join me. Whispering Winds is already aware you will be attending."

Andrew and Daniel nod to me.

"Andrew, please fill me in on what you have found and then Daniel, you can follow him."

"A search was run on she-wolf deaths and kidnappings stateside and on an international level. There has been an uptake in aggressions against shewolves in the last six months. At this point no one has been able to locate who is involved in the attacks and kidnappings. All the she-wolves who have been targeted are 17-20 in age and mixed species. Just like our she-wolves. I have reached out to the Alphas of some of the closer packs, I am hoping we can arrange a meeting soon and brainstorm how to locate the people behind all this. As with you, Keith, I have not located any clues or next steps at this point. Interesting to note, though, Jasmine was attacked during a trip to the mall with her friend Ashley and guard Claire."

My head snaps up at this news. Why hadn't Jasmine mentioned the same happening in her pack? Was it an isolated incident or have more members of her pack been subject to the same behaviors? This explains her eagerness to assist my pack. That girl has some questions to answer when we meet this evening.

"Thank you, Drew, I was unaware of the events with Jasmine. She neglected to tell me about it, but perhaps it will be covered during our meeting this evening. Dan, what do you have for me?"

"I ran our normal background checks on all packs we are associated with on both positive and negative levels, there are no obvious changes in patterns or behaviors, except for the Night Fall pack to the Northwest. It seems there has been an increase of hybrid and mixed couples moving into their pack. I made a call to the Alpha of the pack, and he told me the new pack members have been arriving from the East. They do not come from one pack in general but said there has been an upturn in mixed species hostilities as well, not just she-wolves. My thoughts are to start looking closer at the packs in that area." "Great work, Drew and Dan. Thank you for getting me this information.

After our meeting with Whispering Winds, we can make a plan on our next move. Until then I am going to think this over. The plan to start checking packs East of Night Fall pack and see if any ping on the radar is a good starting point, since we have nothing else to go on, it is the best lead we have."

Drew and Dan nod at me in agreement.

"I will let you guys get back to what you were doing before calling this meeting. Be ready to go by five o'clock. I would like to get to the dinner a little early and see if I can't get some answers from Jasmine about her ordeal in town."

Drew and Dan nod again, get up from their seats and leave my office.

Why would Jasmine be targeted? Based on the information from Drew she fits into the profile of victims, plus she is a high-ranking wolf. For the millionth time today, my fingers find their way through my hair, more questions than answers arise. My mind is fatigued with all the thoughts running through it, hopefully answers will begin coming our way.

Checking the time on the wall clock, it appears there are a few hours before we need to leave. It would be best to get a nap in, so I am fresh this evening and able to keep up on the conversation.

I secure all the information on my desk in my file cabinets, then head to my room once I am satisfied my office is secure.

Chapter 25:

Alpha Keith Meets Moon Goddess

(Alpha Keith's POV)

Dragging my tired body into my bedroom the door closes solidly behind me, automatically locking as it shuts, it is designed this way so if there is an emergency with the pack, no time is wasted on making sure my area is secure.

Going farther into my chamber, my shoes are kicked off as soon as possible, even though they are the most comfortably designed, my feet are aching after my surveillance of my border today. My feet are finally able to breath and stretch out, I wiggle my toes, easing the cramps that are starting. Sitting down on my bed, socks are the next order of business to get off, they are damp from all my activity today.

My bed is so comfortable, and I cast a longing glance at my pillows, even though my bed looks welcoming, a shower is the first thing in order, I am sweaty from my patrol this morning.

Regardless of my baser desires, it is time to drag my unwilling body into the bathroom. This space has been designed for comfort, the shower is large enough to accommodate three adults, and my body size is close to taking up space for almost two, finally the temperature is adjusted to a relaxing warmth. Leaning my head against the marble tiles, I stand under the cascading stream and let it massage my sore muscles. After half an hour, I reluctantly drag myself out of the shower as the water begins to turn cold.

I dry myself off and don't bother to put on any clothing, there is no need for it since my plan is to grace my bed with my presence. Quickly crossing my room, I throw the blankets back and slide under the covers of my bed and sink into the mattress, letting it hug my body. Soon I am fast asleep, lost in the world of dreams and mixed realities.

A large field spreads out around me, in the distance there are snow-covered mountains, a light, cool breeze is blowing over the field and around my body. I look down and see I am in wolf form; this is the perfect time and place to let Aspen run free and enjoy himself. We run toward the mountains and stop by the banks of a babbling stream. Aspen is thirsty after running around the meadow, chasing small flying insects in a game of tag, he takes a long drink of the pure chilled water. Never have I had such amazing water as this. We lay down by the banks of the stream and nap, the perfect combination of exercise, warmth, and chill lulls us to sleep, this is a much-needed dream after all the issues the pack is experiencing.

The feeling of fingers running gently through my fur, jolts me awake, but there is no threatening presence around me, Aspen is content to remain where he is. There is a soft giggle to my left.

I turn my head and there sits a woman with shining silver hair and diamond eyes, wearing a loose light blue gown. Her eyes shine with kindness and mischievousness, a small smile plays on her lips. She is beautiful, there are stories about her visiting dreams, but have never experienced it myself, I am in the presence of the Moon Goddess herself and have completely shut down.

"Hello, Alpha Keith," comes her melodic voice. I have never heard a voice that sounds like tinkling harp music, she has me completely mesmerized, locked into her being. "We have some things to discuss. While I am happy to sit here and pet my dear Aspen, you need to shift back, please. After everything going on at your pack Aspen needed to relax, it pleases me to see he was able to run and enjoy himself, but work needs to begin." Her eyes hold nothing but seriousness.

I instantly shift back to human form and a blush brightens my cheeks, when my dream started, we were already here in wolf form and there were no clothes next to us, it didn't seem important at the time but now, I am sitting naked in front of the Moon Goddess, completely mortified to be in this position; she is to be respected and highly regarded. I look down in shame at the circumstances.

"Keith," Moon Goddess giggles. "You are fully clothed now, there is no reason for embarrassment. Besides, I made you my child and have seen you in all forms and stages of dress, your reverence for me is appreciated; now look at me, my pup. We have a lot to discuss, since you will need to awaken soon to go to your engagement."

I sit up straight and give her my full attention. "I am ready, Moon Goddess."

"There is great strife in the realms. The supernatural world is at war with itself, sort of a civil war. There are those who want purity of species and detest all who have mixed-blood. I know your pack has been affected by these people. I am sure you have heard rumors of a collaboration fighting to separate all species into their own lands, this rumor is accurate. It is made up of high-ranking officials of werewolves, witches, vampires, and all other supernatural creatures. The attacks happening on your land is because they are searching for the Midnight Wolf."

This catches my attention; I turn to look at her with a questioning glance. "Midnight Wolf? Isn't that just lore?" Confusion evident in my voice, these were stories told to me at bedtime.

"All lore has some basis of truth to it. It just gets changed with generations of retelling; however, the Midnight Wolf is not lore, it is prophecy; a prophecy that is coming to fruition as we speak."

My mouth falls open at her revelation. I never thought I would be living in a time when a prophecy would come to light. It is still unclear why she is speaking to me; perhaps it is because my pack has been hit due to the hunt for this wolf.

"Does the Midnight Wolf reside in my pack?" I question, mixed emotions coming through in my tone. Fear that one of my pack is being hunted, anger that there is a group working against the supernatural and killing them off as they see needed, uncertainty at what the future is going to hold for us all, thankfulness that the Goddess thought to explain this to me.

"No. Let me give you some history. Thousands of years back, when I first created my beloved werewolves, there was a push to eradicate all of you. The vampires and witches did not want the challenge of another supernatural species usurping their power and hold. There was a war between the three worlds and many perished in the fighting.

"Finally, the heads of the three largest supernatural groups came together for peace talks. After days of discussion, it was decided to invite the heads of all the other supernatural species. They decided as a large group to name a ruler over all supernaturals. The issue was no one understood what it meant to live the life of another species, due to this issue it was agreed to take each head of the groups and put them in a challenge against each other.

"This challenge covered strength, knowledge, compassion, understanding, deductive reasoning, ability to lead, war maneuver, and much more. In the end, the werewolf leader was chosen and named king of all supernaturals. His first order of business was to name a council made up of representatives from all groups so each one had a voice. There were some who disagreed with this and after 100 years they were able to bind together to overthrow the king and council. They disbanded the entire hierarchy and left each group to fend on their own, against each other.

"Throughout the years there have been attempts to reestablish the royal line and rename a council. All attempts have failed. As the prophecy has said, when the strife between the masses is at its worst there will rise a Midnight Wolf, this wolf is to be the Queen over all supernaturals. There will be many trials and tribulations to get to the palace. The Queen will have protectors from each realm, who will train and fight for her, with her. The wolves protecting her will be of my ancient army—do you have any questions at this point?"

"The Midnight Wolf is a female; that is why my she-wolves and other packs she-wolves have been attacked," I state softly, understanding slowly creeping over me.

The Moon Goddess nods her head, then continues. "The Queen will be of mixed-blood and hold the powers of both her parents. You are one of her trainers, Keith, one of her protectors. For years you have been near your Queen, raised with her in a way, all orchestrated by me; your Queen is Jasmine Oscuro, her wolf, Brooke, has already recognized you as a protector and will accept you easily. It is important to train her and Ashley fully, they have training, but they must learn the ways of all species and varying tactics;

Ashley is the head of my army, Jasmine's main protector and the Blood Wolf. The Blood Wolf's piece of the prophecy is to be merciless in the final war. This will be the war that ends all separation. The prophecy says the ground around her will match the color of her coat, she will spare no one and be the strength that saves the Queen."

I am doing my best to accept all that is being said, so much information to process has been given, what I thought was a childhood story is reality. My reality.

"Jasmine and Ashley no longer have anyone to train against, they are stronger than the Alpha and Beta of Whispering Winds. You will soon pair with a powerful witch and together train them; it is imperative they work seamlessly. Jasmine holds the witch and werewolf powers. When you met Jasmine this afternoon, she was training, but it was her wolf performing the magic."

I look at the Moon Goddess in surprise. I have never heard of a wolf able to do magic. This is a lot to take in and process, I don't have time for doubts, though. "I accept my role, Moon Goddess, but I am concerned about what will happen with my pack?"

"While you are training and as you leave for battles, your Beta or Gamma will remain and lead the pack. Although I think with information soon to come to light, your Beta will always want to accompany you in battle. You will be returning often enough you will not need to give up your Alpha role. I would not want to take that from one of my most loyal wolves. Your pack warriors will be assisting in the battles, and you will be in command under Ashley. There is much training to do. Plans must be made soon, and training started. We do not have long before war is knocking on our doors."

"This is a lot to take in but I understand, Moon Goddess, failure will not lie at our feet. Myself and my pack is loyal to our Queen, we will do all in our power to assist Jasmine and Ashley, we will become stronger together. I will give my life to protect all realms."

"It is time to wake up, Alpha Keith. Go in strength, my son."

My eyes open and I bolt up with a start, running my hand down my face. Looking around me, I am back in my room. My dream plays quickly through my mind, all the information received, I take a deep breath and steady myself, time to get ready.

Chapter 26:

Dinner at Whispering Winds

(Jasmine's POV)

After our run-in with Alpha Keith, Brooke and I call it a day for training and return home to meet up with Dad and resume my studies and shadowing, preparing me to take over the Alpha position. Many reports have been coming in from other packs regarding missing she-wolves, fitting in with what Alpha Keith was explaining to me today, this is concerning and needs to be investigated more. I finish working with Dad in his office just after four in the afternoon. There should be more than enough time to get ready for dinner tonight, it is nice not having to spend a lot of time on my hair, I want to be downstairs no later than five to welcome guests.

While working in the office Dad makes a call, apparently to the Alpha of Red Crescent and invites him and his team. I would have liked to let Keith know so he wasn't taken by surprise, especially since this dinner is to discuss happenings in his pack and it is unknown if he wants to involve other packs besides Whispering Winds, but there is only so much I can control.

Even though this evening is a casual dinner, it is important to look nice for our visitors. My mind has settled on the perfect outfit, I move into my closet and find my favorite beige shirt dress with turquoise belt and grab the shoes that match the belt perfectly, since it is my favorite accessory item.

Looking at the clock, there is just enough time for a quick shower, not that I did much in Dad's office, the shower is more to calm some anxiety of the dinner party, running to the bathroom, the water temperature adjusts quickly to my preferred setting, then I jump in, washing my worries down the drain for the time being; the water will help make my hair stay slicked down while putting it up too. In no time at all I have finished and dry off with my favorite soft, fluffy cream-colored towel, finally I wander out to my room and slip on my clothing for this evening.

Pulling my hair into a French twist, I secure it with turquoise pins to match my shoes and belt. The ends of the pins are shaped as flowers. I think this goes perfectly with my ensemble. I finish the look with some turquoise stud earrings and a teardrop necklace, which falls into the hollow just below my neck. While make-up has never been a favorite of mine, a little mascara finds its way onto my eyelashes along with a dab of gloss for my lips, subtle but striking.

Looking critically at the finished product in the mirror a smile spreads across my face. I feel classy and confident in this outfit, it is time to get this evening started. I leave my room and make sure to lock the door behind me, this is a habit when we have multiple guests at the house but with all the new information we have, it should become a regular thing.

I head to the staircase and begin my trip down to the main floor, Mom and Dad have made it to the lobby ahead of me. Drawing the attention of my parents from the clicking of my heals on the stairs, Mom looks my way and smiles.

"Jasmine, honey, you look beautiful."

"Thanks, Mom. You are looking stunning yourself as always. Better be careful or Dad might get cranky around the young pups tonight," I tease.

Mom laughs heartily at my joke, and Dad gives me a look of mock offense. We are all still chuckling when there is a knock at the door.

"I'll get it," I reply and walk over to the door.

I open it with a large smile on my face; after all, we are allies and close friends with everyone coming to dinner tonight. Our first visitors of the evening are Alpha Mason, Luna Rebecca, Future Alpha Ryan, Beta Clark with his wife Lacey and Gamma Richard of Red Crescent Pack.

"Welcome, ladies and gentlemen," I greet with a bright smile, "we are so happy you were able to be present this evening. We do know it was short notice, so we appreciate your ability to be flexible. You are the first to arrive, but Alpha Keith of Midnight Moon pack along with Beta Andrew and Gamma Daniel will be along shortly. Please come in and have some beverages in the parlor." I stand aside and motion them through the door.

"Always happy to come and see some of our favorite neighbors," booms out Alpha Mason, while patting me on my head. He has always been a big, jovial man and I can't help but like him despite his habit of patting me. Luna Rebecca nods her head enthusiastically beside him, with a wide smile on her face.

They make their way over to my parents along with their Betas and Gamma. Turning back Ryan is still standing at the door, this seems odd to me, he has been here many times since our families are close, he has never behaved like this before.

I raise an eyebrow questioningly and look at him. "Is there something I can assist you with, Future Alpha Ryan?" I ask gently.

He looks at me and shakes his head. "No. I just don't really have any desire to be here, I was pulled along by my parents. They seem to think it is good for future relations with your pack," he responds back in a bored tone; he then pushes by me into the lobby.

I am slightly taken aback by his revelation and his obvious lack of desire to be included, he never seemed to dislike our company before. I cannot imagine being this blasé about things happening in ally packs, especially knowing I will be taking over my pack. Looking at Ryan's retreating back and thinking over his bizarre behavior, there is another knock at the door, pulling me out of my head. I look at the clock, 5:15. Well, all our guests took the invitation to arrive early to heart. Good.

Opening the door to Alpha Keith, Beta Andrew and his wife Katie, also Gamma Daniel and his wife Lexi, an excited smile graces my features. I of course know all of them and instead of a formal welcoming, they all take me into a big group hug. This is more the type of dinner atmosphere I was expecting.

"Welcome, everyone, it is so good to see you all again. Before we go in just a friendly heads-up; Dad invited the Red Crescent pack too, they are already here, arrived just before your group. Come in and enjoy drinks in the parlor before dinner," I offer, stepping aside to let them pass.

They are familiar with our home and do not need to be directed where to go, I place a hand gently on Keith's arm to indicate I would like him to stay back.

"Keith, since I know why you are here and the issues you have been having, I would like to ask you to keep an eye on Future Alpha Ryan. His behavior is off, and I have an unpleasant feeling about him," I whisper.

Keith nods his head, but does not ask me any questions, he just trusts and accepts my observation and request.

Keith offers me his arm, smiling at me, grasping it we walk into the parlor together. "So good to see everyone after so long. Ahh, Alpha Alexander, so nice of you to invite us to your home, Alpha Mason, so good to see you here as well. Future Alpha Ryan, nice of you to join, no doubt getting ready to take the reins of the pack and let your parents enjoy retirement," Keith calls out in a friendly manner. "Lunas and ladies, you all look lovely this evening. Now, I have this little minx here on my arm, but where is her partner in crime, and the partner in crime's brother?"

No sooner had the words parted Keith's lips than he was jumped on by the very said brother. They mock battled like this for a few minutes, playing as boys will play when reuniting after not seeing each other for a while, their antics get laughter from most of the group and a grumpy expression from Ryan. Drinks are being passed out to everyone while they continue to be the impromptu entertainment, their drinks set on the bar for when they are done.

Drinks have been finished, most people enjoying the company of those around them, then Dad directs us all to the dining room.

"Since this is an informal get-together, the seating arrangements have been left open, everyone may choose to sit where they please—just not two to a seat." Dad finishes with a wink, getting another round of laughter.

We mill around for a few minutes choosing our seats. Finally, Dad is settled at the head of the table, with my mother to his left. Next to Mom is Beta Mark, Patricia, and Gamma Simon. To Dad's right is Alpha Mason, Luna Rebecca, Future Alpha Ryan, then his Betas and Gamma. Alpha Keith and crew, along with myself, Zeke and Ash, have taken up the last seats at the table. I sit in between Gamma Simon to my left and Alpha Keith to my right.

"Looks like we are all settled. Let's begin our feast and get to the unfortunate business that has brought us all together this evening." With that Dad summons in the dinner and changes the jovial mood to business.

Chapter 27:

Business and Dinner

(Jasmine's POV)

The feast our kitchen has prepared on short notice is making my mouth water in anticipation, murmurs of appreciation and delight fill the air, making me proud of the hard work everyone put into this evening's event, our pack has wonderful wolves dedicated to it. The assembled party digs in and begins to fill their plates.

Before us lays choices of salmon on cedar planks cooked in citrus, quail with a huckleberry juniper sauce, and elk marinated in wine for a couple days, then slow-cooked, mixed greens salad filled with garden vegetables, seasonal vegetables sautéed in truffle oil, roasted tri-colored potatoes, and freshly baked dark sweet dinner rolls; after a few moments the clatter of serving quiets down. Folks have begun sampling the food and are passing along praise to the chefs in the kitchen. They really have outdone themselves, but I always think they do.

Dad clears his voice from the head of the table. "Now that we are all situated, let's get down to the bare bones of this impromptu dinner. Whispering Winds recently had an issue, in which an unknown individual attempted to kidnap Jasmine."

At this revelation there are many surprised gasps. Watching the room carefully, I am observing the reactions of each individual, I am surprised to see no response from Keith, Andrew and Daniel; the most astonishing reaction to this admission, though, is the smirk that appears on Ryan's face.

"Why weren't we notified so we could secure the borders and help locate the offenders?" asked Alpha Mason, sounding taken aback and hurt at the lack of communication between our packs, for something so significant, especially with our families being so close.

"The attempt took place off pack grounds, there was no concern about border compromise. Jasmine, Ashley, and Claire managed to capture the offenders; said offenders were interrogated and sentenced for their crimes. I do apologize, it would have been good manners to include both your packs in on this information. After the event we went into immediate investigative mode, and we were focused on that outcome. We should have never left our family out of the loop, though."

Alpha Mason and Alpha Keith nod their heads, giving appreciative smiles. It is easy to assume had the same events taken place in their packs, they would have responded the same way. I see Keith give me a look of disappointment from the corner of his eye, I can only assume it is because I did not share this information during our meeting earlier today, although based off his reaction, he most likely knew the attempt occurred. A guilty smile crosses my lips and is sent his way as an initial form of apology, we will speak later.

Dad continues. "Recently it has come to my attention Midnight Moon is also experiencing some issues among their pack. I thought it best to also invite Red Crescent and see if they are by any chance having the same issues. I think it is best, if agreed upon by all packs, to come together and find the root of this evil befalling our area." Dad looks around the table, to see the serious faces of all surrounding him. He looks to Alpha Keith. "Alpha Keith, if you would like to update us on the happenings in your pack, we would appreciate it."

Keith swallows the mouthful of food he has and takes a sip of wine to clear his mouth. "Thank you, Alpha Alexander. Over the last six months we have been having she-wolves of mixed-blood, either killed or kidnapped. We performed a complete run of our borders, but there is no sign of entry, or smell of intruders. We have done some investigating and found on an international level, other packs have been experiencing the same issues, with she-wolves aged 17-20. It appears they may be looking for a she-wolf who is about to shift, or has recently shifted and remains hidden, although we are not sure why she would remain hidden. We have also found many mixed supernatural couples and mixed-blood wolves are moving from the Northeast into the Northwest packs, due to increased hostilities in the area. We are attempting to see if we can locate any specific pack the aggressions may be coming from."

Dad and I share a knowing look at this last comment from Alpha Keith. Broken Moon is in the Northeast, we know for a fact they have hostilities against non-pure bloodlines in the species.

"Fortunately, we have not been experiencing any of these issues, although we do not have many mixed couples or supernaturals in my pack. The few we do have are all male, so there is little reason for us to be attacked. Red Crescent is on board to help track down this individual or group; eradication of any supernatural being is heinous to say the least. In the next few months, I will be turning over the Alpha position to Ryan. Ryan, will you continue to assist Whispering Winds and Midnight Moon to find the perpetrator?" Alpha Mason asks his son.

Ryan raises his gaze from where it has been locked onto his plate and focuses on his father with an unpleased glare, his body stiffening even more than it already is, his hands, next to his plate ball into fists. "It appears you are not giving me much of an option, asking me in front of both packs; however, I will assist them as I am needed. With our pack being free of this threat, I do not understand why our resources need to be utilized, we should make sure our own are cared for first."

All present turn startled eyes on him at his response. Even though he has agreed to assist, his resistance is obvious to all involved.

I look over to Alpha Mason wanting to see his response to Ryan, he has turned bright red, there is a vein throbbing in his forehead, his eyes narrow down, drilling into his son, his fingers are white at the knuckles from grasping the table so tightly, the Alpha's Adam's apple moves up and down a couple times before words leave his mouth.

"If the prospect of helping our allies is so odious to you, Ryan, as well as the thought of helping the supernatural world and the hybrids of it, then perhaps you are not meant to lead our pack. I will begin looking for another successor immediately," Alpha Mason snarls back to his son.

It appears there is more tension between the Alpha and his son than is known to the rest of the group, this reaction is not normal for Alpha Mason.

With this Ryan jumps up from his seat, knocking over his wine glass, sending it shattering to the floor. "If that is the way you want it, Father, then do as you please. I do not feel the need to assist those who are too weak and ignorant to assist themselves. I have a stronger calling than being Alpha to your pack!" yells Ryan as he throws his napkin on his unfinished plate, not bothering to watch for the broken glass, with that Ryan storms out of the house.

Absolute surprise at the sudden turn in events is written on everyone's faces. No one dares glance to anyone else in the room, the shock of what has just occurred slowly settles, and mouths begin to shut as we get our bearings back.

Alpha Mason turns to the group, embarrassment written clearly on his and his Luna's features. "We apologize for our son; it is best we take our leave for the evening. Trust our pack is at your call for any assistance, we stand with you and not against. I will deal with Ryan at home and ensure he stays in the pack borders." Alpha Mason's group rises from the table, and everyone stands to bid them goodbye.

I escort them to the front door with my father, Alpha Mason looks at me with kind eyes.

"Future Alpha Jasmine, Alpha Alexander, I will investigate my son's comings and goings for the last six months. His entire attitude about coming to this event tonight and his outburst have concerned me. I will update you on any information we gather. Again, I apologize for Ryan." With that he takes his leave.

Dad and I return to the dining room and take our seats. The atmosphere in the room is somber and tense.

"Please, everyone, finish your meals, and let's continue to discuss next steps. I will ensure to keep Alpha Mason in the loop and update you all with any information he passes on to us. Alpha Keith, is there any additional information you would like to include for us to consider?"

Chapter 28:

Coming Forward

(Alpha Keith's POV)

"There is additional information I would like to bring forward, now that it is just our packs; please do not misunderstand, Alpha Mason is trustworthy, I am just not sure how up to date he is on the information that needs to be discussed. It is imperative for me not to speak out of turn and thought it best to keep the information closer to the belt until all the players are known to me. Please forgive me if I assume too much," I inform the group.

Alpha Alexander gives me a questioning look before speaking. "We would need to know what information you have prior to knowing if you need any forgiveness, young Alpha. Please feel free to share. All in this room can be trusted, as well as the pack. If you so desire, we can retire to the secure meeting room on the eighth floor."

"No, no. Your trust in your pack is enough for me to continue forward."

Clearing my throat my gaze floats around the table, landing briefly on each individual. There are so many ways to begin this discussion, but the best choice is unclear to me still, so I choose to begin by addressing Jasmine.

"Jasmine, if you don't mind me asking…it is known by many you recently had a birthday, I believe it was your 18th, did you receive a wolf on your birthday?" Hesitation at asking the question stutters my words slightly.

This group is an extension of my own family but recently there has been some space between us as I took over Midnight Moon and put all my concentration into that move.

There are gasps heard around the room, but Jasmine is only smiling at me, thankfully, she nor anyone else in her family and close circle is upset by the question. It is said never to ask a question you don't already know the answer to, and this answer I have no doubt in.

"Of course, she didn't receive a wolf, Keith, she has her mother's powers, you know, a mixed-blood child can only possess the powers of one parent. Don't make our lovely Jasmine downhearted by reminding her. Why such a question?" asks Beta Katie, somewhat flabbergasted by my boldness.

"No, it is a fair question," Jasmine interjects quietly. "A question I will be very happy to answer; Alpha Keith, I did receive a wolf on my 18th birthday, her name is Brooke. She told me you would be coming to speak with me soon, I just didn't think it would be this soon or that you would be so forward in your questioning." Jasmine giggles lightly.

Andrew, Katie, Daniel, and Lexi all look at Jasmine openmouthed. They are the only ones in this meeting who did not know the identity of Jasmine yet.

"Please allow me to explain; I was visited by the Moon Goddess prior to our engagement this evening, she informed me of the prophecy's history along with my and my pack's roles in assisting in the outcome of the prophecy. It was not my intent to be forward, but it escaped me how to broach the subject more delicately." At this point I get up from my chair and assist Jasmine to stand. The entire table is watching us, captivated by what is happening.

Kneeling before Jasmine there is once again audible surprise from the others in the room.

"I swear to you, Queen Jasmine, my loyalty and the loyalty of my pack, we will stand beside you through any endeavor, through any battle. I have been summoned by the Moon Goddess to train and protect you, to train Ashley and serve under her as a commander. With the breath and life I have in me, I swear these things to you, my Queen."

I am still kneeling before Jasmine when there is a clearing of a throat. "Queen Jasmine? I think there are a few of us in this room that are unaware of all that is happening, if no one minds, can we please be caught up to the same place as everyone else?" Andrew asks, bewildered.

Neither Andrew nor any of my ranked staff have ever seen me kneel in front of anyone, not even my father while growing up. I look around the room and then between Jasmine and Alpha Alexander.

"Who would like to explain everything?"

Jasmine smiles at me and says, "Perhaps we can all contribute, it is a detailed story with many parts, that is as long as you stand up and stop kneeling in front of me."

A smile finds my lips also and it is sent back to Jasmine, finding her humbleness endearing. Standing up I drop her hands; for a moment I had forgotten I was kneeled before her, this only solidifies Jasmine is a Queen; otherwise, Aspen would refuse to bow or kneel to anyone.

"Well," Jasmine begins, looking around the group, "what do you all know of the prophecy of the Midnight Wolf?"

"It is a legend, not a prophecy, or that is what I have always been told. It is a bedtime story for pups," offers Lexi.

Jasmine nods her head to Lexi, "That is what we have all believed for generations, even my father thought it to be only a bedtime story told to him by his grandfather, but we now know differently."

She beckons Ashley to come over to her, quickly Jasmine says a spell over the two of them and at the same time they shift into their wolves. My eyes widen at the amazing sight before me. The wolves of these ladies are beyond imagination.

Slowly approaching the wolves my hands reach out to them, then pause to let them decide if they will allow my touch, both wolves grant me to touch them, their fur is soft and deep, the color vibrant, their markings undeniable. I swallow hard and begin to feel the stirrings of excitement, the Moon Goddess has seen me fit and worthy to train them and protect the Queen, I have been honored and blessed. Let our destiny begin and guide us where we are meant to go.

The girls shift back, fully clothed, apparently the spell Jasmine performed was so they would be dressed when changing back to human form. Very wise. "It is not legend; it is a prophecy. I am the Midnight Wolf and Ashley is

the Blood Wolf. It is said, yours truly is to be the Queen who will unite the supernatural world and do away with those attempting to segregate and annihilate the mixed-bloods. I come from two blood lines and hold the powers of both blood lines."

"Yes, our Queen," they all chorus in unison, heads bowed to Jasmine.

"Please, there is no need to bow. I needed to make sure you understand this is not jest, but reality."

"Jasmine, if I may, now that the prophecy has been established and undeniable proof given to the validity of the claim, may we move on to other subjects? It is not my intent to rush anyone but there is still more to cover, and it is getting late," I politely request.

"Of course," chirps Jasmine.

"I was not surprised at the mention of your kidnapping attempt, which you noticed at dinner, because during his investigation, Beta Andrew discovered it, then brought it to my attention. It was my intention to speak to you about it after the dinner, but it has been covered now; however, it didn't go unnoticed, while I was giving my brief you and Alpha Alexander exchanged a glance at the mention of people leaving the Northeast packs. Is there information you have on these occurrences?"

Alpha Alexander begins speaking. "After interrogating the rogues, we knew the plan they were supposed to follow. The rogues were hired by someone else to kidnap Jasmine. We were unable to pull information from a cellphone they had been given, except for the location of the drop-off place. We sent a text to the individual, confirming Jasmine had been caught and was secure in the designated spot. Turns out the person sent to retrieve her was also not the main source of the attempt but a go-between, Jasmine opted to go with the person sent to collect her, to uncover more information. She ended up at the Broken Moon pack in the Northeast, Alpha Blaine of Broken Moon put her in the dungeons and was going to kill her. Jasmine escaped from the dungeon and made her way out of the pack lands, Alpha Blaine attacked us on neutral soil to try and get her back, but we fought them off, well, Jasmine ensnared the Alpha, Beta, and top warriors in tree roots, we have the one sent to collect her in our dungeons."

"Why does it feel like there is a vital part missing?" I ask cautiously, not wanting to overstep any boundaries.

"Because there is, Father was trying to spare me embarrassment. Alpha Blaine was my mate and he rejected me because I am of mixed-blood. He is part of the group pushing for segregation and eradication. There is someone behind him, though, and we are trying to find out who that is," Jasmine adds in. "Broken Moon is a pack of hired mercenaries, for a bigger fish or school of fish."

I do not know what to say or how to react, all I can do is reach out and pull Jasmine into a tight hug. She is already showing so much strength and bravery, to speak of her rejection without breaking down, to admit it to us in this room. My heart breaks at what she must have endured, while my protective side raises again, death will find this wolf.

After a few minutes Jasmine steps back and gives me a sheepish grin. "I think we have planning still ahead of us. If you all would like, we can go back to the parlor and discuss what's next over drinks," suggests Jasmine.

We all agree and make our way back to the parlor, looks like it is going to be a long evening. It is good I had a nap that was somewhat relaxing.

Chapter 29:

Leaving Red Crescent

(Ryan's POV)

We have arrived, I watch as my parents, their Betas, and Gamma walk through the front door of the Whispering Winds pack, fighting back my urge to walk away from this entire evening, this is the last place that should be graced with my presence, no desire resides in me to sit and share a meal with these people, who dare call themselves werewolves. I do not understand why my father continues to not only align himself with them, but befriend them, these people who spit on our pure blood. When the time comes, when I am in control the alliance with be terminated.

Apparently, I have been standing in the doorway lost in thought for too long because the insipid little thing, who is the future Alpha of this "pack," is asking me if I need help. If help is needed, it absolutely would not be from this nasty girl standing in front of me. I allow myself a moment to show my dissatisfaction of this situation, in my reply to her, the shocked look on her face pleases me to no end.

Here we are, standing in their parlor, me trying to get through pre-dinner drinks, and the complete juvenile antics of those around me. There are at least a few dozen different ways I would rather be spending my evening, instead of trapped with this lot. My father, the jovial buffoon, appears to be enjoying bhimself, and my mother is eating up the attention of other ladies her rank. It is nauseating. Oh, finally dinner is being called, time to come out of my corner, this night should be done quickly now that the meal is being served.

Of course, it doesn't go quickly, dinner is a disaster. How dare my father ask me questions about how I will run the pack in front of others, others who have no business being involved in such talks. Questioning my alliances in a place I cannot be open about them, it is beyond me to control myself and my father has just informed me he is going to replace me as successor to him. My blood is boiling, bile rises in my throat, my wolf is coming to the surface, it is not safe for me to remain here, I jump up from the table and leave, not even bothering to give these pretenders a farewell.

My father fails to see it as odd I want to take my own car and not ride with the group. He thinks it has something to do with me being young and wanting to show my independence. How ignorant can one man be? No, there is a bag packed in the trunk, my desire to leave coming to the forefront, and I am on my way out, out of this cesspool, unfortunately called home.

Apparently, someone mind-linked the warriors, because an escort stays with me until I pass through the main gates of the pack lands. Who in their right mind would want to remain on these grounds? Good riddance! There is no desire to stay in this tri-pack area in my heart or body, my calling is far away from here, with a group more like-minded.

An hour of driving passes me by when it becomes necessary for a break. I pull off to the side of the road and stretch out my limbs. There is one last thing to do prior to continuing my trip.

Facing the general direction of my pack lands my voice comes out strong, carrying across quiet night, "I, Ryan Marshall Reed, of Red Crescent pack, cut all ties, binds and loyalties to Red Crescent pack." Needing to see if it worked, I try to mindlink my mother, nothing, absolute quiet, it worked. My ties are cut, no longer a member of Red Crescent pack, free to go and seek out my own destiny.

A satisfied smirk pulls at the corner of my mouth, it is beginning, and this wolf will be on the forefront of the battle. Sliding back into my car to continue on my path, it is time to make the call I have been dreading since leaving the dinner. The phone rings three times, then is picked up.

"Hey, this is Ryan…. Things didn't go well at dinner…. I was there for most of the evening…. I can fill you in later. Look, my father is not going to name me Alpha any longer…. He didn't like my responses to some questions he asked…. I know this causes a few issues, I thought we could plan around those issues, though…. No, I cannot go back and play nice…. I am not in the pack anymore…. There is no need to yell, I just called to see if I can come to your pack…. I am about an hour out, we can discuss this in detail when I get there…. Yeah, thanks. See you in a bit."

The call went better than anticipated, which could mean he is using this time until my arrival to plan my death, or think of new ways to torture me, he has also been known to use those who displease him as training tools for his youth army. That doesn't bode well for me. My wolf has always been on the smaller side for an Alpha wolf and now, with me throwing away my Alpha position, he may be smaller yet. I will find out the next time I shift into Gadreel.

The Alpha I am about to meet with and become a member of his pack is merciless. If he is not happy with me, it will be me paying the ultimate price, me being tortured and most likely killed. It is important, prior to my arrival, to make sure I have all my plans in place, he is not a patient wolf. Ideas of how we can fix the issues I have caused flow through my mind, there are a few that aren't too bad, but the details need to be worked out, let's see how well I can sell it to the Alpha.

Finally, arriving at the main gate of my destination, my car rolls to a stop and I roll down my window, letting the patrol wolves see who it is. They wave me through without any issue, the Alpha must have let them know to expect me and to let me through. Pulling up to the main house, there is no one awaiting my arrival; it is not uncommon. Finding a place in the garage, my car is nosed in, I get out and grab my bag out of the back end slinging it over my shoulder. Slowly my feet find their way to the main door of the packhouse, even though being here is my choice, there is no hurry in me to get the face to face started. Pushing the ringer on the door it swings open, giving me sight of a furious Alpha Blaine.

Alpha Blaine reaches out and grabs me by my jacket collar, yanking me into the house. "Ryan, you have got a lot of explaining to do, and you had better not leave out any detail, no matter how small you think it is," he growls at me in disgust.

I do my best not to start shaking in his grasp. I clear my voice. "Well, let me put my bag down, then we can meet in your office and full details will be given." "You are on the second floor, same room as always. You have ten minutes."

With that Alpha Blaine stomps off towards his office.

Chapter 30:

Tri-Pack Planning

(Jasmine's POV)

Making our way from the dining room to the parlor Katie and Lexi are excitedly asking Ash and me questions about our wolves and complimenting how beautiful they are. Amazement at the revelation this evening is still fresh in their system, soon they will comprehend the full extent of what is occurring, the weight of what we are facing.

Entering the parlor, we choose our places and are all sitting comfortably, I help Dad hand out beverages before taking my own place on a loveseat next to Ash, this is our regular place when in here. Soon all idle side talk ends and we begin discussing strategy, training, and possible next moves.

"It seems odd to me Alpha Blaine has not made any attempt to recapture me or try to attack Whispering Winds. It has been months, it would make sense he would want to get some sort of revenge for the escape and battle that occurred, especially based off his reputation." Not that I want any of those things, but after the night we had at Broken Moon, I would have anticipated some sort of attack or attempt.

The others in the room are nodding their agreement, this does seem odd. "We will keep our defenses up and send a scout to the Broken Moon pack to monitor their movements, visitors and set up telecommunication surveillance.

They will not make any moves without our knowledge. Zeke, you are in charge of setting up the spy-type equipment we will need to make this happen," Dad directs to us.

Zeke pulls out his ever-present tablet and begins to get to work, the look on his face reminds me of a kid at Christmas, this is his forte and he is letting his nerd come out full force; it is wonderful to see.

"Just to make sure the equipment is set up correctly, we will send Zeke with the team, after everything is functioning and secure there, he will come back to the pack. We will need him here, no one else comes close to his level of expertise with technology."

With a plan in place, we begin discussing the events of the evening, the conversation I had with Ryan, and some of his behaviors.

"I never knew he harbored such resentment towards our packs, he used to be close to our group. We will have to speak with Alpha Mason to find out what Ryan has been up to in the last few months," Keith speaks out.

Before he can continue the phone rings. Dad picks it up.

"This is Alpha Alexander of Whispering Winds pack; how can I help you this evening?... I see…. Alpha Mason, excuse my interruption, but before you get too far into your story, I am going to put you on speaker phone. The remaining dinner group is still here discussing plans, and this is vital information…. " Dad gives a "help me" look to Zeke, who approaches him, pressing a few buttons on the phone. Dad gives a look of thanks to Zeke, then turns his attention back to the conversation. "—-Go ahead, Mason."

"Thank you. As I was saying, when we returned to Red Crescent, Ryan was not here. We checked around the pack lands for him but did not locate him. We decided to check his living quarters to see if there was anything in there out of the ordinary. We found he had some missing clothes, gym bag, laptop, cellphone, other personal items, and money has been taken from the safe in my office. About ten minutes ago Ryan broke his bond with the pack. I know I should have called sooner, but his mother has been frantic and now she is inconsolable. We have no idea where Ryan has gone. We are doing a more detailed search now of his room, office, and online activities from his work computer. We are hoping to pull his phone logs from his cellphone and look at those too, see if they give us any idea what he has been up to."

Silence looms around the room as we take in this information, finally Dad responds.

"I appreciate the call, Mason. Please send our best to your Luna. Let me know if there is any way we can support you and your pack. Alpha Keith is indicating the same for him. We have Zeke, who is a computer genius, if you need help with the technology part. I know this is a difficult time for you, but we need to get together and plan. We also have something significant to share with you and your higher ranks. Can we meet tomorrow?"

"How much longer are you all going to be planning this evening?" "I would think a few more hours."

"If it is all the same to you, Alexander, I am already on my way with my Beta and Gamma. If we were not able to reach you by phone, I was going to have the guards wake you. I thought this was significant enough. We will be at your border gate in about thirty minutes. We can plan with you tonight."

"Very well. I will let my guards know you are coming."

"See you soon." With that Alpha Mason disconnects the call.

Dad places his earpiece back into the cradle, then turns back to the room.

Simon clears his throat. "Alpha, I know Ryan left pack grounds. I mindlinked the patrol and they escorted his vehicle until it left our main gate."

"Thank you, Simon, that takes care of any concerns of him still being on pack grounds. I am worried about him breaking ties with his pack so easily, I think we may have a possible coup attempt on our hands with that young wolf." Dad is looking off as he says this, lost in thought.

"Why would Ryan break ties, then attempt a coup when he was in line to take the Alpha position in just a few months? It would seem there is more going on than an attempt to take over." None of this is making sense to me and I think it best to voice my questions while we are in this group.

There are several nods of agreement in the room. We are all lost in our own train of thought, thinking over all the information and conversations that occurred tonight; trying to find an explanation to all that is happening, a knock at the front door brings us back to the moment at hand.

"I will go get the door," I say, setting my drink down on a side table then departing the room.

I reach the main door and open it to Alpha Mason and his higher ranks.

"Good evening, Alpha, Beta, Gamma, we are in the parlor, having discussions over beverages. Please follow me if you will and I can get you a drink and place to sit."

"Thank you, Jasmine. Sounds wonderful. I hope this is not burdensome to your family."

"Not at all, Alpha. We were planning on a longer evening as it was. I just want to let you know I am truly sorry for what you and your Luna are having to go through, it cannot be easy for either of you."

Alpha Mason casts his eyes down, a grim look on his face. He places a large hand on my shoulder and squeezes gently, that is all the response needed from this man.

We make it to the parlor and drinks have already been prepared for the gentlemen, Dad knows their beverages of preference. Once we are settled again Dad restarts the conversation.

"Mason, I wanted to let you know Simon had a patrol ensure Ryan left pack grounds, he is not on Whispering Wind territory. I was telling the group I am concerned about Ryan breaking ties with your pack, and there could possibly be a coup attempt in the making on his part, but Jasmine thinks there is something deeper happening since he was going to be Alpha in a few months. I am not sure if you are in agreement with any of these thoughts, they are the only possible answers we have been able to reach so far."

"Unfortunately, I agree with both of you. Ryan took a large sum of money from the safe, enough to secure practically anything he wants. He knew there was a large amount in there because I was not able to make a deposit at the bank on Friday and was holding it until Monday. He has already planned against the pack, by taking that money."

"We have been trying to think of a plan or idea to be ready for if he plans on striking. With Ryan being young I think it would be sooner than later."

"I agree, Alexander, if that is his plan. While we are caught on this, why don't you go ahead and fill me in on what you said you had to tell me. Maybe it will help with the planning."

"Alright." Father reclaims his seat and takes a long sip from his drink. Looking over to Alpha Mason he continues. "Everyone in the room from Whispering Winds and Midnight Moon already knows, we are catching you up. It came as much of a surprise to me, to us, as I am sure it will be to you. The legend of the Midnight Wolf is indeed a prophecy. A prophecy that is being lived out at this moment, we are a part of the prophecy, you and your pack included."

Alpha Mason stops what he is doing and looks at my father. He sets his drink down and readjusts so he is sitting on the edge of his chair. A light sweat has begun to bead his brow.

"Are you sure about this? How can that be?"

"Jasmine and Ashley had their 18th birthdays three months ago. We didn't invite anyone outside the pack because we were not sure Jasmine would have a wolf, as you know she has her mother's witch powers. Well, she does have a wolf; Jasmine is the Midnight Wolf and Ashley is the Blood Wolf. We just found out this evening, Alpha Keith is one of their trainers and one of Jasmine's protectors. Jasmine's wolf told her the prophecy has started, while she was being held at Broken Moon." Father goes on to fill the men in on the entire story and I do not believe their jaws could have dropped any farther to the floor by the end of it.

Alpha Mason turns to me. "Is there any way we can see your wolf? I do not disbelieve your father, but I would like to see for myself."

I nod, say a quick spell, so when I turn back, I will be clothed and shift into Brooke.

Alpha Mason and his staff fall to their knees before me. "Queen Jasmine, I swear to you on my blood, you have the loyalty and devotion of the Red Crescent pack. We will stand with you in all matters, our Queen."

I shift back and beckon them to stand. "Thank you for your loyalty and devotion. Let's plan the best way to protect you and your pack at this moment."

"Yes. I got it!" exclaims Zeke.

We all turn to face him. He blushes darkly and apologizes under his breath before continuing.

"Each pack should send warriors to the other packs, enough so that each shift has at least one member from all three packs on it. This way, if an attack happens the warriors can mind-link back to their packs, allowing for faster response time, and location of the attack. If Ryan attacks, he will probably do so thinking no one has made any plans to protect the pack."

"That is an amazing plan, Ezekiel. I think you do indeed have it," Dad says proudly.

"Mom or I can also put a defensive shield up around the packs. I have been thinking about Alpha Keith saying he was unable to pick up any abnormal scents on his pack borders. Just in case there is someone who can hide their scent the barrier will be an extra level of security," I offer.

Alpha's Mason and Keith agree, from here we make detailed plans and decide who will be going to which pack. Simon has let us know there is plenty of room in the warrior bunkhouse to accommodate the incoming group.

Planning took another couple hours, with a plan in place and all parties feeling more confident, we part ways for the evening. I am exhausted and make my way to my room. Sleep is calling and Keith has set an early morning training session planned for Ashley and me already.

Chapter 31:

Plans of Broken Moon

(Alpha Blaine's POV)

Here I sit in my office waiting for Ryan to hurry and come back downstairs, rather impatiently. His phone call was the worst news I could have received this evening. I was counting on him getting the Alpha position in a month or two, so our plans could be set in motion.

We wanted Whispering Winds to let down their guard, and once Ryan became Alpha, we would set up base on his pack lands and attack. Now all the planning I have put in has gone to waste, because of some hotheaded kid. I am fighting my desire to slit his throat and watch him bleed out.

I am putting off contacting my grandfather until I have heard all that Ryan has to say. I am still not certain this Jasmine girl is the correct person to be going after. Grandfather believes she is and has stopped all searches. I do not agree with this move, and at this point I just have to go along with him. Things have been very tense since I lost her a few months ago. Grandfather has not let me forget my mistakes, especially rejecting her. At least my wolf, Samael, feels the same way about her as I do, he has not held the rejection against me.

There is a knock at my door, bringing me out of my internal thoughts. "Come in!" I bark out. I am sure it is the young pup. I do not want him being too comfortable here. He has been a convenient ally, pawn in the game, if you will, but he is no friend.

The door swings open, and Ryan struts in confidently. He comes right up to my desk and leans against it. "Ready to talk now, Blaine?"

I jump from my chair, and over my desk, grabbing Ryan by his throat on the way over, I slam him into one of the armchairs on the other side of my desk. "When you address me, you will address me as Alpha, do you understand, pup? Right now you are a rogue, you have no pack and no rank. So mind yourself and begin convincing me why you should not die by my hand tonight," I growl out at him.

Ryan sinks back in the chair, but cannot get out of my grasp. Fear finds its way into his gaze and finally he lowers his eyes in submission. It is about time he knows his place. I do not know why my grandfather likes him so much. He is weak and is now weaker not being an Alpha.

I let loose of his throat and lean against my mahogany desk. I would rather be sitting in the matching leather chair, but I have a feeling I may need to physically put this pup into his place again.

I turn hard, cold eyes onto Ryan. "You better start, pup, because my patience is gone."

Ryan clears his throat and starts. "I was at Whispering Winds for most of the dinner. My father was upset with me because I did not appreciate him putting me on the spot in front of other packs and discussing pack issues in front of them."

"What pack issues?" I interrupted.

"Um, well, if I would keep the alliances and assist them in finding the people responsible for killing mixed-blood supernaturals," Ryan responds meekly.

"Why did you have a problem answering those questions? They regarded the alliances with the packs in the room. You are amazingly inept. If you would have kept your head and agreed, we would be in a good spot instead of scrambling as we are now. You have singlehandedly turned this mission upside down. You better have a plan to get yourself out of this."

Ryan gulps nervously and pushes back further into his chair under my cold stare, but continues. "When I left no one knows where I went. I gave no indication and left no clues. Whispering Winds only cares that I left their pack grounds. My father and mother are already planning on finding a new replacement for Alpha. I did not threaten anyone when I left. I am sure they all believe I am throwing a fit and will come back home in a few days, with my tail tucked between my legs looking for forgiveness."

"Get to the point, pup," I growl.

"They will not suspect an attack. We can have the witch you know hide our scents and tomorrow night we can sneak onto the pack lands—I know the weakest spot—and attack them. Right now I am still the named heir to the pack. If my father dies, I become Alpha. Why not help him die? We can take over, before he ever has an opportunity to reach out to the other packs."

"You don't think the other packs will be suspicious that you came back and have had the Alpha spot turned over to you?"

"I will tell them I am only the acting Alpha. Tell them my father had to return to Europe short notice because my grandmother is on her deathbed."

"This could work. Let me think about it. Go to your room and rest for

the night. You have bought yourself a little more time, pup."

Ryan gets up from his chair making sure to leave as much distance between us as possible and heads towards the door. He stops and looks back at me. "I will make this right, Alpha." Then continues out of my office.

I sit for a moment thinking over the plan. I have no choice but to call my grandfather on this. He would be the one to send the witch to us, if I ask for her assistance, she would deny me.

I know I am going to have to wake him up, but this is something I cannot put off until the morning. I decide mind-linking will give me the best results. "Grandfather, I need to speak with you urgently." I wait.

"What could you possibly need to discuss at this time of night, insolent child?"

"Ryan Reed is at my pack. He broke his ties with his pack and is not going to be given the Alpha title to Red Crescent. He did have a plan to attack tomorrow night, kill his father, take over as Alpha and tell the other packs his father was called away short notice to Europe because of his mother being on her deathbed."

"Why do you all feel the need to destroy my plans and my destiny? Sounds like there is already a plan, so again, why did you wake me up?"

"I need you to reach out to your witch friend and see if she will hide our scents. This will allow us to get across the border undetected."

"Fine, I will send her to you but make no mistake, she is not my friend, a mere acquaintance attempting to reach the same end. Do not bother me again."

It appears tomorrow we will attack Red Crescent and get our plan back on track. I need this to go smoothly because I have no doubt in my mind my grandfather will kill me if I fail him one more time.

I mind-link Clark and my head warrior, to come to my office. I need to set plans in motion and we have less than 24 hours to attack time.

Chapter 32:

Surveillance

(Ezekiel's POV)

I opted not to sleep last night. I am not only being fueled by adrenaline and the desire to get back at someone who hurt Jasmine and my sister, but also by the time the planning session was over, I still needed to gather all the surveillance equipment and run checks on it prior to loading it into our vehicles. I figure I can catch a few hours of sleep in the car on the way to our destination.

The plan is to get on the road and be in place, with equipment running prior to wake-up time, for the Broken Moon pack. That means we are leaving no later than one in the morning. I have my travel cup full of coffee, the SUV loaded, pillow in place, shifting from foot to foot, waiting for the rest of the team. They will be riding there with me and I will bring the vehicle back. We do not want a car sitting around, unmanned, causing suspicion.

I hear a noise behind me and turn around. To my surprise Jasmine is walking towards me.

"Well, good morning, My Moon. Why are you out of bed so early?" I inquire with a tired smile on my face.

Jasmine looks at me, her eyebrows are raised, there is a slight smirk on her face and her eyes are looking at me knowingly. "I know you didn't sleep last night, Zeke. I figured I would get up this morning, and place a couple spells on you and the team. I want to hide your scent and do a protection spell. I didn't want to do it last night, because I want to give you guys as much time being covered by the spells as possible," she responds with a yawn.

"Thank you for thinking of us. It didn't occur to me to ask you to do this. I know Alpha Keith has an early training scheduled for you."

"He does, and truth be told I didn't sleep well. I feel apprehensive and I am not sure why. I want to be able to do all I can to ensure you are safe. If I didn't have this training I would go with you and place a spell on the site you are setting up to keep it hidden. Don't forget, even though there is a good distance between our pack and theirs you can still mind-link, or at least I was able to."

Both Jasmine and I turn when we hear someone clearing their throat. What is it with the women in this family, being so darn quiet? Before us stands Luna Abigail.

"Well, my dear, I had the same thoughts as you did about the protection spells. I am going to be accompanying them to their setup site. No need for you to do any spells, I will do them once we get within distance."

I am amazed. Before I can say anything else, the rest of the team shows up. We go over the plan once more as a group and load into the SUV. I can't help but smile to myself, the Luna and Future Alpha have the biggest hearts and concern for their people. We are indeed a blessed pack.

I settle into my seat and lean my head against the door, in no time at all I am asleep.

I feel a gentle nudging in my side. I look over and Luna Abigail is smiling at me.

"We are about twenty minutes out from our park site. I wanted to make sure you had time to wake up and clear your mind before we get moving. Here is your coffee, I warmed it back up for you."

I smile back. "Thank you, Luna, I appreciate the thoughtfulness."

Luna just pats my cheek, as she has done since I was little, and joins back into the conversation of the other pack members.

I sit up and stretch as best I can in the crowded back seat. A yawn passes through my lips and I take a welcomed sip of my coffee. Thank goodness the Luna controls the element of fire and was able to warm my coffee; otherwise, I would be suffering drinking it cold.

I look around us and vaguely recognize where we are from our visit a few months ago. Well, if you can call that a visit. We are planning on setting up on a hill to the north of the pack. This vantage point will allow us to see over the wall, with a clear view of the packhouse and main gate.

The equipment I have brought will allow us to magnify in and see things even clearer. I am planning on tapping into the phone lines, once we get everything else set up, and I will do my best to think of a way to get ears into the house. I am hoping I can figure out the layout of the house and patrol routes from our area.

The car takes a turn and makes its own road through the grass, into the woods. We stop in a heavily wooded area, it shouldn't be patrolled since it is outside the pack grounds, but we can't be too careful, they did attack us off pack grounds.

We get out of the vehicle and Luna calls us around her. She places scent blocking and protection spells on the group and then does another spell to hide the vehicle.

"The spells are only good for 72 hours. Gather all the intel you can on this pack and then return. Zeke will be back to get you all," she reminds us.

Once Luna is done we all grab the gear out of the car and prepare for the four-mile hike in. We are doing our best to stay under the radar.

After about an hour and a half of fast-paced hiking we make it to our destination. I set down the equipment I have been carrying and begin to strategize the best setup options. I like this area the best, we have a canopy of trees protecting us from overhead view, right up to the edge of the cliff. Thank goodness the leaves have not fallen yet.

With a plan in place I start directing the placement of the gear. I begin unpacking the cases, set up the scopes and site everything in. I show the rest of the team how to use everything and some basic trouble shooting, just in case. The only thing left for me to do is plant listening devices in the house.

Utilizing the wide-angle telescope, I view the packgrounds below us, security is heightened, vehicles are coming in and out, personnel are moving about sporadically. Unfortunately, I still do not have a plan. I turn to the group.

"I need to get listening devices into the house. I am not sure how I am going to do that. Security is pretty tight around their border right now. It looks like they have a lot of movement happening. It will be difficult to sneak in and out with all the activity occurring. I am open to any suggestions."

I look around me and all I see is blank faces looking back at me. When you send in aggressive beasts it is difficult to find a plan for a finesse job.

"Zeke," Luna begins. "If it is too crowded to get in and out physically, why don't we use some magic?" Luna opens her hand and there appears a couple dozen small winged bugs. "I can send these into the house through an open window, each has a specific destination to head to, and after 72 hours they will disappear. No trace of equipment and if the pack scans, they will not be picked up."

"Luna! You are brilliant! Thank you for coming to our rescue," I exclaim with excitement and relief. "You will need to show Jasmine that one. It is very handy to have." I smile at our Luna.

Luna smiles back at me, raises her hand to her mouth, whispers something to the bugs, and then gently blows them into the wind. We watch as they are carried away and the Luna guides them. They make their way into an open window on the second floor.

I do one more check of the equipment, take a quick peek through one of the scopes at the main pack area, then the main gate. There is a lot of movement in and out. I have a feeling of foreboding.

"Keep your eyes on the activity. I feel something significant may be happening. I want you to mind-link in every thirty minutes with an update," I direct the men remaining behind.

They nod to me in understanding.

I turn to the Luna. "Shall we go now, Luna? Everything is set and the men know their mission. I think we have done all we can."

Luna turns towards the men. "I have the utmost faith in you men. You all make us proud every day. We look forward to your updates. Stay safe." With smiles on their faces the men bow their heads to our Luna in respect.

With that we turn and begin our four-mile walk back to the SUV.

Chapter 33:

Surveillance 2

(Luna Abigail's POV)

Zeke and I are making good time back to the car from the surveillance site, the vehicle is in view, I am looking forward to a relaxing drive back with Zeke. He is a good boy, always has been. I am proud of all the knowledge he has gained and is using to benefit our pack.

I stop in my tracks, the hair on the back of my neck standing up. There is danger vibrating though every living organism around me. I look around me slowly and catch a bright light from the corner of my left eye, coming from the trees. Without time to think, I jump on top of an unsuspecting Zeke and tackle him to the ground, wrapping him in my arms we roll twenty feet to the right. There is an explosion off to our left, leaving a huge pit in the ground, any closer and we would have been dealt serious injuries.

I jump back to my feet and send several energy balls into the trees. I am not sure who our attacker is. I am assuming it is a witch, based off how we were attacked, but I still do not know if they are standing, flying, in a tree, or exactly where they are, I also do not want to start a fire in the forest. The energy blast will momentarily stun them. After sending in the energy balls, I follow it with a wave and much to my dismay I am face to face with Victoria, as the water carries her out of her hiding place.

Victoria is one of my council members. We have been having issues with her over the last couple months going against council policies and laws. At our next meeting I was going to direct she be watched to see if she is up to any dark magic or mischief. It looks like I should have requested it sooner.

What is she doing at Broken Moon, her coven is not in this area. The fact she is attacking us does not bode well. She is a strong witch, who only controls one element, a strong element, but she is not varied in attack strategies, meaning I am stronger. Zeke has taken a protective stance next to me, ready to engage in battle.

Still looking forward, I softly speak to Zeke. "Mind-link the Alpha and let him know what is happening. Link the guards on the mountain and tell them to stay put, do not respond. They are protected there and we need the information they are gathering."

Zeke lets me know he understands by making a grunting noise.

I capture Victoria in a restraining spell and walk up to her. I levitate her off the ground, and turn her so her head is pointed at the earth. I do not want her to be comfortable. This position will make it difficult for her to breathe and more than likely give her a headache. At this moment I do not care, she tried to kill me, I am playing with her just until I get my information.

"What are you doing here, Victoria? Your coven is nowhere near this area and there are no covens within 100 miles."

"I could ask the same thing of you, Abigail. Why are you here? What possible business could bring you out this way?"

"Simple, I was putting eyes on the pack that attempted to kidnap my daughter. I want to make sure they are behaving themselves. They thought it was a wise idea to threaten the safety of a witch's family, this allows for me to monitor them, and use the power of the council to deal with them as I see fit. You know that. Now explain yourself."

"I would, but I just don't feel like it."

At that moment Victoria's eyes make a quick movement and a rock is slammed into my stomach. The air is knocked out of me and I hunch over from the pain and lack of air. I am bent over sucking in air, trying to gather back my concentration, but my spell holding Victoria is broken, and she goes on the offensive once she feels it loosen. She sends more fireballs at us. Luckily she is only able to control fire. I respond to her by wrapping her up in a tornado and ramming her into a tree.

"Zeke, run to the car and get it started. I will hold her off and then we need to go quickly!"

Zeke takes off running, Victoria has recovered and tries hold him in a restraining spell with one hand, while continuing to throw fireballs at me with her other. I have no greater desire at the moment than to burn her with her own power, quite literally. I put up a wind wall and direct the current back towards Victoria. Her own fireballs are thrown back at her and she has to let Zeke go to protect herself.

As she is dodging her fireballs and knocking them to the ground I send in the wind wall and use it to hold her to the ground. I back towards the vehicle keeping an eye on her.

Once to the car I jump in and yell, "Go, Zeke, get out of here, go, go, go!" Zeke hits the gas pedal and we peel out of the area we secured the SUV. I am looking out the back window to see if she has managed to get out of the wind trap yet. I see Victoria flying to us quickly. I open the moon roof and stand up through it. I use my powers to build a back protective wall around the vehicle.

Once the wall is in place I begin sending my own fireballs towards Victoria. I have managed to knock her out of the air a few times. I have never battled from a moving car before. This is a new experience. Zeke is swerving the SUV around the road trying to make it more difficult for her to hit us, unfortunately it is also throwing off my aim.

Victoria manages to send a fireball over the top of the protective wall. I watch horrified as it hits the front end of the car. There is a massive explosion and I am torn from the top of the vehicle and thrown 100 yards away, slamming against a rock. I hear cracking and am struggling to get in breaths. I fear I have broken a rib, and hope it does not puncture anything.

I see the car roll over and over and over. I cannot see any movement inside the SUV and I am not sure if Zeke was thrown out or not. "ZEKE!" I scream his name hoping for some type of response.

I am lying against the rock, struggling to breathe, tears streaming down my face, as I imagine the worst fate for Zeke. Victoria's face comes into view and there is an evil smirk plastered over it. She is saying something to me, but I am unable to hear the words.

Next thing I know, I feel something slam into my skull and my world goes dark.

Chapter 34:

Countdown to Attack

(Alpha Blaine's POV)

I stand on the balcony outside my office, looking down on the commotion. I run my hand through my hair, scowling at everything playing out before me.

There is too much: too much noise, too much movement, too many wolves congregating in larger groups, too many weapons being out on display. This is not the way I prepare for an invasion, this is a mess and rushed planning. If we are being observed, we are going to give away our plans before we get out the gate.

I grip the balcony rail until my knuckles are white and let out a massive growl. All movement below me stops and hundreds of eyes are on me.

"Let's pretend we have done this before, prepare and act accordingly. Do not give away our plans," I snarl out to the crowd below.

The atmosphere of the scene below me begins to change to one of practiced calm. My pack does not normally do short-notice movements. I make it a point to scout the pack we are invading, research the guard movements, find multiple points of entry and then attack after careful planning. That is why my pack is so deadly. This plan is being put together sloppily and all based on the intelligence and information of a pup, who has not proven his loyalty to us. I am uncomfortable following him in blind. I will make sure he does not leave my side, during this invasion.

I stand above my pack observing, running through our plans as I watch the work progress. I am momentarily brought out of my thoughts by a swarm of bugs flying around my head and into my office. I let out a huff and move back indoors, closing off the entrance to the balcony. I don't need any more bugs in my office, just another nuisance to me in my already agitated state.

I move behind my desk and look over the map of the area we are heading into. Ryan has marked the entry point. Only one point. No backup plan, no optional point of egress. One way in and he is not anticipating a way out, because he is positive the plan will work. I study the paper before me, looking to add onto the already established plans. I will not lead my wolves into a battle I cannot leave if things do not pan out for us. We are deadly, but Red Crescent is not weak and they have very strong allies. I will not go in unprepared.

I look to the clock on my desk and see we are approaching the noon hour. I am waiting for the witch my grandfather said he was sending. I thought she would be here by now, I need to fill her in on the plan so she can tailor her spells to the mission. So far it has been working to our advantage and we have not been tracked. I smirk as I think about all the Alphas who cannot fight the terror invading their packs. I thrive on the panic and destruction I am causing.

The balcony door crashes open, in flies a very disheveled Victoria, her red hair is pulled out of its normally very neat bun, giving the illusion her head is on fire, by the anger in her eyes, I would say I am not far off. She has cuts and scrapes over her body and burn marks on her dress.

"What an entrance, Victoria, as always. You could at least make an effort to be presentable when you arrive here," I snap condescendingly.

"My entrance into your doghouse should be the least of your worries. I would think you and your mutts would be running better perimeter checks. I am amazed you have managed to make it this far into the plan without ruining it," she mocks me back.

I look at her questioningly. Victoria does not say another word, she simply makes a beckoning move over her head with her hand. In flies the unconscious forms of two individuals. The male looks familiar, but it is difficult to place him, the female reminds me of my mate, but she is older.

"Who are they and why should I be concerned with them?"

"This is the Luna of the Whispering Winds pack and high witch on the Witches' Council, the pup next to her, I am not sure, but he was accompanying her. I saw them coming out of the woods, I think they were doing surveillance on your pack. I searched the area and did not find anyone else."

My eyes widen at the information given. Of course, Whispering Winds would keep an eye on this pack after the issue with the soon-to-be Alpha. I hate to admit Victoria is correct, but I should have placed better security and checks. At least she took a look around the area.

"If you don't mind giving me the specific area you located them, I will have my wolves do another check on the ground. I appreciate your assistance with this. Did you get any information out of them before they passed out?"

"No. I had to blow up their car before I was able to capture them. They happened to be inside when I blew it up."

I mind-link my guards. There is a knock at my door and I summon in the guards.

"Take these two to the dungeons." I motion towards the Luna and her accomplice. "Make sure the male is secured with silver chains and give him a good dose of wolfsbane. As for the female place her in our witches' cell and make sure she is also chained. Place four guards on each cell, and add extra security to the outside of the dungeon."

"Yes, Alpha" comes their curt replies.

"Once that is complete, get a patrol of six guards and do a detailed border check on the neutral side of the Northwest border. That is the area these two were found in. Victoria did an aerial surveillance and found nothing. Just to be secure I want a ground check done, and a report back prior to the planned departure time. This attack is dependent on what you find."

"Yes, Alpha," they chorus again.

I wait until the guards have taken the prisoners out of my office. I will have to deal with them after we return from our mission.

I turn back to Victoria. She is leaning against my desk with a smug look on her face. I detest this witch, but she is necessary at the moment.

"Now they are taken care of. Let's get back on track. We are going to continue as though the plan is still a go. I do not want to be playing catchup. If you care to turn around I will go over the plan with you in detail."

She gives me a bored look, but turns around and gives the map her attention.

Chapter 35:

Moving Forward

(Alpha Blaine's POV)

The guards have completed their perimeter check and linked in to me. The area is clear. No tire tracks, no scents, except those of the prisoners, and no equipment. The light is green to continue on with the mission.

I call Ryan into my office and once again I am left waiting for the bothersome pup. He needs to learn his place again when dealing with me. I am not the type to be kept waiting. Finally there is knock at my office door.

"Get in here, pup, and make it quick!" I yell.

The door opens and in slinks Ryan, again with a cocky, confident air about him. I do not know why he is so pleased with himself. His direction at every turn has been corrected. He does not know how to lead from the front and keep his men calm. Not that he has any men here. My men are already drawing numbers for who gets to kill him.

Ryan saunters up to me, gets directly in my face and sneers, "Remember, Alpha, when we get into the main packhouse, I am the one to kill my father. Keep your mutts away from him. I want the death of my mother at my hands to be the last thing he sees before I rip his heart out."

I look Ryan back in the eyes and simply bring my fist up, hitting him on the left jaw, the force throwing him to the ground. "I told you once before, pup, watch how you talk to me. You are a rogue, no pack, no rank. I will not tolerate you or your insolence. Next time I break your neck, mission be damned."

Ryan looks up at me from the floor, while massaging his sore face. I didn't use enough force to break his jaw, he is fine, just being weak as always.

"Get yourself up off the floor. You are a disgrace," I spit at him.

Ryan gets himself up and has enough sense to keep his eyes adverted to the ground. "Yes, Alpha," he struggles to get out.

I am sure his pride and ego are taking a significant hit, having to submit to me. Good.

"I called you to my office to let you know we have captured a witch and a wolf, snooping around the area. We know the witch is the Luna of Whispering Winds. We do not know who the male wolf is, though. We need you to identify him for us. My guards did a detailed land search on the neutral side of the perimeter, while the witch helping us did an aerial search. Neither search found any other wolves in the area. Looks like the Luna was wanting to make sure we were behaving ourselves after kidnapping her daughter. The mission is a go."

Ryan looks at me in disbelief. "If you have the Luna of Whispering Winds here, you can bet if she isn't back to the pack at a designated time, he will be on you and take her back. You are ruthless, but do not underestimate Alpha Alexander. He is a force to be reckoned with."

I throw my head back and let out a loud, harsh laugh. "What kind of Alpha sends his Luna to do the dirty work?"

"The type of Alpha who is searching for a reason to kill you" comes Ryan's response. "If the Luna came, there are only two people he would send with her as an escort, Beta Mark or his son, soon-to-be-Beta Ezekiel. It was only by chance your witch found them; otherwise, you would have never known. It was not a dangerous mission she went on."

"Let the Alpha come for her. It will please me to end the entire family. The Oscuros are a blight on this earth and need to be wiped clean. I will start with the Luna once we return from our mission. This Ezekiel, would he also be called Zeke?" My eyebrows narrow in thought, trying to place our prisoner.

"Yes, Zeke is what his family and friends call him. I am surprised your witch was able to capture them. She must be very strong."

"She blew them up in their car and knocked them out," I respond, bored with this conversation. "This male wolf we have with us is one of the wolves who came to assist Jasmine when she escaped. He is the one who secured Saul and took him away. That is why he looked familiar to me."

Looks like I am holding two aces over the head of Whispering Winds. I cannot wait to use my cards to my advantage. The prisoners will have to wait, though. This mission is my priority.

Chapter 36:

Surveillance 3

(Lead Warrior's POV)

I get a mind-link from Future Beta Ezekiel. He tells me they are under attack from a witch, but the Luna is keeping her at bay. Our direction from the Luna is to maintain our position and do not respond. The intelligence we are gathering is more important. I relay this information to my men, and we are all having a difficult time maintaining our place. We want to assist and protect our Luna. It is ingrained in us.

I decide to mind-link with our Alpha for further direction. "Alpha Alexander, this is Miles."

"Yes, Miles, what do you need?"

Through the mind-link I can tell the Alpha is stressed about something. He must be aware of what is occurring, but it is my duty to ensure my thoughts are accurate.

"I received a mind-link from Ezekiel saying he and Luna were under attack and our direction from the Luna was to maintain our location and not respond. Is this your direction as well, Alpha?"

"At this time, that is my direction. Have faith in your Luna, men. She is correct, what you are doing is especially important."

"Understood, Alpha. I will pass on this direction. The audio should be coming through anytime now. The Luna sent in bugs, literal bugs, as listening devices into the packhouse. Transmission will be a minute or so delayed, but still real time."

"Thank you, Miles. Link me with any further developments."

"Yes, Alpha."

"Okay, men, the direction from the Alpha is to maintain our position, to have faith in our Luna and to update him through mind-link with any new developments. We are going to start communicating through mind-link only. I am sure there will be a perimeter check now that there has been a clash. Let's make sure there is no reason for them to suspect we are here."

The men all nod in understanding. The Luna has put her faith in us, and we will not fail her. She is leading by example, and she is fearless. I am honored to follow her.

There is an explosion in the distance. We all turn in the direction with wide eyes.

"Zeke," I try to mind-link.

There is no response.

"Zeke," I try again.

I get a very faint response. "Car. Blown up. Injured. Where is Luna?" Then nothing but silence.

I feel a cold sweat come over me.

"Alpha, there was an explosion. The car was blown up, Zeke is injured and unsure of where the Luna is."

"I can feel her pain. The Luna is injured but not dead. I am heading that way with warriors."

"Alpha, there is a lot of activity at the Broken Moon pack. Let me look through the scope and update you on what I see."

"Very well. This way I can make sure I have enough warriors with me to take them back if I need to."

I run over to the scope and look through it. I start by looking at the front gate and working my way to the packhouse. This pack is preparing for some type of a big movement. I am not sure what they are up to, or where they are headed but it does not bode well for the pack they are going after.

I get to the window the Luna sent the bugs in and I pull back in surprise. I settle myself and look again. I begin to shake in rage at what is folding out in front of me.

"Alpha, I am looking in Alpha Blaine's office window. A witch with red hair has just flown in, she looks like she has been in a fight. She has the Luna and Ezekiel with her. They appear to be unconscious, and she has some sort of shield around them to make them move at her will. She just dropped them on the floor at the Alpha's feet. They are having a discussion. There is someone at the door. It is the Alpha's guards. They are taking the Luna and Ezekiel out of the room. Most likely to the dungeon. Wait, they are looking at the door again. What the hell!!! Alpha, Ryan Reed just walked into Alpha Blaine's office."

"Good work, Miles. We are getting audio now. Hold position and continue monitoring. At this moment you and your team are extremely valuable right where you are. We will work up a plan after listening to audio and get back to you."

After breaking the link with the Alpha, I catch a scent in the air. It is not the scent of my men. I look around and give a sign for all motion to stop. We all pause. From the trees come six wolves. I do not recognize them, while we are outnumbered, I trust in our training and continue to hold my position for any sign of attack or aggression.

The wolves look around for a while and finally the lead wolf speaks. "I don't see anything here. Let's link the Alpha and tell him all clear. Time to head back and kick some ass at Red Crescent."

There is a round of whooping and hollering at this comment. The wolves move away. We wait another ten minutes before moving.

"Alpha, a patrol just came through doing a security check. The head guard said something about kicking ass at Red Crescent. I think we know where they are going now."

"Thank you for the update, Miles. You all stay safe and alert."

My men and I get back to our surveillance. We are now keeping an eye on the entrance to the dungeons as well.

Chapter 37:

Counterattack Planning

(Alpha Alexander's POV)

I am pacing in my office, unable to sit, balling and un-balling my hands into fists. As I pace, so does my wolf inside my mind, we are fighting every instinct to run to our mate, protect her, save her, and kill those who dared to harm her. I also know if I drop all the other plans to run to her rescue, I will have to face her wrath. I am a strong man, but the wrath of my mate, and the power she holds is enough of an incentive to do as she has requested.

Punching the wall behind my desk and then spinning around, I turn furious eyes to Simon, pinning him down and demand, "Where are we with the audio? Miles said it should be coming through at any time. I need to know what is happening. Enough idle time, a plan must be made. The Luna and Zeke need to be brought home!"

Simon shifts his weight and stands a little taller. He is monitoring a computer Zeke set up prior to departing. Simon's knuckles are white as he grips the edges of the stand-up desk. Simon takes in a deep breath and lets it out slowly, he is remiss to tell me no data has come through yet, he does not want to deal with my impatience and rage.

We all hear a ding come from the computer and Simon uses the mouse to click on a file. The room is suddenly full of Alpha Blaine's voice. It seems Zeke put surround sound in my office. This does make it easier for everyone to listen to the live audio. We have some catching up to do, but the file is there and complete. Simon makes sure we will be listening from the beginning.

Just before Simon begins the recording, I motion for him to stop. I am receiving a mind-link from Miles. I didn't expect one so quickly. Miles fills me in on what is happening at Broken Moon. My wolf is in a frenzy now. I do not know how much longer I can control him from taking over. I grit my teeth and demand he go to the back of my mind. It is difficult to concentrate with him yelling at me to go to our Luna.

"Miles just linked. Broken Moon is being assisted by a witch, and apparently Ryan Reed is there. Mark, get Alpha Mason on the phone, or better yet, ask him to join us. He should be able to get here in a few minutes in wolf form. Let the border guards know he is coming and not to stop him. This is urgent."

"Jasmine," I mind-link. "I need you and the group with you at the training grounds to come to my office now. There are new developments."

"Yes, Father" comes her terse reply.

Within minutes I have sweaty, and blood-soaked, Jasmine, Alpha Keith, Ashley, and Beta Andrew in my office. All of them carry intensely serious faces. "Luna and Zeke have been taken prisoner, Broken Moon is gearing up for

a movement to Red Crescent and Ryan is with them. Alpha Mason is on his way, in just a moment we will listen to the audio coming from Alpha Blaine's office," I push out through gritted teeth. My emotions are not stable, I can feel my wolf pushing to take control and save our Luna. We need a plan, a double plan. We cannot leave Red Crescent without support.

I look over to Jasmine, her eyes are beginning to glow, wind is starting to swirl in the office. I run up to Jazz and gently grab her by her shoulders, bringing her out of her enchantment. She places eyes on me that are glowing white, ringed with blue.

"We will get her back, Father, and there will be blood spilled tonight. Both at Red Crescent and Broken Moon. There will be hell to pay for attacking my family again."

A shiver runs down my spine, while a cold sweat breaks out on my brow. I have never heard Jasmine speak like this, the hostility in her body is overflowing. It is as if her voice, Brooke's, and the ethereal sound of her witch's blood all mix together. I am afraid revenge is her driving force, instead of the safety and wellbeing of all packs. I make a mental note to talk with her regarding this when it is just the two of us.

Ashley comes up behind Jasmine and wraps her arms around her shoulders. "We will get them back, Jazz. Do not worry on that account. Come back to us, reground."

Jasmine relaxes at the coaxing of Ashley. I am comforted to know there is a presence next to Jazz that can bring her back. Moon Goddess was wise to choose Ashley to be by her side.

I look around the room and see many anxious faces. Such a small show of power from my daughter has a group of high-ranking male wolves shaking before her. It is a good thing none of our enemies can see into this office. As I am musing, I receive a mind-link from the border patrol.

"Alpha Mason just crossed over and is coming to you at full speed."

I look back to the room, "Alpha Mason will be here momentarily. I suggest we wait to begin audio, since his arrival is imminent. I will ha—"

I don't get to finish. The door to my office slams open, there stands a winded red and sweaty Alpha Mason. Jasmine takes him a glass of water. He nods his thanks to her and downs the glass in one go. Mason clears his throat, turning his attention to me.

"I apologize for my lack of decorum, but from what I gather this is urgent. If I may be so bold, in your home, Alpha, let's not waste any more time and get down to work. Looks like there are two simultaneous plans to make up."

"I couldn't agree more, Mason. To work it is, my good man."

Simon clicks on a few buttons, and the voice of Alpha Blaine once again fills my office. I feel anger and hatred rise in my system, hearing him speak of my mate. I grip the edge of my desk, small pieces breaking off in my grasp. I grit my teeth and struggle my way through the taping.

Chapter 38:

Counterattack Planning 2

(Alpha Mason's POV)

My blood surges in my veins, and the pounding of my heart is deafening to my ears. I see red and do my best to control my breathing and anger. My wolf is clawing at the edges of my mind to break free, causing a massive headache.

How could my son turn on his mother and me? How could my son turn on his people? How could he turn on our close family friends and allies? Listening to him tell Alpha Blaine how he plans to end my life is nauseating. He is literally bringing death to his people's door. The only good part of the entire audio is when Alpha Blaine knocks Ryan on his backside and makes him submit.

Momentarily forgetful of my surroundings I let out a deep growl, followed by a mournful howl. My body is in shock and there are too many emotions running through my system now. As the howl is let out, a single tear escapes down my cheek.

Ryan cut all ties to the pack when he left, regardless, he is still my son, and the betrayal is all too fresh and cuts deep. It is now time for me to put that aside and protect my Luna and my pack. Ryan chose his side, and I will not let his mother find death at his hands, not while there is a breath left in me.

A gentle hand is placed on my shoulder, comforting me in silence. It draws me back to the reality we are in. I am not alone, but with a room full of wolves who understand my pain. It is good to be among friends at a time like this. I take in a steadying breath and turn towards Alpha Alexander.

"Where do we start? You must bring your Luna and Zeke home, but Red Crescent also needs to be protected, my Luna needs to be safe."

"You are correct, Mason. My initial plan, off the cuff, is to do a small split of forces. We know the manpower Alpha Blaine is planning on sending to Red Crescent and what he is leaving behind to defend Broken Moon. The young Alpha is greatly confident, it is to our advantage, he is unaware of the surveillance we have on him," Alpha Alexander begins.

I nod in agreement, letting him continue.

"The best plan may be for Whispering Winds to leave half our warriors here, to protect, in case Alpha Blaine makes plans on the move to attack all three packs at once. The others and I will accompany you to Red Crescent. Half of Midnight Moons warriors, with agreement from Alpha Keith, can stay in place and the other half accompany him, Beta Andrew, Jasmine, Ashley, and Claire go to Broken Moon, to rescue our loved ones. As clarified before, this is just off the cuff, please feel free to add in any thoughts."

Alpha Alexander looks around the room as so do I. Many people are deep in thought, thinking over the suggestion. At the moment my mind is not in the correct place to yay or nay any suggestion. All I want is blood, blood of the one who has turned, and threatened the existence of the person who bore him life.

My attention is called back when Alpha Keith begins speaking. "With all due respect, Alpha Alexander, I would be honored to turn control of my men over to you. It may not be my place to say such things, but you being there to bring your Luna home is important and necessary, it will comfort the both of you. Please take my men or yours and I will go with Alpha Mason to defend his pack."

This young Alpha continues to amaze me. All evening he has been silent through the audio, stepped to the back and let us old war dogs have our say. The only moment he comes forward is to make sure an Alpha is by the side of his Luna. This is an Alpha I can stand beside with pride and honor.

"Thank you, Keith, your thoughtfulness is appreciated. What if we do some of our original plan, mixed in with the new. The warriors staying in place remain the same, but a quarter of the warriors from Midnight Moon and a quarter from Whispering Winds accompany me and the others accompany you to Red Crescent. That way if there is additional manpower needed mind-links can be sent to both packs. Also, Abigail's sister, Meredith, will be arriving any moment. She has agreed to accompany you all to Red Crescent, since we know they are being assisted by a witch. A little fire to fight fire will be helpful."

Looking around the room all heads are nodding in agreement. Determination is set across everyone's features.

"As an Alpha it is difficult for me to be humble at times but thank you all so much. You could have ended all support to my pack and gone after your Luna and Zeke, but instead, we have all worked together to find a way to protect all. I am not sure I can express my appreciation, forever, Red Crescent is in your debt." Tears are clogging my throat as I manage to get out my statement.

Alpha Keith clears his throat. "There will be time for sentiment later, right now we have plans to make and put into effect. We have limited time to make our manpower changes." Keith winks at me as he finishes his statement, making it clear, between us, he is trying to save me face, Alpha to Alpha.

We straighten our shoulders and begin putting our plans in motion. I mind-link my Beta and let him know what to expect, then join the group, this promises to be a long night.

Chapter 39:

Broken Moon on the Move

(Ryan's POV)

Alpha Blaine has crossed a line with me, at the moment, I am unable to stand up to him. What was I thinking revoking my ties to my pack? Now I am a rogue and Alpha Blaine is using it to his advantage to control me.

He will get his in the end, oh, yes, I have plans for him too. As soon as I dispose of my mother and father, have the Alpha title connected to me, and my power back, Alpha Blaine will feel my teeth on his throat. The light leaving his eyes will be payment enough for all the embarrassment he has caused me. A smile spreads across my face thinking of my payback.

Right now, I am standing in the very back of one of six formations, each formation has 100 wolves. My rightful place is in front of all the formations, with Alpha Blaine and that damned witch. The irony of the situation is not lost on me. We are trying to separate the species of the supernatural world, yet we still need to rely on the help of the other species to make it happen.

Each company of wolves is directed to a five-ton truck. The distance is too great to run all the way in wolf form and have enough energy to battle once there. We are going to drive until about an hour away, by vehicle and go the rest of the way as wolves.

Once we settle in the back of the massive military-like trucks, the witch comes around and does a spell to hide our scents. Alpha Blaine does not allow her to do a protection spell. His thought on this is that if his warriors are ignorant enough to do something that causes them to fall in battle, then that is a consequence they need to pay. He says it roots out the weak for him.

The trucks start up and we are on the move. Anticipation and excitement run through my system. My wolf and I are ready to lead Red Crescent, to bring a new era to the pack. I don't have much cleaning that needs to be done to make my pack a pure wolfpack, but I relish the opportunity to cleanse it.

Watching our surroundings carefully, I realize we are almost to the rendezvous point. I shift to my wolf and leap from the back of the truck. The men are yelling at me to come back, all the vehicles come to a screeching halt. I do not care. I will be with the leads of the pack when we attack. This is my right; this is where I belong, and no one is taking that from me.

I arrive at the entry point, turn back to my human form, then find bushes big enough to sit behind to ensure I am hidden from any patrols and wait. Soon I feel the aura of Alpha Blaine around me. He yanks me to my feet.

"What. Are. You. Doing?" he snarls into my face.

Smiling at him, I enlighten him. "I will be one of the heads going into this attack. I am here to end my father and mother and take my rightful place as Alpha of this pack, at this time I am still the rightful heir. Do not relegate me to the back of one of your formations. I may be rogue now, but I will soon be your equal."

"You will never be my equal, you may be an Alpha, but that is it," he snarls back to me.

Alpha Blaine lets me go.

Turning our attention back to the task at hand, I am where I belong. I was hoping the witch would stay back, but apparently, she is accompanying us, just in case we need her assistance. She is strong, I will give her that, she did take down Luna Abigail. Maybe she can be helpful.

Cautiously we cross the border of Red Crescent. Once all the wolves have crossed over, we wait and listen. If we have been detected a loud howl will go up from the Alpha. Generally, they can sense when there is a breach on the border, but we have been spelled to help with that.

We wait on high alert, for about ten minutes and no warning goes up. We proceed forward closely observing our surroundings. It is obvious Red Crescent is not anticipating an attack. There is no increased patrols, none of my fathers heightened security measures, all is calm. Confidence is surging through me; I have planned this attack to perfection. Won't Father and Mother Dearest be so surprised.

We move farther in, until we are at the edge of the tree line surrounding the packhouse and grounds. All the lights are turned out in the cottages and packhouse, everyone is asleep for the night. We don't plan on slaughtering the entire pack. I need someone to rule over, all the wolves with us are a show of power, more than anything.

We pause and surveille the area, making sure we are not being watched. We begin hearing small grunts coming from the back of the ranks. Alpha Blaine spins around, furious. His orders have called for absolute silence. He scans the back of the ranks, but nothing seems out of order.

Just as we are about to move forward, bodies drop from the trees above us, and begin engaging the warriors. How? How were they prepared for us? How did they plan this? We are surrounded, there is no escape route open to us. I guess I will have to fight, before killing my father. So be it, and I move forward to engage in battle myself.

Chapter 40:

Battle at Red Crescent

Alpha Mason and I look over land maps of his area. We pinpoint the weakest area and believe this is where Ryan will enter and attack from. There is a large wood at the edge of the packhouse and grounds. Perfect for staging, prior to battle.

This is where my men and I will be located, along with a mix of Red Crescent and Whispering Winds warriors. Communication is key for us and we are doing our best to make sure all areas are covered.

Meredith arrived with three other witches, this way we have a witch that can control each of the elements, I was not aware she is considered a warrior witch and specializes in battle strategies and power usage. Thankfully, Meredith was able to spell my men and me so our scents are hidden.

The element of surprise is the most important part for us. We want to surround the warriors and cut off any means of escape for them. The battle with Ryan ends tonight. I hear soft footsteps coming from behind the woods, sniffing the air, there is no scent. Their witch spelled them also.

Patience is the hard part now, waiting until the formations have settled, and lulled into a calm. I look down from my perch in an oak tree and see the leaders of the pack. Ryan is standing at the front and excitement is rolling off him, he is barely able to stand still, shifting from one foot to the next.

I direct my men at the rear of the formation to take out the last line of warriors. Jane, one of the witches, is with this group, she has placed a spell on the back line obscuring the view. My men can take them out and not be seen by the rest of the pack.

Watching the movements below me, it is time for us to jump into action. I mind-link the group and give a signal, as one unit, we drop from the branches above and engage in battle. Mind-links have been sent to the warriors on the pack grounds, the battle is starting.

I land behind Ryan and Alpha Blaine. Coming down I land a hard blow to the kidneys on Alpha Blaine. I hear the air burst out of him. He quickly shifts into his dark gray wolf, and lunges for me. I sidestep his attack and shift into Aspen, my fur is golden, and while battling Alpha Keith we appear as good and evil in our coloring.

Alpha Blaine lunges for me again and this time I meet him head on, our wolves crash into each other, we swipe, claw, and dig at each other's bodies with our paws. The metallic taste and smell of blood is heavy in my mouth and the air around me. I manage to bite into one of Blaine's shoulders. His wolf growls at me and knocks me off with a blow from his head.

Aspen stands back to his feet and initiates the attack, this time. He latches on to Blaine's hind leg, breaking it, he lets loose and sinks his teeth deep into Blaine's hind quarters. Blaine will not be able to walk for a while. His wolf will heal him, but not too quickly. I circle around, baring my teeth, and lunge, but suddenly, I am thrown into a tree. I feel a cracking in my back as I fall to the moist earth below me. I sink into the leaves, and struggle to get a breath in.

A woman with red hair is standing before me, an evil smirk crosses her face. "Oh, poor little doggy is about to be put down," she lashes out in a demeaning tone.

I see the energy ball forming in her hands, unable to move, I close my eyes, waiting for the pain. The fire never comes, it doesn't hit or consume my body, opening my eyes I see the woman pinned to the ground by tree roots.

I look around and smile my thanks to the witch helping, she only nods in response. Aspen has used this time to heal us, a great deal. We are not completely healed, but enough to get back into the battle and be effective. I am looking for Alpha Blaine. I see him near the front, dominating some of the younger warriors.

Aspen is having to fight his way to the front. Blaine's warriors are strong, and fight without mercy, I will give them that, but there is a weakness to them. They are too confident in their skills; they do not think anyone can stand against them. A wolf jumps on my back. I flip him over, slamming his body to the ground and use my claws to behead him. Just as I finish with him another wolf claws my side. I wince from the pain, but reach out and claw him across the chest, pouncing on his wolf, I get him to the ground and manage to break his neck. The fight continues like this, as I slowly make my way to the front of the battle.

Finally, Blaine is in my sites. He has one of my young warriors in his grasp. I leap forward, bringing my jaws shut on his shoulder. Blaine drops the warrior he is holding, growling out in pain and annoyance. He delivers several blows to my head with his alternate arm, and I let loose of him. We circle each other, with bared teeth. I begin to lunge at him, when I feel teeth sink into my hind leg, pulling me back.

Looking back momentarily, I see Ryan's wolf attached to my back leg. I kick my other leg back, delivering a blow right between Ryan's eyes. He lets loose and I have just enough time to evade Blaine's lunge. Recentering I prepare to engage again with Blaine. Aspen is crouched, muscles ready to send us launching forward, when an arrow lodges in Blaine's shoulder.

Blaine falls to his knees, on the field before me for just an instant. He is back on his feet but has shifted to human form. The arrow must be silver, for that to happen. Blaine pulls the arrow from his shoulder and sprints into the trees. I choose not to go after him. The silver has weakened him, and he is out of the fight.

Surveilling the area, I find Ryan engaged with his father. Two other wolves are assisting him in attacking the Alpha. Aspen leaps forward to come to the assistance of Alpha Mason.

Chapter 41:

Battle at Red Crescent 2

(Alpha Mason's POV)

Beta Andrew of Midnight Moon and Beta Mark of Whispering Winds are by my side along with Meredith, anticipating the battle ahead of us. Both men's eyes glaze over, and I know it is time. There was no warning our boundary border had been broken. The witch they have with them must have spelled them.

Giving the order to move forward, all the wolves with me move stealthily ahead. Meredith placed a spell around the grounds, so it looks like my pack is not wise to the attack planned by Ryan and Blaine. We have moved into position just, five feet in front of the leading pack members.

Keith drops down behind Blaine and Ryan, landing a hard blow to Blaine. Meredith drops the shield, and we are all exposed. Jumping into the battle. The look on Ryan's face is priceless. They are surrounded, no way out but to fight. This pack will not fall to the likes of them. We will stand for justice.

Andrew shifts, jumping on to who I assume is the Beta of Broken Moon. They are exchanging blows and bites, teeth bared and saliva whipping out of their mouths. Andrew's mouth is tinted with blood from a strike he made to his opponent. It is time I also engage.

Mark is fighting with two of the other wolves near the front, and Meredith is sending a tornado through the second line of their pack, taking wolves, high into the air and then dropping them. There is a wolf charging her from the right, and it does not appear, Meredith sees him coming. I jump into action and tackle the wolf, tearing out his throat.

Engaging with the next wolf, I continue fighting. Looking around I see Ryan has a hold on Keith's leg, Keith kicks him off, and I run to end this battle with Ryan.

Making my way to Ryan I head butt him, while he is still dazed from being kicked by Keith. He flies several feet away, I approach slowly, allowing Ryan to clear his mind and get to his feet. This battle will be one on one, if he can defeat me here, then the pack will belong to him.

Ryan crouches down and lunges for my neck. I stand still, at the last moment I raise my large paw, delivering a strong blow to his head, knocking him down. We go on this way for a few minutes, when I see another wolf approach from my left. I move to avoid his strike, but his claws just catch my ribcage. Nothing that will not heal quickly.

Looking back to Ryan, I see it is now three on one. I have faced greater odds; it appears my son does not want me to leave this battle alive. The three of them attack at once. Since Ryan has become rogue, he is not as strong as the others, I focus on the strongest wolf, engaging with him.

As the three wolves leap into action, I see a wolf come in from the right and take out one of the wolves, leaving me with Ryan and the one I was originally planning on attacking. They lunge at me and I land a solid blow to the wolf, dislocating his shoulder and leaving deep gashes, his blood flowing heavily and shoulder barely hanging on by strands of sinew.

Ryan misses me, not anticipating me fighting with the other wolf first. He comes around and reattacks. I meet him head on. His lips are pulled back, showing his canines, covered in blood and saliva, his eyes are dark, obviously his wolf is in control. They are on the same mission. To end me and lay claim to this pack. Over my and my wolf's dead body.

Chapter 42:

Battle at Red Crescent 3

(Luna Rebecca's POV)

As Luna of this pack, I refuse to be hidden in a saferoom while our warriors and my mate fight for us. Especially against our son, our traitorous son. A tear runs down my face thinking about him. I heard the audio, Mason left his link to me open, and I heard the entire tape. I know what our son had planned for us. My lip curls thinking about it, as my cheeks become the background to a waterfall.

Locating Beta Female Lacey, I walk up to her. Using my Luna tone on her, "You stay here with the pack members and protect them with your life. I am going to fight with the warriors."

The look Lacey gives me is one of pure panic. Smiling at her, I try to ease her fears. "We have three packs, fighting out there. I will be with my mate. I must be by his side on this one. The threat is coming from our own son. Between my mate, Alpha Keith and all the Betas, I am going to be completely protected. We ensured enough wolf power to keep them at bay."

"Yes, Luna. I will watch out for our pack here. Go and do what you need to do. Please be careful. Goddess watch over you."

With that I leave the saferoom. I have no intention of finding my mate. He will be livid to find I have left the packhouse. Finding my way back to our room, I go to the back of my closet, reaching up to a shelf, I pull down my bow and arrows. Mason doesn't know, but I continue to practice my fighting abilities. It is the only secret I have from him, but I refuse to be a weak Luna.

Quickly I change into clothes more appropriate to battle in, then hang an amulet around my neck and tuck it into my shirt collar. Meredith gave the amulet to me, to hide my scent and give me some protection. She is the only one aware of my plans. I tie my hair back and run out the door, knowing the battle has already started.

Sneaking around the packhouse border, I pull my wolf to the front with me. While using my bow and arrows, I am unable to shift, but I need her heightened senses. We sniff the air but are unable to smell anything. Both sides have had their scent hidden. This may be more difficult than I initially thought. I do not know all our ally warriors enough to tell them apart from the enemy. My plan is to focus on the wolves I know, this way I can help eliminate some of the threat. My heart sinks a little knowing I am unable to help all our allies.

I move forward, hiding behind a smokehouse. This building is close enough to the battle I can use my weapon of choice, but far enough away there will be question as to where I am hiding. Lifting myself to the roof of the building I take cover behind a chimney.

Peering out from behind my brick protector, I see Keith battling with who I assume is Alpha Blaine. Ryan comes out of nowhere and attaches himself to Keith's hind leg, Keith is able to kick him off and evade the attack from Blaine. This is my chance. I steady my bow and nock an arrow. I site in on my target, right as I am about to let loose the building below me begins to shake. The arrow releases, I have no idea who I have hit, if I hit a target at all. I am unable to look because this smokehouse is coming down.

I leap from the roof and roll to the side as the building collapses. Through the smoke comes a red-haired woman, with fireballs in each hand, she has a sinister smile on her face.

"Why, if it isn't the Luna, of the dirty mongrels. I hope you had your fun before you meet your end. One less bad puppy to deal with." She begins laughing, as she raises one hand above her head to let loose the flame.

Refusing to go down without a fight, I pick up a large stone next to me on the ground and hurl it at her. She is momentarily unfocused, allowing me to get to my feet, in a better stance to battle. My resolve is set, I will die here if necessary, protecting my pack and my people.

From behind the witch comes a large wave, washing over her and knocking me from my feet. Looking up I see Meredith emerge from the tree line, a deep scowl on her beautiful features.

"Of course, it is you assisting them. Vile bitch, you will pay for turning your back on your people and attacking my sister."

Meredith binds the other witches' arms with water ropes and then encases her in a tornado, sending her high up in the air. "This should hold her until the battle is over," Meredith informs me as she sends death glares to the tornado above us. "I will be dealing with her personally. Let's get back to the battle."

We head off to the battlefield ensuring to remain hidden as we approach. Peering out from behind our most recent refuge, I see Mason and Ryan exchanging blows. Their wolves are entangled. I hear Mason let out a growl of pain. Ryan was able to sink his claws into Mason's side. Fear washes over me.

I step out from behind our building, pull up my bow and nock an arrow. It is difficult to see from the water in my eyes. Taking in a deep breath, I let the arrow fly. In no time Ryan falls to the ground, I let out a strangled scream and run forward, uncaring about any danger facing me.

I get to Ryan and fall to the ground next to him. I hold his head in my lap, brushing his hair back from his face. My arrow held true and landed in his chest. Mason comes up and falls to the ground on his knees next to me. We hold our son, as the light leaves his eyes. My wolf lets out a mournful howl at the loss, and my body shakes from the sobs wracking my body.

As I kneel there, surrounded by our allies, holding the body of my son, the warriors of Broken Moon begin to retreat. I stand on shaky legs and view the field around me. Bodies litter the ground, there are moans coming from all around. Blood stains the earth and assaults my nasal passage.

The warriors link us, stating all Broken Moon warriors have left our grounds. I mind-link the medical staff and let them know the grounds are clear and to send out medical staff to attend to the wounded. I will take care of Ryan on my own.

Chapter 43:

Battle at Red Crescent 4

(Alpha Blaine's POV)

The rogue wolf has been causing nothing but problems for me. He has a skewed view of what he is entitled to from me. He is entitled to nothing. I have a bad feeling about this mission we have been sent on. My wolf is uneasy in the back of my mind, cautioning me to stay hyper-alert.

We cross the border into Red Crescent, no alerts go up from our entry. We have managed to cross into their territory unnoticed. Our witch seems to be pulling her own weight, the quicker we can get this over with, the quicker we can get rid of her. Following Ryan's lead we make it to the edge of the woodlands, edging the open field before the packhouse and family houses.

I hear noises coming from the back of my wolves. I turn around scowling at the back line. They know my rule is total silence. Nothing seems out of place. My wolf is growling at me, saying something is off. To get out now, retreat with the men. I am about to put up an order when bodies begin dropping from the trees.

I take a heavy blow to my kidneys. They were expecting us! I send out a quick mind-link. Engage, no mercy. I turn and strike at the wolf who attacked me. I recognize Alpha Keith of Midnight Moon, I am momentarily surprised to see him here, regardless battle is battle.

Keith is stronger than I had imagined, he is a worthy opponent. He has delivered strategic injuries to me; I am down for the moment. His wolf is circling me, sizing me up for a final blow. Before he can advance on me, he is picked up and thrown into a tree. I see Victoria come up to him, ready to end him, but another witch intervenes. They have more than one witch to assist them? So much for taking out Luna Abigail.

My wolf has managed to heal me enough for me to get up, continuing to combat. I have battled my way back to the front of my warriors with Ryan in site. Finally, I am beside him, continuing to fight. We are dominating some of these young warriors, trying to make our way to Ryan's father.

Suddenly there are teeth gripping into my shoulder. I drop the young wolf I have in my hands and begin punching the wolf biting into me. Finally, the wolf lets go. I turn around to see Keith has fought his way back to us. He attempts to lunge at me, but Ryan latches on to his back leg, Keith manages to kick him off and avoid my counterattack. As we circle each other I feel a stinging pain in my shoulder. I look over and see an arrow sticking out. I change back into my human form against my will; the arrow must be silver. I am unable to link my pack, so I get up and run into the trees, grabbing the closest warrior to me.

Once in the safety of the trees I have the warrior link our Beta, but he does not respond. I do not know if he is dead or alive. I direct the warrior to remove the arrow. The pain is awful, but I will not make a sound, I refuse to show weakness.

I have the warrior call for a retreat, meet at the secondary rendezvous point, egress through any exit available. We then make our own way out of Red Crescent territory. The trek to the meeting point was long, by the time we arrived, most of my energy was gone and I had no choice but to use the assistance of the warrior with me. I need to get the silver out of my system.

As wolves come in I have them line up in formation, this way I can take accountability. I can barely stand as I finish accounting for everyone. Sweat is rolling down my body, I have a headache throbbing behind my temples, that is only secondary to the burning and throbbing in my shoulder. My stomach is rolling with the mildest movement. We have lost 250 wolves, my Beta and Ryan being among them, and Victoria is not with us. I am not sure if they are all dead or if taken captive. This information only adds to my nausea.

Pulling myself up into the truck, I lean into the seat and close my eyes, time to get back to Broken Moon. I have two prisoners to deal with, but they can wait until tomorrow. My grandfather still needs to be informed of the failure. The silver in my body is more comforting than the thought of telling him of our failure.

CHAPTER 44:

RESCUE FROM BROKEN MOON

(Jasmine's POV)

It has been decided by the group for me to take lead on this rescue mission. I am the only one out of the group, with knowledge of the layout of the grounds and where the dungeons are located. My nerves are on edge, I can hear my heartbeat in my ears, pounding away. Closing my eyes, I take deep breaths in through my nose, and out my mouth, recentering myself.

We are thirty minutes out from Broken Moon's boundary.

"Miles, are you there?" I link.

"Yes, Queen."

"Please update me on what is happening on the grounds. We are not far out now."

"There is increased security at the entrance to the dungeon, appears to be six guards on the outside, and the same inside, based off counting those going in and coming out. The front gate has been enhanced with two extra guards, and there are four additional patrols roaming. It does not appear they have any actual direction, so where they go and when cannot be mapped."

"We will be approaching from the Northwest border, does that appear to be the best place to enter from?"

"Yes, Queen, best option, not as many guards or patrols."

"Thanks, Miles, that is all for now. Hold you position and stay alert." "Yes, Queen."

Looking back to the rest of the group, "All our plans are still a go. Some increased manpower, but not enough to deter us. The highest rank on site appears to be the Gamma, who I did not meet."

Our vehicle comes to a stop, and we unload. Dad, Ashley, Claire, myself and twelve additional warriors gather into a small group so I can hide our scents. Only one spell can be completed, or I won't have enough energy to do any more if needed in the cells.

Viewing the group, upon completion, they all have their game faces on. We are going in to bring back our family and put a little hurt on this curse of a pack. This action alone is going to lead to an escalation in aggression between our packs.

"Young One, once over the border stay close to the walls, do not go into the shadows of the trees. Deception is at play, but we can outsmart them," my wolf informs me. Brooke has been silent most of the trip to Broken Moon, I assumed she was preparing and settling. "If you must shift, do not use your magic in wolf form. We must keep it to ourselves for the time being, no matter what happens, promise me."

"I promise, Brooke, you make it sound so ominous."

Brooke just gives me a sigh and goes to the back of my mind. She is not being her normal, supportive self today, worry begins to wash over me for her. I push it to the back of my mind for now, we will speak when this mission is taken care of.

We come to the border wall.

"Miles, is it clear for us to enter over the border wall?" I link.

"Yes, Queen. There are no patrols in your area. The closest one is a mile off, and they do not appear to have scented you."

"Thanks, Miles, alright, from here on out mind-link only, no audible, stay close to the border wall and avoid the trees. Brooke has given me a warning."

Nods come from all around me. We send up a grappling hook and secure it. The wall is too high to jump to the top, even in wolf form. I go up first and drop down to the other side. It is hard to believe I am breaking into this pack when a few months ago I was doing everything to break out.

Settling into a position, where I can view all directions and secure those coming over the wall, I link the rest to let them know to come over. One by one the team makes it over. The last wolf grabs the grappling hook and rope. We begin to move out keeping close to the walls. Brooke has come back to the share space at the front of my mind.

"Young One, I am giving you my power and heightened senses. We will fight together."

Once she finishes, I feel my body tingle and foreboding take over mind and heart. Things here are not as they appear.

Chapter 45:

Rescue from Broken Moon 2

(Jasmine's POV)

Silently, we creep towards the doors of the dungeon, peering out from behind our hiding spot, I see three wolves patrolling the outer door. Using wind, the way my mother showed me, I wrap the three guards in cocoons, silencing any cries they attempt to make, and send them to the top of the building where they are hidden from sight.

Slowly creeping out from behind the shack, we make our way to the dungeon doors. We are completely exposed, we stay in a tight group, not exposing anyone's back, our eyes never stop scanning our surroundings.

Reaching our destination, I peer around the stone wall, three more guards sit at the table directly in front of the door. Their heads fall to the table, under the influence of a sleeping spell. Three of our warriors pull them out of sight, swap clothing, and secure them, then take their place at the guard table. By wearing their clothing, our wolves will smell like the guards, not causing suspicion if someone happens by.

Remembering how the dungeon door squeaks, giving away any element of surprise, we pop the hinges, silently making a gap large enough to fit through. Once we all clear the door, we ensure it is back in place, but leave the hinges out. If we need a quick escape, we will be able to just kick the door down.

I approach the stairs, cautiously looking over the railing, there are no guards in sight. Beginning my decent, I motion for the rest to follow. Halfway down, there is a noise to my right, snapping my head in that direction, I see our first guard. Putting up a hand to stop the others behind me, I crouch down as low as possible. The guard walks by, stinking of fresh blood and sweat, my stomach churns. Please don't let this be the blood of my mother or Zeke.

The guard enters a room, none the wiser to our presence. Dropping my hand, I get up from my crouched position and continue to the bottom of the stairs. Peering down the hallway to my left, there are no guards visible, same to the right. Where are they keeping Zeke and Mom?

"Let's try the room the guard went into, then we can search the rest of the cells. Remember, Miles thinks there are six guards down here, so far we have only accounted for one," I mind-link the group.

We surround the door, then try the handle, of course it is locked. I send a surge of wind towards it and knock it open. The guard spins around, mouth open and eyes wide. Using the little extra time, I have I pin him to the back wall, as the rest of the group enters the room. Quickly, the other two guards in the room are rendered useless, cuffed in their own silver shackles.

Squatting down, I look directly into the eyes of the first guard. "Where are you keeping the witch and wolf from Whispering Winds?" I snarl out.

The guard's response is to spit on me, with hate-filled eyes.

Instantly my father lashes out and decapitates the guard, his wolf has taken over, snarling at the other two he growls out, "The Queen asked you a question, unless you want to end up like your friend, answer her." Saliva is dripping from his fangs, and all can tell he would love to have the blood of these wolves soaking them as well.

The guard closest to my father gulps in fear. "They are separated, opposite ends of the dungeon. The witch is on the second floor, East side, the wolf is on the same floor, West side."

That was far too easy, extracting the information from them. My sense of foreboding is spiking again.

I place a sleeping spell on the two guards and turn to the rest of the group. "This is too easy; something is not right. There was plenty of time for them to mind-link, while we dealt with the first guard. We need to rescue them at the same time. Dad, you, Claire and four guards go to get Mom, the rest of us will get Zeke. Keep the link open, and silent unless something urgent comes up." I receive nods all around.

The guards at the front of the building need to be updated. I send a mindlink to everyone, including Miles, "Keep on your toes, we may be compromised. We captured three guards down here, but they gave up the positions of their captives too easily. We are splitting up and rescuing Mom and Zeke at the same time. Prepare for a hot out."

"Yes, Queen."

Checking the hallway, our group leaves the room we are in. Heading back to the stairwell, we make our way to the second floor, once in the lobby area, we split into our teams and head out in opposite directions.

"Young One, prepare for a fight, it is coming soon, there are allies at Broken Moon, who know who we are."

I link the group. "Brooke told me a fight is coming soon. No mention of where the fight will be or when. She said Broken Moon has allies who know my identity."

Silence is all the response back; Ashley looks at me with hard resolve in her eyes. We have trained for this, now we will see how effective we are in a real fight.

Chapter 46:

Rescuing Ezekiel

Our group makes it to the West wing of the dungeon, slowly we continue on our way, peering into each cell as we go. Zeke is not responding to mind-link. I am not surprised, though, he has probably been shot full of wolfsbane and put in silver restraints, every part of my being hopes they did not give him too much and that he is alive.

The smell down here has not gotten better since my forced stay. A shiver makes its way down my spine at the thought. My mind is pulled back to the present when I pick up the sound of a faint heartbeat. Joy surges through me at the sound of it, and the smell that finally reaches my nose. We have found Zeke.

Next to me, Ashley perks up also. She has sensed her brother; she turns to me and gives me a smile. We continue, cautiously to his cell, there are still three guards down here, we don't know where they are. There is a loud smack, which resonates through the area, followed by a groan full of pain.

"Alpha said we can't touch the witch, so this wolf will have to do until the Alpha returns. He is a strong one, how is he still conscious?" an unknown voice breaks the silence around us.

The only response is a grunt. There are at least two guards in with Zeke. At the moment, they are distracted by their torturing of him, we can use it to our advantage.

Motioning for the rest of the group to stop and stay put, I move to a position where I can view the cell. One guard stands in front of a kneeling Zeke, the other stands behind him, fisting his hair and keeping his head pulled back. I notice a large gash over Zeke's right temple, pouring blood down his face, his eyes are swollen shut and large bruises make him look like a racoon, his lip is split in a few places, and his breathing appears labored, he may have a broken rib or two if they have been doing any body shots. Zeke's hands are encased in silver shackles, with chains attached to the ceiling keeping his arms far apart, his ankles are also shackled making it so he cannot stand.

To our benefit the cell door has been left open. Stepping back, I look at the rest of the group and nod my head. Holding up my hand, I show three fingers and drop them, once the last finger is down, we rush the cell. Ashley jumps on the wolf holding her brother's hair, pushing her claws and hand deep in his chest, withdrawing her fist, she holds his heart, spitting on him as he falls to the cell floor. Ashley's wolf, Grace, is not taking any prisoners, especially where her brother is concerned. She is the blood wolf.

The other guard has his throat slit; our warriors are looking at Ashley with wide eyes. They have only ever seen us spar for practice, this is the first time to see our wolves in action, even though we aren't completely in wolf form.

Turning my attention back to Zeke, I notice his body is slumping forward, his head lolling, chin on his chest, arms stretched above. One of our warriors finds the keys on the guard missing his heart and quickly unlocks the restraints, catching Zeke in my arms as he falls forward. His eyes open, just a slit, then a smile appears on his face. My Sun and Moon, thank Goddess. Then he falls into slumber or unconsciousness, we are not sure which one.

Wanting to be as gentle as possible on Zeke's body, I float him in the air, Ashley and the warriors surrounding us, our group makes its way back to the main area of the second floor.

We are the first to arrive. I gently lower Zeke to the ground and kneel beside him, I run my hands over his body, pulling forward my healing powers. I do not have much time to do a complete job, but I can start the process to help him. Hopefully his ribs can heal enough, I don't have to worry about sending a broken bone into a major organ, while we carry him out.

I won't be able to use my magic to get him out. One of the guards will need to carry him. Both of my hands need to be free to use my magic if it is needed. Since we don't know what shape my mother is in, I will assume she will also be out of commission.

Chapter 47:

Rescuing Luna Abigail

(Alpha Alexander's POV)

Jasmine has split off with her group to find Ezekiel, my group and I head in the opposite direction to find Abigail. As we cautiously make our way down the cell corridor, I send up a silent prayer to the Moon Goddess. *Please, Goddess, allow my Luna to be safe and unharmed, please be with my wolves, keep us all safe, to continue fighting this evil against you. Please bring us all home to our families.*

This corridor seems to be vacant; this is highly unusual for a high-profile prisoner. We know they are aware Abigail is a Luna and the head of the Witches' Council, whoever it is they have working with them made sure they knew. It would be genuinely nice to find the person who did this to my Luna and show them my displeasure.

I link the group with me. "Be on high alert, things are not right here. There should be at least one guard on our Luna, not an empty hall." Curt nods are my response.

The farther we go down the passageway the more my heart begins to sink, thinking they have moved her, or lied about her being here in the first place. We make it to the end of our aisle, and we can all see why there are no guards on her. Abigail is floating in the air, face down, eyes closed, there is no scent coming from her. Whatever spell has been placed on her keeps us from detecting her.

Reaching out for the cell door, I yank my hand back quickly as sparks fly out. There appears to be a barrier around the cell. It does not seem we will be getting the Luna out quickly. I send two guards down the hallway, to find a breakroom, or guard shack, hoping against hope there is a way to break this barrier and get to Abigail.

Impatience is settling over me, when there is a loud clank, and what little lighting is in the area shuts down. Isn't that nice, the barrier around my Abigail's cell is an electric forcefield and has been shut off with the electricity. Amazingly enough her cell bars are not silver, and we are able to break the door open.

Walking up to Abigail, I reach a hand out to touch her, and gently whisper her name. There is no response to my call, but her body moves when my outreached hand touches her, pulling my hand towards me, I notice her body moves forward. By suspending my Luna, they have given us an easy means of egress with her. I smile to myself, thinking they inadvertently helped us.

Guiding the Luna through the cell door carefully, we head back down the corridor. Claire and the guards have the Luna and me surrounded as we make our way back to our meeting area, we continue to progress with caution. I cannot push away the feeling something is off.

We reach the main area of the second floor at the base of the stairs. Jasmine is on the floor next to Ezekiel, doing a healing spell on him. He must be in a bad way for her to take her time to do the spell now. I just hope she doesn't drain her energy.

"Don't worry, Father, I am not going to drain my energy. I just needed to heal his ribs a little, at the very minimum before moving him again," Jasmine pipes up, her eyes glittering.

I must have a shocked expression on my face, how was she able to hear me? I wasn't mind-linking or speaking out loud.

"I can just hear you, Dad. I am not sure why. This is odd, and I am not sure why it is happening. I can't hear anyone else."

"We will look into it more when we get back. Is there any way you can get your mother out of this spell? Since she was mobile, I didn't want to risk having your team come down to us."

Jasmine stands up and walks over to us, she looks over her mother, touches the forcefield around Abigail. She closes her eyes and begins to chant, opening her eyes they are glowing white, tinted with blue. Once she finishes the chant,

Abby is gently placed upright, her eyes open, and the force holding her swirls up her body and away.

Abigail gives us all a radiant smile. "Oh, my loves! You have all come to rescue us. Let's leave this dreaded place and deal with some rats." Her eyes fall to Ezekiel and her smile falters. "Oh, my brave boy, what have they done to you? I will not rest until they pay," Abby vows as a single tear runs down her cheek.

We begin our ascent of the stairs. Jasmine in the lead, Luna and Zeke being carried by a warrior, in the center, surrounded by the rest of the group.

Chapter 48:

Leaving Broken Moon

(Jasmine's POV)

We make it to the top of the stairs, then begin heading to the door, it is still off the hinges so we will need to be careful when opening it. "We are headed towards the door with Luna and Zeke. Status update, please," I link the guards we left at the front of the dungeon.

"It has been quiet, too quiet. Something seems off. There is hardly any movement around the grounds. I would expect more, even with most of their warriors gone."

"Keep your guard up. We are coming out, the toughest part will be leaving this building, it is completely open, and we won't have any cover. Zeke is injured and unable to fight, one of the other guards is carrying him, we are down two men."

"Copy that. We have the opening secure."

We open the door and cautiously step out; we need to regroup before we head out of the dungeon.

"Place Zeke down and let's regroup. Mom, do you think you will be able to fight with us if needed?"

"Absolutely, Jazz. They did not injure me in the slightest, I am fit to fight with my pack."

"Alright, I will take lead, Luna will be at the back, Alpha to the right, Claire take the left, Ashley beside me. Max, please carry Zeke, the rest of you please fill in the extra spaces. We need to keep the group tight and protect Zeke as best as possible.

"Miles, we are getting ready to head out of the dungeon. We need your eyes as we make our escape," I mind-link the warriors on the hill.

"At the moment all is clear."

We form our group to begin our trek back to the border wall we entered over. Our careful departure has been going well so far. Miles has not seen any wolves or other threat. We are nearing the tree line. Chills run the length of my spine and Brooke yells in my mind.

"Down now! Prepare to fight!"

"Drop!" is the only command I yell out, every member in my group hits the ground.

As we do arrows fly overhead and lodge in the earth behind us. From out of the tree line comes roughly thirty wolves, snarling, teeth bared, waiting to feel our flesh sink beneath them as our blood fills their mouth.

"Everyone shift except Max. Keep the circle tight as long as possible. Claire, stay with Max and keep Zeke safe," I link to the group.

There is a silence over the field as Ashley shifts, followed by angry howls and growls.

"Queen, I don't know where those wolves came from. It is as if they appeared from thin air. I see no one in the trees" comes Miles' voice.

I don't have time to respond. We are getting into the thick of battle. Bringing up my hands I send a rolling earthquake towards the wolves, using the roots of the trees to secure them to the ground. No sooner have I done this than they are released. I look back questioningly at my mother.

Mom begins a chant and a barrier dissolves before our eyes, showing us a small force of wolves, witches, and vampires. We have our work cut out for us.

My claws come out, but I remain in human form. Brooke still cautions me against shifting. Crouching down into a fighting stance we prepare for the onslaught of aggressors.

Three wolves charge to me, each aiming for a different part of my body, I remain crouched down, until the last possible moment then, in a blur Ashley is in front of me tearing the throat out of the first wolf with her jaws, while she has her paw sunk deep into the chest of a second wolf. Both fall lifelessly to the ground, red staining the earth below.

At that moment, all hell breaks loose. Everyone left hidden in the trees charges our group. My mother and father are a force to be reckoned with. Mom is using her magic to throw all manners of beings this way and that. Those who manage to get by her are met by the incredibly angry wolf of my father, and he is showing no mercy.

The rest of the warriors are cutting their own swath through our enemies. Suddenly one of our warriors is thrown high into the air and slammed to the ground. His neck is at an odd angle, and he does not move. We close in around him and continue to battle.

A breeze blurs by us, and another one of our warriors goes down, his throat has been sliced. Mom sends a tornado around the group and catches three vampires in it.

I set up a protective shield around the group, Mom supplements my powers with her own. The two downed pack members are picked up and we make our way to the main gate. No point in going over the wall now, our cover has been blown. As we continue towards the gate, fire and energy balls batter our shield to break it.

We need to reach our vehicles soon, I am not sure how much longer I can hold this shield, even with Mom's help. I have used a lot of energy already in this trip.

The gate is just ahead of us, unsure how we are going to make it through the gate, when I see a wall of wolves there. Our shield almost drops as a loud explosion sounds behind the wolves at the main entrance and they fly in all directions. A man and two women walk through the gate, defensive postures in place.

"If you want to get out of here and back to your pack, I suggest you follow us," the man calls in our direction.

"Follow him, Young One. He is one of your trainers. So good he found us when he did. Always has had a flare for the dramatic," Brooke informs me.

Nodding to the group we head towards the gate, keeping the shield in place. We are still under attack from the force behind us.

Making it to the cars, we must drop the protective shield to get into the vehicles. I am helping secure Zeke and the other pack members into the back of one of the SUVs when I hear my mother scream. I jerk my head up to see what is happening.

My father is on the ground, arrow lodged in his left clavicle. He is beginning to shift back to human form, the arrow must be silver. My mother is lying next to him, crimson blossoming on her chest, Ashley in front of them holding just the body of a vampire, his head rolling away on the ground. The three newcomers are in front of her making another protective barrier.

"Everyone in the cars, NOW! Ashley, grab Mom, Max, help me with Dad." We rush into the cars with our dead and injured, speeding away from

Broken Moon, still under a foray of arrows and fireballs.

My father is lying over my lap, eyes closed, not responding to my calls and pleas. Mom is lying over Ashley's lap, there is no heartbeat, her skin is turning pale, her lips blue. Streams fall from my eyes, and pain courses through every fiber of my being. I let out a howl/scream, letting the world know of my loss and grief.

I close my eyes and lay my hands over my father's chest. I know you should not remove anything that is punctured into the body, but the arrow is silver and is poisoning my dad. Taking in a deep breath, I pull it out, and place a shirt over his chest applying pressure. I close my eyes again, and focus on his injuries, sending any remaining energy I have left to help fight the poison in his system.

All I am thinking is I can't lose them both, as I sink into darkness.

Chapter 49:

New Reality

(Jasmine's POV)

There is brightness shining on my closed eyelids bringing me to awareness. My heart aches, head is pounding, throat feels raw, eyes feel heavy and swollen, trying to peel them open takes a lot of internal fortitude. I roll over to my side to grab my alarm clock, wanting to see what time it is, but my muscles scream at me in protest. I let out a groan and flop back onto my back.

"Jasmine, you're awake! Oh, thank Goddess! I have been so worried about you, haven't left your side since we returned," Ashley cries out as she sees my movement.

"Ash, where are Mom and Dad?"

Silence meets my inquiry. Finally, my eyelids lift, and I turn my head to look at Ashley. She is curled up in my armchair, next to my bed. Knees pulled into her chest, arms folded over the top, tears run down her face, her eyes are swollen, and she looks as if she has lost her family, trepidation moves into my soul.

"Jazz, what do you remember about rescuing Zeke and Luna from Broken Moon?"

"Not too much right now. We got them out of the dungeon and made it back to the entrance. We regrouped there, and started our exit, while doing that we ended up in a battle, but someone helped us at the gates, and we got out. Is there more?"

Ashley unfolds her body, moves to the edge of the seat, and grabs my hand in hers, squeezing tight, she clears her throat. "Jazz, when we got to the cars, we were still under attack, your dad was hit with a silver arrow in the left clavicle, yo—"

"NO!" I scream over the top of her.

Ashley's breath catches. "I am so sorry, sis. He is in the clinic now, the doctors say he should be fine, but there is more. Once your dad was hit with the arrow your mom moved to protect him. At that same time a vampire was coming by to take his heart, he got your mom's instead. I was too late to save her, but the vampire is no more."

A sob tears itself from by chest, my world feels void and empty. I scream out, Ashley jumps onto my bed and wraps me into a tight hug. Our tears mingle together as she holds me and lets me grieve.

The door slams open and in limps Zeke. He sits on the edge of my bed and pulls the two of us to him. No words part from his lips, he just holds us and gives the extra support we need.

After many moments of being held, I have cried out my tears, giving a hiccup cough, I pull back and look at the two, who are like my siblings. "I need to get started on Mom's funeral. Why was I allowed to sleep while this was going on?"

"Jasmine, you passed out while attempting to heal your dad's wounds. You have been unconscious for three days." Ashley looks down at her lap and plays with her nails, she looks back up to me. "We had your mom's funeral this morning. We didn't know when you or your father would regain consciousness. I am sorry we did not wait."

"Help me up and get dressed. I need to visit my mom, see where she is laid to rest. Dad will need me by his side, to be there when he awakens."

Ashley helps me up from the bed, with some help from Zeke, as I hold on to them for support I look to Zeke.

"I am so happy you are okay; sorry I cannot express more joy for you."

"My Moon, do not apologize, take care of you right now. We can talk later." I nod, then turn towards my bathroom. I hear the door of my room shut as Zeke leaves. Ashley assists me into the shower. I stand there, letting the water run down me, hoping it will wash away my pain and despair. Finally, I get out

and move to my closet, throwing on the first items of clothing I come to.

Ashley leads me out past the pack garden, and into the forest. We come to a thicket my mother loved, filled with wildflowers in the spring and summer. She and my father would frequently picnic here, she felt close to the earth. This was the perfect place for her to rest.

"This is perfect, Ashley, thank you for making sure her resting place was one of her happiest places."

I walk forward and fall on my knees next to the mound of freshly turned earth. I place my hand on the stone at the head. Tears water the earth and I feel my heart break again.

"I will avenge you, Mother. I will train and take down our aggressors, I will rise and be the most just and fair Queen to this supernatural world. This I swear to you, your death will not be in vain!" I shout out to the heavens.

Ashley falls beside me, "I swear this oath too, My Queen, we will avenge our mother."

We hold each other and rest there, saying our goodbyes.

The sun is beginning to dip down, and the forest is darkening. It is time we left this place and get to Dad's side. Slowly we get up, stretching our sore muscles and make a slow trudge to the pack hospital.

Chapter 50:

New Reality 2

(Jasmine's POV)

The pack hospital looms before me, the building as modern as any out there, the entrance is especially intimidating to me tonight. Generally, this is a place I thrive in, a place I am able to help others. Today it is a place I am visiting my last surviving parent. A place that once he awakens, I must give him the news of Mom's passing.

A deep breath down to the bottom of my lungs helps me steady my nerves. Ashley places her hand on my shoulder and gives a gentle squeeze of encouragement, turning grateful eyes to her, we give smiles of understanding to each other. Thank Goddess I have her with me, to be a support and strength to get through this.

We step through the doors, find our way to the elevator, and go to the third floor. Stepping out of the elevator we make our way to the Alpha wing. Yes, a whole wing for an Alpha, if they are injured enough for a stay there needs to be room for the guards, family and any staff that needs to come in.

Eventually the door looms in front of us. I reach out a shaky hand and push the handle to open it. The door swings open, Ashley and I walk through. Heads snap up and guards take a defensive position at the unexpected noise. Once eyes take me in and my identity is processed, the guards drop their protective stances.

"Queen, it is good to see you up. We were not notified you had regained consciousness or that you were coming to see your father. Our apologies for your reception," Miles comments to me, stepping forward from the group.

Giving him a warm smile, "I am very pleased to see you all taking such good care of my father and protecting him. I want to thank all of you who assisted in the rescue of the Luna and Zeke, also those who went to assist Red Crescent, not to forget those who remained here, to protect the pack and our lands. Without all of you, we would not be the strong pack we are. Miles, I would like you to please call in a replacement for yourself and then come to my father's room."

"Yes, My Queen."

Ashley and I continue down the hall to dad's room.

"I guess Zeke didn't let anyone know I was awake. Maybe he wanted to give me time, before being overwhelmed with everyone," I say, giving a side look to Ashley, with slightly raised eyebrows.

Her only response is a slight shrug of her shoulders

Room 1 is before us. I always found this odd since it is the only room on this wing, everything else is offices and a kitchenette. Slowly I push the door open, the lights are all down in the room, but I notice a scent coming from there, I sniff the air picking up the smell of my Aunt Meredith. Once the door is fully opened, I walk through and see she is curled in a chair, in the corner of the room.

Making my way over to Dad's bed, I look down on his sleeping figure. He has an IV line started in each arm, with fluids running through both. I look and notice one is normal saline and the other is saline with a morphine drip going in. They are probably keeping the pain caused from the poisoning of the silver arrow at bay, not to mention the pain of having the mate bond break.

Sucking my lips into my mouth, I bite down on them, as tears spring to my eyes at this thought. I lift a tentative hand, bringing it to my dad's face. Gently I push the hair off his forehead, then lean down, pressing a gentle kiss there. As I stand there, touching my dad's hair, I feel relief flow through my being for the first time today, peace, knowing I have not lost him too. Seeing him has made it a reality and not a hope.

I reach down and take my dad's hand in my own, holding it, like the lifeline it is to me. Slowly I sit down on the mattress next to him, watching the rise and fall of his chest. Changing my breathing to match his own and count out his respirations. Twelve, good, nice number of respirations.

"Dad, I know you and your wolf are healing, rest is needed. I love you, Dad, when Ashley filled me in on what I couldn't remember, I was so happy to know you are still with me. Please come back to me when you are ready. Take your time, heal your body and heart. I will be here when you decide the time is right to return." With that, I raise his hand to my lips and leave a gentle kiss on the back of it.

There is the sound of rustling coming from the corner, Aunt Meredith sits up and blinks her eyes at me, seeing but not comprehending. Eventually a huge smile graces her face, and she leaps off the chair pulling me into her arms. She keeps me in her embrace for many minutes, no words, just soft sobs, and tears. Once she has managed to compose herself a little, she pulls back and cups my face in her hands.

"Oh, my sweet girl. I am so happy you have returned to us. Ashley told me what you did to save your father. All your energy must have been used up, and you needed the rest to recuperate. How are you holding up with everything?" she sniffles out.

"I went and visited with Mom before coming here, I...it just doesn't seem real, she can't really be gone. We saved her, Auntie, we saved her. I failed her, I failed her and Dad." I break down again, tears streaming down my face, every beat of my heart sending pain through my body.

"Honey, you did not fail anyone. You were all in a battle, lives are taken in battle, battle does not care if someone was just saved or not. What you did was get your people out of there, left no one behind, and protected them, healed them. You gave everything you had to keep your people safe. You showed what it is to be a Queen," Auntie says, as she places a finger under my chin, so my eyes will meet hers.

"Listen to her, Jazz, she is correct. I couldn't be prouder of you," a rough voice grasps out.

We turn amazed eyes to my father's bed. He is awake! I rush to him, falling on his chest, taking him into a gentle hug. I feel his hand on my back, giving a squeeze back.

"Oh, Dad! I... I have to. "

"I know, Jazz, I can feel it. I know she is gone from the earth, only the earth. She will always be with us, we just have to look a little harder to see her, baby girl."

Chapter 51:

Preparing for Prophecy

(Jasmine's POV)

The doctor has come into the room to give Dad a check-up, now that he has awoken and is able to respond to questions about pain and mobility.

"Alpha Alexander, it appears the silver arrow caused some damage in the collarbone your body is not able to heal. There is going to be reduced movement in your arm, and it will affect you when in wolf form. I am not sure how badly until you shift and see how it moves. I do want to keep you here overnight for observation, since you just woke up, but if everything goes well, you should be discharged tomorrow. It is nice to have you and our Queen back." The doctor leaves the room, giving one last backward glance before shutting the door.

"Jasmine, I am tired, I want to rest some more. You have had quite the time too, and need your own rest, please go back to the packhouse, and continue recovering. We have a lot of work to do once I am out of here, we will be hitting the ground running." Dad looks down at his blankets before continuing, "I also need a little time alone, to mourn your mom." A single tear escapes his eye, running down his cheek.

"Okay, Dad. Rest well, I will see you in the morning." I give him one last hug on my way out with Ashley.

Once out the door we see Miles coming towards us.

"I apologize for not coming sooner, Queen, there was some trouble getting coverage. We have increased patrols around the border. It is no excuse, though."

"It is fine, Miles; I would like you to please take Ashley and me to the families of the warriors lost. I want to pay Dad and my respects to them. It needs to be done now, since we were unable to visit previously."

"Yes, Queen."

We leave the hospital together, heading to the first house. By the time we head back to the packhouse we have visited thirteen families, between the two we lost and eleven lost at Red Crescent.

Miles opens the front door for us to enter through and we run directly into Alpha Keith, Zeke, and three strangers. Alpha Keith has a mixture of emotions running over his face as he looks at me and I am not sure if he is upset with me or not. I give him a small smile, while looking directly into his eyes. The smile holds small amounts of innocence and guilt. Although I am not sure what I have to be guilty about.

"Jasmine, it is good to see you up and around, only wish I would have been notified so I could accompany you and make sure you are safe. Though I do see, you were not going around without some sort of guard. Thankfully. It is very important now, you do not go out alone, now that we know a good amount of the forces against us." With this statement Keith opens his arms to me.

I run into them. The brotherly hug and concern are exactly what I needed at this moment.

Pulling back, I look over to the three new individuals standing silently by, watching our interactions. The male, who appears to be the leader, has ebony hair and piercing pale blue eyes. His skin and the skin of the other two is very pale, almost transparent. I take in a subtle sniff of the air, then it hits me. They are vampires. Brooke said to trust them, though, so I will.

Making my way over to them I extend my hand out. "I am Jasmine Oscuro, daughter to Alpha Alexander, who is unable to meet you now. Thank you for your assistance at Broken Moon. I have no doubt we would not have been able to make it out without your help. We are deeply indebted to you. "

"The pleasure was ours, our Queen. I see you are humble; we can appreciate that. We happened by the area when we were on our way to your pack. We noticed your scent and stopped to assist. We are here to assist in your training. I am Maverick and behind me are Angie in the red, and Muerta in the black." His demeanor is very formal and correct. It will be interesting working with this trio.

"Assuming, since you have been here for three days, you have already been given quarters and they are acceptable?" I receive a quick nod in response. "Very good, Ashley will be training with us. Have the three of you and Alpha Keith already worked out a training plan for us?"

"Well, Queen," Keith starts. "Turns out your Aunt Meredith is also one of your trainers. All of us have figured out a new training plan and we want to start at five in the morning. If you have no objection to the time."

"Five in the morning it is. Guess I had better get up to bed if I plan on kicking some mixed species booties in the morning. Ashley, rest up as well." I depart with a wide smile on my face.

This is the start, preparations are beginning. There is no stopping the prophecy now, and what is more, I wouldn't want to.

Chapter 52:

Broken Moon Regroups

(Alpha Blaine's POV) Complete and utter disaster.

My intuition was telling me not to trust the rogue wolf, not to follow him into this battle. I allowed myself to be pushed by him and my grandfather. Now look at the devastation I need to build back from. My warriors are depleted, not just from the battle at Red Crescent, but from the infiltration by Whispering Winds. I lost a total of 422 wolves, not to mention the other species my grandfather sent to assist us.

Slamming my fist down on my desk it cracks under the force, splitting in half, I push myself away and jump out of my seat, stomping to my office door. My wolf, Samael, pushes forward in my mind, it takes everything I have to keep him from taking over.

Ripping the door off the hinges, I yell down the hallway, "GAMMA, ERIC, GET TO MY OFFICE NOW!" I hurl the door to the side, breaking it to pieces.

In seconds my Gamma and Eric have entered my office. Their brows are arched over their eyes in looks of questions and concern. They are heeding the call of their Alpha, but not sure if they are going to survive this meeting. The fear they are trying to keep tamped down pleases me. They are strong, but not stupid.

"As you know Beta Clark lost his life at Red Crescent. The wolf who took him down is one of the current Betas of either Midnight Moon or Whispering Winds. The fact that both allied with Red Crescent to face off against us, and their audacity to infiltrate my pack puts all of them at the top of my list for attacking. They will feel the pain of my teeth and claws."

"I called you both in here because I need a new Beta. I am moving Gamma Rodney into the Beta position and Eric, you are taking over the Gamma position. There will not be a ceremony for this. We must begin regrouping and planning now. My grandfather will be here in the next few minutes, and I must deal with him. I want you both to gather all the information you can for me on the three packs. Especially on the Oscuro family. My grandfather believes their daughter Jasmine is the Midnight Wolf. Find me proof."

They are dismissed after that, quickly departing my office. I glower at the empty space my door used to be. I guess I am going to have to use one of the conference rooms when my grandfather comes. He waited until I healed from the silver in my system to make his visit, said he would not deal with me while I was in a weaker state than normal. I learned a long time ago that wolf has no real love towards me, but I continue to hope I can earn his approval.

My head snaps up at the sound of footsteps near my office door. Around the frame I see the figure of my grandfather emerge. Swallowing hard, followed by a calming breath, I move forward to meet him at the door.

"Grandfather, good to see you. Let's go across the hall into the conference room so we can close the door for our conversation."

"Appears you still need to learn to control your emotions, Blaine. What did breaking your door and destroying your office do to help the cause or your pack? Nothing is what it did," Grandfather expresses disdainfully as he looks around my office at the destruction I have caused. He turns without another word and makes his way across the hall.

Following him silently, I close the door behind us and take a seat across from him at the small table. Slowly I look up, not making eye contact with him. "Grandfather," clearing my throat nervously I continue, "they were prepared for us. They knew we were coming. The only thing they were not aware of was the help of the witches and vampires."

"I am aware they handled you as if it was your first altercation, making you tuck tail and run. A group of, what, maybe a dozen, was able to infiltrate your pack, rescue the captives and fight their way out when outnumbered by multiple species? I would say your foresight and planning was highly poor."

I continue to look at the floor, Grandfather has never allowed me to look him in the eyes, even as an Alpha.

"I meant what I said about killing you the next time you failed me," his dark voice echoes out, causing my heartrate to increase and my mouth go dry. "Unfortunately, the wolf I was going to replace you with perished in the battle at Red Crescent. Today, I will not have the pleasure of tearing out your throat and feeling your blood run down my claws and paw. It appears I need you after all, a rather displeasing thought indeed. Wait here until I give you further instruction. Do not plan any attacks. I will once again clean the mess you made and get this plan back on track."

"Yes, Grandfather. There is a positive to this, though. We were able to take down the Luna of Whispering Winds and injure the Alpha with silver near his heart. We have not heard if he survived or not yet."

"Alpha Alexander survived. What you fail to think about, though, is you poked a sleeping beast in him. His Luna was the only thing keeping him calm. You also killed the mother of the Midnight Wolf, and she will be seeking blood for retribution. The place we are in now is more dangerous than any other time. All caused by your mistakes. I will allow you to remain with the title of Alpha, but all your moves from now on will be under my order."

"Yes, Grandfather," I whisper out, keeping my head down. I hear rustling from the other side of the table and notice Grandfather has gotten up from the table. Quickly standing, I come around the table to meet him and show him out.

Grandfather takes me by surprise, reaching his hand out towards me. I slowly reach out to take it into my own. As our hands are clasped together, in an awkward handshake, Grandfather lands a solid punch to my right side. I hear a couple ribs break, and my breathing becomes difficult. Suddenly there is a kick to my knee, bending it backwards with a pop and dropping me to the floor, followed by an up cut to the jaw. I am laid out on my back. Grandfather comes over, places his foot on my broken ribs, pressing down, cracking more, and sending bone into soft tissue and organs.

"This is why you lose battles; you do not think of all the ways harm can befall you. Let this be a lesson," he sneers at me in anger and disappointment. Grandfather then turns and leaves the room.

Once again, my meeting with him ends with me finding my way into darkness.

Chapter 53:

Unexpected Visit

(Jasmine's POV)

It has been three weeks since we made our rescue attempt at Broken Moon. The coolness of November is heavy in the air, stinging the lungs with any deep breath. It revitalizes me and reminds me I am alive, there is something worth fighting for, and a large amount of supernaturals counting on me.

I stretch out my arms, preparing for our early morning training, then move to my legs and my back. The program planned for Ashley and I has been amazing, the knowledge and work ethic of my trainers is unbeatable. I know I am stronger than I have ever been, I feel it in every fiber of my body. Confidence in all my skills has grown, Aunt Meredith is one bad girl witch, my mom knew a lot and had more powers, but Aunt Meredith specializes in combat. Between the two of them, I feel more powerful for the teachings, taking a moment I think of my mom and how I would love to continue to have her teaching me.

Shaking my head, I come back to the present. Taking off on a warm-up run, I continue to think over all the events happening. In two days, we will be hosting numerous Alphas from around the United States, then a couple days past that is my first appearance at the Witches' Council. It is time I let my true identity be known, time to unite the packs and the other supernaturals. War is looming for us; we know some of the forces against us hold high-ranking positions. We just don't know if the collaborative has members in all the highranking forums or not.

Zeke is working on doing a detailed background on all of them. His priority is to do checks on all the Alphas and guests that have RSVP'd for the meeting. We need to know who we need to be watchful over during our event. At the moment we have 96 packs committed to coming.

Dad and I discussed him turning the pack over to me, since he is hindered by his injury and a possible liability in battle. He does not want to risk the pack. I let him know I would give him an answer after my trip to the Witches' Council. He seemed to agree with this, since it isn't too far out in the future. I am going to need to take command eventually anyway, he will always be there to step in and watch over the pack as I go to battle.

It saddens me to see him depressed, losing a mate is never easy on the one left behind. Let this meeting be his last hoorah as an Alpha, but his heart is not in it. I just don't know how to help him.

The rest of the team approaches the training field and I throw a smile their way.

"Don't tell me you already went for a run," Maverick groans out.

The first few trainings we had with him, Angie and Muerta were difficult, now we have increased our speed and strength, there is not much Ashley and I miss. Many times, we defeat the three of them, from what I understand they are among the strongest of their kind, and their coven is top ranked.

"Absolutely I did, Maverick. I have some stress with all these meetings coming up and I am excited to get started and let out my aggressions on someone," I laugh out, sending a wink his way.

"Well, um, I think Alpha Keith has lead on training today," Maverick says, throwing Keith under the bus.

I laugh out loud at the vampire's sheepish expression, while Angie and Muerta shake their heads sadly at him. He will be hearing about this from those two for a while.

Ashley comes running up to the group. "Hey, everyone. Alright, ready to go, just finished sparring with Zeke, he is building his strength back up well. He got in a few great hits today," she beams with pride. Zeke has had a lot to come back from and he is making remarkable progress.

"The two of you are not normal. You have both already had complete workouts and consider it a warm-up. I am so glad I cannot see inside your minds," Keith grumbles out. He is not the happiest this morning. "Let's get started, there is a lot to prepare for with this meeting coming."

We all fall into place and begin our training, two hours later we have completed, dripping in sweat and muscles burning we all head back to the packhouse.

Walking up the path from the training field to the house, we come around one of our outbuildings, and see a massive black SUV sitting in front of the house. Looking around at the others, no one recognizes who it belongs to. Putting my nose up I sniff the air, Keith and Ashley following my lead.

"I do not recognize the scent, how about you guys?"

Ashley shakes her head no, and Keith looks concerned and angry.

"What is it, Keith?"

"Elder Charles of the High Wolf Council is visiting. I recognize his scent. I do not like or trust this wolf; our guards should be up," Keith growls out.

We continue our progress towards the packhouse and enter. Dad is standing in the lobby with an older gentleman, I assume this is Elder Charles, Dad's posture is stiff and guarded. Elder Charles turns around, looking at us, his cold, gray eyes piercing me.

"Ahh, Jasmine Oscuro, just the wolf I came to see."

Chapter 54:

Elder Charles

(Jasmine's POV)

An uncomfortable silence looms in the air. Dad, Keith, Zeke, Ash, Claire, Mark, Simon and I all take seats at one end of the long oak conference table, while Elder Charles sits at the other end with his assistant. Even his assistant sits three chairs down from him, it seems no one wants to be close to this man.

I take a long, hard look at Elder Charles, who has caused so much turmoil by his presence. He sits very straight and still in his chair, his gray hair is parted to the left and gelled back, way too much gel, a sharp narrow nose sits perfectly on his face, but his mouth is in a constant frown of disapproval and his eyes hold little to no emotion. He isn't a tall man, in werewolf terms, only about five foot ten inches, and he has a slender muscular build. Importance and irritation oozes off this wolf.

While I am taking him in, he is returning the favor and looking me over at the same time. He does not approve of me, that is very clear in his facial expressions and eyes. I send him a smirk and look that tells him I know what he is thinking, and I just don't care.

Elder Charles clears his throat, "Jasmine, it seems your presence on this earth has caused some issues between Whispering Winds and Broken Moon.

It has come to my attention this pack has attacked Broken Moon twice. What is the cause of these aggressions?"

I cannot hide the incredulous look that has pushed forward on my face. If he had done even the most cursory research, he would know the answers to this. I do not trust him.

"Well, Elder Charles," I begin, trying very hard to keep my temper in place, "it is custom that when one pack kidnaps and imprisons the daughter of an Alpha, there will be retaliation for those acts, acts of war. When that same pack imprisons the Luna and future Beta, it is also customary there will be a rescue attempt mounted and carried out. All of these actions have been reported and documented, I am surprised they were not brought to your attention prior to your visit," I manage to calmly get out.

"You are a very disrespectful she-wolf, you should be punished for your insolence to me," he snaps at me, standing from his chair.

My father also stands from his chair and growls out, "She has said nothing to you that I would not have said myself, in the same tone and affect. I am not sure why you are here or what the underlying motive is, but you will not threaten my daughter with words or actions. Now, if you would like to resume your seat and have a discussion, I am open to that; otherwise, you will need to take your leave of my lands, and there will be a complaint filed with the council regarding your actions."

Elder Charles sends a nasty look my father's way but sits down in his seat. He folds his hands, cupping his chin in between his index fingers and thumbs, while taking a moment to think. "There has been rumor Jasmine is the Midnight Wolf and Ashley is the Blood Wolf. Is there credibility to these rumors?"

I sit looking at him, attempting to formulate an answer. Brooke has been against me letting out our identity, but we are going to expose the truth in two days anyway.

"Young One, it is alright to let him know. The prophecy has started and there is no reason to conceal our identity any longer. It will not matter if he tells the other Alphas they will want to see for themselves anyway," Brooke directs me. "Be wary of this wolf, he hides a secret, his intentions here are not pure and honest. Stay close to Ashley and Keith and keep your guard up," Brooke continues to caution.

"There is truth to those rumors, I am indeed the Midnight Wolf." I do not want to give him more information than what he is asking for. He does not need to know all our plans.

"Are you aware of the prophecy that surrounds you and Ashley? Are you aware of the consequences if that prophecy comes to fruition?"

"You mean the fact that there would be no division among the supernatural world, that all species are accepted, respected, and have a voice? Those consequences?" I question back to him.

"The fact you will singlehandedly bring a massive war to all the species and be singularly responsible for the death of thousands."

"We are already at war, Elder Charles. There are attacks, regularly against mixed species, packs having members run from their grounds because of the blood that runs beneath their skin. I am not bringing a war; I am ending an attempt to create division and an unfair class structure to the supernatural world." I am losing all patience with this wolf.

"You are naïve and overly optimistic. Women are too emotional to oversee anything, but the house. Alpha Alexander, we need to speak about who will be taking your spot as Alpha of this pack, I do not find Jasmine to be suitable. Also, from now forward, you will desist with any attacks on Broken Moon. The aggression you have shown against them has been uncalled for," Elder Charles spits out at us.

"Elder Charles, as a single member of the High Wolves Council, you alone cannot make those decisions. It must be decided by the entire group, after an investigation. You are going against your own customs and policies. I think this meeting is over with. We will ensure your car is brought around and fully prepared for your departure," Dad snarls to him, standing from his chair, indicating this meeting is indeed finished.

"I will be staying, Alpha Alexander. You want an investigation, you will get one," Elder Charles sneers back.

"Very well, I will have a room prepared for you," Dad says, as he walks out the door, turning his back to the Elder, showing significant disrespect to him.

Elder Charles turns to me. "This pack is now on my list. I will be watching you, and any little misstep will be noted, and sanctions will be brought against you."

"Noted, sir. I believe there is a pack member outside the door waiting to show you to your quarters. If you will excuse me, I have important matters to attend to." The remaining group steps around him and out the door.

Mind-linking Claire, I let her know what I need from her. "Follow the Elder and keep eyes on him. He is up to something here. I do not trust him."

"Yes, Queen. I have concerns about him myself." With that last link she breaks off from the group to prepare for her assignment. I have complete faith in her abilities to get the information we need.

"Well, shit," Zeke grumbles beside me.

Turning to him, he has his face down looking at his phone screen, sweat beading on his brow. I lift an eyebrow in question. Zeke does not usually swear or break out in the sweats. He is usually collected and calm.

"What is the matter, Zeke?" I question.

"Broken Moon just RSVP'd for the Alpha Meeting. They will arrive tomorrow, a day early."

Chapter 55:

Arrival of Broken Moon

(Jasmine's POV)

I am pacing about in my dad's office. Sleep eluded me all night, so today this she-wolf hybrid is a tired, cranky, hot mess from the word go. My emotions are still in some turmoil after the meeting with Elder Charles yesterday and now the anxiety of having to be face to face with Alpha Blaine eats away at me. "Jasmine, perhaps you should take Brooke out for a run with Ashley and Keith, try to work off some of the anxiety that is eating away at you, my dear,"

Dad gently suggests to me. He understands where I am coming from.

"I ran this morning before the training session with Keith, Maverick and Aunt Meredith. We even trained for an extra hour because of my anxiousness. It cannot be run out of me today, Dad. I feel, deep in my bones, something is amiss, and we don't see it. I am concerned."

"I called the High Wolves Council yesterday after our meeting and explained what occurred. They will be here about the same time as Broken Moon. Elder Charles does not know of their arrival plans, and they would like it kept that way. They have been having difficulty with him lately."

I turn towards my dad quickly. "We are going to have the entire council here for my shift? Well, it will give us time to view each of them. We know the person who made the kidnaping plans is from the city. There is no better way to start the investigation we wanted than to look at the council members up close and personal," I grump out, not liking the way things are going and the drastic change to our plans.

"I was thinking the same thing, Jazz. Use them to our advantage to deal with Charles and get information on them at the same time. We will need to increase security, but you have enough protectors around you, I will not assign any of our warriors. Is that alright?" Dad asks me gently.

"If you don't mind, would you please assign Miles to me? I appreciate his insight, also because he is known to be a warrior and not part of my 'group,' people may be more open about saying things to him."

"Good idea, Jazz. I will let him know of the change." Dad looks at me for a moment before continuing. "I am stumped by Elder Charles' protection of Broken Moon. I have made it a point to place their rooms at opposite ends of the packhouse. I do not want them to be next to each other. I am also moving Claire into a room next to Charles since you have her following him. I would ask you place a scent hiding spell on her to assist."

"I already did last night, Dad. I will make sure to redo it this evening, after the Elder has gone to bed. Claire and I discussed it."

"Very good, Jazz. You are doing an amazing job, I am so proud of you, you will be an amazing Queen."

"Thank you, Dad," I whisper and stop my pacing at his office door. "I think it is time I prepare for the arrival of Broken Moon and the Elders. How long do I have to get ready? I will need to mind-link Ashley and Keith also."

"Almost two hours. Just go for a business look, Jazz. No reason to get fancy, we will put on a show tomorrow for the majority of the group showing up then."

"Alright. Thanks." I leave the office and head to my room, letting Ashley and Keith know the plan.

Two hours later I am headed down the staircase. I opted for black slacks, a turquoise silk blouse and heels matching the shirt. I am wearing no jewelry; I do not know how the welcoming of Broken Moon is going to go. Usually, I do not worry about make-up but today I went ahead and applied some foundation, mascara, and blush, keeping the look natural. I placed my hair in a French braid and then put the ponytail part into a bun at the base of my neck. I hope my look says all business.

I walk out the front door, and take my place next to my father, on the marble staircase my mother had put in. I feel her with me now, giving me strength. Together we stand tall and proud, awaiting our guests. The door opens behind us and out steps Ashley, Keith, and Mark. Mark stands on the other side of my father; Keith is next to me, and Ashley stands behind me to the left. I would prefer her next to Keith, but she won't leave my back exposed.

Elder Charles makes his way out also, he is taking it upon himself to be part of the welcoming committee. He stands apart from us on the other side of the landing, letting his separation and displeasure with us be known.

I breath out a sigh of relief when the first to arrive is the rest of the High Wolf Council. I glance over and see Charles pale, at the sight of them he quickly covers it up and places a fake smile on his face. He can't hide how he has placed himself, however, and the council has taken notice.

The remaining four men and two women of the council make their way to the top of the stairs and stop in front of my father.

"Alpha Alexander," the man I recognize as head high council member, Elder Gary, addresses my father, "it is a pleasure to be invited to your lands for the Alphas' meeting. I realize we arrived a day early but we have some additional business to attend to. We greatly appreciate your hospitality and look forward to meeting with you once we are settled in."

"Elder Gary, the pleasure is all ours. May I present to you my daughter, and future Alpha of Whispering Winds, Jasmine."

I reach out my hand to the elders in welcome. They take my hand and gently acknowledge me.

"On my other side is my Beta, Mark, and next to Jasmine is Alpha Keith of Midnight Moon." My father pauses as they shake hands and make small talk with the others. "Your rooms have been prepared and we will have pack members take your bags to your rooms for you. You are welcome to stay and greet Broken Moon when they arrive, or you may get settled in. I will leave the choice up to you," my father finishes, giving them a broad smile.

"I think we will choose to wait and welcome Broken Moon, thank you," Elder Gary states after discussing with the rest of the group. "Ah, Elder Charles, we weren't expecting you to be here already. The invitation only came in late yesterday afternoon. We would have thought you would travel with us." Elder Gary pins him down with a harsh look.

Clearing his throat nervously Elder Charles responds, "Well, I was closer to Whispering Winds than I was to the High Wolf Council, so I didn't want to backtrack to get here."

"Very well. Why don't you at least show some decency and come stand with the host to welcome the other pack?" Elder Gary's question is stated as a command and gives no room for argument.

Elder Charles moves next to us but takes his place at the end of the council line. For five minutes there is uncomfortable silence, until two vehicles pull up in front of the stairs. Out of the cars steps Alpha Blaine and five others. I do not recognize any of them from either encounter with Broken Moon. My blood boils beneath my skin, how am I supposed to graciously greet this wolf and his packmates?

I want his blood staining the marble in sacrifice to my mother, to avenge her.

I glance over and see the same emotions run across my father's face before he hides them away. He is an Alpha first, and in front of the council. He will behave accordingly for now. I will do the same, follow in his footsteps and support him completely.

Alpha Blaine climbs the steps and stops in front of my father. "Alpha Alexander, pleasure to be here," he sneers out. "Thank you for the invitation to the meeting. It should be informative. Let me introduce you to my new Beta, Beta Rodney and Gamma Eric."

Father nods his head in recognition to them. Then clasps Alpha Blaine's hand in a handshake.

"Thank you for making the meeting, Alpha Blaine. I hope it is as informative as you think it will be. You already know my daughter, and future Alpha, Jasmine."

I nod my head in recognition but refuse to reach out my hand to him in welcome. I am sure I will have to answer to the council for that later. Father introduces the rest of the group to Alpha Blaine and lets them know their quarters are prepared and their bags will be delivered to them.

Alpha Blaine lands his hard, cold eyes on me. "Jasmine, I would like to speak with you in private, after I have settled into my room."

"You will not meet with my daughter alone, at any point in your visit, Alpha Blaine. You already had her kidnaped and attempted to kill her once. It is enough we have invited you into our home, do not push your welcome," my father snaps at him harshly.

Next to me, I feel Alpha Keith bristle and Ashley is letting out a low growl.

"Very well, Alpha Alexander, if I may speak with Jasmine and you after I have settled, I would appreciate it."

"Bring your Beta and Gamma, I will have mine there as well as Ashley and Alpha Keith. I would also request to presence of the council as well," Dad grits out.

"The council will be pleased to sit in," states Elder Gary.

"We will meet in an hour, then in the first conference room on the first floor. I will have lunch delivered in there," my father says and moves aside, letting our guests enter the packhouse.

Chapter 56:

Meeting with Alpha Blaine

(Jasmine's POV)

Choosing to stay in the clothing I had on during the greeting, I make my way directly to the meeting room to oversee the setting up of the space. We always have the room set up with a large oak meeting table and comfortable black leather chairs, but today we are bringing in lunch for multiple people and need a space to place a buffet.

I opt for the buffet, thinking it will allow everyone to eat as much as they want, as they want it. Also, this gives me an opportunity to set up a surveillance system with Zeke, prior to their arrival. While it is not exactly on the up-and-up, hopefully we can get some information off facial recognition. Zeke can also watch their body language and movement to report back later. The conversation itself is not as important to him, we plan on recording it regardless. I do not trust any of our visiting guests who will be in the meeting.

Ten minutes left until the deadline for the meeting time, my father walks through the door of the room, taking a glance around. "Very nice, Jasmine. There should not be anything for the guests to complain about during this meeting regarding food. How are you feeling? I will be beside you, regardless of what happens. He will not lay hands on you."

"I am more curious to see what Alpha Blaine could possibly have to discuss with me. I do not fear him anymore, Father. I am stronger and the bond was broken months ago."

Dad pulls me in for a comforting hug, he rests his chin on my head and just holds me for a moment. This is exactly what I needed. This moment of comfort and understanding, strength being offered in silence.

Someone clears their throat behind us, Dad and I turn to see Elder Gary standing in the doorway, with a pleasant smile on his face.

"Sorry to interrupt your moment, Alpha and Jasmine. I tend to be a little early to all appointments."

"No need to apologize, Elder Gary, we appreciate you and the rest of the council agreeing to sit in on this meeting." My father smiles back at the elder. "Please help yourself to the buffet Jasmine set up for us and take any seat you would like. I tend to go with relaxed seating in meetings such as these."

"Thank you. The food does smell amazing and may be some of the reason I am here early. I am famished after our travels," Elder Gary chuckles, as he moves to the buffet table to get himself a plate.

In ones and twos, the rest of the group arrives for the meeting. Everyone has managed to fill their plates and find seats at the table.

Dad is at the head on the farthest end of the meeting table. I am to his left and Mark is to his right. Simon sits next to Mark and beside me is Alpha Keith, Ashley stands behind my chair. The seven council members have divided among the two sides. Alpha Blaine sits at the head of the other end and his Beta and Gamma sit on either side of him. He does not appear happy about having his back to the meeting room door, but I just cannot find any empathy for him.

"Now that we are all here and settled, I guess it is time to start this meeting. Alpha Blaine, you requested to speak with my daughter so I will turn the table over to you," Dad states firmly.

"Thank you, Alpha Alexander. Jasmine," Alpha Blaine begins, turning his soulless blue orbs towards me, "I think we got off to a bad start. I wanted to discuss with you our mating bond. I was hoping this could be a private conversation since it is sensitive." He clears his throat. His entire demeanor screams arrogance and falsehood.

"I am not interested in discussing our mating bond. You rejected me, while holding me in a cell, stating my mixed-blood was not pure enough for you, and you wanted me to feel the pain of rejection prior to you killing me for entertainment. I am not sure how I could have misread the situation and would even entertain the idea of attempting anything with you except malice. Especially after you held my mother and Ezekiel captive and attacked our allies," I respond back, without hesitation. The audacity of this wolf!

Next to me Alpha Keith places a calming hand on my shoulder. A loud growl rips through the room and Alpha Blaine jumps to his feet. "Get your hands off my mate! You do not touch what is mine!" he rumbles out, from deep in his chest.

In turn I jump up from my chair, letting my Queen aura out. "I am not yours; I will never be yours, we broke the bond. You rejected and I accepted. You have no claims, and I will not tolerate you coming onto my lands and threatening my family. If you are unable to control yourself, you are free to find your way out the door and back to your lands," I vent out, my anger has risen to new levels, a low growl comes from me, followed by one from Ashley. I stare down the Alpha who dared confront me.

The glaring match goes on for a few moments. Elder Gary is looking between the both of us. The rest of the table is quiet and tense. On alert to see where this meeting will go.

"Jasmine, Alpha Blaine. I know this is not my house, but please take your seats" comes the clear direction from Elder Gary.

I look over to the Elder and see sternness in his eyes, but still gentle. I decide not to push it and resume my seat. Eventually Blaine does the same.

"Alpha Blaine, did you in fact reject Jasmine, in the manner she just stated?" inquires Elder Gary.

"I did, Elder."

"Then Jasmine is correct, you have no claims. I am surprised you still feel a mate pull. It is obvious Jasmine does not." Elder Gary gives a side glare at

Elder Charles during this comment, but continues. "The real discussion we should be having is why there is so much aggression between your two packs. Obviously, the rejection is part of it. The council will decide, as a whole, what punishments, if any, should be handed out to your packs. Alpha Alexander, would you please start with Whispering Winds testimony?" Although this request is made pleasantly enough, it is very clear it is an order.

Father covers all the happenings from the attack at the spa, to my kidnapping, to Mother's death. I feel myself tear up at the mention of her death but manage to keep my face emotionless. There will be time to mourn when I return to my room. The elders pay close attention to my father's monolog.

Once Dad is finished the council allows Alpha Blaine to give his explanation of all the happenings. I am wondering how he is going to pass off being hired as a mercenary to kidnap and kill me.

All the sides are given, and the Elders sit quietly. It appears they are mindlinking with each other regarding the matter at hand versus going to another room for privacy.

Eventually Elder Gary clears his throat. "It is the decision of the council, though not unanimous, Whispering Winds acted within the laws given by the High Wolf Council. Any act of aggression brought upon Broken Moon was justified and played out with thought to the least injuries possible."

"Broken Moon, we have concern about you initiating these aggressions. Alpha Blaine, your pack is going to be put under surveillance by the council, we will be sending an Elder to reside at your pack to watch the working of your pack." A smirk appears on Blaine's face at this information. "Elder Thomas will be coming to your pack. Make sure accommodations reflecting his rank and importance are made for him," Elder Gary finishes.

The smirk falls from Blaine's face. Does he have a contact in the Hight Council?

"Furthermore, Alpha Blaine, you will no longer pursue Jasmine. The mate bond was broken appropriately, and she does not want to make amends. You must accept and respect her decision on this matter. If we find you continue to harass her, there will be punishment set forth."

Alpha Blaine lowers his eyes in acceptance.

Elder Gary looks around the table at everyone. "If Alpha Alexander agrees, I am calling an end to this meeting. I have a report to write up and send off to my office."

"I agree with Elder Gary. This meeting is over. Dinner will be served at seven o'clock in the main dining room."

Everyone stands up from their chairs and makes way to the door. As I make my way out, Ashley next to me, a hand grasps my elbow.

"This is not over. I will win," hot breath breathes into my ear.

Turning my head toward the voice, I see Blaine is the one holding me. I calmly reach over, grasping the fingers pushing into my skin, and bend them back quickly, hearing them snap.

I give him a scowl, "Any part of you that touches me will either be broken or ripped off. Do not touch me." With that I walk off down the hallway heading to my room. Eyes burning into my back as I make my departure.

Chapter 57:

Secret Meeting

(Alpha Blaine's POV)

Pacing back and forth in the room they have given me, I can't help but think back on the events that have occurred today. Nothing is going according to the plan my grandfather devised.

Grandfather is the only reason I am at this pack, the only reason I accepted the invitation to the Alpha meeting. I am sure it was pure accident I received an invite in the first place. It is doubtful Whispering Winds want me anywhere near their lands and home.

What is going to happen now? I have been directed, by the High Wolf Council, to no longer pursue Jasmine. Getting her to accept the mate bond was the entire basis of the plan. Grandfather thought she would still be pining away for me. He couldn't have been more incorrect. The fire in her eyes made me a little frightened. Samael wanted to bow to her in submission, my wolf never wants to bow to anyone. It is hard enough lowering our eyes for my grandfather.

"Blaine, we need to meet and talk. I have made a few changes to the plan. We will meet by the lake to the north. It is in neutral land. I give you thirty minutes to get there," Grandfather links to me.

I have no choice but to go. I am beginning to see the power standing against us in this battle of separation.

I stop my pacing and find my shoes. I am not sure how far the lake is from the packhouse and there is no way I can change into my wolf form to make the run. Walking out my door, I notice the entire hallway is silent, no lights are shining under the doors. How long was I lost in my thoughts?

Now outside the packhouse I pick up my pace and begin jogging north, towards the lake. I run through the forest and break through the tree line to see the moon shimmering off the liquid glass beneath it. There seems to be an aura of peace in this place. It feels nice after all the conflict I have had ruling my life.

"Over here, Blaine. Don't waste any more time looking at the lake. It is just a body of water, same as any other. We have plans to firm up."

"Yes, Grand... Elder Charles." I almost forgot his rule of not calling him Grandfather outside of my home and mind-linking. It is a good thing I caught myself. Although the glare he is sending my way tells me I did not catch it soon enough.

"Wooing Jasmine to agree to be your mate is off the table, not just because of the order of the council, but she obviously does not feel the mate pull any longer. That is too bad, it would have been easier," Grandfather begins his monolog. "I have reached out to some of our allies, and they have agreed to assist us. Unfortunately, none of the witches left to our disposal are as powerful as Victoria, but she is either dead or captured. I haven't seen her since Red Crescent.

"We have a mix of vampires, witches, werewolves, fae, and trolls. All agree, the sooner we can take the Queen down, we can finish our separation of the species and the Collaborative can dissolve." Alpha Charles is rubbing his hands together in excitement as he continues to lay out the new details.

"During the second day of the Alpha meeting, when folks are feeling calmer, we will attack with the forces. We will kidnap Jasmine, and you will forcefully mark and mate her. Trapping her to our side. After you kidnap her, a witch will be there to bind her magic and portal you to Broken Moon. There is no chance of Whispering Winds getting to you before she has been marked and mated," he continues with an evil smirk on his lips.

"Once she is yours, I do not care what you do with her. She can live in a cell for all I care or die at your hands."

"Elder Charles, we do not know for sure Jasmine is the Midnight Wolf and the Queen of the prophecy. Why do you continue to push forward as if she is?" I inquire, tired of his assumptions.

"Jasmine admitted to me she is the Midnight Wolf. I do not need to see her wolf form, when the words came from her mouth. We need to stop her, before she has a large following and fulfills her destiny. We must ensure the species fail to unite. They are easier to control separated," he sneers at me.

"Your ignorance in these matters continue to amaze me. Have faith in me, my boy, and you will get your rewards in the end. I may be proud enough to claim you as my grandson to the masses," he promises, with a sly glint in his eye.

I cannot believe he said that out loud. Especially after ensuring I kept quiet all these years.

"Very well, Elder Charles, what is going to be the sign the battle is beginning? What type of assistance do we have, what are the numbers?" I concede, his acceptance has been all that I have craved in this life.

Chapter 58:

Start of the Alpha Meeting

(Jasmine's POV)

Today is the day all our guests will arrive, Whispering Winds will be inundated by packs from all over the United States. It is going to be a long day of greeting them all to our place and ensuring their initial needs are met. Hopefully the barbeque planned for this evening will also go off without any mishaps.

I can't believe these are the thoughts running through my head, as I narrowly miss an incoming fist from Keith.

"Where is your head, Jasmine? I never get that close to landing a punch," Keith gasps out, winded from two hours of intense training.

"Sorry, Keith, I am thinking of the arrival of the packs and guests to Whispering Winds today. I guess I am a little preoccupied with everything going on. It has been a busy week." Next thing I know I am flat on my back, the cold eyes of Maverick looking down at me.

"Every time you lose focus, your leave yourself open and vulnerable to attack. It is important you are always aware of your surroundings and changes in the atmosphere around you. How else are you to tell if a magical creature has decided to go invisible to plan a sneak attack? Just as I did now," Maverick lectures me, as Keith nods in agreement.

"Alright, I understand. I guess I did need that lesson. Now is definitely not the time to be letting my guard down. It is much preferable to learn from you two now than a harder lesson down the road." I smile at them.

They offer me their hands and help me up. Then they both turn to deliver hits to my body. I am ready and use my magic to stop the hits, I step out from between them, and then release the spell allowing them to collide roughly together. I let out a giggle.

"I learn quickly, boys!" I shout over my shoulder as I depart for the packhouse.

They quickly catch up to me, broad smiles on their faces.

"Our little pup is growing up," Maverick teases as he wipes away a fake tear. "I can already see the crown on her head, using her sass to lead the world."

I laugh out loud at his antics. Who knew a vampire could be this funny.

Ashley and Aunt Meredith didn't train with us this morning because I gave them alternate tasks to attend to, after receiving a late-night visit from Claire.

"Do we have everything in place?" I ask quietly. I am not sure who is listening in on our conversations when we are out in the open.

"Yes, we do. I made all the calls last night. Not one group declined to come. I think they are curious about you and the prophecy," Keith replies to me, all the humor gone from his face.

"That is fine. I am happy to use my 'mysterious nature' to draw them in, like flies to a light," I say with a mock sinister face.

Keith and Maverick just shake their heads at me.

"It is time to go doll yourself up, Mysterious One," Keith quips back.

I roll my eyes at him and run up to my room. It is six o'clock now and I need to be with my dad to meet our guests at 7:30.

After a quick shower, getting dressed, then doing hair and light make-up, I manage to be just on time. Skidding in next to Dad at the top of the staircase, I place my heels on my feet. There was no way to run down the stairs safely in those things. I prefer barefoot to these torture shoes anyway. I turn and give my Dad an innocent smile. He smiles back gently, and I hear a chuckle rumble from his chest.

The first Alpha to arrive is Alpha Peter of Night Fall pack. According to Keith, this pack has been taking in a large number of mixed couples fleeing from their pack lands. I will need to make sure to find time to speak with him.

"Alpha Peter, nice of you to make this meeting. May I introduce my daughter, and future Alpha of Whispering Winds, Jasmine," my father politely makes the introduction.

"Honored to meet you, Jasmine. I would appreciate a moment to speak with you and your father in private, if the opportunity arises during our stay," Alpha Peter requests, his eyes maintaining contact with mine, as he holds my hand in a friendly shake.

"We will make sure an opportunity arises, Alpha Peter, I also want to speak with you. If you don't mind, Alpha Keith will also be joining us."

"That will be fine, Jasmine, thank you for your generosity." He gives one last smile, drops my hand gently and continues.

The next four hours are a blur of greeting Alphas, shaking hands, and playing nice.

In all we have representation from 110 packs. We were not expecting it, but we did have five confirmations from Europe. It is amazing this has gone to an international level, but thinking on it, it does make sense. Separation of all supernaturals would include Europe too. I guess my initial thoughts were a little too narrowminded. This was a good wake-up call.

The lunch barbeque is well underway and the Alphas are milling around getting to know one another or catching up with old friends. Most brought at least their Lunas, if not also their Betas and Gammas. It is a wonderful turnout, I am excited, but nervous all at the same time. The prophecy seems to be moving ahead at an increasing speed, whether I am ready for it or not.

Managing to grab hold of Keith's arm as he passes me, I whisper into his ear, "What time are our special guests supposed to be arriving? I do not want to be late greeting them."

"Worry not, Mysterious One," he teases me, with a smirk on his face. "They will not be here until nine this evening. They want to arrive under the cover of dark and keep their identity hidden until the start of the meeting tomorrow. They have agreed to a meeting, directly after their arrival."

"Very good. Things are progressing quickly. We need to keep on our toes. Are we sure Elder Charles does not suspect he is being followed?"

"I traded out with Claire the other day and he gave no indications."

"Jasmine, just the young wolf I was looking for," a loud voice calls out, pulling Keith's and my attention over to the person.

Alpha Peter is walking towards us, plate and a beer in hand. His walk is one of ease and casualness. I continue to analyze him as he approaches.

"Would you and Alpha Keith mind sitting with me and chatting for a bit?"

"Not at all, Alpha Peter. Choose a table, while we fill our plates, and we will be right with you," I respond with a beaming smile. "Thank you, young lady."

Keith and I quickly get our plates and drinks, we forego any alcohol, knowing we have a long evening ahead. We make our way back to Alpha Peter and see he is also joined by my father.

"Hey, Dad," I acknowledge as I take my seat, Keith nods in respect.

"Hi, honey, I see Alpha Peter also reached out to the two of you." Dad has a sparkle in his eye. He is not upset, but amused our attention has been capture by this unknown visiting Alpha.

"I needed to speak with you three; I have been hearing a lot of rumors up North. I figured the best way to confirm them was to ask at the source, so here I am. I don't know how to put this delicately, so I am going to be blunt, and I apologize now if it comes out offensive. " For the first time Alpha Peter seems nervous, as he plays with his napkin and picks at his food.

"As you may know, I have been having an influx of new pack members from the East. The one major thing each new pack member has in common is that they are either mixed-blood or mixed-race couples. There are whispers among them, the Midnight Wolf prophecy is coming to fruition. Are you all aware of the prophecy?"

We all nod our heads in the affirmative to Alpha Peter and he continues.

"I have heard there are increased hostilities between Whispering Winds, Midnight Moon, Red Crescent and Broken Moon. The first three being banded together against the last. The influx of people to my pack have been escaping the tyranny of Broken Moon. The only mixed-blood in the group is you, Jasmine.

"Are you the Midnight Wolf? Is this why this meeting has been called? I hope it is so, I want to let you know, if this is the course we are going, you have my packs loyalty and sword, Jasmine. We will stand with you at all costs."

Tears begin to shine in my eyes. The people are beginning to speak, to let their displeasure known. The time is ripe for us to move forward. I reach forward and gently lay my hand on top of Alpha Peter's.

"The rumors you have heard are true. We have called this meeting because the prophecy is moving forward and picking up speed. Soon we will clash with those trying to segregate the supernatural world. I am honored to have your loyalty and your sword, Alpha Peter."

Alpha Peter nods to me. Looks around the table and gives a big smile. "I imagine you all have a lot to do, I have taken up enough of your time. Jasmine, I will keep your confidences close to me and let you make your announcement as you see fit," he finishes, standing from his seat.

The rest of the table also stands out of respect.

"Thank you, Alpha Peter. I look forward to working with you."

With one last nod, he walks away. We watch his retreating back for a moment, then resume our seats.

"Let's at least finish our meal before we starve from lack of sustenance," Dad jokes with us.

We continue to eat in silence, thinking over Alpha Peter's impromptu meeting with us.

Chapter 59:

Late-Night Arrivals

(Jasmine's POV)

The barbeque has lasted well into the evening, it seems all the folks gathered here are enjoying themselves. We have made sure there is no lack of food or drink for the group and are happy to let the festivities continue as long as the people want. The more engrossed in the festivities they are, the less likely they are to notice or question when some of us leave to welcome our visitors.

"Alright, guys, I am showing 8:40 on my watch, let's start slowly leaving the festivities a few at a time. We don't want a mass exodus and start people talking. Dad already left the party about an hour ago claiming fatigue. Simon will stay in place to wish everyone good evening as they depart," I mind-link our core group.

"As we get away, meet in the eighth-floor meeting room, most of the guests are staying on the third and fourth floors, so we are putting our guests on the sixth floor. No one should accidently wander up there. Surprise is going to be our friend here, so let's make stealth our ally tonight," I finish up.

"Sounds like a plan," Ashley links in. "I am going to grab Zeke and we can wander off together. No one will question us leaving together, especially since he is still recovering from his stay at Broken Moon, the assholes."

Looking at Keith, I update him on the links, we try to contain our laugh at Ashley. Now that she has accepted her place as the Blood Wolf, she is no longer the unsure girl she was, now we have quite the fierce protector in our group.

After about ten minutes, Keith walks up to me and places his arm around my waist. Our ruse is, I am his Chosen Mate, especially with all the drama during the meeting with Alpha Blaine and Keith standing next to me during the welcoming of the Alphas. No one would complain about us wanting a little alone time, especially this time of evening. We whisper to each other and smile as we depart. There are some who give us looks of approval on our way out.

Finally, we are all gathered at the designated meeting spot. Maverick saunters in flashing everyone a gleaming smile.

"Everyone should be arriving shortly. They are all coming together at the same time. The plan is to glimmer into this room, as long as I am here, they will be able to make it," he tells us with mock importance.

Mark ensures the door is shut and secure, we don't want anyone inadvertently walking in. No one should be on this floor without authorization, but we can't put anything past some folks at this point.

I switch from foot to foot and look anxiously around the room. Dad had a buffet brought up, so our guests would be able to eat upon arrival if they chose. My nerves are getting more and more frazzled the longer we wait. I feel as if I ate butterflies for dinner instead of ribs. Dad places a calming hand on my should and pulls me into his side for some extra comfort. The Goddess must look favorably upon me to still have one of my parents present and I am so thankful.

After what seems like an eternity, but is only a few minutes, the atmosphere around us changes and becomes semi-electrified. Blinking once I open my eyes, and a group of supernatural beings stand before us.

Maverick walks up to the group. "Ah, Damien, so good to see you all made it safely. Any issues getting everyone here in one go?" he asks the coven member responsible for bringing everyone.

"Completely uneventful, except for this witch, who wanted to debate why portals are better than shimmering," Damien motions to his left, dismissively toward a petite brown-haired lady. "Once I took over her mind, though, there were no more issues," he states with a thin smile on his red lips. I am trying to figure out if the red in natural or stained from a meal before travel.

Aunt Meredith lets out a giggle. "I see the two of you are still getting along as well as ever. So good to see some things don't change. This should be entertaining for us, and a lesson in patience for the two of you."

"How about if anyone who would like to grab a plate does so, then finds a seat at the table. After we get that completed, we will make introductions," Maverick suggests.

Thirty minutes later everyone is settled in. Maverick stands at the head of the table. "Let's get started here. I will start to my left and go around the table."

I semi-tune out during this part. There are fae, witches, warlocks, vampires, trolls, werebears, and elves all represented here, all the members sit on the high councils for their kind. Awe runs through me at the group gathered to ensure safety of the supernatural world.

Maverick is done talking and looking at me, I stare back at him with a blank expression on my face. He lifts one eyebrow and continues staring. Finally, it dawns on me, my turn to talk.

Slowly I stand from my seat, a blush heating my cheeks and look around the room again. "Thank you all for coming short notice. We are gathered here due to a threat against the supernatural species. We have discovered there is a collaborative of supernatural who want a segregation of all species and have been attacking those of mixed-blood and mixed relationships. Initially we were only able to definitively confirm werewolves, witches and vampires working together to cause this segregation. Recently we uncovered some of their members are high ranking in the councils. For example, one is a High Wolf Council member, one is an Alpha of a dominant pack, and one is a High Witch Council member." There are a few gasps at this information.

"There has been a trusted member, shadowing the werewolf council member and she learned there is a plot to attack the Alpha meeting on the last day using soldiers and warriors from the werewolf, witch, vampire, Fae, and troll communities." Anger stirs in the faces of those around the table.

"Has everyone here heard of the Midnight Wolf prophecy?" I inquire.

Ember, the head fairy, speaks up. "Everyone at this table has heard of the prophecy, Young One. As a matter of fact, I believe we were all around when it was first foretold." She smiles. There are many affirmative nods around the table. "What does this have to do with you, though, sweet girl?" she asks kindly.

"Well, I am the Midnight Wolf and Ashley is the Blood Wolf. The last part of the plan of these aggressors is to kidnap me in the middle of the chaos, have a witch make a portal to send us to Broken Moon pack, so the Alpha from there can mark and mate me against my will."

A growl rips through the room.

"That bastard already stole my wife; he will NOT steal my daughter too!" Father bellows, slamming his fist onto the table.

With Father having his outburst I fill the group in on the battle we had against Broken Moon, those involved and the death of my mother, during the rescue attempt. There is a silence around the room, and after finishing the saga I slide back into my seat, doing my best to keep the tears from falling, reliving that horrible day.

"I have been hearing the Midnight Wolf returned. The winds have told me they have seen her. You have the support of the Fae. It is imperative we stop this. Do you think this attack will be the ultimate battle?" Ember asks.

"I do not believe it is, ma'am, I think this battle is to attempt to shift the momentum towards the evil side. If they can turn Jasmine to side with them, then the battle is lost," Keith adds in. "Meredith, Maverick and I have been training Jasmine, Ashley, and some of our warriors to enhance their battle tactics. We have been chosen protectors and trainers by the Moon Goddess."

"Why are we just now being brought into the planning?" asks Morg the troll.

"My plan was to start with the Alpha meeting and initially introduce myself there, then two days later do the same at the Witches' Council. After those two dates Maverick was going to assist me in reaching out to the rest of you. With this new plot against us, we needed to change the original plan and quickly. My intent was not to exclude anyone." I direct my answer to everyone seated around the table.

"May we have a moment to discuss all this?" Morg requests.

"Absolutely. Would you like me to take out all my group or just the were-wolves? Aunt Meredith and Maverick can answer many questions you may have," I offer.

"Just the werewolves for now, please. It is clear the werewolves are going to be a part of this battle regardless of our decision."

"That is understandable, and we will grant your request. We will be in my father's office, just knock on the wall when you are ready."

All the werewolves in the room get up and go next door into Dad's office.

"What will we do if they decline?" Dad asks as soon as his office door shuts behind us.

"Then I will bring in the majority of my wolves as planned anyway and reach out to Red Crescent to assist as well. We would have to pray to Moon Goddess the power we have will be enough to overcome," Keith answers thoughtfully.

Taking a seat in one of the nice armchairs, I close my eyes and lean my head back. My stomach is rebelling against me, and the butterflies have turned into an inferno eating its way north. My head is throbbing, and my eyes burn from holding in tears, wiping my hands on my pants doesn't seem to be helping keep the moisture off them. Hopefully a few deep breaths will help to bring calmness to my system.

There is a knock on the wall, and we all look at each other around the office, prior to collecting ourselves and heading back to the meeting room. Maverick opens the door for us, and we file in one after another and resume our seats.

Morg stands from his seat and addresses us. "We all agree, it is necessary to assist in this prophecy. Maverick and Meredith were very informative and let us know the plans you have once the prophecy is brought to fruition. Do you know who you will place on the Royal Council?"

"My plan is to let each of the species send three representatives of their choosing to the Royal Council. It is important to ensure the council members I have helping guide me have the faith and trust of their people."

"It sounds as though you have put a lot of thought into this, Jasmine, and you have the best interest of all at heart. You are someone we can support. We pledge to you our loyalty and swords. We do not have much time to assemble those needed prior to the attack date. Please show us to our rooms now so we can start making proper arrangements. How many wolves will be assisting?"

"Whispering Winds and Midnight Moon positively. Night Fall has sworn their loyalty and sword to me, I will speak with them tomorrow. Red Crescent will also be asked, but they lost a lot of warriors in the attack from Broken Moon. Besides those packs we are not sure who is with or against us."

"Again, Jasmine, you have shown us you are putting just as much into this battle as we are. Shall we meet again tomorrow evening at 6 P.M. for an update?"

Everyone nods in agreement.

With an initial plan in place and an agreed-on meeting time tomorrow we all depart to head to our rooms for a night of rest. Hopefully sleep will find me easily. Once the groups agree to support us, my anxiety lets loose of my body and calm flows over my being.

Tomorrow promises to be another long day.

Chapter 60:

First Day of Meeting

(Jasmine's POV)

Four in the morning comes early, especially since sleep, once again, eluded me. Training is still happening for me, even with all the Alphas here for this meeting. The only change we did make was to ensure our training was held out of sight of any visitors. We are still wanting to keep the talents of Ashley and my wolves quiet for the time being. Let the enemy guess what our powers are instead of putting them on display.

I still have not shared with anyone that Brooke is able to do magic while in wolf form, it is best to keep some things to yourself, no one else knows about, kind of an ace in the hole. Trust is not a factor when it comes to my trainers, but you never know if there is a spy about.

Two hours fly by, while sparring three against one. We thought it best I do some training without Ashley, just so I do not end up only developing a fighting style that had to include her in it. Keith, Maverick and Aunt Meredith have been putting Ashley through the same type of training as well. Reasons like this are why I couldn't ask for a better team around me, they are making sure I am an all-around weapon on the battlefield. The unsure, young girl in that first fight on my birthday is gone.

Thoughts of today's meetings are going through my head, as the massaging spray of the shower runs over my body. Ashley and I are going to share our wolves with the werewolf world today. No more secrets, well, not as many secrets hiding in the pack. How are the Alphas going to take this new revelation that is going to be sprung on them? The threat is real and needs to be discussed. Especially with all we know.

Finding an outfit for this morning is the difficult part ahead of me. I still need to appear professional in my appearance, but I also do not want to destroy any of my nice business attire. Hopefully there is something in my closet that is older, that will not be as much of a loss to destroy in a shift. An outfit is already sitting at the ready for post-shift.

Twenty minutes later I am walking through the main entrance of the meeting area. There are already a few Alphas present and they chat with me, on my journey towards the front of the room.

Dad looks up from the main table and sends a smile my way. "Good morning, Jasmine. How was your training this morning?"

"It was great, Dad. Is there anything you need help getting ready before the start of the morning? I see the kitchen staff has done a lovely job setting up morning snacks and beverages for those in attendance." Peering over the offerings set out, I choose a fruit bowl and poppyseed muffin.

"Everything is running smoothly and set up. This event has been planned out well. While we are in this meeting the ballroom will be prepped for the evening's events. Great idea, Keith had to host a ball, after today, so we can catch idle chatter in a relaxed and unguarded atmosphere about the prophecy and who will really support us," Dad whispers to me, so the others in the room are not able to hear.

"Where are your protectors, Jasmine? I thought we agreed you would be more cautious," Dad asks, while lowering his eyebrows and pursing his lips.

"Miles is outside, Ashley is finishing getting ready and Alpha Keith is on his way right now. Miles and I thought it was best if he hangs back a few feet. It gives others the opportunity to approach him, but keep me safe. Besides, we knew you were in here already, along with Alpha Peter," I respond back with a smile on my face and a slight blush at being reprimanded by my father in front of other Alphas.

"Of course, of course. You always have everything planned out and are being responsible. I should learn my lesson by now you are a strong, smart, independent woman, but I still see the little girl," Dad laments, attempting to cover up his misplay and save a little face for me.

The door swings open forcefully, slamming into the wall behind it, looking up, we see Alpha Blaine stomping down the aisle towards us, his new Beta in tow.

"Alpha Blaine, nice to see you here this morning. Please try to be a little gentler on my property, I don't want any holes in my walls," Dad growls out to him.

"I will keep that in mind, Alpha Alexander. Do you mind telling me why you have one of your members following me?"

"I do not have anyone following you, Alpha Blaine. My wolves have tasks and chores to do, your whereabouts are not one of them. Why do you assume there is someone following you?"

"There was a woman near the lake last night, while I was there, no scent was discernable on her. We know Jasmine is able to hide the scent of wolves, thought perhaps you all had a hand in it."

"Alpha Blaine, the lake is a very popular place, and is neutral territory. There were probably many more wolves than you realized there with you. The woman more than likely went to meet a lover and mistook you for him at first. If you are going to accuse my daughter and me at every turn, perhaps this meeting is not the place for you, or your members," my father quips back pointedly.

Alpha Blaine sends a glare my way, keeping my face neutral to his accusations, I send a shrug his way in response. My actions instantly infuriate him, and he lets out a massive growl, while closing the two steps between us, and grips my shoulders forcefully. Brooke is snarling and growling in my mind.

"Let me tear him apart, Young One. How dare he touch his Queen in such a way!"

My father jumps up from his seat, and Alphas Peter and Keith, with Miles right behind them, run to the front of the room. I raise my hands up to shoulder height to stop them all from interfering. At this point, we have the attention of all the members in the room.

Looking Alpha Blaine directly in the eye, I calmly but forcefully address him. "Alpha Blaine, you will take your hands off me. Do not touch me, ever.

This one time, you will get a pass, but the next time, you fail to remember, you will be missing a hand or arm, is that clear to you?"

After a few minutes' standoff Alpha Blaine drops his hands, "This is not over, Jasmine, do not think it is even remotely over, in the end I will have the final say and laugh." He turns around and walks to a seat near the back of the room.

Not fully trusting him, I watch him the entire time, before letting my guard down slightly. This is not the way I was hoping the morning would start.

The tension in the air slowly dissipates and the other Alphas and guests take their seats. There are soft whispers around the room as those who were present for the altercation catch up others who missed it. Many eyes turn my way, as I sit next to my father, head held high and proud.

Ashley comes in and stands behind my chair. "I smell anger on you, Jazz. What happened to cause this?"

"Alpha Blaine thought he needed to get a little handsy earlier. I dealt with him and had lots of support. I was in no danger."

Ashley looks back to where Blaine is sitting, she curls her lips and sends a growl towards him in warning. His response is to raise his eyebrows and smirk, then turn to his Beta and whisper something in his ear. We may not have had anyone following him before, but we would be now.

Alpha Keith comes over and takes a seat next to me, leaning over he places a kiss on my cheek, then places a hand on my thigh. We are doing our best to keep up appearances from the last few days. It is a great cover as to why he is around me constantly. The council members all come in together and sit at the table set up for them to the side.

Once everyone is seated, my father stands from his seat and clears his throat. When he sees he has everyone's attention he begins. "Welcome, all, to this Alpha meeting. Just a few housekeeping chores to start off with, the restrooms are to the sides of the building, near the back, there is a buffet set up, so please partake as you desire from the offerings. Staff will be in and out making sure it continues to be stocked. As you all know, after today's meetings we will host a ball, starting at 7 P.M. Any questions before we get started?"

Silence hangs in the air.

"Very well, let's get on with business then. We have called everyone here today to discuss an issue that has been growing. There seems to be an increase in aggression against werewolves of mixed-blood or mixed-species relationships. I have had the opportunity to speak with Alpha Peter of the Night Fall pack and he says he has noticed an influx of new members being displaced from the East of his pack lands. Alpha Keith of Midnight Moon has reported many she-wolves of mixed-blood, about ready to turn, being kidnapped or killed from his pack. He did a full perimeter sweep and was unable to find any entry point or abnormal scents on his land. Have any other packs been experiencing occurrences such as these? Please stand and explain your issue one at a time, then we can discuss the problem further once everyone has had a chance to speak."

An older Alpha in the middle of the group stands up. "I am Alpha Steven of Howling Wind; we have been experiencing the same issues as Night Fall. We have had an influx coming from the south into our lands. When they arrive, they are badly beaten, and we have lost a few due to their injuries. We sent out scouts, but none of them ever returned. I still have an investigation going forward on this matter."

Once Alpha Steven sits down another Alpha stands up promptly.

Chapter 61:

The Reveal

(Jasmine's POV)

The last Alpha to stand up and tell their tale is number 82 of 110 packs represented, three packs from Europe reported issues as well. This appears to already be a global issue. The force with which this hatred and cancer is moving through the supernatural world is breathtaking and so very sad. How can such anger and distrust live in people's hearts?

After the last Alpha has sat down and we ensure there are no others who wish to speak, Dad stands back up.

"Thank you all for speaking out to the issues darkening the lives of your packs. We all are feeling the strain, even here in Whispering Winds. My daughter was kidnapped, imprisoned, threatened, rejected, and then escaped and fought a battle, a few months later my Luna and future Beta were captured by the same pack. My Luna was imprisoned, but the Beta was tortured and is still recovering, due to the amount of silver and wolfsbane in his system. We had to battle our way out and, in the battle, we lost warriors and my beloved Luna. All because of being mixedrace. This is a blight on our world, one that needs to be eradicated," Father continues in a low voice, as tears threaten to spill as he tells our tale.

Clearing the emotion from his throat, he raises his head and looks out across the sea of faces. "How many in attendance today have heard of the prophecy of the Midnight Wolf?" Dad's question brings around hushed conversations and whispers. Many are looking at Dad as if he is telling a joke.

"Seriously, you are joking, Alpha Alexander. The prophecy is no more than a glorified children's bedtime story. Is the loss of your Luna making you crazy with grief?" yells out one of the Alphas in the room.

There is some light laughter at this inquiry, and I let a growl that shakes the walls of our meeting space escape my lips at the disrespect shown to my father.

Many heads rise in surprise at my growl and the force of it. I am angry they have made fun of my father and my mother's death. I will not stand by and allow these pompous people to belittle my father. Rising to my feet, I send a glare out over the population of the room. Ashley has moved to my side, and Alpha Keith has also risen.

"My father was attempting to bring you all into this slowly and gently, but since you deem it appropriate to mock him, I do not care much about how you perceive it. There is a threat out there to the entire supernatural world. Many of you stood up and spoke about the plights of your own packs. Well, allow me to give credence to my father."

With that I allow Brooke to come forward and shift into my Midnight Wolf as Ashley shifts into Grace, her Blood Wolf.

Across the room you can hear the gasps and amazement. Many people jump from their seats and there is a general air of chaos at this point. The noise and pandemonium is too much for me at this point and I again rock the walls with a growl. This has the desired effect, and everybody stops what they are doing, turning back to the stage.

"As you can see the prophecy is true. My daughter is the Midnight Wolf and Ashley is the Blood Wolf. The prophecy has begun, and we are in the thick of an ever-growing violence. There is a collaborative out there of highranking members, who want to see a permanent separation of the species and are working diligently towards that outcome. You are all here so we can make a plan to combat this threat," my father firmly speaks out to the group.

"How is she to be a Queen when she has no pack lands? Who is supposed to give up their lands so she can rule?" comes a question from the crowd.

"This evening at the ball, I will be handing over the Alpha position of Whispering Winds to Jasmine. It has long been known she is my heir and has completed all her training under me. None of you have to worry about giving up your lands," Dad assures them.

Alpha Mason stands, "I will also be turning over the Alpha position of Red Crescent to Jasmine this evening. I have been looking for a new heir and I see no better qualified than our future Queen. My trust in her and those chosen to rule beside her is unwavering." He finishes with a bow to me, in return I nod my head, acknowledging him. To be honest this is unexpected news from both Alphas, and my breath is caught in my throat.

"Remember to breathe, Young One, it would not be a good show to pass out on this stage. We are ready to take this on. They recognize we are strong and capable," Brooke encourages me.

Next Alpha Peter stands, "I swear the loyalty, sword, and claws of my pack, Night Fall, to the Queen. We will stand beside her and fight our enemies until the last breath leaves our bodies. We will not stand idly by and watch the segregation of our world."

"I too swear the loyalty, sword, and claws of my pack, Midnight Moon, to the Queen. I have been chosen by the Moon Goddess to be a protector and trainer to our Queen, my pack and I will lay down our lives for all. Who else stands with us! Who else will fight beside our Queen?!"

Alpha Keith follows behind Alpha Peter. Brooke raises her head high and proud, looking out over the audience with confidence.

Slowly one Alpha after another stands, until 80 packs have sworn loyalty to me, and promised to fight for the supernatural.

Council Member Gary stands from his chair. "You have the support of the High Council, except for Council Member Charles. He is the only holdout, but we have suspected him of playing against us for a while now." With this revelation many growls go into the air. "Please have a couple guards detain Council Member Charles and hold him in a cell until we are able to question him further," Gary requests, as Charles turns surprised eyes to him.

Father nods, Miles steps over and takes hold of Charles, while Dad is mind-linking for another guard.

"Let go of me, pup. There is no need to take hold of me as if I am some criminal. It will be proven I am innocent of these allegations once an actual investigation is done. This is highly insulting," Charles huffs out and attempts to pull away from Miles.

Surprisingly Alpha Blaine has remained quietly in his seat through this entire ordeal. It makes me wonder about the true relationship between him and Charles, it appeared they were as thick as thieves. Perhaps he is supposed to be a sleeper Alpha, to ensure the attack goes off, as they think it is planned tomorrow. We will be keeping an eye on him.

Once all the commotion has died down, and Charles has been escorted from the room, Ashley and I walk from the stage into a side room. We shift back and dress quickly making our reappearance in a matter of minutes.

"Now that a semblance of calm has made its way back into this room, let's continue to discuss the topic at hand. There are many who did not vow loyalty or aggression in this matter, and it seems there are more questions to answer. We would be pleased to answer any questions you have," I address the crowd, with a smile on my face.

As I settle back into my seat, the discussion has started again. It looks like it is going to be a long meeting day for all. Hopefully we can answer all their questions adequately.

Chapter 62:

Adapting to Deceive

(Alpha Blaine's POV)

The change of events happening is something else to watch. Councilman Gary just called out my grandfather for being against the council and the werewolf population. Choosing to maintain my seat and not make any further spectacle of myself, I watch it all unfold. It takes a lot of control not to rise and voice my opinions regarding the segregation. I take note of the packs who do not swear loyalty to the Queen, either myself or my Beta will need to speak with them this evening.

The old man was correct in pursuing Jasmine, she is indeed the Midnight Wolf, a beautiful wolf. Our plans would go much more smoothly if she was on our side, if she was by my side. With Grandfather in their cells and the council out to hang him, I am in charge of the werewolves in the collaborative now. Maybe it is time to be the proverbial wolf in sheep's clothing, a smile crosses my face at this thought.

Now that there is a new direction in mind, the continuation of this meeting is wearing on my nerves. I need to get back to my room and plan for the changes, adapt to the new mission; however, I need to make it appear there has been a change in my attitude.

There will need to be a meeting between myself and the heads of the other supernaturals Grandfather called in for help. Although it leaves a bad taste in my mouth to work with them, they have made it clear once the war is over, we part ways for good.

Finally, we are being dismissed from this meeting. Time to square everything away, I link my Beta and Gamma directing them to follow me to my suite, I also link one of my guards and ask him to round up the heads of the other groups to meet at the lake after ten this evening. I should make an appearance at the ball and set the new plan in motion.

Arriving at my room, I ensure the door is securely shut behind us before speaking. "The events at the meeting today have given us a new opportunity. One I plan on taking full advantage of." My Beta and Gamma just look at me, no emotion on their faces. "Now that Grandfather has been detained, I can give the appearance of having been deceived by Grandfather and work myself back into the good graces of Jasmine. Once she is willingly with me, bringing her over to our side will be easier. Forcing her has too many risks associated with it. The attack will still need to happen tomorrow at the meeting, but I am going to fight by the other wolves instead of against them. I need the two of you to let the other heads know what is going on now, and that I will explain the rest to them this evening once I can get away from the ball."

Without a word they leave the room to follow through with the instructions I gave them. I have no doubt my orders will be done exactly how I asked. They know the punishment for failing me. Now it is time to prepare myself for the ball and begin my plan to thwart the prophecy.

About two hours later I descend the stairs to the main floor of the packhouse and make my way to the grand ballroom. It is amazing what Alpha Alexander was able to put together in such a short planning time. Casting glances around the room I see my Beta and Gamma have been able to make it back from their tasks.

Continuing to scan the area, I see a couple of Alphas near the back of the ballroom. They are particularly interesting to me, because by the end of the meeting day, they still had not opted to support the future Queen, they also had not sworn to fight against her. I need to know what their plan is, or how they are leaning at the very least.

A waiter passes by and offers me a glass of champagne, I accept the glass and make my way over to the Alphas. "Good evening, gentlemen. I must say, I hope the dinner is worth getting dressed up for." I chuckle as I walk up to them. They seem slightly guarded as I approach.

"Alpha Blaine, nice to see you opted to join us this evening. We didn't think balls were your sort of atmosphere, especially after your confrontation with the hosts this morning," Alpha James quips back to me in a bored tone.

My wolf does not like his tone with us and wants to lash out, it takes a massive amount of control to keep him in his place.

"All a significant misunderstanding. After the happenings in the meeting today, I firmly believe Jasmine and Alpha Alexander indeed were telling the truth about not having me followed, it is a better assumption the council was having Council Member Charles followed. Once an opportunity presents itself this evening, I will ensure to rectify the misunderstanding."

"Why would you be meeting with Council Member Charles? He is a traitor to werewolves, wouldn't anyone meeting with him also be a traitor?" inquires Alpha James.

The other two Alphas stand there, listening to our back-and-forth, but not offering any input of their own. Samael wants to rip his throat out and end it there, this Alpha is making it difficult to begin showing my change of behavior, hopefully it isn't this difficult all the time.

"You could assume such a thing; however, that would be rather closeminded of you. Did it ever cross your mind that Charles was not completely honest with me in our dialog and told lies to bring me close to him?" I ask, while I push down the utter disdain I have for this wolf before me. It is taking all my power to remain civil. Is this change in mission worth it?

"That is a well-presented hypothesis, sounds like you have put a lot of thought into it before coming down here this evening. Time always tells the true colors of a soul; my bet is yours is still as coal black as always. Have a good evening, gentlemen, I must make my departure and find my Luna before the start of the evening's events."

Without leaving an opportunity for me to defend myself or a backward glance, Alpha James leaves the group.

Turning back to the remaining Alphas, I flash them a smile and shrug my shoulders, in response to what just occurred. Neither one speaks, but cast guarded looks my way. This is going nowhere quickly so I excuse myself and make my way to the balcony. Hopefully fresh air and distance from others will help to calm Samael, until I have full control again.

Chapter 63:

Change of Alphas

(Jasmine's POV)

Once the meeting lets out, I find Maverick and ask him to have Muerta follow Alpha Blaine, even though it is not necessary to explain my reasoning for the request, I do so anyway. We couldn't risk placing Claire on him, after the confrontation we had this morning, and everyone else I trust to do the job in the pack is known to him.

Luckily Maverick is only too happy to assist us with this task, and when he informs Muerta of the request a rare smile slides across her face. It appears she misses being in action, and life in the pack is too sedentary for her liking. Glad we were able to spice up her world a little. Knowing we have a skilled and trained individual keeping an eye on him makes me feel a little better.

Time is starting to slip away from me, and I really need to get ready for the ball, and the Change of Alpha ceremony. It is hard to believe Alpha Mason chose me as his heir to Red Crescent. I will need to figure out how to blend the packs seamlessly. Luckily Alpha Mason and my father have the same leadership style and their pack and ours are regularly together for events.

Once inside my room I head directly to the shower, there is not much time to dawdle in there and enjoy the liquid massage on my sore body. My dress for the evening reminds me of Brooke's coloring, but it shimmers as the light hits it. Dad chose this dress well for me, it is an empire waist, and falls smoothly to the floor, simple but stunning. Rushing to make sure I make my entrance on time, I opt for a simple French twist and place a silver-looking clip in my hair. Of course, it is not real silver, that would be painful. I decide on simple, natural-looking make-up and finish with a silver-looking choker with a blue moon stone in the center and matching earrings.

Finished, I throw on my black flats and rush out my door, making record time down the stairs; however, I do pause and slow my descent when I get to the second floor. Cannot have the wolves seeing me in my "hot mess" moment.

My father, Council Member Gary, Alpha Mason, and Alpha Keith are waiting for me at the bottom of the stairs.

"Jasmine, honey, you look amazing. Your mother would be so proud of you, and all you have accomplished. I have no doubts you will guide this pack to its rightful place in the future. I am proud to call you My Queen."

"Oh, Dad," my voice catches in my throat and I have to clear it. "I may be Queen, but I am first your child, your daughter. I am thankful to have your guidance and support as I take this new journey in life. Without you, I would be lost, Dad. You are my anchor." I run into his waiting arms and wrap my arms around his waist. Thank the Moon Goddess, he is still here with me.

"Jasmine, Alpha Alexander, it is time for us to go in and begin the ceremony. We should not leave the guests waiting too long," Council Member Gary reminds us gently.

We break apart from the hug, I wrap my hand around Dad's elbow, and we get ready to enter the ballroom.

The stage for the ceremony has been set on the back deck. We are not able to fit all the wolves from our pack, Red Crescent, and the guests into the ballroom; this allows all pack members to watch the Change of Alpha ceremony. After the ceremony we will go and greet the wolves outside.

Dad leads me to the stage, and we stand facing Gary, we are positioned so our backs are not to either group, Alpha Mason and Alpha Keith stand behind us. Council Member Gary clears his throat to get everyone's attention, then begins.

"Welcome, everyone, to the Change of Alpha ceremony. Tonight, Jasmine Oscuro will become Alpha of Whispering Winds and Red Crescent, as chosen by the Alphas currently sitting. Are there any objections to Jasmine being named Alpha?"

There is a pause to allow anyone to step forward. I steadfastly keep my eyes on Gary, everything in my being wants to look and see if Alpha Blaine is here and ready to cause a scene.

"Very well, let it be known there were no objections. Jasmine Oscuro and Alpha Alexander Oscuro, please come to the ceremony stand. We approach the table that has been set up, a white-and-gold tablecloth covers the wood, on top sits a gold chalice and bowl, encrusted on the outside is diamonds and blue topaz, next to them is a gold dagger with diamonds and blue topaz on the handle; these are the packs ceremonial items.

"Do you, Alpha Alexander Oscuro, willingly change your position of Alpha to Jasmine Oscuro?" asks Gary.

"I do, High Council Member Gary, freely and without doubt, I turn over my title and pack to Jasmine Oscuro," responds Dad, his eyes glistening with pride.

"Jasmine Rose Oscuro, do you willingly accept the title of Alpha to Whispering Winds pack, do you swear to the Goddess to protect, love and give your life to them? Will you help them to prosper and be well?" Gary directs to me.

"I swear this to the Goddess, High Council Member Gary. I will not only lay down my life gladly for this pack, but for the entire supernatural world." "Please hold out your left hands."

We hold out our left hands to Gary. The left hand is closest to the heart, so this is the hand chosen to use during the blood bond. Council Member Gary picks up the dagger and makes a small cut on my palm, he does the same to Father.

"Please place your palms together and grasp the other's wrist."

We do as requested. Once our hands are grasped together, I feel a wave of energy and strength engulf my entire being.

"The Moon Goddess looks favorably on this transition of power and title. Whispering Winds, I present to you, your new Alpha, Alpha Jasmine Rose Oscuro."

A cheer goes up in the air, Dad lets loose of my hand and pulls me in for a hug.

Dad changes places with Alpha Mason, and we do the entire ceremony again, no complaints or objections for this change either. In a matter of minutes, I have become Alpha to two packs. I am thankful for my anchors, because at this moment my life is fluid and ever changing as the rivers around us.

Stepping down from the stage, we enter the courtyard to meet and greet my pack members. I receive many well wishes and congratulations, the outgoing Alphas receive many thank-yous. Soon the pack members have dispersed, and we find our way back to the ballroom.

Once back inside, we mingle through the crowd, soon dinner is served, and we all sit to enjoy our meal. My stomach has had butterflies in it since the meetings this morning, and I find it difficult to eat much this evening.

"Jasmine, are you feeling alright?" Dad asks me, his eyebrows are furrowed, mouth is set in a line, and eyes shine with concern.

"I am fine, Dad. Just a lot today, and then the ceremony. Just butterflies in the stomach is all."

Dad smiles at me and goes back to his discussion with Alpha Mason.

"You are doing wonderfully, Young One. Many people have faith in you and support you. I understand the nerves, but their faith and trust is not falsely put in you. I only caution you to be careful of those who appear changed. Do not harden yourself but listen with you mind and heart," Brooke speaks to me.

"Thank you, Brooke, I will heed your guidance. This has been a full day with an amazing evening. What I really want is to escape to my room and think it all through," I confide to my wolf.

She just chuckles and goes to the back of my mind.

When I come back to the present after my discussion with Brook, the dance floor is being set up and a staff member is standing in front of me with a questioning look.

"I apologize, I was speaking with my wolf and did not hear your question," I admit to the young wolf, a blush creeping up my neck and face.

"It is alright, Alpha, I was wanting to know if you were done, so I may take your plate," he asks again.

Giving a smile, I nod my head and back away from the table, allowing the staff to continue their chores.

Chapter 64:

The Ball Continues

(Jasmine's POV)

The dance floor is set up and the band is playing. Dad comes up to me, "Jasmine, may I have this first dance with you, my dear daughter?"

Giggling, I give Dad a curtsy and nod in agreement. He whisks me away to the dance floor and the band begins a waltz. I love moments like this with my father, when the world is a little at bay and we can just be family. We don't say much to each other, we enjoy the moment.

Once the music resides, Dad walks me back to our table. I am about to sit down when someone grasps my elbow from behind. Keith lets out a low growl and Father takes a defensive stance. There is only one wolf who elicits this type of response from these men.

I turn and look into the icy-blue eyes of Alpha Blaine. "I distinctly remember telling you not to touch me, or you would lose a body part, Alpha Blaine. What did you not understand about that?" My voice is cool and aloof. I have no patience for this wolf. I want him out of my packhouse and off my land.

"I do apologize, Alpha Jasmine," Blaine begins. "I was hoping I could have a dance with you, congratulate you on your new title and position, perhaps even bury the ax and make amends." He gives me a smile that has no effect on me. This man makes my skin crawl and my body scream to run away.

"You may have one dance, then no more. As far as burying the hatchet goes, I am not sure that is possible, our history is a little too much to overcome so easily." I refuse to bow to his requests, especially this soon after a very public confrontation just hours earlier.

Alpha Blaine leads me to the dance floor, we are followed by Alpha Keith and Dad. They do not trust this Alpha either, his motives are suspect. I see Muerta standing at the edge of the crowd keeping an eye on the events unfolding. Once to the dance floor, I attempt not to cringe as Alpha Blaine places his hand on my waist. We begin to take the steps in time with the music.

"I really must apologize, Alpha Jasmine. It is clear now, you and your father were not having me followed, but the council was having Charles followed. I am afraid many of us were fooled by that man, myself included. The events of this morning were highly surprising and opened my eyes to my folly. I know I have a lot to make up for to you, and I promise, I will do whatever it takes to earn your trust. I cannot change the past, but I hope for a better future." He smiles down to me.

Looking in his eyes, I do not see an ounce of honesty there. I am not sure what game he is trying to play, but I refuse to be a part of it.

"Alpha Blaine, it is well known a leopard does not change its spots. Not for a moment do I believe you were ever fooled by Charles, but a very willing participant in his acts of hate and segregation. I have no desire to work on a better future with you, because to you a better future is the segregation of the species, something I do not agree with and will not tolerate."

Alpha Blaine does his best to put a shocked look on his face prior to responding to me. "Charles led me to believe he had the support of the council behind him. I followed through with all the actions because of that belief. When I witnessed the spectacle in the meeting today, I realized I was indeed mistaken. I realized my error."

"Do you forget the words you spoke to me right before you rejected me, Alpha? Do you forget the conditions you placed me in? Do you forget how you treated my mother and Beta Ezekiel? Do you forget your attack on Red Crescent? Do you forget all your actions, made without Charles' input? No, you are not changing, you are playing a game and I refuse to go there with you. I am aware of the type of wolf you are, and you will not be changing my opinion of you." I stand firm in my convictions and do not give him an inch. This is my first actual act as an Alpha.

"I was really hoping you would choose to work with me. Take steps to have a peaceful resolve. I see I have damaged any chances of that." As he makes this revelation the song is ending, he puts me into a deep dip and whispers in my ear. "One way or another, little Alpha, you will be by my side, and I will break you to submit to my will."

He stands me upright, bows deeply and departs the dance floor, leaving me standing in the middle. At this moment I am too livid to be embarrassed.

Alpha Keith rushes up to my side and places his hand around my waist, in a protective way that signals all others to stay back. Ashley stands on the other side, protecting me there. Keith's eyes take in the entirety of the ballroom, sensing no threats, he drops his hand and takes a step away.

In an attempt to save as much face as possible, I address the crowd. "Thank you all for coming this evening and supporting the change of Alphas, and for working with us to battle the threat that faces the supernatural world. The Goddess has blessed us with amazing allies and friends. It is time I make my departure for the evening. Please continue to enjoy yourselves, have a wonderful evening and I will see you tomorrow for the last day of meetings." Turning on my heel, I leave the room, closely followed by Keith, Ashley, Zeke, and my father.

Chapter 65:

Late-Night Conspirators

(Alpha Blaine's POV)

Jasmine is much stronger than I have given her credit for, it is obvious my plan is not going to work. Guess we go back to the original plan Grandfather laid out for us. Something must work; we have hit a wall at every turn and the one individual there every time is Jasmine. She will break, she will serve her purpose at our side and then die.

Checking the time, there is still half an hour before we need to meet. I quickly change out of my tux and leave my suite to head out to the lake. It feels as if I have eyes on my back, turning around slowly in a 360-degree circle, I survey my surrounding. There is no one in the area, there is no scent here either. Perhaps I am just being paranoid with what happened to Grandfather.

Setting out at a fast jog from the packhouse, I make it to the lake just in time. I walk around the edge of the lake until I come to a rocky outcrop. The heads of the species fighting with us are assembled, waiting on me.

"Good evening, I apologize for how long it took me to get here. Ensuring the secrecy of this meeting was important, so I took some extra steps to make sure I was not being followed. We need this plan to go off without a hitch."

They all nod their heads to me.

"Your Beta told us there was a change to the original plan and you would update us. What is this change, Blaine? We don't like changes this close to attack time." Hisses, the leader of the vampires. She makes my blood run cold, her eyes are open, but vacant, there is no emotion in them, not even hate.

"Then you will be happy to know we are back to the original plan. I was hoping Jasmine would accept a changed man front, after they took Charles away this morning, but she didn't accept it. The plan is still on. We will attack during the morning meeting. Most of the Alphas will still be tired from the ball this evening and sluggish in response," I attempt to placate the vampire. "Jasmine will be a little more difficult to take then we originally thought.

Today she revealed she is the Midnight Wolf, and the Blood Wolf is with her also." Murmurs go around the space at this revelation. "Jasmine also has another protector, who is an Alpha, and very skilled at fighting. He almost took me down in battle at Red Crescent. We will have to fight through these two before we can even attempt to bind her and portal out."

"Did you see any other witches besides Meredith and Jasmine?" inquires the head witch.

"I did not. The only supernaturals I have seen at Whispering Winds, besides us, is the werewolves invited to the meeting. Eighty packs swore loyalty to Jasmine today. I attempted to speak with some of the Alphas who did not decide either way, but they were not open to speaking with me. There is a limited number of warriors here. Most of the Alphas did not bring warriors with them since this is a peaceful pack. The numbers and power we have behind us should ensure a quick win."

"Let me deal with the Blood Wolf," the head troll chimes in, "she should be no match for the strength of my trolls. We can quickly subdue her and the Alpha, then contain Jasmine, while the witch puts a binding spell on her."

"My witches can handle them just fine; we do not need the assistance of you trolls. Stay with the original plan will you. You may have strength, but we have power, dark power, that puts your strength to shame."

"None of us want to be working together, but it is a necessary evil, a means to an end. Once we have managed to win this war, we can all go on our way and never interact again," I remind the group. "The last thing we need is a pissing match to see who the better group is. Our mission is to get the Midnight Wolf, and that is what we will do," I finish.

"This meeting is over. We all know what we need to do and how to do it. Let's get this phase over, so we can have victory." Again, all I receive is nods as they leave the area, via different routes. I cannot get the feeling of eyes watching me out of my mind. Again, I search the area and see nothing, there is no one about and the only scent is that of the members who just left.

The jog back to the packhouse goes quickly, while walking up the stairs to my suite, I link my Beta and Gamma, letting them know the original plan is back on. A voice clears behind me, turning around I see Beta Ezekiel also walking up the stairs, still in his tuxedo.

"Congratulations on the new title of Beta. Hopefully you heal fully to be able to perform all your duties for the position." I smile at him.

"I am healing just fine. Pretty late for a run on a territory that isn't yours. What are you up to, Alpha Blaine?" Ezekiel asks me suspiciously.

"Just stretching my legs before bed is all. Have a good evening." I turn and continue my way to my suite, very aware of the eyes boring holes in my back as I depart. It is going to be sweet victory to see them all bleeding out tomorrow. A smile finds its way to my face at this, thought. Sweet dreams will be mine.

Chapter 66:

Last Meeting Day

(Jasmine's POV)

We have done our best not to deviate from our normal routine, just to ensure if someone is watching us, we do not put out any warning signs. We have called a final meeting, for after training. Muerta didn't have time to update us on what she saw and heard last night, and we need to be prepared for anything they throw at us.

Looking off to the east, there are large thunder clouds darkening the sky, making the daylight seem like dusk. The smell of rain is heavy in the air and the energy around me screams to be ready for a fight. A breeze whips, tendrils of hair that have fallen out of my bun, around my face. On the breeze, a message is delivered to me.

"Our Queen, the evil ones will attack today. This is an important battle, but not your final battle. Prepare and have faith in your team. With doubts, you will fail, with hope succeed."

As quickly as the message came it was gone again. The breeze fell into an eerie calm. I hastened my pace, wanting to get back to the packhouse as soon as possible.

Even though I knew I shouldn't have, I left for the training area without Keith, Maverick or Ashley. There will be a lecture waiting for me once they have caught up with me. We have been training in a different part of the woods, so there is certain confidence no one would know or followed us here. My safety shouldn't be a big concern right now.

Rushing through the thicker part of the forest, lost deep in my thoughts, I am brought to a dead stop when I hear a deep unfamiliar voice.

"The witches think they always have the answer with their spells and magic. Sometimes power is the key, and that power comes from brute strength. It is time the witches learn a lesson, a hard lesson not soon forgotten."

Witches? What witches? Who is this speaking and why hidden? I quickly place a scent-blocking spell on myself and sneak up to the nearest tree, so I can see and hear better. Whoever this is has not detected me yet. Peering cautiously around a large oak, I see a group of ten trolls having a secret meeting. None of them are the trolls Morg brought to assist us with the battle.

"Young One, we should not be here. You are putting us in danger, if we are found out there is no one to know where we are. We are strong but cannot take on this many trolls alone. Three is our limit," Brooke snaps at me in my head.

"I know, Brooke, well, not the part about the trolls, but I need to hear what they are saying. It could benefit us."

"But Angor, we are supposed to be working towards a bigger goal. Won't teaching the witches a lesson go against that goal?" a smaller troll asks, as he bows his head to the apparent leader, Angor.

"My end goal, while the same as the others, has a different path. I will not take orders from wolves or witches; I will not be dismissed by them either. Their arrogance is why we need to be separated from them, so we can survive. Do not get me wrong, we will fight, we will kill wolves, but we will kill all wolves, not one side or another. We will also kill all those who think we are fighting with them. The less to deal with in the future is the better for us," Angor finishes. There are many nods of agreement around him.

Now is the time for me to leave, it looks like their meeting is about to end. I start to back away from the tree when a hand comes down on my shoulder. I jump, doing my best not to squeal and turn, while sending out an energy jolt. Maverick moves aside and smiles at me in mischief. The next thing I know we are standing in the meeting room of the packhouse, many angry eyes directed at me.

"Jasmine, what were you doing leaving all your protectors behind? You should have waited for them to accompany you. Thankfully Maverick was able to shimmer to a close location and bring you back. From the way you got back, I would have to fathom you were in a not-so-safe place," my father begins lecturing me, his eyes are hard, as he stares me down. Even though he is not Alpha of the pack anymore, he is still my father and very capable of making me feel small when I make a mistake.

"I worry about your safety, dear girl, especially with Alpha Blaine and his minions still on this land. I did not want to come off angry, but my worry has been eating at my heart and stomach. Come give your father a hug, to calm me down. I am glad to see you are safe and unharmed." He opens his arms to me, and I run into them willingly. The Goddess has blessed me with his continued love and support.

Looking around the room, the eyes of Maverick, Muerta, Keith, Ashley, Zeke, Mark, and Simon are still bearing down on me. Clearing my throat, I look down at the floor and take a deep breath.

"I owe you all an apology. I should have waited, as I have promised to do, it won't happen again," continuing to keep my eyes on the floor in front of me.

Boot-covered feet appear in my line of site and a finger gently lifts my chin. "Do not ever look down when in our presence, Queen. We care about you and worry about you. We have sworn to lay down our lives for you and protect you. It is difficult to do that when you slip away," Keith tells me softly. I give him a small smile in response.

"If it is any consolation, I did get some information. There were a group of trolls in the woods, having a meeting. They plan on killing all other species present, regardless of side they are on."

Many surprised looks are sent my way. Before anyone has the opportunity to speak the door to the room opens and our visitors walk in, ready for the morning meeting, unaware of all that has transpired minutes before their arrival.

"Have we interrupted?" Morg asks, while surveying the room. His eyes land on Keith and me, then go to each member present.

I stand frozen in place, I can only imagine the somewhat compromising and rather intimate display is being put on in front of them, with Keith holding and looking at me in a gentle manner.

"Not at all," I respond, taking a step back from Keith. "We were just discussing a conversation I overheard in the forest between a group of trolls," I explain honestly.

"Please tell us more about this conversation, Jasmine," Morg requests.

"The troll who appeared to be in charge is named Angor. He and the others do not like being told what to do by other supernaturals, specifically the witches and wolves. They are planning on killing as many as they can from both sides at the meeting today," I explain again.

"Yes, this sounds like Angor. It is good to know who they have recruited, or semi-recruited. Luckily, he and his group will not be much of a bother. We can neutralize them easily." Morg nods to me, seeming unphased by this new information.

"Muerta, please tell us about what you learned last night from your surveillance. For those who do not know, I have been having Muerta follow Alpha Blaine, since we placed his grandfather in a cell," I continue to push the meeting forward.

"Blaine left his room around 9:30 P.M., I was invisible and hiding my scent, but he still felt like he was being watched and took many precautions to ensure he was not being followed. He met a group of supernaturals around the lake at the Northern border. No names were used as they had the meeting. We know the troll, thanks to Jasmine, and I recognized the vampire as Helena, as for the witch and Fae, I could not even guess. The trolls wanted to deal with Jasmine, Ashley, and Keith, but the witches told them no, they have dark magic they are planning on using. All members also know of the identity of the ladies being the Midnight and Blood wolves, which is not surprising since they shifted in the meeting, but they will be prepared for the shifts."

We all stand silently as Muerta finishes her debrief, lost in thought and what the plan will be moving forward.

Chapter 67:

Last Meeting Day 2

(Jasmine's POV)

The entire room is silent, while every member thinks over different ways to approach what we know. Zeke walks over to the wall of the meeting room with the pack lands map hanging on it.

"Jasmine, can you please show me where the trolls were camped, and then Muerta, show me where Blaine had his meeting."

Muerta and I approach the map and point out the requested locations for Zeke. He takes a few moments studying the map, before turning to the group. "With the little knowledge we have from Muerta and Jasmine, coupled with the location of Blaine's meeting place and the Alpha Meeting building, I think the best promise for us to remain undetected, but have the best defense is to set up in these specific areas." Zeke points out specific areas on the map while continuing to speak.

"Since Morg has already said he can take care of the other trolls, it would be ideal to take them out of the game, before the attack even occurs, we can send a few of our warriors with them so they can mind-link back when it is taken care of or if there are any difficulties. We can have Muerta continue following Blaine to make sure he doesn't do one last set of rounds prior to departing for the meeting." We all give nods of agreement and let him continue, uninterrupted. Muerta departs to do her assigned task.

"Since we know the witches are wanting to use dark magic to subdue Jasmine, Ashley and Keith, our witches and fairies can set up a joined group, here in the meeting building and here on the North perimeter of the lands. Vampires can take the West and elves can take the South. We can mix in warriors from the packs to help enhance the numbers of fighters, plus have a few dozen in the meeting hall, behind a shield, put in place by the witches. Ashley and Keith will keep their place next to Jasmine, as it has been from the start. The only thing I do not have a plan for is if they happen to be able to get Jasmine into a portal."

"That is easy, young Beta," Talis, our visiting witch, informs us. "One of the witches can portal to the same place, since we already know where they are heading, or Maverick, Angie or Muerta can shimmer there. There are ways to make it to her. Blaine is most likely unaware you have a vampire trainer and that they met up with you on his lands. The benefit goes to us." She gives a warm smile to the room. "As for the dark magic, only a few can harness it, and we can bind them. We happened to bring our black magic specialists with us, assuming it would be used."

"Alright, Talis, if you would take the Northern border with Ember, then Meredith can handle the meeting hall. Morg, you and your clan can return after dealing with Angor, to assist as needed. Simon and Claire, please get the warriors dispersed as directed and as quietly as possible, make sure they know they are following the orders of the supernatural in charge. Alpha Keith, if you would please direct your warriors the same, and allow Claire and Simon to direct them to their areas," Zeke finishes.

"My warriors will do as you command, they are after all sworn to the Queen. Zeke, this is a great plan. My only suggestion is to mix all the supernatural species. That will only make us stronger. Use the talents and strengths of all, instead of just one group."

"You are correct, Alpha Keith, that will make us stronger. Talis, what do you need to be able to bind the witches using black magic?"

"Alpha Keith, Ezekiel, while I agree with your plan, I need my witches to remain together as much as possible. The original split suggested by Ezekiel is going to be difficult enough dealing with black magic and containing it. I think having joined forces is a goal to work towards, but not use today. We need to train together more, before we do that." Nods of agreement are seen around the room.

"Then it appears we have a plan. Is there any more input?" I look around the room and everyone remains quiet. "If needed, Ashley and Keith will go through the portal with some warriors, if there are more needed, we have three vampires who can shimmer some others. That will be the backup plan if things go wrong. I have faith in all of you, and today victory will be ours. We are on the side of right. Let's call an end to this meeting and get our fighters in place. I will see you all on the other side."

Everyone gets up from their seats and makes their way out of the room. Before I can depart with my group, Talis calls out, "Ezekiel, if you don't mind, please stay here for a moment."

Ezekiel pauses at the door and sends a questioning look my way.

"The rest of you go, I will stay with Ezekiel and walk with him to the meeting hall. Ashley and Keith, please wait for us in the hall." Zeke and I turn back towards Talis with inquiring looks. "Do not worry, young Beta. I know you are still healing, due to the silver and wolfsbane used on you by Broken Moon. I just want to help you. Jasmine is a talented healer, but I have a few extra gifts in that area. Let me help you join this battle completely healed."

Zeke's eyes brighten at Talis' statement. A huge smile spreads across his face, while he nods enthusiastically and walks towards her.

Chapter 68:

Last Meeting Day 3

(Jasmine's POV)

Alphas continue to filter in the room and find their seats. Many look the worse for wear today. They must have all enjoyed the rest of the ball last night, and the wine Father and I supplied had more impact than they expected it appears. Luckily there is plenty of coffee available in our meeting room to assist in chasing off some of their ailments.

Alpha Blaine walks in with his Beta and Gamma, sending a loathsome look my way. I match his glare and refuse to break away first, if this is a battle of wills, I will win it. He sends me a sinister smile and turns away to take his seat near the back of the meeting hall.

Keith places his hand on my leg, in a motion of support, of course he saw the entire exchange. My thought is on the door behind where Blaine is sitting. It is not the main door the other Alphas are coming through and is hardly used during this meeting. Would he be bold enough to use that as an entryway for his warriors? My plan is to keep an eye on him and his behaviors during this meeting. We know they are planning on attacking sometime this morning, but we do not have it nailed down any further than that.

"Zeke, can you ask Aunt Meredith if she knows how to lift a barrier spell?" I link.

Thankfully Zeke is part of the warriors in the building, so I still have a way to communicate with everyone.

"She says that isn't a problem and just let her know when you need it done and where."

"The where is going to be the entryway behind Blaine. It is possible he is bold enough to use that for his warriors to come in from."

The meeting has been in progress for a couple hours now, Blaine is starting to move about in his seat more, fisting and un-fisting his hands, he does a move where he pretends to be stretching, to cast a look over his shoulder. My hunch is starting to pay off, the time must be getting close. Blaine's signs are subtle, but still there.

"Zeke, have Aunt Meredith do the lifting spell now, everyone be on alert, the battle is about to start."

While linking Zeke and our warriors, I tap on Keith's leg and nod towards the back of the room. He turns and gives me a wink and a smile. It seems he is excited for this battle to start, at the least ready for it.

Watching the back of the room, I notice an energy wall dissolve and expose those hidden previously. It is difficult to see how many opposing forces are in that room and if there is a portal set up to allow more in as the battle continues. The other wolves in the room need to be warned. I jump from my chair, a scowl marring my face, and angrily point to the back of the room.

"What is this?" I yell out. "Who dares bring warriors into this meeting hall? Who dares attempt to attack Whispering Winds during a peaceful meeting? Stand now and show yourself!"

As a collective all the heads turn, looking in the direction of my pointed finger. Growls break out around the room, as they see they have been betrayed. All the wolves in attendance are on their feet, ready to battle, the after-effects from the wine last night forgotten.

Blaine jumps to his feet, followed by his Beta and Gamma. "That would be me. The Collective will not let this happen, the species will be segregated, and the blood lines purified. We will no longer have mixing of the races. Starting with the death of all the Alphas here."

With that his warriors rush into the room, followed by witches, fairies, and vampires.

The Alphas in attendance let out more growls, some shift, while others elongate their claws and snouts, then begin engaging with the threat before them. Aunt Meredith drops the shield, and our people enter the fight. Ashley and I remain in our human forms for now, while Keith has shifted into Aspen. We stand in a tight circle, backs towards each other, prepared for the onslaught about to hit us.

Ashley is merciless, even in human form, she has elongated her claws and is ripping out throats as fast as they come at her. The bodies are beginning to pile up and she is covered in red. Keith, or Aspen, is not looking much better, also covered from head to toe. He is a force to be reckoned with, tearing down foe after foe. I could not have better protectors around me.

Currently, I am taking on a couple wolves. I recognize them from Broken Moon, they are quick and powerful, working in tandem perfectly. Brooke is sharing my mind space and has pushed her strength forward for me. I dig my claws into the shoulder of the closest wolf and send him flying to the back of the room. While in the middle of the throw, I feel a stabbing pain in my hip, looking down there are claw marks deep in the tissue, blood running down.

The wolf comes in for another attack, and I block it, sending out my right hand, I catch hold of his neck, using more power than I realize, I end up decapitating the wolf. As soon as that wolf is down there is another one coming at me. The onslaught seems to never end.

Aunt Meredith is working with two witches and a Fae to bind a dark witch. I did not realize how much power it took to contain them. The witches are doing a chanting spell, while the Fae is blocking any attack the dark witch is able to send off. Luckily not all our attacking enemies have dark magic, but there is a good number. It will take Aunt Meredith and the others a while to bind them all.

Looking up there is a witch sending a fireball towards Ashley. I throw up a block around Ashley with one hand and send an energy burst to the witch, sending her through the back wall. Her scream of frustration tears through the building and in no time, she is back, attacking with a vengeance. She is quick sending off the fireballs, now all directed at me. She appears to have the fire element, wonderful, I call on the water and bring in a wave that washes over and immobilizes her. That should work for a while at least.

As we continue to battle a link comes in from the warriors with the trolls, "We have eliminated the threat to the East, coming back now to help engage at the packhouse. Sounds like quite the battle." There is no time to respond back now, Blaine and three witches are making their way towards me.

Since the meeting hall is already destroyed from the fighting, I call in roots from the surrounding trees. They break through the floorboards and wrap around the witches with Blaine, securing them in a tight papoose. Before my eyes, the witches begin to glow, and the roots turn black and fall away. My jaw drops open, of course the three with him are dark witches. I begin sending white energy balls at them to deter them. Mom told me during our trainings these will cause the most damage to a dark witch.

Two of the witches have gone down, and are screeching in pain, the sound painful to my sensitive ears. Quickly I conjure muzzles to place on them to quiet the sound. In the time I took to do this Blaine and the other witch have almost made it to me. Keith is currently battling five wolves and Ashley has her hands full with Blaine's Beta, Gamma, and a couple others.

The pain in my hip is increasing, causing me to have not as much mobility. Brooke has been working to heal it, but she says the claws of the wolf had something on them, and it is more difficult to heal. I have been fighting for over an hour, while still losing blood. Another wolf throws himself at me, in an attempt to tackle me. I use the forward motion of his body to help propel him into the far wall, where one of our warriors rips out his throat.

There continues to be a large influx of enemies, not sure what to do, I send a large earthquake through the building. The interesting effect is anyone who swore loyalty to me as Queen is not hindered by it, only our enemies are at a loss for footing and stability. Ashley doesn't miss a beat and jumps on top of Blaine's Gamma, decapitating him, letting out an angry howl, she stalks towards his Beta, prepared to hand him the same fate.

While most of the enemy is still down, I call up more roots and secure some of the invading force to the rubble beneath them. Many were quick to return to their feet and the fight. Ashley is attempting to finish the battle with the Beta, while Keith has pounced on those down around him. My focus has been on directing the root systems, and not paying close enough attention to what is going on around me. I hear my name, screamed in fear, from Aunt Meredith's lips.

I snap my head in her direction, as I do, I feel a body slam into me, causing enough force to make me fall backward. Only there is no wall or floor that I fall into, as I raise my startled eyes, I see Blaine jump behind me, as I continue to fall, a never-ending void below me.

Chapter 69:

Return to Broken Moon

(Jasmine's POV)

My body feels as if it is falling through space, the blackest night surrounds me, all I can hear is the crackling sound of energy. I have never been in a portal before, the most I have done is a small shimmer with Maverick. A new experience to add to all my other new experiences since turning 18.

Why does my mind jump to these silly thoughts? Perhaps it is a defense mechanism, who knows. My situation is not good, Blaine jumped into the portal behind me. I am sure we are heading back to Broken Moon. Who knows what horrors await me, once we get there?

My leg is not healing so I will not be able to depend on my agility to fight, magic is going to have to be my go-to. How many am I going to have to fight off once we get to our final destination? Am I going to be back in a cell, and if so, what type of modifications have they made to it? I know escaping this time around will not be as easy as before.

"Young One, we can do this together. Have faith in your pack and protectors, we planned for this, they are coming to save you. Your leg has stopped bleeding and is starting to heal slightly. I called on your healing powers and it cleansed your system of whatever it was they used on you. I would use it, only as you must. Do your best to rely on your magic."

All too soon the falling feeling ends, and I tumble across a hard wooden floor. I spring to my feet and crouch down into a defensive stance, then look at my surroundings. There is a large four-poster king-size bed to my left against the wall, two doors across from the foot of the bed, I turn to make sure my back is not to those doors. More than likely, it is the closet and bathroom, but there could still be guards or warriors in them. A large chest of drawers with a mirror attached is up against the wall, next to the bed. I can break the mirror and use the glass as knives if I need to. Next to the dresser is another door, this must be the exit door.

Knowing there is not much time until Blaine comes through the portal, I run to the door and try the handle, of course it is locked. My best bet is to wait for him to get here and start attacking the minute he breaks the portal walls. Crouching back into my defensive stance, I wait. A few seconds later, Blaine appears, standing on his feet, a victorious smirk across his face.

Irritated by that smirk, I send a tornado at him, picking him up in the air and slamming him back to hard floor. The surprised look on his face is priceless. He must have thought I would be defenseless and scared. Not with all the training the last few months and the anger for the death of my mother. I feel I am in a much better place to deal with Blaine than the first time I was here.

Blaine slowly picks himself up off the floor, his shoulder has a bulge sticking out the front, good, his collarbone is injured. He snaps it back, letting out a small grunt. Behind him a witch begins to leave the portal.

"Hurry up and bind her, dammit!!" Blaine shouts at her.

Knowing what is coming my way, I begin sending white energy balls at her in as rapid fire as I am able. The witch begins to back up into the portal.

"You are on your own , wolf. I got her here. If you wouldn't have been so impatient, she would have already been bound." With that the witch is gone, along with the portal opening.

With my focus being on the witch, and getting bound, I fail to see Blaine sneak up next to me. He swings landing a hard blow to my left cheek, feeling a crack as he does. Pretty sure my jaw has just been broken; I will let Brooke heal it as I deal with Blaine. He comes to attack again, and I put up my hands using a force field to slam him into the far wall of the bedroom. As he slides down, I begin to throw fireballs at him.

Managing to not get hit by the fireballs, Blaine rushes me. I send a couple more fireballs his way, but he dives before they are able to hit, when he dives, he manages to catch my ankle and pull it out from under me. I fall on my backside, hard. Using my other foot, I send the heel of my boot into Blaine's nose, blood pours down his face. and he loosens his grip on my ankle.

"Stop fighting, Jasmine. The poison in your system is going to take away your energy. It is inevitable you will be mine, make this easy on yourself and accept it," Blaine growls at me.

I am not able to respond back, due to the hit I took to my jaw. I growl as I send him slamming into the ceiling, then ricocheting to the floor. His head slams off the hard floor, creating a gash above his right eye. I glare at him in defiance.

The bedroom door slams open, three wolves rush into the room, straight at me. With one hand, I let my claws grow out, with the other, I send one of the wolves back through the door, slamming into the wall across from the door. Drywall falls down around him as he slides to the floor. Turning, I dig my claws into the side of one of the wolves trying to attack me. As I have my claws in him pain erupts in my injured hip again. Looking down, Blaine has his claws deep in the already broken flesh, the last wolf grabs me, and sticks a syringe in my neck.

My claws retract, letting the wolf stuck on the end of them loose, he swings around and delivers a fist to my face, my nose cracking and blood pooling into my open mouth. My muscles are all relaxed and I feel myself falling to the floor, unable to remain standing.

"Young One, they used wolfsbane on you, a very high dose, I am not able to withstand the effects this time. Your magic still works if...you...ca. "

With that Brooke is gone. My eyelids become heavy, and I am firmly in the grasp of sleep.

Chapter 70:

Aftermath

(Alpha Alexander's POV)

Total chaos reigns over the meeting hall at this moment, on our side witches and Fae have teamed up to bind the dark witches, the wolves are protecting them, so they do not have to worry about being attacked while concentrating on their task. Trolls, vampires, and elves are outside the building fighting, also with wolf support. The aggressors are merciless and are only out for blood and death.

Bodies litter the floor, and the hardwood is now stained red. Meredith is working to bind her second witch with the lead Fae. I move in to help protect them, one of our warriors on their detail was levitated and slammed through the hall wall. Surveying the area, Jasmine is fighting off a couple witches, while Ashley and Keith are next to her fighting off whatever being is attacking.

A wolf lunges at me from my left, and I meet him head on. My attention is focused on the wolf and the battle at hand, managing to get the wolf on his back, I am focused on tearing out his throat, when I hear Meredith scream Jasmine's name. I whip my head around, decapitating the other wolf, in time to see Jasmine being pushed into a portal and Blaine jumping in behind her. A loud growl leaves my mouth.

Maverick, Angie and Muerta rush into the building at the sound of my growl, seeing Jasmine is gone. Maverick runs over grabbing Meredith and my hands, Angie grabs Keith and Ashley, while Muerta grabs Miles and Zeke, as we begin to shimmer away, I see four witches opening portals and warriors running into them. We are on our way to bring Jasmine back. I just pray to the Goddess she is able to fight off Blaine until we get there.

In what seems like only seconds, we are standing at the main gate to Broken Moon, Maverick gives me a smile and speaks.

"This is the farthest we have been on Broken Moon territory, so this is as close as we could shimmer."

I nod my understanding to him. Soon Angie and Muerta have finished shimmering with their wolves.

"Let's huddle up quickly. Ashley, you are going to take lead here," I command the group; no argument is given.

"The best bet is going to be to stay as close to the walls as possible," Ashley starts. "Ashley, if I may…," interrupts Meredith, "I can do a cloaking spell on us, along with a scent block. It may give us quicker access to the packhouse."

"Excellent idea, Meredith. Thank you for offering. Once Meredith cloaks us and hides our scents, I still want to remain close to the border wall. Less chance of running into patrols this way. They will be watching the walls but hiding in the trees for cover. Once in the packhouse we will scent her out. Let's move, we have no time to waste."

Meredith quickly places the spells on us, and we move out. We manage to get through the main gate, without any difficulty. We hug the border wall and make excellent time trekking towards the packhouse when sirens begin to sound. Blaine put in motion sensors, while his wolves and others cannot see us the sensor picked us up easily.

We stop and hold our position, there are no wolves responding to the alarm. "Last time we were here, the opposing forces were cloaked as we are now," I whisper to the group, reminding them of what we experienced.

Keeping the spells in place, we cautiously begin moving forward again, this time on hyper alert.

Breaking through the tree line, into the open field leading up to the packhouse, we continue to proceed with caution. It is unsettling there are so few warriors on post here. Did Blaine send the majority of his warriors to Whispering Winds? Was he so sure of his victory, he left his pack unprotected, or at least inadequately protected? As a former Alpha this is horrendous behavior, the safety of the pack comes first.

The packhouse door looms in front of us, Meredith brings her hands up and sends air to push against it. Without a sound the door opens, allowing us entrance, no one the wiser of the breach, as far as we know. We still have not seen a soul in the area. Proceeding into the lobby, the group stops and sniffs the air.

My eyes darken and my wolf begins to push forward, my control of him is slipping fast, a growl rips from my throat. All I smell on the air is blood, blood of my daughter. I race up the stairs, towards the scent, the rest of the group following close behind. When I get to a large wooden door, I do not hesitate, I bust it down and push my way inside, the rest of the group taking the perimeter and watching the door.

In no time at all I have Blaine pinned against the wall, my claws wrapped around his throat, as his feet try to find solid ground. "What have you done with my daughter?" I growl out, my voice more of my wolf's than my own. I wait impatiently for his answer.

Chapter 71:

Return to Broken Moon 2

(Alpha Blaine's POV)

"Take her to the cells!" I growl out to my men. "I don't want to touch her until she heals from her wounds." I sneer at her in disgust. My men don't need to know she caused me some significant injuries. "See if we can get a witch here to bind her now. The one we had ran off." The she-wolf put up a good fight, even injured from the start.

I know time is running out for us, by my calculations we have at least three hours before anyone from Whispering Winds can get here. I need to put plans in place now, the only support I have here is a few of my warriors, all our coconspirators are still at Whispering Winds fighting.

Hopefully I will heal and be able to mark and mate Jasmine before that timeline is up. "Get in my office now," I link the head of security. Reminds me, I need to look for a new Beta and Gamma. I have been going through a lot of them since being brought into the Collaborative by my grandfather.

A loud pounding sounds at my door. "Come in," I bark out at the offender. In walks my massive lead warrior, he was put in this position when I took the old one and made him my Gamma. Glaring at him, I get straight to business. "Whispering Winds is expected to arrive within the next three hours, most likely with a large group of warriors, to reclaim their Alpha. We need to be prepared with the manpower we have on hand."

He nods in understanding.

"Their Alpha is currently in our cells, until she heals. Afterwards, she will be brought to my chambers. We are waiting on a witch to arrive to bind her powers. I need to make sure she has escorts on her at all times, except for when I am in my chambers with her."

"Understood, Alpha. I will make a plan and put it into place right away."

As we are discussing our plans, one of the new sensors I had installed blares out a warning. My warrior pulls out his cellphone and pulls up an app he has saved. He turns the phone around to me.

"There are cameras in the area, this is where the alarm is sounding from."

I view the screen and I do not see anything out of place.

"Paul, are you on guard at the main gate?" I link to one of my warriors.

"Yes, Alpha. I heard the alarm sound, but we have had no movement at the gate. Everything has been clear here," Paul links back to me, knowing what my next question would be.

"How sensitive are the sensors? Paul says there have been no issues at the front gate."

"There have been a couple times they have gone off after sensing a falling branch or leaf. I was hesitant to turn it to heat sensor mode in case we ever had to deal with vampires," he explains.

"The thought process is good. Probably a limb then, the area is heavy with trees. Go ahead and get the plans in order. We do not have much time."

Once again, I am left alone in my chambers to think about what to do with Jasmine. The Collaborative needs her wolf on our side, or we are fighting an uphill battle. I am becoming impatient, waiting to hear about the witch, and to get the plan rolling. Running a hand through my hair, then punching the wall, I am taken by surprise when my door bursts open.

Spinning around, I see Alpha Alexander march into my room, the people accompanying him skirt around the room and secure it, along with the doorway. Before I can blink, I am slammed against the wall and Alexander's claws are around my neck, his spittle is hitting my face as he growls at me. He is speaking to me, but the words have not penetrated the questions I am asking myself. How did they get here so quickly and how did they bypass my security?

Alpha Alexander shakes me roughly, bringing my attention back to focus on him. "I asked you where my daughter is, you deplorable bastard! Answer me before I make it so you can never answer anyone again!" He finishes his statement by slamming my head back against the wall and squeezing my throat tighter.

Closing my eyes, I send a quick link, "Breech, wolves in my chambers and on grounds, breech."

There must be a way to save time, until some of my warriors can get to me and secure the dungeon. Scanning the room, it appears there are more wolves now than before. How can this be? Looking closely, I see three of the members shimmering in and out of my chamber, each time with more enforcements with them. Shit, vampires, how did they get vampires? There is nothing else left for me to do, looking at the Alpha, I give a sinister smile, and say, "I will never tell you where I have hidden her away. She is mine and will remain mine, for all time." Then I laugh in his face.

I am awaiting my promised death, but it never comes. As Alpha Alexander lets out a deafening roar of anger and tightens his claws, a fist strikes me, in my already broken nose, followed by another to my jaw, followed by the sound of cracking. My last thoughts are thinking my jaw is broken, as darkness takes over me.

Chapter 72:

Return to Broken Moon 3

(Alpha Keith's POV)

"My apologies for stepping in and denying you your kill, Alexander, but we can use him for questioning as well. He is the one who has been leading the raids in the area, perhaps we can find out who the members of the Collaborative are from him."

Alexander glares at me, as I shake out my hand from the punches I delivered to Blaine.

"Your logic is sound, but my emotions want to slaughter him. He has repeatedly attacked Jasmine and I must protect my daughter at all costs. His blood is being called for by the spirit of my wife. He will die at my hands."

"Very well, but prior to his death, take him to your cells and question him; torture him until you have run out of ways to make him pay for the pain he has caused your family."

"Very well," Alexander sighs out. "Maverick, can you please take him back to Whispering Winds and place him at the opposite end of the cells than Charles? We will question him once we have Jasmine back home safely."

Maverick steps forward and grabs an unconscious Blaine, shimmering out of our site.

"Ashley, you still have the lead here. Where would he place Jasmine if she is not in this room?" I direct to the rest of the group in the room.

"The best bet would be the dungeon, it will probably be guarded, by whatever warriors he has left in place. There has been no resistance to us in the packhouse. I doubt she is here, also her scent is only strong in this room due to her blood." We all nod in agreement to Ashley's statement.

"The trek from here to the dungeon is open and we will be vulnerable to any attack during that time. Last time we were here, that is how they started the battle, but they were expecting us then. Keep a close formation and watch each other's backs. This time, we destroy all in our path. Broken Moon and the Collaborative will receive a message."

With Ashley's final words we head out of Blaine's chambers, heading to the cells, where we hope to find Jasmine. If she is not there, I am not sure where we should begin to search. We will have to cross that bridge when we get there.

In no time we have managed to find our way to the front entrance, prior to heading out Ashley, Alexander, Zeke, some of the warriors and myself all shift, we want to be prepared from the onset. Meredith opens the door for us cautiously, Muerta and Angie slip out first and give the "all clear" to us.

Ashley leads the way towards the dungeons, this is my first trip here since I was at Crescent Moon for the last battle. They were not joking when they said our trek would be completely open. There is nowhere to get cover if an attack happens. They were lucky to lose so few fighters that day. Very telling about how strong this core group really is.

Soon we approach the dungeon doors with no resistance. Meredith looks at the door, then mumbles a chant and the door explodes inward, making a statement about our arrival. We jump through the opening, into a vacant landing. Putting my muzzle into the air I sniff, the other wolves are doing the same. Soon I pick up Jasmine's scent, nudging Ashley in the side, I point in the direction with my paw.

We leap down the staircase and make haste down the corridor, all of us having the scent now. Ashley slows the group down as we begin to approach openings, where opposing forces could be hiding in wait. It is very odd we have met with no resistance, on our way to her cell.

Rounding a corner, we are able to see a cell guarded by at least a dozen wolves, not being able to see the inside of the cell we cannot tell how many total we are dealing with. We know Blaine's warriors are trained to be merciless and go for the killing blow.

Ashley lets out a massive growl and jumps forward without hesitation, her jaws snapping and claws attacking at any wolf near her, soon there is blood covering the floor and I waste no time joining her. Once the wolves are cleared from the area, we see Jasmine, unconscious, in a heap on the floor. The guards apparently brought her here and dumped her.

Meredith walks forward and checks over the locks and bars, soon we have entrance into the cell. Stepping forward, I pick Jasmine up from the floor gently, and bring her to Alexander. He pushes her hair back from her face, seeing a massive black bruise on her jaw. I am assuming her jaw is broken, she has many other injuries as well. I am concerned about what they have given her for her to be this under, the only option we have is to get her back to the packhouse and to the infirmary.

Muerta comes up, grabbing onto my arm, and grasping Alexander's hand, before I know it we are at the pack hospital, right behind us Angie arrives with Meredith and Zeke, out from a portal walks Ashley, Miles and few warriors. Ashley sets up a perimeter of the grounds, as a doctor comes running towards us.

Chapter 73:

New Arrival

(Ashley's POV)

Alexander has refused to leave Jasmine's side for the last week, Zeke has taken over all duties of the pack, with the assistance of our father. Honestly, he is doing a remarkable job, Jasmine was wise to name him her Beta. Miles has taken up head on the patrols, while I give direction from Jasmine's hospital room. I refuse to let anyone, other than Keith, Claire, or Miles, take guard duty at her door.

Keith has been ensuring the training of the troops continues with assistance from Muerta and Angie, while Maverick and Meredith have been making the rounds of the other supernatural realms, explaining what has occurred. They are accompanied by the heads of the groups, who assisted us in the battle at Whispering Winds. Meredith was given permission by Alexander to act as a representative of the pack, this is significant since, she is of another species, and it speaks loudly as to the dedication of the Oscuro family to uphold the rights of all supernaturals.

Cracking open the door just a few inches, I peer into Jasmine's room, Alexander has a chair pulled up next to her bed, he is holding her hand with one of his, and brushing the other through her hair. His eyes continue to leak, as he places a gentle kiss to her brow, begging her to wake up. Jasmine is still unconscious, they gave her a large dose of Wolfsbane mixed with silver, a dose large enough to take down three normal wolves. Thankfully, her wolf has some resistance to wolfsbane, or the outcome could be much worse.

Meredith brought in a healer witch, to assist the doctors in Jasmine's recovery. Her jaw, nose, eye orbit and wrist had fractures in them, her hip was damaged by multiple stab wounds, some of them causing injury to the bone. Once the witch, or I should say, once Ivy was able to reduce the amount of silver and wolfsbane in Jasmine's system, the doctors were able to flush the rest out. Thankfully her body is healing at a normal pace for wolves, but slower than she normally heals.

Closing the door, I resume my guard stance and scope the area. There are half a dozen wolves at the main entrance, another six at the alternate entrance, we increased our border patrol by double and Zeke set up a new security system. Until Jasmine is able to retake the reins, we are doing our best to keep her safe.

"Ashley, there is a shifter at the main gate, requesting to meet Jasmine, what would you like me to do with him?" links in Miles, from his post.

"Have him wait there. I will have Claire come relieve me so I can speak with him, Zeke will accompany me. Please make sure to treat him kindly until we get there, we have all been on edge this week."

"Yes, ma'am."

A new shifter here? Who can this be?

"Ashley, this shifter is an important part of our team," Grace speaks up. "Goddess has held off sending him because he is very powerful. With his arrival, the big battle is not far off."

Grace retreats to the back of my mind. Unlike myself, Grace is not very outgoing, she is about her mission and at the moment she feels she has failed Jasmine and Brooke; however, I mirror those same feelings.

"Zeke and Claire, we have a visitor at the main gate requesting an audience with Jasmine. Grace came forward long enough to tell me he is a part of the team Goddess has put together. I know nothing else about him right now. I am headed to the main gate, Zeke, please come with me and Claire, if you could trade out guard duty with me that would be wonderful," I link out.

"Be there in just a minute to trade out with you," Claire responds quickly.

Looking up Zeke is walking towards me. I raise a questioning brow at him as he approaches.

Shrugging his shoulders, he sends me a sideways grin. "I was already on my way here to check on My Moon, when you linked, figured I would be here soon enough, there was no need to link back."

I return his smile and move forward, wrapping him in a tight hug. Having my brother by my side through this is the best gift from the Goddess, another person who knows my strengths and weaknesses without judging me. He will never hear it from me, but he is my grounding presence, no need to let it out and see his ego inflate.

While in our platonic embrace, Claire arrives and clears her throat. "Kind of difficult to defend our Queen, when your arms are not available to fight," she comments in a dry voice.

Rarely do I give acknowledgment to her comments. Like everyone else close to Jasmine, Claire feels she let her down too.

Zeke and I turn and walk away, to our meeting at the main gate, leaving Claire to glare at our backs.

Soon we arrive and meet up with an anxious Miles. "No disrespect, but the only person I know more intimidating than this guy is Jasmine. Keith is on his way over also, with the aura coming off this stranger, I thought it might be best to have another strong figure available."

Miles looks down towards the ground with this revelation, a blush creeping up to his cheeks.

"No worries, Miles. You have been wise to do so, I can feel his aura from here. Grace said he was powerful, but I didn't think it was going to be this powerful." A nervous chuckle leaves my lips. Wiping my hands on my black cargo fighting pants, I take in a deep, calming breath. Grace told me he is part of our team, I shouldn't be this nervous, he is obviously our ally.

"What have I missed out on?" Keith's voice calls out through the air. He is running towards the front gate, at a good pace. Apparently, Miles had a hint of urgency in his voice when he called for him.

"Nothing so far. We just got here and have not met with the stranger yet. Perfect timing," I respond back. "Let's not keep him waiting, though, Grace will be upset with me for taking my time in welcoming a part of our group."

We head into the waiting area, Miles shutting the door behind us. Before us stands a six-foot-eight giant, his body is lithe and muscled, glowing with a natural tan color. He turns to look at us, as we enter the room and his deep chocolate eyes fall to mine.

"I apologize for imposing on your pack at this time. I know your Alpha is recovering from injuries. My name is Nóox, or Rain, if you prefer. I am a thunderbird shifter, sent to you by the Goddess." He runs his fingers through his straight, long, nightshade hair, while casting an unsure glance our way.

A thunderbird shifter, the Goddess is smiling down on us as her favored people. No kidding he is powerful, Grace, he is as close to being a god or demigod as is possible, without being one. I am trying very hard not to stare with an open mouth at this man before me. Looking from the corners of my eyes, I see the same surprise on Zeke and Keith's faces, at least I am not the only one.

"Welcome, Nóox," I smile to him, "my wolf, Grace, told me you are to be part of our team. I am Ashley, Jasmine's lead protector, and the Blood Wolf to my right is Ezekiel, Beta of Whispering Winds, and to my left is Alpha Keith, another protector and leader of Midnight Moon."

"Very nice to meet you all." His voice is deep and husky, baritone if I had to give it an octave. "As I said previously, I know the Queen is recovering, but it is imperative I speak with her."

"Please follow us and we will take you to her room. I must inform you, though, she is still unconscious. She was given silver and wolfsbane while being held captive. We are only waiting for her to wake up. We can introduce you to her father, though, he is with her in her room."

"Thank you. I believe that will be the best option."

We set out on our way to the hospital. While in route, I link Alpha Alexander and let him know what is occurring.

Chapter 74:

Interrogating the Enemy

(Alpha Keith's POV)

Alexander has sent Claire and me to interrogate Charles and Blaine, stating he is not in a good position to question them himself. It is probably the best call; they would most likely end up dead if Alexander was here. He does not have much control over his wolf right now. The introduction of Nóox to him was almost disastrous, thankfully there is a strong aura accompanying Nóox and Ashley was able to vouch for him, based off Grace.

"Which one do you think we should deal with first?" I attempt to start some type of dialog with Claire. She has really receded into herself since Jasmine was injured. Claire sends a cold look my way, her eyes screaming at me to just let her be.

"I think, Alpha, you should let me take lead on this. I am the Gamma of this pack and the lead female warrior, well, I guess third now that we have the Midnight and Blood wolves here. Regardless, I still know my job and I am very good and very effective at it. Who knows, you may learn a few things watching me." Ahh, there seems to be some jealousy and feelings of being replaced there. It can be difficult to have your status change overnight.

"Very well, I am happy to step back and let you run the show, Claire. Allow me to remind you, though, I am an Alpha, and will be shown the respect of one, no matter if you are having an internal struggle regarding your place and duties. As far as that goes, Jasmine thinks highly enough of you to name you, her Gamma. At the moment, roles are not clearly defined, due to the constant chaos that has ensued. Trust me, though, when I tell you, once this is done, Jasmine will ensure roles are set out and clear."

Claire has enough sense about her to lower her eyes to the ground, looking ashamed. "Yes, Alpha, please accept my apology. I forgot my tongue for a moment." Raising her head, Claire looks at me with wide shimmering eyes. "When do you think she will wake up? Do you think she is in pain?"

"I think she will awaken when the Goddess deems it the right time. I do not know all that is eating at you, Claire, but please remember, we all did what was in our power to protect her. We retrieved her back and are healing her wounds. She fought to buy us time so she would not be marked and mated. Have faith, she will return to us as good as ever, the Goddess has a plan for her." I am trying to believe those very words as I speak them to Claire.

"You are correct, Alpha; we all need to have faith in the Goddess. Let's do our part, by getting answers out of these devils."

Claire straightens up and marches forward, a mission to accomplish. Following her, I am thankful to not be on the receiving end of her wrath. Whispering Winds is a pack of strong supernaturals, thank Goddess I am allied with them.

Claire leads me to the dungeon; it is ingeniously hidden on the pack grounds. If I were to attack to reclaim hostages, I would have a heck of a time finding them. We make our way down to the third level of cells. At the far end, sitting on a bare slab of concrete is Blaine. He looks a little worse for wear, his left eye is swollen shut, with a deep gash over the top, his collarbone still has a large lump on it, maybe rebroken once it healed. He is shackled to the slab, unable to walk around the cell, from the placement of his knee, he wouldn't be able to walk regardless. There must be a small dose of wolfsbane or silver in his system, keeping him from healing, but not putting him out.

"Blaine, we have come to talk to you today." I smile, noticing Claire has stripped him of his title. This should be fun, let's see how this goes.

"That is Alpha Blaine to you, she-wolf. Mind your place, before I make you mind it," Blaine growls out, with what little energy he has.

"It is doubtful you will make me do anything; however, you will be answering questions for me today. If I do not like your answer, or your answers are not forthcoming or dishonest, then you will face punishment, that will make your current wounds feel like child's play. Am I clear, Blaine?"

Blaine raises his head and spits on Claire, she lashes out, causing his head to twist to the left painfully. A small trail of blood leaks from the corner of his mouth. Blaine runs his tongue over the new wound, refusing to make any sound, he sends daggers with his eyes, towards Claire.

"Tell us what you know about the Collaborative, who the main players are and what your role was in it," Claire directs to him.

Blaine looks at her, his look full of hate. "I do not know what you are talking about. I have no knowledge of a Collaborative or whatever it is you are referring to."

"Nice try, you showed your hand on that one, while at the Alphas' meeting. You admitted in front of 110 Alphas to being a part of it. Don't go back on what you said now. Have a little integrity, have a little saving grace, you are losing it all so quickly," Claire quips back.

"Look, all I know is my pack gets contacted to do jobs, paying jobs. We are a pack of mercenaries. We don't ask questions, we just do the job and most of the time we don't know who the employer is, we never meet them. If we happened to do a couple jobs for the Collaborative, I would never know it," Blaine says with a confident smirk on his face.

"Well, we can confirm it. We have a money trail connecting you to them. As a matter of fact, we have all sort of documentation and photographic proof, connecting you to them. I really don't need you to tell me, I just was looking to see how you would be during this discussion. Now I know we can trust nothing you say. That means the only thing you are good for is a torture experiment. Enjoy your stay." Claire turns around, walking through the door of the cell and back to the stairs. There is a clanging behind us, as the guard closes the cell door.

Climbing the stairs to the second level, we walk the opposite direction to the very end of the cell block, there sits Charles, dirty and tired. He has not been as manhandled as Blaine, but he is recovering from bruising as well, small cuts and scrapes all over his body.

"Charles, just the wolf I was looking to have a conversation with today!" Claire says, in an almost joyful voice. "Do you plan on playing nice this time, or should we do some more pain therapy on you?" she chirps out, smiling at Charles. "No matter what you have planned for me, I have nothing to tell you. No information will come from me, you will remain in the dark."

"We aren't in the dark, though, Charles. When you made that plan to have your Collaborative pals attack the Alphas' meeting, we did find out some of the groups you are working with. See, I was shadowing you the entire time, I witnessed your meetings with the heads of the groups and with Blaine. I heard your words, there is nothing you can deny to me. It is because I know these things without a doubt in my being that I am able to play with you the way I have. Tell me, what hurt worse in the cuts, the acid or the lye?"

"Get out of here! Your pack will be destroyed, and I will find you to keep as my personal toy bitch." Charles lunges at the cell bars, causing Claire to let out a slightly sadistic laugh at his expense.

"Very well, Charles. Until tomorrow."

Claire leaves the cell block, as we approach the staircase once again, we hear a voice call out to us from the opposite end of the cells from Charles. "Gamma, come here to my cell, I have information to negotiate with."

Looking at me, Claire raises and eyebrow and heads towards the cell.

Inside is a man I have never seen before, it is unclear how long he has been here, this is a good time to keep my mouth shut and ears open to learn something.

"Oh, Saul, I forgot you were a guest of ours here. You may give me all the information you have, but there will be no negotiations for it." Claire glares at him, no empathy in her eyes for this wolf.

"If I am correct, you are not getting answers from your other captives. I can give you the name of the man who hired me, and his supporter," Saul attempts to entice Claire with his information.

"Saul, we already know who hired you. You were with him when Jasmine made her escape from Broken Moon. We also know who his supporter is already. You have no information that is valid to us. Hey, enjoy your nonexistence down here. Maybe we'll speak to you again in another few months." Claire waves as she walks away from his cell.

"No! Don't leave me down here! I can help, I can help!" Saul pleads as Claire continues to walk away, unphased by his outcries.

We reach the main entrance to the dungeon and head outside.

"Well, we didn't get any new information today, but they will continue to be encouraged to share with us." Claire smiles at me.

"That is fine. The next time we come to speak to them, I would like to take lead."

"Sure, Alpha Keith, no problem."

I leave Claire standing at the entrance to the dungeon and make my way to the hospital. Time to check on Jasmine and the rest of the team.

Chapter 75:

Coming Back

(Jasmine's POV)

"Brooke? Brooke, are you there?" I call out to my wolf.

"MMMmmmmm" is all I hear coming from Brooke, she is whining as if she is in pain, but the odd thing is the whining isn't in my head like normal, it is coming from my right. Momentarily I am confused and not sure what to do, finally I snap out of it and call out to her. "Keep whining for me, girl, this way I can find my way to you, keep calling out to me. It is too dark to see you in this place."

Brooke continues to whine, as I make my way through the inky blackness. Luckily for me the floor is smooth, so there is nothing to trip over, as I roam about in the dark, following the sound of my wolf. In this strange place, no heightened senses assist me, no smell, no night vision, no increased hearing. Loneliness surrounds my soul, being separated from Brooke.

Do not panic, slow steady breaths, Brooke is calling out and we will find her. My heartrate is picking up, pounding against my chest wall, causing discomfort. My breaths are shallow and quick, making me dizzy as I attempt to navigate my way. There is a thin layer of cool sweat covering my face, back and palms, my mouth is dry and negative thoughts are beginning to invade my mind, without the calming presence of Brooke there. I must hurry and find her; my life is at risk without her.

Falling to my knees, I begin crawling through the darkness, sensing she is close to me. Reaching out my hand, my fingers find soft fur, running my hand over the fur, I call out, "Brooke, is that you, girl? I have missed you so much." A whine is my only response. "You rest," I begin as I pull my body closer to her, picking up her head and laying it in my lap. "We will be here together, until you are ready. Take all the time you need to heal. I will not leave you; we are back together. I love you, Brooke, please don't leave me." Lowering my face to her head, I leave a kiss there. Soon the sounds of her soft snores fill the air around us.

While Brooke is resting, I try very hard to remember what occurred for us to end up in this odd place. Thinking is giving me a headache and soon, I find myself next to Brooke, curled up in her fur, fast asleep. It doesn't seem like we have been asleep for long when I feel a wet tongue against my cheek. Sitting up, Brooke is next to me, and she seems to have recuperated.

"You found me, Young One. Thank you for bringing us back together. It was difficult overcoming the silver and wolfsbane in our system. We were in a dangerous place, when we first arrived here, but we have been moved to a safe place, and outside sources helped us recover. Do you remember how we were injected this time?"

"I tried to remember, but it gave me a headache, causing me to fall asleep. Brooke, how did we become separated?"

"We are in a deep healing space in your mind. Protected from any influences by the external world. This allows us to heal from the poisoning, as well as the mental and physical assault we had. While here, we maintain two bodies, but will reunite when we go back. Our memory will most likely be fully restored then too. Are you ready to go back?"

"Yes, I am. We have a pack to lead, and I miss everyone. There is still a battle to prepare for."

Wrapping my arms around Brooke's neck, we hold each other close. It feels as if our bodies are being pulled into a vortex, heading toward the center, and being funneled back to our lives.

Finally, the swirling motion has stopped, there is a soft mattress under me and a strong hand, holding firmly onto mine, a soft snore reaches my ears.

Slowly, I blink open my eyes, the room is in darkness, but my night vision has returned. Looking down to my right, it is my father's hand and snores.

A smile graces my lips and I gently call out, "Daddy. Daddy, wake up."

His head snaps up at the sound of my voice, he looks at me with such concern and then overwhelming happiness. He grabs me into a bear hug. "Oh, baby girl, I was so worried about you. Thank the Goddess you came back to us." Dad cries out in my hair. Holding on to him for dear life, I do my best to absorb his strength and love. "It has been the longest week of my life, watching you lay there, unconscious, fighting to survive the poison put in you. I couldn't even help you, I couldn't help my child, but I never left you, I never went away from your side, honey."

Tears well in my eyes, as I grasp my father tighter. A week, Brooke and I were gone for a week healing. It is time to get out of this bed and back to training. While Dad and I are still in a strong embrace, the door to my hospital room busts open, in runs Ashley and Zeke, Keith on their heels, and Meredith yelling behind them to not all attack me at once. This is my family, this is what I came back for, to protect.

While everyone is talking to me and welcoming me back, I see Claire standing just outside the door. "Claire, it is good to see you. Please come in."

She enters the room but keeps her eyes downcast. This is not how Claire behaves, what is bothering this girl?

"What is wrong, Claire? You seem off."

"Alpha, you should not be worried about me when you just awoke from a week long coma. I want you to know I will not fail you again, I will protect you with all that I have."

"No one failed me, Claire. We were in the heat of battle and things happened. This is why we planned the way we did. I ended up with a few physical wounds, but he was not able to mark or mate me. You all saved me," I tell her in a quiet voice. Brooke was correct, my memory did come back.

Claire lifts her head and looks me in my eyes. She must have seen what she was looking for there, because she smiled and then wrapped me in an unexpected hug.

Laughing with my family, there comes a knock at my door. "Come in," I call out.

Miles opens the door and is followed in by an amazing specimen of a man. I lift my brow in question, and look at Miles, while tilting my head to the side a little.

"Alpha, this is Nóox, or Rain. He came to us while you were in coma. Ashley said Grace vouched for him. If this is too soon, I apologize, but he sensed you were awake and asked to be brought to you immediately."

"You did the correct thing, Miles. Thank you for doing as he requested. Apparently, everyone else forgot we had a guest," I tease with a smile on my face, eyes lighting up. "Please come in, Nóox; Miles, would you please grab a couple more chairs, one for Nóox and you."

"You want me to stay, Alpha?" Miles asks in surprise.

"Of course. You are part of the family, you have been by my side, during every moment. Without you and the rest of this group, I would not be here now."

Miles nods and leaves the room.

"Well, I guess the welcoming is over, and it is back to business as usual. Who would like to catch me up on all that has happened, after Nóox tells his tale?"

Chapter 76:

Nóox

(Nóox' POV)

Miles, one of the Queen's chosen warriors, escorts me to her room. Even though the Blood Wolf has vouched for me, and the Queen's father has accepted me, I am not left alone. Until the Queen herself gives the final approval, my status goes no farther than a guest here. I have to hide a smile, knowing our Queen is well looked after.

Entering through the hospital doors, I need to steady myself. Hospitals have always brought out the worst anxiety in me, even though more than death occurs in these walls, the smell that accompanies death is the prominent smell that assaults my nose. My thunderbird has a definite aversion to death, our nemesis comes from the underworld and this smell always is on him.

Wiláu, or Arrow, my thunderbird, is highly unsettled. I am doing everything I can to keep him down. The last thing we need to happen is for Wiláu to make an unwelcome appearance. The plan is to keep him hidden until the major battle. The Goddess is not comfortable with the dark witches called in to assist the other side, hence my arrival to Whispering Winds.

As we approach the door, there is more noise than normal coming from it, Miles smiles and opens the door, entering the hospital room, introducing me to the Queen. Even coming out of a coma, she is breathtaking and has a strong sense of power coming off her.

Looking around the room, I am not sure how we are going to fit any more bodies in here, but the Queen has asked for two more chairs to be brought in. Again, a smile crosses my face, this Queen holds all these people dear and refuses to send any on their way. She is also saving me from having to tell my tale many times over. The Goddess has not chosen wrong in picking this woman to rule the supernatural.

Two more chairs have been set in the room, Meredith has vacated her seat, allowing me to be closer to Queen Jasmine. Settling myself, I look into the green eyes of my Queen and give her a warm smile before beginning my story.

"Queen Jasmine, my name is Nóox, or Rain, whichever is easiest for you to say or remember. My name comes from my people's native language. My family has seven sons, I am the fourth son, all of us are warriors, but I particularly was chosen to serve the Goddess, and she has sent me here to help train and battle with you, there is concern about the dark magic the other side is using and my people are trained our entire lives to battle the evil," I begin my tale, speaking in a low, calm voice.

"Nóox, it is nice to meet you, I am not sure where you have journeyed from, but welcome to Whispering Winds. Hopefully pleasant accommodations have been made for you while I continued to recover." Jasmine smiles at me, the warmth lighting up her eyes.

"Yes, my Queen, everything is great. Thank you." Now that the initial pleasantries are out of the way, my story can continue.

"My people are thunderbird shifters; we are best known for fighting against the forces of the underworld and any dark magic. It humbles me to be sent here to assist you, and when the time comes, my people will stand with you to bring down our threat. We will be able to help protect you from the air, looking around the room, it does not appear you have any such beings that can assist with that."

Giving me a slight chuckle Queen Jasmine addresses me. "You are correct, Nóox, there are no such beings in our army at the moment. The closest we have are vampires and witches. Although I believe the fae are with us now, just no fliers that we know of yet. We are honored to have you with us and look forward to your training. Let's begin tomorrow morning, shall we?"

Many voices raise in protest to the Queen's suggestion of beginning training tomorrow, clearing my throat the room instantly goes quiet.

"If the Queen feels she is ready to train, we should support her in this. Her wolf will not let her push too hard after her ordeal, and our Queen can always forego the physical training and work on the magic aspect if necessary."

"Thank you, Nóox, finally a voice of reason on my side. That's right, people, listen to your Queen! Nóox, welcome to our wonderful hybrid family, you are a perfect fit."

Laughter has her eyes shining and a large smile is spread across her face as she teases those closest to her in this room. A light blush makes it way to my cheeks at her praise.

There are not many people I answer to as a thunderbird shifter because of our power and strength, thankfully Wiláu does not object to us following our Queen. He has accepted her, due to her nature we have seen so far, it is amazing how quickly we developed a protective constitution for her. The Goddess showed me what our Queen went through, and it will not happen again. I am amazed she has not let the ordeal change her negatively.

Standing from my chair, a smile graces my lips as I return my Queen's gaze. "Thank you for meeting with me so quickly after waking up. It is time for me to go back to my room and rest for tomorrow and allow you time with your family. When should I arrive for training in the morning?"

"Well, Nóox, training will be at five in the morning, but it is my duty to inform you that since the Goddess has named you a protector and sent you here, you are part of this family, and there is no leaving us to run back to your room. I suggest sitting back in your chair and getting to know everyone. Specifically, Keith, Maverick and Meredith, they have been doing the majority of the planning for training." My Queen points back at my chair, with a smirk on her face, while the rest of the room just nods, it is different to be accepted into a group this easily.

I sit back in my seat, look around the room and begin the daunting task of remembering names, faces and positions. Finally, a sense of belonging settles over me, and Wiláu is calm.

Chapter 77:

Late-Night Rescue

(Jasmine's POV)

The hospital finally let me discharge out to go home. My suspicion is they just wanted the constant flow of visitors in and out to stop so other patients in the hospital could rest. It feels good to know my pack loves me and is happy to have me return to them.

Once all my well-wishers have moved on for the evening, Dad and I make our way upstairs to our floor. Fatigue is quickly taking over my system, but the thought of a shower has been teasing my mind since waking up in the hospital. Kissing my father goodnight on the cheek, I open my bedroom door and head directly to the bathroom, my craving overpowering my body's desire.

The shower is a little slice of the heavens, put here by the Goddess. Clean and in the most comfortable pajamas available in my room, I slide under my comforter and snuggle into my sheets and pillow, in no time, my eyelids shut, giving way to a dreamless sleep.

"Queen! Queen! Are you able to hear us?!" barely makes it through the haze that is clouding my brain, making it very difficult to concentrate. No one else has a key to my room besides Dad, and he isn't going to yell out Queen to me. He would just shake me awake if it was imperative. The urgency of the voice won't leave the fog of my brain, though.

My eyelids begin to open, just as a pounding begins on my door. There is yelling behind it coming from Ashley, I jump out of bed and rush to the door as another message comes through mind-link.

"There has been a breach in the dungeon. Repeat, breach in the dungeon. Patrols are out looking for the escapees currently. Queen, we need you at the cells, please."

Throwing the door open, Ashley storms in, while I run to my closet and throw on the closest clothing.

"Ashley and I are on our way to you now," I respond back, while grabbing my shoes, shoving my feet into them, then grabbing Ashley's hand on the way out the door. "Ashley, get the rest of the group together, including Nóox, and meet me at the dungeons." As I am giving Ashley direction, Keith runs out of his room on our floor. "Great, Keith, escort me while Ashley gets the rest of the group together. There has been a breach at the dungeon."

Keith falls into step beside me as we rush down the stairs, out the front door and straight to the dungeon. Miles is standing at the opening waiting for us, concern etched deep into his features.

Hearing us approach, Miles looks up, "My Queen, we are not sure how the prisoners escaped. The guards on duty state there was no breach through the front door. No one was aware they were gone until the routine check. We don't know specifically when they made the escape, but we do know it has not been more than an hour."

"What prisoners are gone, Miles?"

Trepidation is finding its way up my spine. There are not many prisoners in our cells, and I am feeling nauseated, hoping my suspicions are not correct.

Lowering his eyes to the ground, Miles scuffs at the earth with the toe of his boot, steadying himself for the disclosure. "Charles, Blaine and Saul are all gone. The odd thing is, the locks on their cell doors have been melted, there were no sounds to alert the guards."

"Melted? When I was captured at Broken Moon, I escaped by melting the lock on my cell. I bet anything they had help from a witch or multiple witches. We know they had dark witches working with them during the attack. They were also able to open a portal to Broken Moon. We need to get to the cells and take a look. Nóox and Aunt Meredith should be here momentarily, send them down to us right away, please."

Giving out directions, Keith and I make our way down to the first empty cell.

"This was the cell we held Charles in."

Squatting down to see better, the lock is indeed melted away, but not to the extent I had melted mine. A couple options come to mind; the first is: The witch only did the amount necessary to open the lock to lessen the chance of exposure, or secondly, the witches we are dealing with are not as strong as Aunt Meredith and myself.

Keith enters the cell looking around the edges. "All the shackles in here are broken, of course it would be silly of them to melt them on a person's body, but I was thinking maybe they were picked. Breaking them is the quickest option, though. Three wolves were broken out in less than an hour. This was a quick job."

Footsteps sound on the stairs above us. Keith and I move to the bottom of the stairs to await the rest of the group. Nóox is at the front of the group, as he lands on the concrete floor, his nose scrunches up in disgust.

"Black magic was at play here. Not strong, but dark, nonetheless," his deep baritone voice echoes through the halls.

"I must agree with you, Nóox, wonderful observation. Jasmine, isn't there a protection spell placed around this area to prevent this?" Aunt Meredith chimes in following behind him. Soon the rest of the group has made it to the landing.

"Yes, Mom put it in place when she came to the pack."

"Oh, honey," Aunt Meredith begins. "When your mom passed the spell would have been broken. You will need to place another one, soon."

Guilt rushes over me at my oversite in protecting the pack, "Very well, I will make sure I get that completed as soon as we are done in the cells."

It completely went over my head that when a witch passes all the protection spells they placed break at their death. Right now, I cannot focus on that, we need to finish in the dungeon.

"We looked at Charles' cell already, the lock was melted, and the chains were broken. We figure they were going for speed, since they were able to break out the three in less than an hour. Saul's cell is also on this floor, but Blaine was held downstairs on the third level, I am most eager to look over that cell." Nods of agreement go around the group.

Soon we stand at the open door of Blaine's cell, the smell of the witches is stronger here, Blaine must have been the last one to be broken out. Sniffing the air, I pick up on the smell of the witch who opened the portal for Blaine during the attack on Whispering Winds, a growl erupts from my throat, causing the group to turn and look at me in shock.

"One of the scents is of the same witch who opened the portal for Blaine," I manage to get out, then duck into the cell Blaine had been held in, searching for any clues or additional information.

"Miles, was Blaine tortured last night, during the last guard check?"

"No, Alpha, he wasn't touched unless it was during interrogations, as directed."

"There is fresh blood in this cell, not much, but still fresh. It appears he was beaten before he was allowed to portal out. Who would have beaten him, though? Saul was not a high enough rank to challenge him, not strong enough, and witches prefer to not get their hands dirty if it can be helped. That only leaves Charles, but why?" I ponder out loud.

"Charles is Blaine's grandfather. I thought I had briefed that earlier," Claire calls out from beyond the cell door.

If she had, I had forgotten. Looking around the group, they all carry the same look of concern.

"Send out notice to Whispering Winds and Red Crescent there will be a pack meeting at noon today. It is mandatory for all to come. Keith, if you need to head back to your pack to brief them, I understand, they are also welcomed to join us here. We can hold the meeting on the training field, so there is room."

Thankfully we never slowed on the training, still anticipating the upcoming battle the prophecy has foretold. Not once did we think just because we had Charles and Blaine captured the threat was over, it was time to begin actual mobilization, increase our training and send out a search party. We need to know where Blaine and Charles have escaped to and what their plans are.

Chapter 78:

Rescued

(Alpha Blaine's POV)

If these mutts really want to break me and make me speak to them regarding any information I know, they are going to have to pick up their interrogation game. The skills they have are weak at best. By this time my pack would have already had all the information needed and the member would have been disposed of. Instead, I am sitting in a cell, eating three meals a day and getting beaten only when they want to talk to me. This is why they will ultimately lose the war; they are not willing to do what has to be done. Compassion is overrated.

The only thing that could possibly break me in this cell is boredom, complete, total, and utter boredom. I have been slow to heal due to the silver shackles and wolfsbane, but the pain is nothing. I have had worse given to me at the hands of my grandfather. Sounds on the stairs above me pull me out of my internal thoughts.

It isn't time for another guard check, they just came through. Hopefully this isn't another pitiful interrogation attempt on me. I peer through the bars of my cell, waiting for the owners of the footsteps to reveal themselves. My eyes pop open in surprise as I see the distinct, intimidating figure of my grandfather present itself. Behind him is Saul and three witches. A smile spreads across my face, we are on our way out of here.

"I wanted to leave you here, but was informed if that happened, then many supporters would turn their backs on the Collaborative. You should thank them for your worthless life," Grandfather sneers at me through the silver separating us.

As we stare each other down, the creaking of the cell door opening hits my ears.

Grandfather enters my cell and stands before me; fury is coming off him in waves. I know I should not speak my mind to him, but this time, I am just unable to hold my words.

"At least I was captured in the heat of battle, instead of being found out due to carelessness. Seems your life is just as worthless as mine." All the scorn and contempt I can muster comes out in those few words.

He moves so quickly I do not see the right fist coming at me until it connects to my stomach, then Grandfather brings his knee up into my nose, the crunching sound assuring me it is broken again, the knee is followed by a left to the jaw that sends me to the ground. Instead of leaving my eyes focused on the ground like all the other times, I glare into the merciless eyes of my grandfather.

The unspoken message of "wait until I am out of this silver and my body is healed, old man" resonates through my body and eyes. One of the witches comes over and breaks my chains, then Saul assists me to stand. The other two witches have opened portals, Saul and I pass through one, while my grandfather and the third witch pass through the other.

Leaving the portal, we find ourselves in a new place, we did not return to Broken Moon. "Where have we come to?" I direct my question to any of the witches with us.

"The Collaborative requested we bring you to a new base of operations. From now on you will be working from here, with more oversite from the Collaborative and less from your grandfather. They see something in you, but feel he is holding you back from your true potential. Welcome to your new home, Vengeance's Gate," the apparent leader of the witches tells me, then they vanish from the room.

Looking over at Saul, we share a confused look. The room we were delivered to appears to be an office. There is a large mahogany desk along the back wall, with a black leather chair seated behind it. On the left wall is a set of double doors that presumptively lead to a balcony or deck, next to the double doors is a black leather couch between two black leather armchairs, a small glass table located in front of the couch. On the right wall are maps and a large table set up to discuss strategy. The room is overall dark, and much to my liking.

Behind us the main door to the room opens, spinning around we see four people entering the room. Saul and I look at them, waiting for them to all be situated.

"Welcome," a tall man with ebony hair and skin speaks to us. "It is nice to see we were able to break you free without any trouble from Whispering Winds. I am Scion, my people come from the vampire race; to my right is Dusk, her people come from the elves race; to my direct left is Murick, his people come from the fae; and this is Elise, a representative from the witches, Victoria will be with us tomorrow. Your grandfather will still be in place to assist us, but with him losing his seat on the council, he is not of much use to us now. We want you to be our main werewolf representative, Blaine. Also, we do request you make Saul your Beta, we know your last couple have not survived your last few battles. Pity, I liked the bloodlust of your first Beta."

"What about my wolves at Broken Moon?"

"We will be bringing your warriors here. The plan is to move them under the cloak of night, and only a truck full or two at a time. The total move will take close to a month. We do not want to cause suspicion in the area. We have members in the area, who will continue to carry out small attacks, as Broken Moon was doing. We need to give the appearance all is normal."

"Very well, I am happy to call Vengeance's Gate my new home, and I am proud to serve next to you all."

An evil smirk crosses my lips knowing Grandfather has been demoted.

The name of my new pack lands is perfect, vengeance will be ours.

"Get yourself settled, rest, heal and at 0600, we will meet back in this room to commence planning. From here on out wolves are not the only members pushing forward. It is time we acted like a Collaborative to take out the Midnight Wolf and her people, that is the only mission we have. I will have a servant show you to your rooms."

"A mission I can support, Scion. We will see you all in the morning."

The servant directs Saul and me to a staircase off the main foyer. We travel up six flights of stairs before we make it to our rooms. Bidding Saul a good evening, I enter my room and locate the bathroom. First thing is to get the dirt of the cells off me.

Chapter 79:

Pack Meeting

(Jasmine's POV)

Sleep evaded me for the rest of the evening, where did our prisoners get away to? Even though there is supposed to be a guard with me at all times due to the heightened security threats, I opted to go out for a run alone, to attempt to clear my mind. Brooke has not been able to stretch her legs for a while now, this run will do both of us good.

Giving Brooke control we take off through the forest, the breeze so refreshing through our fur. The feel of the earth, cool and spongy under my paws, the smell of rain fresh in the air, the bite of the wind on our snout. Winter is almost upon us, the positive is this region tends to have mild winters, lots of rain, but little snow or ice. Our forces will continue to train, so the elements and terrain will not be an issue.

Brooke slows down to a walk, we are still deep in the forest, looking around I realize she has brought us to our old training area.

"Brooke, why did you bring us here?"

"Young One, we have been doing much training, but none know of my ability to perform magic while in wolf form. It would not be wise to lose those skills. We are here so we can continue to practice in secret. We need to add this back into our daily training, this could be imperative during the war."

"Correct as always, Brooke. Are we healed enough to go back to sparring?"

"Yes, Young One, you may spar today. I am excited to see what Nóox has planned for our training, it is not common to be coached by a thunderbird.

The Goddess is looking down on us favorably, we are pleasing her in our actions and behaviors."

"It is good to know I have not disappointed her. Some of the actions taken against Broken Moon were not pure of heart. There was some revenge there too."

"Yes, but we did not kill anyone in cold blood. Blaine is still alive because you will not kill without a valid reason. Young One, your heart is still pure."

An hour later, Brooke is giddy with all the effort we have put forth. She really enjoys using magic, this is the only new aspect for her, she has never been hosted to a human with this power, the battles and upcoming war are all old hat, the normal of her reemergence.

"Oh, Young One, my mind is clear, this training has been fun. It is time to return to the packhouse and prepare for our training and pack meeting," Brooke sighs through our link. Back to business as usual. "Young One, there is another presence here, it is new, but I am not sure where it is coming from."

I spin in a full circle slowly, looking over the area around us, sending out a spell, there are no areas of hidden magic, the grounds are clear. Behind me there is a rustling of...wings? Placing one foot behind the other, I aboutface, my eyes falling on an enormous, beautiful bird; before my eyes, the head falls backwards and the feathers fall to the ground, leaving in place a fully clothed Nóox.

Luckily Mom found a spell that would allow Ashley and me to shift back clothed, so we wouldn't run into awkward situations such as this. We shift back to human form and look into the deep chocolate pools that belong to Nóox.

"My Queen, I apologize for startling you. You left the house without an escort, as you have agreed not to do, Wiláu and myself did not want to leave you unguarded. How many people know your wolf can perform your magic, My Queen?"

"Please, call me Jasmine. How many people know? Well...there is you, me, and our animals. Thank you for coming to watch over us, you were correct in your actions, where I was not." The need to explain myself is strong, so the words continue to leave my mouth. "We needed to clear our mind after viewing the cells, sleep wouldn't come back to us, so we thought a run and some training was the best plan." My eyes are lowered to the ground, as if we were a child with our hand caught in the cookie jar.

"Escaped prisoners can cause stress, especially when their whereabouts are unknown, plus you have the looming pack meeting, to tell your pack about them. The supernatural world needs you, now more than ever, please, your safety is paramount. Now that I am privy to your secret, it would honor me to accompany you on these early morning runs and trainings. We will keep this between ourselves. Your wolf has not exposed this yet for a reason, and we must trust her fully."

A smile breaks out across my face and my eyes raise to meet his again. "Thank you, Nóox, we plan on training prior to our group training every morning. If you have any suggestions, we would be more than happy to hear them."

He just nods to me, and we depart the area, headed back to the main training grounds, leaving now we will make it just on time.

Three hours later, my body is exhausted, the group insisted we take training easy today, but I quickly overruled that thought. Now, it seems maybe they were in the correct mind frame. A hot shower is calling out my name and then preparations for the pack meeting take precedence.

It is time Red Crescent was also informed about what is going to be happening with their pack. Zeke and I have managed to sit down and hash over the plans. We included input from the Beta and Gamma of Red Crescent as well as Dad, Mark, Simon, Keith, and Claire. Midnight Moon is going to also join the meeting even though all the information does not pertain to them, they will be excused after the information regarding the escaped prisoners and the plans moving forward regarding the war are discussed.

Noon comes quickly, and even though the majority of the information is put together and prepared, I still feel as though a couple more hours would be wonderful. Staring out across the field at the many pairs of eyes on me, my heartrate picks up and my palms become sweaty. Public speaking is not my forte, but it is something that I must adapt to.

Clearing my voice, I begin to address the crowd, "Thank you, Whispering Winds, Red Crescent and Midnight Moon, for coming today." A light giggle goes through the crowd and a smile graces my lips. "I know it is a mandatory meeting, but your efforts to be here are still appreciated. First, for those who are not aware, we would like to make introductions to the cadre on the podium. The member will step forward as I call out their name and what their role is. I am Alpha Jasmine Oscuro of the Whispering Winds and Red Crescent packs; I am also the Midnight Wolf."

Whispers begin circulating around the grounds.

"Silence would be appreciated so we can move through this swiftly," I remind the packs.

Within ten minutes, introductions have been made to the entire group on the stage. The Beta and Gamma from Red Crescent are on stage with us, we thought it would help the pack feel comfortable to know members are present who know them and the pack, during our discussions.

"The reason for this meeting is to inform you all, three prisoners were broken out of the dungeons last night. Saul, Charles, and Blaine were all set free from their confines. There were no injuries or deaths caused to any wolves, it appears the individuals responsible for the break-out used witches to portal in and out. A protection spell has been put into place around all three packs to keep this from happening in the future. As long as I am alive the spell will hold. Currently trackers and warriors from all three packs are out looking for these individuals. We have eyes on Broken Moon, watching for any abnormal behaviors or movements from them."

Concern and fear are the main emotions etched on the faces of those in the crowd before me.

"There will be an increase of traffic to Whispering Winds. This pack will be the main staging area for training of all supernaturals, who will be fighting in this war. In a week's time, we will host the heads to all supernatural communities, please ensure to be hospitable, but also keep a heightened sense of security about you. Any abnormal or questionable behaviors should be directed to any member currently standing on this stage."

The crowd continues to actively listen.

"Training will move to twice daily for non-warrior wolves, all warrior wolves will train three times daily, while alternating patrols and other duties. Training will include how to battle against those who possess magic, such as witches. Aunt Meredith and I will be two of the trainers for this. Maverick and his team will work with us to teach defense against vampires. Our goal is to go into this war as prepared as we can be. Are there any questions regarding the escape, security or training?" I open the floor to the wolves in the group before me.

Murmurs are heard spreading around the field.

"Alpha Jasmine, will warriors who have retired be allowed to go back into the warrior ranks and have more advanced training?" comes the first question.

"If a retired warrior wants to come back to the ranks, they will be welcomed back, assuming they meet the requirements. It is not being mandated at this time, though."

"What are we going to do about the children and elderly? Are there enough bunkers to house everyone? Is our medical staff adequate for what we will be facing?" inquires another voice.

"Ezekiel has been taking a census so we have real numbers to determine our bunker situation. Based off these findings we will build more if needed. We will be visiting the hospital and speaking with the doctors and nurses to see where any short falls are and building up from there. Our children will be taught basic self-defense tactics just to help ensure their safety."

The group before me remains quiet after the last question was answered, we wait another five minutes to give everyone a chance to speak.

"The times before us are critical, we will be having regular meetings to keep everyone updated. If questions come up before the next meeting, again please address them to any of the members standing on this stage. Midnight Moon, thank you for joining us today, if Alpha Keith gives the okay, you are all dismissed. Whispering Winds and Red Crescent, please remain, we have additional information regarding the merging of our packs to discuss."

Stepping back from the podium, Alpha Keith takes my place. "Midnight Moon, you are dismissed back to your duties. Thank you for making the journey here today. Beta Andrew and Gamma Daniel will be your points of contact, when I am not on pack grounds."

"Everyone may take a ten-minute break and then reassemble, if you have been asked to stay," I call out.

Chapter 80:

Pack Meeting 2

(Jasmine's POV)

After ten minutes has come to an end the members of Whispering Winds and Red Crescent are assembled in front of the podium again. Watching the emotions play over the faces of the members, it is easy to tell anxiousness and uncertainty are the main emotions at play, hopefully we will be able to dispel most of those feelings with this meeting today.

"It has been a couple weeks now since Alpha Mason named me as heir to Red Crescent and turned over the Alpha position. He has been kind enough to continue running the pack along with Beta Clark and Gamma Richard, while I was recovering from my ordeal. A plan has been put into place, with input from your outgoing Alpha, your Beta and Gamma. Today we are discussing the future of Whispering Winds and Red Crescent."

Throughout the crowd nods are seen, along with a few side comments.

"A new packhouse will be built on the boundary line that used to exist between the packs. This will allow easier access to both packs, the exact location is not known yet, we plan on scouting soon, to decide on placement. The current packhouses of both packs will remain. The plan is to utilize the first two to three floors for pack members and the other floors to accommodate longterm guests. Pack members will not be forced to move from current housing, family housing will be built closer to the new packhouse for those who wish to move."

As I pause, there are again side comments going around the group, but most seem to be positive.

"When the war has come to an end and I am crowned Queen, the combined packs will become the Royal Pack, until that time, we will go by the combined name of Whispering Red Winds. Beta Clark and Gamma Richard will continue to carry on as the Beta and Gamma until we are able to build the new packhouse and become the Royal Pack. At that time if they choose, they can remain as dual Beta and Gamma, or retire. A complete inventory will be conducted of the former Red Crescent, Beta Ezekiel and Beta Clark will be running this, please assist them as requested. Under this new pack all members will retain their current ranks. It behooves us to have duplicate bunkers, hospitals, schools, kitchens, and warriors. When we combine to the Royal Pack, no one will be displaced. Standing true to the rule I was raised under, members will be allowed to test for any staff position that is open, as long as the requirements are met. Information will be going out in the next couple weeks with the openings. Any questions?"

"Alpha Jasmine, how are we planning to feed the expected increase in supernaturals? Most of the food for both packs is raised and grown locally."

"This is true. We located fifteen acres on the boundary line, split by the old line. With the merging this land is open, allowing us to prep it for orchard and garden use. The Gammas have spoken with those who raise the meat, and we will increase our herd size, the managers are already looking at purchasing more. Alpha Keith has also agreed to assist in supplementing since many of his warriors will be training here full time. In the meantime, we will need to purchase from the local economy. Meetings will be held with all kitchen staff to discuss dietary requirements of guests staying with us, so far all members have been impressive ensuring proper nutrition for the protectors and trainers sent to us already. Did this answer your question?"

"Yes, Alpha."

"Anyone else have anything for any of us?"

"Will we need to expand our schools to allow for the other supernaturals coming here to send their children? If this is going to become the base camp and then Royal Pack, it is presumptive an increase in children will be seen."

"I will have a better answer regarding that for you after the meeting next week. There are still some things that are not worked out, and that is one of them. It is on the radar, and one of the priorities we will be discussing. What I would like is for teaching staff to email former Alphas Alexander and Mason with information regarding needs and concerns. They will be the points for education concerns. Next?"

"Alpha Jasmine, I mean no disrespect, but you are a female Alpha, an unmated female Alpha, who is supposed to take up the duties of Luna under you, if your father is heading up the education platform and your Aunt Meredith is an appointed protector and trainer?"

"No disrespect taken, that is a fair question. Luna Rebecca has been gracious enough to offer her assistance, and we have accepted. She will retain her title as Luna, not to be preceded with former, she is working under my authority."

With this announcement a cheer goes up amongst the crowd. Luna Rebecca is very well known and respected by both packs, to many in the former Whispering Winds, she was a second mother and a second Luna. That is how close our families are.

"Are there any more questions for us?" A span of a few minutes is allowed to go by. "Very well then, if anything does come to mind, please feel free to reach out to anyone on this stage. Have a wonderful day, you are all excused to go back to your duties and business." I give them all a last smile as I back away from the podium and turn to the group behind me.

"Luna Rebecca, Ezekiel, Angie and Aunt Meredith, can the four of you please get together to plan the conference next week? It would be best to have everyone arrive Friday morning and depart Sunday late afternoon, meetings to begin on Friday at 1 P.M. Please make sure to invite the heads of all supernatural groups. I would appreciate a ball planned for Saturday evening, if we can make that happen on short notice. Thank you."

They depart the training field, heading back to the packhouse, conversation already flowing between them. I have no doubts this will be planned exceptionally well, and Luna Rebecca will most likely end up with the brunt of the work, while the other members have split duties.

"Dad and Alpha Mason, if the two of you could please begin with walkthroughs of both schools today, then develop preliminary plans to present at the conference next week, that would be very helpful."

"Absolutely, Jazz, we will saunter over to the schoolhouse now and start. Most of the kids should be out of school for the day and I will mind-link the principal to meet us." Dad gives me a kiss on the forehead before moving out.

Alpha Mason gives me a beaming smile, also followed by a kiss on the forehead. Goddess has blessed me with an amazing support system.

"Gamma Claire and Gamma Richard, I need the two of you to please get together and plan the schedules for the warriors to either attend or run trainings. Do not be afraid to use higher ranks on patrol if needed, to include myself. We all need to pull extra duties to make this happen. As additional warriors come in, we should feel some of the burden lessen on our pack."

Curt nods are received from them both and they move away to begin their process.

"Beta Clark, you are solely in charge of the gardens and pastures, they are the most squared-away areas, and the managers are well on the way to ensuring we have what we need in place. Just act as the point of contact for me, please."

Clark places a hand on my shoulder and gives a gentle squeeze, smiles at me, and moves to take care of his assigned detail. He has been like an uncle to me growing up and it pleases me to be able to keep him in his position.

"Miles and Muerta, the two of you are responsible for setting up surveillance on Broken Moon and locating our escapees. I will need daily updates on this. Miles, correct me if I am wrong, but isn't our equipment still in place from our previous surveillance mission?"

"Yes, Alpha, it is still in place. Beta Ezekiel set it up so the elements would not affect it. We had agreed prior to setting out that day to leave it in place long term."

"Wonderful, let's pull the audio and video from the day of the escape, see if anything has been happening. I doubt they would go back to Broken Moon, but they may try to move the warriors out, to a new location. If they are smart, they will make these movements over an extended timetable, so watch for anything that is out of normal for that pack."

"Yes, Alpha."

Alpha Keith, Maverick, Nóox, Ashley and I remain standing on the stage.

"Well, I guess we can visit the kitchens. We have a representative from all groups on grounds. Is anyone familiar with troll, fairy or elven diets? We will also be the team responsible for setting up training plans, not the rotations, but the actual plans."

"The kitchen staff should still have menu ideas from when the allies were here during the Alphas' meeting." Ashley offers up.

That is correct, they did pass on dietary restrictions and such while they were here, that had slipped my mind. We will just need to have this staff share with the staff on the other side of the pack lands.

"Alright. Once we finish at this kitchen, we can scout for a good packhouse location on our way to the other kitchen, two birds one stone, am I right?"

Everyone nods in agreement, we head off to the kitchen, maybe we can sneak away with a snack while we are there.

Chapter 81:

The Collaborative

(Alpha Blaine's POV)

BEEP. BEEP. BEEP. BEEP.

What in the hell is that annoying sound? Why is it sounding in my cell? It takes a couple minutes for my fog-covered brain to realize we aren't in the cell anymore. A soft mattress lays beneath my body, covered by a deep burgundy comforter, my skin is clean, along with my hair and teeth, strength is beginning to reenter this tired and beaten body of mine.

A smile spreads across my face, as I stretch out, hands hitting the headboard and groan in pleasure at my new surroundings. The memories of last night come flooding back. I am free of Whispering Winds, free to carry out my revenge on them. How dare they imprison me!

The Collaborative has decided to back me and demote my grandfather; what a glorious morning this is. There is no time for me to lay here and bask in all that occurred. We have a meeting to begin planning the downfall of our enemies, of my ex-mate. Excitement runs through my veins. I jump from the bed, feeling more energy than my body actually has, and move towards the closet.

Exiting my room to find the meeting hall, I soon realize this place is a labyrinth. A house servant had shown Saul and me to our rooms last night, and I did not pay attention to the route we took, soon I run into Saul, also wandering around this maze, trying to find his way out.

"Good morning, Saul, my new Beta, you don't happen to remember where the staircase is, do you?"

"No. I thought I was going in the correct direction, but I seem to be getting turned around."

Saul and I turn our heads at the sound of soft footsteps in the hallway, rounding the corner is a petite blonde girl, probably no more than 14 years old, her blue eyes land on us and widen in surprise.

"Pardon me, Alpha! I apologize for not making it to your room before you were ready to depart. I am here to show you to the conference room, sir," she blurts out in a quiet voice, keeping her eyes focused on the ground in front of her.

"Very well, let's be on our way then. I do not want to keep the others waiting," I snap at the young girl. It is because of her we will be late, and I despise being late. I will make sure to have a different servant assigned to me.

The young girl bobs her head, turns on her heel and begins to lead us towards the stairs. We were on the opposite end of the floor, if this is to be my new packhouse, I will need to make sure I know all the ins and outs of it. Being lost in my own home is not acceptable.

Soon, we are in front of the office door, the door is sitting open, welcoming in all those to attend the meeting. Saul enters behind me, as he passes through, he slaps the young girl knocking her to the ground. "Do not ever fail in your tasks again, servant!" he growls out through clenched teeth, my laugh proceeds us to the meeting table.

One of the witches with Victoria jumps from her seat and uses her magic to slam Saul against the wall. She is quick to get in his face and screech at him. "That is my daughter, you dirty dog, she is not a servant! I will gut you here and now."

She pulls out a silver knife and holds it against Saul's abdomen. Victoria sends a spell her way, holding her hand.

"Enough, Elise, he was not aware. If this occurrence happens again, I will gladly let you rid us of one more mutt. Come back to the table." Victoria sends me an evil sneer. "This is not the best way to start off your first day, Blaine. I despise being here to begin with, but the power the Midnight Wolf is gathering is too much for any one supernatural to defeat on their own. Even my dark magic."

"How did you get away from Red Crescent?"

"The same way you got out of Whispering Winds. Now let's get to work. The sooner this is done, the sooner I can be away from here and treat for any fleas we may have acquired during this visit." Her animosity drips off her.

Off to my left I hear a thud, looking over Saul is on the floor. As the witch leaves him to come back to the table, she delivers one last good kick to his ribs, powerful to be sure as I hear a crack and Saul's face confirms the pain.

"Ah, Victoria, you were not here last night when we informed Blaine, he is now the main representative for the werewolves and Saul is his new Beta. Charles has been demoted. Please show them a semblance of respect. I know the two of you do not have the best working relationship, and none of us want to work together, but we have to meet our common goal, before we can thankfully segregate," Scion tersely remarks to the head witch.

Victoria sends him a nod, noting her understanding. Apparently, Scion is the head of the Collaborative.

"Thanks to the attack at Whispering Winds all trolls have stepped out of any supporting role to this endeavor, apparently the entire group sent was killed before the attack even started. We are not sure how they were discovered, but they were. So, we are down one significant group. The plan moving forward is to do smaller attacks over a lengthened timeframe, against all allies to the Midnight Wolf. The attacks will be done by specific groups, no intermingling of species." There is a pointed look to each of the members at the table.

"It is best if they are not aware of all the groups working together. Also, no species will attack the same species, except maybe the wolves, since Blaine already has a history of attacking other packs. Once we have whittled away at the allies, we can plan the last final attack against the Midnight Wolf and her followers." Scion looks around the table, he isn't asking for any questions or further ideas, he is ensuring we accept his direction.

Never being one to follow the expected path, I decide to voice my questions. "Last night you said this pack was to be the new base of operations.

If that is so, are the other species going to be coming here to train? Will all the attacks branch out from here? Also, exactly where is here?"

"Here is 50 miles southwest of Broken Moon. Yes, the plan is for all attacks to occur from this pack, this is the most centrally located pack area and when we are ready to attack Whispering Winds, we will be close enough not to exhaust our resources. Training will be occurring here. Once you are able to explore your new grounds you will see each species has their own building, kitchens and training area, no intermingling. When the war is over you will take over the rest of the buildings. It can be the hub of the werewolf world," Scion sighs out, acting like I don't have a brain in my head and am slow on the uptake.

Gritting my teeth, I just send the vamp a nod.

"Our first attack will occur in three nights. The vampires will be attacking Alpha Peter of Night Fall, one of the first to swear his allegiance to the Midnight Wolf. Soon he will regret the allegiance he has declared, and his oath will be made good."

Finally, the momentum is changing for me, I am in the inner circle, right where I belong. Let hell reign down on those who oppose us and let me be at the forefront to see the fall of the mighty. I smile to myself in satisfaction and begin to daydream of the massacre that awaits Night Fall.

Chapter 82:

Allies

(Jasmine's POV)

Once again, my body is up before the alarm goes off, even with the earlier hour. The early mornings and late evenings are beginning to catch up with me, but my mind will not shut off, allowing for more sleep. Staring at the cloud ceiling above me is accomplishing nothing, I let out a heavy sigh and swing my legs over the side of my bed, stand and stretch, then make my way to my desk in my room.

It has been two days since the pack meeting and tasks were handed out. Thankfully everything has been going smoothly and reports are coming in with all the requested information. The pack is looking a lot better than initially expected. Alpha Mason left Red Crescent in a good way when he handed it over, I didn't really expect any different.

An hour has passed since sitting down at this desk to accomplish some work, time for me to get ready for the first part of my training. Quickly stripping out of my nightclothes, I climb into my windowsill and jump, shifting midair and using my magic to gently lower me to the ground. Running towards the tree line, Nóox is there waiting for me. Once he sees me, he shifts into his thunderbird and takes to the skies, it is amazing to watch, and Brooke is speechless every time we see it.

The wind is swirling around my body, gently coaxing me into the tree line, it is as if nature is impatient for Brooke and me to be in her midst. Brooke gives in to the gentle pull and happily runs into the trees, our solace from the world. Running toward the training grounds, we notice the wind picking up again, then the faint voices of our hidden friends reach my ears.

"Our Queen, your allies are in imminent danger, you must protect them, or all will be lost. Evil is rising, building strength." Just as quickly as they came, they are gone.

Digging my paws into the ground harder, we make it to the training grounds in record time, Nóox is leaning up against his favorite tree waiting for me, Brooke lets me shift back quickly.

"Nóox, the wind spoke to me again during my run here," Nóox arches an eyebrow at me, but does not say anything or move, "they told me to protect our allies, they are in imminent danger and evil is rising and building strength. I think it best if we cancel this training and head back to the packhouse, awaken the others and get a plan in place. They did not tell me how long we have."

"There are voices in the wind that speak to you?" Nóox finally asks. "Yes, it started on my birthday after my shift. They welcomed me as

Queen. They usually only speak when there is a warning or advice to give. I guess that is why we are called Whispering Winds, and I couldn't change the name too much when combining packs."

"I know of these voices; you are indeed special, My Queen. We will go back at once and make a plan to protect those who swore allegiance to you."

Brooke quickly takes over, having me shift back into wolf form, as she runs back home, I mind-link those in my group who are connected to me.

"Wake up, everyone, there is an urgent matter to discuss, please get those who are not connected via link and meet in Dad's office, Nóox is with me, but gather the others and do it quickly, please."

"We will do as requested. Do we need to contact those at Red Crescent?"

"No, we hear you loud and clear. It is going to take some getting used to being connected. Appreciate you thought of us and keeping us in the loop. We will meet you in the office as soon as possible" comes the voice of Beta Clark. Knowing my directions will be taken care of, I turn my attention back to Brooke and the run we are on. May as well enjoy what I can of this outing be-fore we need to be serious, hopefully it will calm my nerves.

We take the stairs at the packhouse two at a time, shifting back midstride, Nóox is right behind me. We make our way up to the Alpha floor and into

Dad's office. Many tired eyes look at us as we enter the office, taking a count everyone has made it, even the Beta and Gamma from the other side of the pack lands.

"I have called you here this morning because the winds spoke to me again. They said our allies are in imminent danger, also that evil is rising and building strength. Zeke, can you please pull up the map of the region; everyone to the map table, please."

Everyone gets up from their comfortable positions to do as I asked. On the way over Ashley hands me a cup of coffee.

"Here, just the way you like it, my dear. We will discuss later why you are even up at this hour, crazy lady."

A soft giggle escapes me at the humor Ashley can still inject in this serious environment. Gladly accepting the coffee from Ash, I take a long drink and we move to the map table. "Zeke, do we have a way to mark all the ally packs?" He punches a few more buttons on the electronics part of the table then hands me a stylus. "Thanks. These are the packs that allied with us during the Alpha meeting we held." I take the time to mark all the packs.

"We do not know where the escapees have gotten off to, but I would think any attack would be concentrated to areas near us or Broken Moon. It is our responsibility to protect them all, but I think we need to put the most resources here and here." Using the stylus, I circle four packs near us and five packs near Broken Moon.

"Aunt Meredith, what type of protective spells can we use that will not deplete our energy?"

"We could use a couple different spells. The Alphas have to be willing to let us put them in place, though. I will reach out to covens in the area to see if they have already set up treaties with the packs and given protection. If not, a call from you, Alexander, or Zeke, to the Alphas could go a long way in making the treaties happen and the spells being completed."

"Great, Aunt Meredith, thanks. It would be best to let the covens know of the threat too. If they are allied with you, then they are at risk also. Maverick, the same goes for your clans."

Aunt Meredith and Maverick give me nods of understanding.

We all concentrate on the map in front of us. Keith is the first one to break the silence.

"Who was the first pack, besides mine and Red Crescent, to swear loyalty to you, Jasmine?"

"That was Alpha Peter of Night Fall, he is located to the West of Broken Moon, here." I point out their location on the map. "He swore loyalty to me the first day of the meetings. Why?"

"If I was an avenging evil force, I would weaken your forces by taking out allies, and I would take out the most loyal first, those who didn't need to be swayed by violent acts," Keith informs us.

Dad, Mason, and the others nod in agreement.

"Night Fall will be the first pack we reach out to then, followed by others in the area. Ashley and I will travel to Night Fall today with Nóox and Maverick, also a couple dozen warriors. We will depart at varying intervals and via different exits just in case we are being watched. Keith, it will be best for you to be at your pack with your Beta and Gamma, there is already a protective spell around your lands. We will let the other packs decide on if they want additional coverage or not. I will add another spell prior to leaving, one that will not allow any with ill intent from entering, pack member or no."

"Why don't you allow Angie and I to travel to Night Fall, then we can come back and shimmer everyone else to the pack? Less likely to be tracked that way," Maverick offers.

"Great suggestion. Let me reach out to Alpha Peter first, this way he isn't overly concerned when a couple vampires show up at his gates."

Maverick sends me a smile that would cause many to shiver in concern, but I know this to be his playful smile. He met Alpha Peter briefly and they got along well.

Surveying the room, all I see are faces, set in concern and determination. We will not let our allies fall; we will lessen the sacrifices their packs have to make.

"Zeke will be in charge in my absence, he will send out troops and representatives as he sees fit. Dad, please support Zeke as needed. We all know what needs to be done, let's move and keep our people safe."

Everyone departs Dad's office, except for me. Making my way to the phone, I look up the contact number for Alpha Peter and dial the number. After a couple rings the line picks up, a very sleepy Alpha Peter on the other end.

Chapter 83:

Night Fall

(Jasmine's POV)

Alpha Peter was very happy to accept our assistance and additional manpower. He has a strong pack, but not a large one, none of us know the numbers coming at us from the enemy. We have a vague educated guess at best, they have been very good at keeping their real numbers hidden.

Maverick's plan to move us undetected to Night Fall worked smoothly. Maverick and Angie drove together, then Angie brought the car back, while Maverick shimmered to Whispering Red Winds and began transporting us over. If the opposing forces have eyes on Night Fall, it appears they only had a visitor for a meeting. This works to our advantage.

Nóox was not a fan of shimmering and has informed us from now on he will fly in his thunderbird form wherever we need to go. He wasn't rude about it, but I still had to laugh at his expression of nausea and dizziness. No one thought it would affect him the way it has. Nóox is doing an aerial patrol, wanting to scope out the area, looking for threats or staging areas. He told me his thunderbird can fly higher than an eagle, but still have clear sight, his thunderbird is like a stealth fighter, amazing at every turn.

The sun is beginning to fade on the Western tree line, the pinks and purples lighting up the horizon are beautiful, the smell of cedar is in the air, calming me. Peace is not a feeling I have been able to enjoy much this year, but I appreciate the small moments I get to experience.

The icy wind begins to nip at my cheeks and nose, bringing me back to the present, pulling my hood tighter around my head, I rush to the guard shack. Alpha Peter has assigned a guard to work with each of us, this way if an event occurs, we are able to be in on the information as it comes in. The warriors we brought already integrated into the pack warriors. Throwing open the door, six guards jump to their feet.

"I apologize, guys, the wind helped me open the door more forcefully than anticipated. I am Jasmine, Alpha Peter said a guard was waiting in here to team up with me?"

One guard stepped out from the others, "My name is Clay, lead warrior to the pack, Alpha Peter has assigned me to you, My Queen. It is an honor to have you here assisting us."

"Thank you, but please call me Jasmine. It is important all packs stay safe during this time. Hopefully we will see you and some of your warriors during hosted trainings at Whispering Red Winds. It is very nice to meet all of you, but let's get going and take the first patrol." I send a smile to all the warriors in the room. It is nice to see this pack allows females to be warriors, there are some who still will not allow it.

"Do you want to run it in human or wolf form, Jasmine?"

"I prefer to stay in human form for now, no one knows we are here, and my wolf is very distinct, difficult to hide her features."

Clay nods in understanding. We head out of the guard shack and begin running to the border, we reach it in a matter of minutes.

"Clay, please pause for a moment. I want to get a feel of the earth here." He gives me a quizzical look but nods all the same.

Clay finds a tree and leans up against it, waiting for me to do what I need. In order to do this correctly I will need to tolerate the chill for a bit, stripping off my outer jacket, shoes and socks, winter wraps its icy hands around me in a gentle caress. Taking in deep breaths to control my heartrate, I close my eyes, put my hands out to my sides, palms towards the earth and connect with her. All my senses increase, the gentle footfalls of a rabbit foraging to my left causes a smile to come to my face, the winds are gentle, peace reigns in this area of the pack lands.

Standing in this spot a little longer, a dark feeling begins to seep into my soul, a hint of death comes in on the winds, all sounds of nature have gone quiet, whatever is coming is not moving by ground forces. What is this smell? It is not rogue, but I have smelled it before. My mind is desperately trying to recall where it has been scented before... Broken Moon. Oh, Goddess, we are being attacked by....

My eyes fly open, and I turn to Clay, Nóox lands forcefully in front of me before I am able to speak to the warrior.

My fearful eyes land on Nóox, "Vampires, I smell the death of them on the air and darkness is coming over the land. Did you see anything?"

"At least 100 strong, no other supernaturals mixed with them. They will arrive at this border in no less than half an hour. I can take out a good number of them from the sky if I let Wiláu take over, he detests vampires."

"Let's get our defenses set up here first. We do not want to give them any forewarning, if possible, but you do need to fight from the sky for us. Clay, mind-link the Alpha and let him know vampires are attacking. Send all my warriors to this border, they are trained to fight them. Maverick needs to get here as soon as possible."

My orders are given out, the last time I battled vampires, my mother lost her life. A shiver runs through me as I think back on that day. No time for this now, we are here to protect Night Fall and that must be my priority.

Maverick arrives in a matter of minutes to our location. "Jasmine, you asked for me as soon as possible, what is so urgent?"

"Vampires are attacking, they smell like the ones who attacked at Broken Moon, like death. Nóox said they are about 25 minutes out. What do you know about them?" As I finish my question, Ashley runs up to us, looking ready for a fight, Grace is shining through her eyes, ready for a battle.

"They are the third strongest clan, run by the darkest lord in vampire history. He is merciless and loves to see the distress and pain of those he attacks. He likes to draw out the death of those who oppose him. How many?"

"Nóox said at least 100. The forces we brought are close to a third of that, Night Fall only has about 50 warriors to assist, none trained to fight vampires. We will need you to guide us on the easiest way to dispose of them, once they are all assembled here. I know this must be difficult for you, thank you for being by my side."

"This is not a difficult choice, My Queen, these vampires cause death and havoc. We are constantly at battle with them, without this war looming. It is my honor to serve you."

Soon all the warriors are assembled in front of me, along with Alpha Peter and his Beta, the Gamma remains back in the second line to lead them and protect the packhouse, where the women, children and elderly are protected. "Night Fall and Whispering Red Winds, we will be attacked by vampires in the next few minutes. I know many of you have not battled vampires before, this clan is merciless and strong. Maverick is going to speak with you, to let you know the best way to slay this enemy." Looking at Maverick,

I send him a nod.

"The best way for us to defeat this clan is to behead them. The head needs to be clean away from the body. Once they are beheaded pierce their hearts, just to be on the safe side. Once the battle is over, we must burn all the bodies, allies, and enemies. The burning must be done quickly to prevent any possible turning of the allies and any rebirth to the clan members."

As Maverick finishes, Nóox lands before us, whispers are heard through the ranks. This is the first time any of them have seen a thunderbird. Wiláu's coloring is similar to Brooke's, he is light blue at the ends of his feathers moving into a dark midnight color, a white streak runs from his eyes, over his head and across his wingspan.

"The vampires are five miles out and closing quickly. Excuse my abruptness, but it is time to spread the defensive line. The vamps are spread over maybe a quarter-mile span. May I return to the sky and begin my attack?"

"Yes, Nóox, you are clear to take any actions you feel are necessary."

With the approval given he transforms back into Wiláu and heads to the skies.

Alpha Peter steps up, "We all heard Nóox, let's spread the ranks a little over a quarter-mile. Ensure to mix in with Whispering Red Winds warriors and remember the direction from Maverick. TO VICTORY, FOR THE QUEEN, FOR THE SUPERNATURAL!"

A loud cry rises into the air from all present.

Ashley, Maverick, Alpha Peter, Beta Cody and I stand at the front, most of the wolves have opted to only partially shift, allowing their claws to grow out, so they can use them to decapitate the vampires, but having the agility of their human form. As the anticipations grow in the ranks, the sky clouds over, thunder sounds around us as a gentle rain begins to fall, soon we see streaks of lightning coming from the sky and hear screams of pain and agony.

We see the first vamp break the tree line, Ashley and I let out a battle cry and race forward together, engaging the first vampires we meet. Ashley is soon shifted into Grace, and blood is flying around her, she has a vampire in each paw, clawing their heads out then using her sharp nails to pierce their hearts. As soon as she is done, she races to the next two. Grace is the most bloodthirsty wolf I have ever seen, but only in battle.

Brooke has come to the front of my mind, giving extra strength. Since I am still in human form, we are using a combination of magic and strength. I call up the roots from nearby trees and wrap them around the throats of the vampires, pulling tightly and running them through the flesh-like wire, then bringing them down to impale the hearts.

Looking to my right Alpha Peter is fighting against three vampires, he is a strong wolf, but not in his element against these creatures. He beheads one, but another catches him by the shoulder throwing him off into a tree. I rush to a defensive stance in front of him, as the two vampires advance on him. Brooke lashes out, removing their heads from their bodies. She purrs inside my head at the feel of their blood on her claws.

The battle continues to rage on, there seems to be a never-ending flow of them, Brooke is still feeling fresh and alert, ready for her next victim, we have a few scratches, but no significant injuries. Ashley and I continue to battle side by side, working our way through the enemy.

I feel a sharp pain in my head and close my eyes for a moment. "Someone is trying to control us, Young One. Poor fool, we are not able to be controlled. Let me locate him, we will need our Blood Wolf."

Brooke scans the area and her eyes land on a powerful male near the back of the group. He is focusing on me, using significant energy trying to take over my mind. I send an evil smirk his way, stalking towards him, eyes never faltering from his figure. Taking down any vampire that dares get in our path, we leave a bloody path to our nemesis.

Once we are 100 yards out, the vamp lets out a loud hiss and flies towards me with an amazing amount of power and energy. Bringing up my hands, I catch him in a tornado and hold him there.

"You think you can hold me, vile beast? We will kill you and all of your kind, your time on this earth is counting down, mark my words."

Grace jumps from my side, claws extended, aiming for his head. Before she is able to hit her mark, the vampire disappears along with the others still alive.

We all look around us, shocked at what has just occurred. We went from the heat of battle to nothing in the matter of a second, my eyes turned to Maverick.

"Vampire version of a retreat" is all he says to me, he moves out and begins to place vampire bodies into a pile, other wolves step in and begin the same.

Grace is highly agitated to have her kill yanked from her in that manner, she is pawing the ground and pacing.

"Take a run, Grace, we will be cleaning up here for a while. Work out your anger, Nóox will keep watch overhead as you calm down." Grace takes off in a dead run.

"Please bring all ally warriors who perished here and line them singularly. If they are from this pack, please mind-link their families for final farewells."

As the bodies come over to where I am standing, my heart grieves for the losses, but rejoices we only lost ten wolves. Using my magic, I conjure up white sheets to wrap them in, we do not want the families to see any injuries sustained. I have made a wooden pyre, to honor those we lost.

The families and pack arrive, saying their final goodbyes. The tears run down the faces of those precious to the deceased. My heart goes out to them,

I know the pain they are feeling and the battle they have ahead of them. Alpha Peter begins the ceremony, his voice softly carrying over the area. Once he is done, each member of the pack takes a torch, and as one they ignite the pyre, sending the souls of the warriors to Moon Goddess.

Once the pack has moved on Maverick and me we light the vampires on fire, staying until all that is left is ash. This pack does not need to deal with any more loss because of these vampires. Silence hangs heavily between us as we watch the flames lick at their pale flesh. Hearing footsteps we turn to see Ashley and Nóox walking towards us.

"How bad were our losses?" Ashley asks quietly.

"Night Fall lost ten warriors. None of ours fell. Maverick, is there any way to send trainers to the packs? We cannot ask the packs to send warriors to us and leave their packs undefended. I don't think this will be the last attack. We need to brainstorm, the best way to train these warriors and keep their lands safe."

Chapter 84:

After Battle

(Jasmine's POV)

Maverick, Nóox, Ashley, and I trudge our way back to the packhouse of Night Fall, we sent our warriors back, when the families departed to make sure they were safe. The woods are calm again and in harmony for being scarred by battle, the threat is gone for the moment.

We enter through the main door of the packhouse and see a quickly thrown together celebration of life taking place, honoring those who fell defending their home. A young boy, about eight years old, stomps his way to us, a look of hate glaring from his eyes. He stops in front of Maverick and spits at him.

"You and your kind killed my father! When I am old enough, I will join the Queen's Army and kill you all to avenge him!"

Gasps are heard around the room. A woman, face red in embarrassment, comes forward and gently grasps the boy by his shoulders. I put my hand up to silently request she not remove the boy.

"What is your name, young man?"

"James, My Queen."

"Very nice name; James, today there has been a lot of loss, a lot of heartache. It is not easy losing members of your family." I kneel to be at eye level with him. "We need to be careful not to blame those who are innocent. Yes,

Maverick is a vampire, but he is not part of the group who attacked this pack. He is part of this Queen's Army."

James sends another scowl towards Maverick, time to try another approach.

"Okay, James, Alpha Peter was at Whispering Red Winds when Alpha Blaine attacked the meeting. Did you hear about this?"

"Yes, Queen. I overheard Mom and Dad talking about it." Sending a sheepish look at me, he whispers, "I was supposed to be asleep."

I nod in understanding and give a conspiratorial wink. "Please call me Jasmine, James, I think we are friends now." James nods his head vigorously and stands a little taller, straightening his shoulders. "We know Alpha Blaine is part of a bad group of people. Would you be happy if other supernaturals accused your pack of also being part of the bad people, because of what Alpha Blaine did?"

"No, Jasmine. That wouldn't be fair."

"That is exactly what you are doing to Maverick and other vampires, by grouping them all in together." Realization lightens James' face, as what we are discussing begins to sink in. "There are bad people in every supernatural group, we all have to be careful about blaming an entire group or species, for the actions of a few. It is the actions we should be focused on disliking and changing."

James looks down at the floor for a long moment, scrunching up his face and nose as he thinks over our conversation. He turns his body towards Maverick and slowly raises his head up to look the vampire in the eyes. "I am sorry I said those things to you and about you." He looks back down at the floor once he is done.

Maverick kneels, reaches out his hand and gently raises the young pup's chin. "James, it makes me happy you listened to Jasmine and chose to apologize to me. That took a lot of courage and strength. It is not easy to admit when you made a mistake and own up to it. I am proud of you, proud of your actions. Your parents must be very proud of the young man you are."

"My dad died today," James whispers out, a single tear trailing down his face.

Reaching out Maverick pulls the young pup into a hug. "I do not know which wolf was your father, but all those who gave their lives today fought bravely for this pack and the supernatural world. Your father is a hero, he stood for what is right. If ever you need anything you can call out to me." Maverick reaches up, looking like he is taking something from around his neck, but there is nothing there, as he brings it over his head a necklace materializes.

"Take this necklace, James, wear it always, all you have to do is rub the stone and call out my name. I will be here in a moment. While it is around your neck it will be invisible."

A large smile spreads across James' face, he turns quickly to show his mother. She sends us a grateful look over James' head.

This must be the plan of the Collaborative. Attack those who are allied to me, with other supernatural species to cause distrust and hatred amongst the species, tear us apart from the inside, then once weak, attack us from the outside. Very smart. Smiling, it dons on me, I just received a lesson myself as I gave a lesson. Thank Goddess for the young pup.

Alpha Peter hastens over to us. "Alpha Jasmine, I apologize for James' behavior."

"There is no need, Alpha Peter. It is best he got it out, instead of letting it eat away at him. The young pup gave me some insight by allowing me a teaching opportunity. This worked out the best, for everyone involved. You should feel proud of the pups, your pack is raising. James listened and corrected his actions. Pups learn from role models, and he must have quite a few great ones to behave as he did at a young age." A smile brightens my face as this compliment is loud enough to be heard in the entire room.

"Thank you for your patience and understanding. It is our honor to serve you." Alpha Peter bows his head in respect.

"We will leave these warriors in place to help supplement and train your pack. The rest of us need to be getting back to Whispering Red Winds. Please reach out to me for anything."

"Well, there is one thing. " Alpha Peter looks down at the floor, his face turning red. "The children would like to see Nóox' thunderbird. This pack has never seen anything like him before and—"

"I am more than happy to let the young ones meet Wiláu." Nóox smiles broadly. "We just need a little room to change over, if any of you are brave enough to pet him be gentle and stroke with the direction of the feather. He will not nip or bite."

The members in the room make a large circle allowing Nóox more than enough room to transform into Wiláu. An audible gasp is heard throughout the room at the incredible size of the thunderbird, he is indeed beautiful and a sight to behold. It is a good thing the packhouse has vaulted ceilings or the roof would no longer be in place. Wiláu allows the children to pet him for about ten minutes and then shifts back. The children jump on the large man, giving him hugs.

We all give our final goodbyes and directions to the warriors remaining in place. We will be receiving daily updates on training progress. Maverick reaches out, holding Ashley and my hands to shimmer home. Nóox, staying true to his word, runs outside to shift and fly back home.

Chapter 85:

Revising Plans

(Jasmine's POV)

Maverick has shimmered us into the main meeting room, he must have sensed my desire to begin the brainstorming session on how to change training and what we can let up in manpower. This needs to be hashed out prior to the large meeting we are holding in a few days.

The core group needs to be notified we are having a meeting; thirty minutes should be more than enough time for everyone to make it to the packhouse. I leave Ashley to reach out to everyone and I make my way to the kitchen, the staff is always very helpful and are happy to prepare snacks and coffee for the meeting. There is no telling how long this session will go tonight, but it is important we make significant headway on it.

Making my way back to the meeting room, Aunt Meredith calls out to me. "Jasmine, honey, wait up. I have someone you should meet and possibly invite to the meeting this evening."

Turning around to face Aunt Meredith, my eyes fall on a tall, thin man next to her. His hair is pale and falls to his shoulders, eyes the color of a summer sky, as he smiles at me a shallow dimple shows in his left cheek.

"Welcome to Whispering Red Winds, I am Alpha Jasmine, how may I assist you today, good sir?"

Placing a smile on my face, I do my best to sound cordial, but all I really want to do is get this meeting started and not play nicely with new guests.

"Alpha Jasmine, nice to meet you. I am Prince Jasper from the Elf Kingdom, my father received your invitation to the meeting in a few days and requested I come earlier to offer our assistance in any way, be it training, additional resources. We are swearing our loyalty and sword to you."

My eyes widen at his disclosure, this is a blessing dropped down from the Goddess. Quickly, I mind-link the kitchen to let them know an elf will be amongst the meeting members and to please make sure there are snacks for him as well. "Prince Jasper, we are just heading into a meeting to discuss training. Your insight would be welcomed. Once the meeting starts, we will update you on all the happenings, with the rest of the group."

This time my smile is genuine, receiving a nod in agreement, I show the prince to the meeting room. Aunt Meredith nudges me in the side with her elbow, giving me a knowing look, of "I told you so." I smile back to her and gently shake my head; she is an amazing woman.

The kitchen staff is leaving the meeting room as Nóox and Keith walk in, finally the entire group is gathered. I have been waiting impatiently for everyone to arrive, it has only been fifteen minutes; however, I am anxious to begin. Standing to my feet, I address the room.

"I know this meeting is short notice, but after assisting Night Fall, we have discovered we need to alter our training plans for our allies. First, I would like to introduce everyone to Prince Jasper of the Elf Kingdom."

Introductions are done by going around the room, and the group introducing themselves to the prince.

"We know the Collaborative has witches, vampires, Fae, trolls and wolves working with them, at least they were part of the group that attacked here. Vampires are the ones who attacked Night Fall, no other species. It appears the Collaborative wants to tear our alliances apart from the inside. Send different species to attack others and bring about distrust once there is separation attack and take us down. Since they are attacking our allies directly, it is imperative we leave all warriors in place to defend their homes. We need to find a solution." Pausing briefly to let this information sink in, Keith takes a moment to speak up.

Aunt Meredith speaks up first, "Is it possible to have one member of each ally group send one or two warriors here, we train them and then send them back to their packs to train the rest?"

"I have thought of that, Aunt Meredith. It is a great idea; the only issue is the amount of time it will take to train all the warriors in the ally group. They will still have to attempt to defend their lands without any insight on how to battle other supernaturals."

Aunt Meredith nods her head and chews on her bottom lip in concentration. "Jasmine, we have, what, 88 wolfpacks allied to the cause? Is there a way we can send one or two warriors from our three packs to assist in training at the home bases? Once we have more allies aligned, we can send wolf trainers to those allies as well. The wolves we have can teach what they have been taught regarding fighting witches and vampires, with the prince here we can enhance our training to include elf. I think the wolves have more manpower resources than our other allies.

"It would be possible for our kingdom to send a dozen trainers, plus myself. Our kingdom is very well protected, it is difficult, if not impossible for other supernaturals to enter without an elf allowing entry. I can contact my father once this meeting is concluded, if that is what the final plan is," Prince Jasper offers, his eyes alert and body prepared for action.

"Your plan is great, Keith; it may be our best option. We can send an elf trainer to the first few packs with our trainers. Once our trainers have picked up the skills, they can take over teaching and then the elves can return home to defend their grounds. Prince Jasper, I would like for you to remain with us and train this group."

Prince Jasper nods his head to me, a smile spreading across his face. "Claire and Richard, I would like for the two of you to meet with Keith's

Gamma and come to an agreement on the trainers we will be sending out to the allies. We will need to notify all the groups at the meeting. The trainers can depart with the allies they will be training after the meeting."

Before I can wrap the meeting up there is a loud pounding at the meeting room door. Spinning around I crouch into a defensive position, the rest of the group falling in behind me, ready to meet whoever is behind the door.

"Enter!" I call out in an authoritative voice.

The office door swings open, and Miles stands before us, a grim look on his face.

"Alpha Jasmine, I have information to give you." Miles scans the room quickly, "Do you want me to relay my information with the group assembled or to you only?"

"The group is fine, Miles, this way we are all on the same page."

Everyone takes their seats and Miles begins his briefing.

"We have been observing Broken Moon as directed, there has been nothing glaringly significant, until I looked over all the data collected for the past few days. To verify the information, Muerta went in observing the pack members and gathering close intel. Broken Moon has a truck come in every evening. This truck is loaded with warriors and leaves. Muerta followed the truck to its destination, she believes there is a cloaking spell on the area. The area looks to be a wooded area, once the truck stopped, for what we assume was a gate, it disappeared. She attempted to enter but was held out by a barrier."

"Thank you for bringing this to us so quickly, Miles. It appears they are abandoning Broken Moon. Aunt Meredith, Prince Jasper, is there any way the two of you can view the area with Muerta in the morning and report back to us? We need to know what type of magic is being used and if there is a way we can break it."

"I would be very happy to escort your lovely aunt to the area and collect any intel we can."

I raise my eyebrows in my aunt's direction. She tilts her head down, a light blush coloring her cheeks. A small smile graces my lips.

"Then we have a plan set, time to adjourn this meeting and get some rest, training comes early."

Everyone stands up from their chairs, stretching their cramped muscles and leave the room.

Staying back, I clean up the refreshment area the kitchen set up, it is not fair to leave a mess for them in the morning. I am stacking dishes on a platter, when a plate appears before my eyes, I jump slightly and turn to see who is in the room with me.

Nóox sends me a smile. "I thought you could use a little help. It will make the task go quickly."

I smile back my appreciation.

Soon the room is clean, dishes are washing in the dishwasher, and tiredness is taking over my body. Nóox and I climb the stairs together, stopping in front of my room. We had our visiting guests, who are part of the core group, moved to the Alpha floor, makes contacting them easier.

"Thank you for your help, Nóox, have a good evening." He nods and continues down the hallway.

Chapter 86:

Vengeance's Gate

(Blaine's POV)

From what I understand, the vampire attack on Night Fall was a failure. Damn! Another failure, at least my pack is not a part of this one, it just goes to show the power of our enemy. We were informed my sorry excuse for a mate was there, she is always causing issues, I should have just killed her the moment I saw her in my dungeon.

There was a driving need in me to make her pay and suffer, pay for the very thought of being my mate, a dirty mixed-breed creature as herself. The dishonor it would have brought to my family name. Now here she is, bringing dishonor to our name anyway. Thwarting all our well-laid plans, bringing my grandfather down in shame and losing his seat on the council. She will atone for her misdeeds, with her life, but death will not come easy for her.

"Alpha Blaine! Do you think you could give some of your attention to the meeting?" Scion quips, bringing me back from my musings.

Sitting up straighter in my seat, placing my elbows on the table, and resting my chin on my folded hands, I do my best to give the impression of interest. This meeting was called due to the decimation of the vampires at Night Fall, it is difficult to understand why we all must be here for their lecture.

"I apologize, just attempting to think of a way to bring down Whispering Winds and their Alpha. I must have gotten lost in my thoughts." I send a disingenuous smile towards Scion.

He glares back, swirling his fingers around at his sides then brings them up quickly; my chair, with me still in it, slams against the far wall, tendrils wrap around my neck, and it feels like bindings are holding me in place. I struggle against the bonds, but the tendrils around my neck begin to constrict, cutting off my air the more I fight. Letting out a muted growl, my challenge is sent towards Scion.

"Do not disrespect me or lie to me, boy. I do not have the patience. The only reason you are here and still alive is because I allowed it; otherwise, you would rot in that cell."

Averting my eyes to the floor, my half-hearted apology comes out as a whisper. How did I manage to fall under someone worse than my grandfather, it seems my life is meant to be controlled.

Scion releases me, my chair and body crash to the floor in an intertwined mess. Slowly raising to my feet, brushing off my pants, pampering my ego and setting my chair upright, I take my seat back at the table, playing the part of a properly chastised minion.

The room is silent during this entire ordeal, no one wanting to call the wrath of Scion down on their own heads.

Looking away from me and clearing his voice, Scion continues with the meeting. "Alpha Jasmine seems to know our plans before we have the opportunity to attack, I am not sure if we have a mole in our midst, leaking out information to her or if one of her people is clairvoyant. My plan is to send one of our own into the lion's den undercover. Blaine, I need you to choose one of your wolves to go in, one she does not know."

"With all due respect, Scion," Dusk's voice cuts through the directive being delivered. "Alpha Jasmine will most likely be suspicious of a wolf just showing up now. Why don't we send in another species to be the spy? I will even volunteer myself. Prince Jasper sent out word a group will be going to Whispering Winds to work as trainers, there is no reason I could not be part of that group," she finishes, a sinister smile creeping onto her face and distorting her delicate features.

Her smile is shared by Scion. "Excellent plan; why would any of them question a trainer accompanying your prince? With your status, you could easily become part of the inner circle, regardless, you will have access to many of their areas. Who is in agreement with Dusk inserting herself into the group of trainers and becoming our spy?"

It is time for me to interject and cast some shadow on their golden plan. "If there is any doubt about you, Alpha Jasmine will have you monitored. That is how my grandfather met his fall from grace and our attack plan discovered. There are beings there who can hide their scent and appearance. What will the failsafe be?"

"We elf can detect such things, our connection to nature lets us know when there is any type of disturbance. A body, hidden or not, will spike our senses," Dusk replies condescendingly to me, she acts as if I am not able to comprehend any thought processes.

"What if the person following you is in the air? Will your senses pick that up?" I mimic her tone. "Scion already said they have a thunderbird shifter working with them, hence the fall of the vampires. What can you do against a thunderbird?"

Dusk sits quietly, glowering at me, there is no doubt in my mind, if she could conjure a weapon and send it through my heart she would. The sooner our species separate the better, I am tired of having to deal with this Collaborative already.

"Enough with this bickering. Dusk, are you able to identify if a thunderbird is following you?" Scion inquires.

"I don't know. I have never seen or dealt with a thunderbird before. This will be a new experience for me, as it was for the vampires apparently."

If the elf had fangs, she would be flashing them at Scion, no doubt in my mind. She doesn't like being told her idea is not perfect and questioned.

"Are there any other ideas to bring to the table?" Scion sends a questioning look around the table. One by one the rest of the group shake their heads, remaining quiet. "Then we will move forward with Dusk's plan; an imperfect one is better than not having one at all. We will need to be available if she needs us for anything. Dusk, as soon as you are able see how your senses respond to the thunderbird."

Chapter 87:

Meeting Dusk

(Jasmine's POV)

Yesterday we welcomed everyone to our pack for the alliance meeting, so many supernatural are attending from across the globe, there was no time for anything else besides a welcoming dinner. Luna Rebecca did an amazing job planning everything out short notice. One would think we had at least a month to prep.

True to his word, Prince Jasper brought a group of trainers with him, the initial introduction and training will start this morning. I have some apprehension about taking so many warriors out of our pack lands, but it is the best plan we have. The people must be safe, leaving packs, town, or cities without protection is not an option. No one knows what the Collaborative is truly capable of and I refuse to leave my allies vulnerable.

Brooke and I are racing to our training area, looking above me, Nóox is out of sight, but I know he is there, keeping a watchful eye. Thank Goddess for surrounding me with an amazing team. He has been helpful while training with Brooke, giving insights, and helping with form. It is nice to have someone we can speak with regarding this specific training. Nóox has become the trusted confidant I have always needed; Keith is too much like a brother for me to let him in on all the secrets of my life.

My nerves are on edge with this large group and me leading it, hopefully this training will help to calm me. We burst into the clearing and Brooke prances happily around the edge. She is always happy to practice our magic and become stronger. We are able to control all earth and wind powers, water has been tricky, but fire is by far our favorite element to learn as a team. Brooke wants to try to direct it through her eyes like a laser. During our training she behaves more like a pup than the ancient soul she really is.

We hear Wiláu land behind us, turning we see the sun shining off his feathers. He shakes his mighty head, while flapping his wings out a few times, his massive talons dig deeply into the soil at our feet. He towers over us in both his thunderbird and human form. Magnificent is the only way to describe him. In a breath, Nóox is before us, Wiláu taking a rest.

"We should work on fire today, Brooke," Nóox directs in his deep voice, while running his fingers through our fur. "I spoke with your Goddess, and she says you are not allowed to channel fire through your eyes." He smiles, I had told him about Brooke's dream. "However, you are allowed to breath it out like a dragon, is that an acceptable compromise?"

Brooke eagerly nods her head, ready to attempt mimicking a dragon. An hour later, all the trees around our training site bear the scars of our training. We have made progress but will need to heal this place before we leave, unfortunately there is not much we can do about the singes on Nóox' head, back and buttocks. Brooke hiccupped, and cast a small fireball out, none of us expected it and Nóox was facing away, taking the brunt of the force. He has assured us he will be fine and training accidents do happen.

"We need to be heading back, My Queen. More training awaits us."

Nóox turns to give enough room, before changing into Wiláu. When he turns, we have a nice view of his very muscular backside. Neither Brooke nor I could tell him we had burnt the clothing off his buttocks, and he was very exposed. We blush at the site and giggle internally to each other.

No one else is at the main training ground when we arrive, shifting back, I begin stretching, it is important to keep my muscles loose and warmed up. Wiláu is doing a patrol check prior to landing. With so many packs and allies here, we have amped up our security and patrol. As our warriors begin to show up at the training grounds, Wiláu lands, shaking the ground beneath us, letting out a screech, causing us all to cover our ears in pain.

Shifting back Nóox looks around at us. "We will train on how to deal with your sensitive hearing. One screech from my thunderbird left all of you exposed to attack. It is imperative, with the war facing us, we are as strong as possible. While it's nice to have an Alpha who can cast a spell to protect you, we cannot count on her being in all places at once."

My warriors slowly stand straight, nodding to the large man before them. They have come to respect and trust him, they know his words are not meant to criticize, but to build them into stronger warriors. After our battle at Night Fall, my warriors would follow him into any war without question.

Prince Jasper walks into the training area, followed by the trainers he brought with him. Beside him stands a petite female, her hair is a shimmery silver, with bright blue eyes and delicate features. She looks up, meeting my assessing gaze, the female elf sends a smile towards me, but it doesn't meet her eyes.

Brooke bristles and growls inside my head. "Do not trust that elf, Young One. Do not trust her but keep her close."

I send a smile back, waiting to see where this training will lead us. "Alpha Jasmine, nice to see everyone assembled and ready for our training.

Today will be an introduction only with an explanation of the way elves fight, not much on the physical side. We are planning on integrating the hand-tohand tomorrow with the other training." I nod to Prince Jasper, sliding my gaze over to the female again.

"Let me introduce you to our top female warrior elf, Dusk, she will assist me in training your group. When she heard of the plan, she was excited and adamant to join us here. There is much we can learn from her. I was thinking while she trains all of you, I can travel and begin training with other allies." Jasper sends me a pleased smile.

Dusk steps forward, holding out her hand to me. "Very nice to meet you, Alpha. You are famous in the supernatural world, being the first female werewolf hybrid to advance as you have. Such an inspiration to all, and I am honored to be teaching you our elven ways."

I take her hand in mine, giving a firm shake in return. "Welcome to Whispering Red Winds, we hope your stay is pleasant."

I introduce her to our core group, the ones she will be responsible for training. Once I get to Nóox, she lowers her eyes to the ground and pales slightly. Interesting reaction to our thunderbird shifter, I wonder what that is about. This one will be watched closely. Time to try my new form of surveillance on this one.

"Alright, everyone!" Jasper claps his hands, getting the group's attention. "Let's start with introductions to the instructor core and then begin with some basic knowledge of how the elves work and fight. It is important to know how your enemy lives, in order to fight them effectively."

Our warriors gather around, creating a circle around Jasper and the rest of his instructor cadre, ready to absorb all the information he is willing to give and better themselves. Keeping my eyes trained on Dusk, I watch her interactions with our warriors. She seems at ease and enjoys training, there is a fire in her eyes, but what does that fire burn for? Dusk definitely has my wolf and myself unsettled.

Chapter 88:

Alliance Meeting

(Jasmine's POV)

Our allies are entering at their leisure into the new meeting hall. We ended up having to tear down the old one after the attack by Blaine and his group. I have mixed feelings about this new hall, on one hand it is nice not having to relive that day every time I walk into the building, but on the other hand my mother and I designed the old building together and it feels like I have lost another part of her to that horrid wolf.

Keith stands next to me, placing a hand on my shoulder, pulling me back to the present. He looks down at me with concern in his eyes. Reaching out his other hand, he pulls out a chair from the table we have set up on a stage at the front of the meeting hall and sits down. "Where were you, Jasmine? You look sad," he quietly asks, leaning into my side so our conversation remains private.

"I was just thinking how Blaine took my mom from me, and now the last building we designed together was demolished because of him also. That wolf has taken so much from so many, and he has never been made to answer for it. I will make him answer, not just for me, but for all the supernaturals."

No other words are shared, Keith pulls me into his side and hugs me, sharing his strength. I rest my head on his shoulder and close my eyes for just a moment, appreciating the fact there are such amazing people in my life. A source of energy when I feel I have none left. They are my reason for fighting, for living, for being the Queen that Goddess has set me on the path to be.

Lips press gently to the top of my head, letting out a sigh, I sit upright in my chair, refreshed for a moment. We notice there are many curious eyes turned our way. Keith and I share a look and break out in wide mischievous smiles. Let them think what they want, I could do significantly worse than Keith as a chosen mate, if that were the case.

The remainder of the group arrives and from the last count we completed, at least one representative from each ally group is present. Time to get these meetings started, standing from my chair, I look over the group assembled before me and clear my throat.

"Welcome to Whispering Red Winds, I am Alpha Jasmine." Gesturing around and behind me, I introduce the rest of the group. "We have come together for the next couple days to discuss the threat that is facing us as supernaturals.

"Recently Night Fall pack was attacked. The interesting aspect of this is the entire offensive group were vampires, vampires known to be associated with the Collaborative. After much discussion we have come to a conclusion the Collaborative is making a drive to pull us apart from the inside, wanting to weaken us before bringing the final battle. They are trying to pit species against species and develop an air of distrust, causing us to disassemble, leaving way for them to push their ideals through without any resistance.

"With this in mind, we have opted to cancel all training sessions held at this pack; we have trained warriors we will send to ally groups to train your warriors. Prince Jasper has offered to begin traveling and training allies on elven warfare. I will open the floor at this time to discussion and questions."

For a few moments the room is filled with side chatter and discussions. We retain our seats, observing those seated before us.

"Alpha Jasmine, if you send these resources out to our packs and communities, won't it leave you at a disadvantage if they choose to attack here?" a question comes from the back.

"We have thought of that. We are positive, even with the decrease in warriors, we will be strong enough to turn back any advances. The majority of the warriors from Whispering Red Winds and Midnight Moon have been trained to fight against multiple attack styles. We know the Collaborative has werewolves, witches, Fae, vampires and trolls associated with them, based on those present when Blaine attacked Whispering Red Winds, during an Alpha Summit. We do not know if others have joined their cause or not. It is our desire to keep all allies fully manned and get the warriors trained as well as possible. It is imperative we keep all your people and homes safe."

Many heads are nodding as I finish my explanation.

"While I appreciate his enthusiasm, how is Prince Jasper supposed to train all the groups? Looking around this room, there appears to be at least 150 represented ally groups," Alpha Peter asks, doubt shining in his eyes.

I understand his concern, especially with his pack already experiencing the first losses. "Alpha Peter, I did not explain myself well. Prince Jasper brought a group of trainers with him; as they are training the warriors, we will be sending out to the ally groups, Prince Jasper and a couple of my warriors will travel and begin training packs straight away. Once the warriors are trained, they will begin training at their designated packs and communities. I apologize for the confusion."

Alpha Peter nods his head in understanding and sends a small smile my way, his shoulders begin to relax some, and he leans back in his chair.

"Alpha Jasmine, please excuse this personal question, but are you planning on taking Alpha Keith as your chosen mate? Is he to be the king ruling by your side, once the prophecy is complete?"

I look towards the back, where the question came from, attempting to find the owner of the voice. Instead, I see Dusk, peeking around the door, she does not appear to see I have noticed her. Why is she spying on this meeting? She was invited to attend as one of the representatives of the elves, and she declined, stating she would begin attending meetings once Prince Jasper set out on his journey.

"The simple, straightforward answer is no. If the Goddess sees fit to pair me with another mate, I will gladly accept, but I will not choose anyone. Alpha Keith has been a part of my family for years, he and Beta Ezekiel were best friends growing up, so I grew up around him, he has been relegated to the part of brother and protector as appointed by our Goddess.

"While I appreciate there will be questions about who will reign with me when I am appointed Queen and concerns regarding an heir once I assume the throne, but the plain fact is, the Goddess has put me on this road, and I trust she has everything figured out to protect the supernatural world. My main focus is all of you, right where my focus should be. My focus is bringing down the Collaborative and saving all our kinds. Our discussions from here forward should be about plans to support each other and fight the Collaborative, to put together contingencies for all possible actions." My voice comes out harsher than I had anticipated it to be, however, I am not going to apologize for it.

There is a war looming before us and it is ridiculous to preemptively discuss my lack of a mate. Our first step is to overthrow the Collaborative and set up a new council, protect the supernatural realm and then focus on the long picture once the people are taken care of. War is what we will focus on for now.

After another three hours of discussions and tabletops we have begun to put ideas into place. The ally group is working well together, thankfully, offering support and resources where others are lacking. As a comprehensive group, we have all we need, we are a force to be reckoned with. The Collaborative has met its match and will be put down. A new era is dawning, an era of a united supernatural world.

Chapter 89:

Dusk

(Dusk's POV)

My alarm goes off causing me to jump, I was awake before the alarm went off, lying in bed thinking over the tasks before me. Training has been happening for three months and still, the inner circle eludes me. Their group is tight knit, and the only ones allowed in on their closed-door meetings are the ones the Moon Goddess sent as protectors and trainers, apparently Prince Jasper was not sent by the Goddess, but volunteered our time and manpower, the cad. The look on our royals' faces will be priceless when we overthrow them and sentence them to death.

Scion is losing patience with me, and that vampire didn't have much to begin with. He is threatening, if I don't begin making headway soon and start offering information to the Collaborative, my appreciation of the consequences will not be positive. What else do I have left to try, eavesdropping at the meeting room door did not work, and I was almost caught because of the sensitive noses of the wolves. Placing a listening device in the room was a failure, apparently their Beta Zeke is a tech genius and has set for an automatic scan to take place prior to all meetings, frying any devices planted.

Oh, if only I had the power to mask my scent and make me invisible, that could make this easier, problem is I never know about the meetings until right before they happen. There is no way for me to get one of the Collaboratives witches here to place a spell on me before that happens.

Time for me to quit wasting my time laying around in my bed. There is snooping to be done and the early mornings are the best time. The patrol wolves are used to me now, know I am a trainer and don't question my movements, making it easy to move around the grounds.

Stretching my arms above my head, I stretch out like a feline and slowly bring my body back to center, throw my legs over the side of the bed, then run my fingers through my knotted hair. A deep yawn takes over as I look around the room, trying to decide what to do first. Restroom. Definitely. Clean up my yuck mouth and use the facilities.

Feeling like a new elf, I head off to the closet and pull out all-black clothing along with a black stocking cap to tuck my overly bright hair into. Finally dressed and ready to get on my way, the clock reads just after three in the morning, excellent sign my mind is going away.

Opening the door slowly, I peek around the edge to ensure the hall is empty. One thing I was able to pass on with greater detail was the layout of the packhouse. This building is massive, Jasmine has me staying on the third floor, this makes it easier to escape outside without being seen.

Fresh air hits my face, the change from Winter to Spring will soon be occurring, the crisp wind has a hint of warmth, a promise of new life, hopefully the change is in the favor of the Collaborative. Pulling myself back from my musings, I rush to the shadows of the walls of the packhouse. Moving along the length of the East wall, I head towards the North, coming to the end of the wall, there is the sound of movement, it carries softly in the early morning breeze.

Looking around the edge of the building there is a wolf headed to the tree line, it is still too dark to see the coloring of the wolf and who it belongs to. This is awfully early in the morning for a wolf to be heading out for a run, if there was a call to combat rogues, there would be a larger response than a lone wolf. Time for me to get to work and deliver something to Scion.

The wolf continues to run to the Northwest, before stopping, mere yards from the border boundary. I climb the nearest tree to me, being careful to remain quiet. Scoping out the scenery below me, the area appears to be a training area, one I had not been informed of. My interest is piqued, what is this wolf up to? Who is this wolf? Suddenly the wind picks up, forceful breezes almost blow my stocking cap off, once able to open my eyes again, I refocus on the area below.

Eyes widening in surprise, there between the trees stands a massive thunderbird, he is beautiful, the wolf runs up to the thunderbird and nips his tailfeathers playfully, then scooting away with a yip, before the magnificent bird can turn around and peck at them. The thunderbird and wolf circle each other for a few moments, then the bird lets out a loud screech, piercing my ears, and works up a great wind with its wings, pushing the wolf back.

To my great surprise the wolf uses its snout to work up a mini-wall of wind to counteract the thunderbirds attack. This appears to be a training between the two, but if this wolf can do magic, then it must be Jasmine. My eyes widen at the realization. Finally, there is something to share with Scion. Now I just need to get out of here undetected, a satisfied smile plays across my lips as I use the trees to make my getaway unnoticed.

Chapter 90:

Seeking Answers

(Jasmine's POV)

The month of May is sitting on our doorstep. Our warriors have been fighting in the residue left over from the Spring storms, one never knows when war or battle will find them, that is why we train in all conditions, it makes us stronger and more resilient. Let our enemies misjudge us, regardless of the arena we meet them in, we will be ready.

Over half of our ally packs have been attacked in small altercations from the Collaborative. Thankfully the training we put in place for them has been beneficial and the losses have been small, it saddens my heart to have any losses, but to know we have decreased the numbers allows me some sleep at night.

Maverick, Angie and Muerta made a month-long trek, going to all the ally homes, so in the event of an attack they would be able to shimmer myself and team along with additional warriors to support the ally. On a positive note, they are able to shimmer more warriors now than when we first started, all three are becoming stronger. On a negative note, they have had to become stronger, due to all the attacks we have been facing.

My pride in my allies is strong, they have faced many small skirmishes, knowing none of them are the end battle, but remain true to the cause and to me. The Goddess has blessed all those who are for the supernatural species, mixed or no. They stand together, support each other, and respond to any call of assistance. Whispering Red Winds has also suffered its own attacks, it seems as if the Collaborative is testing us, seeing what our strengths and weaknesses are, trying to wear us down for the final battle. We seem to be mainly attacked by witches, our group has been discussing why this is occurring, but have no resolute answer yet.

My hands grip the wooden edges of the map table, before me is a map of the region, markers in place to show which allies have been attacked and by which species. Zeke came up with a color-coding schematic for me and each marker represents a specific set of information. I look down on the map, trying to find a pattern, any clue as to what the next move may be, can we preemptively strengthen the forces? Where will the next attack be? When will the next attack be? I stare at the map until my eyesight goes blurry. Slamming my fist on the table edge, I run my hands over my face, rubbing my eyes and taking in a deep breath, fatigue is settling in my brain and cohesive, logical thoughts are getting difficult.

I had the kitchen place a permanently stocked cart in my office, our meetings have become sporadic at best. Refilling my coffee cup, from the evergoing coffee pot, my hands wrap around and absorb the warmth. "Zeke, are you awake?" I link my Beta.

"What do you need, My Moon?"

A smile spreads across my face at the nickname he has used since we were children. "I need someone to go over these maps with me, I can't find the pattern or correlation, you are the best at this."

"Give me a couple minutes to get up, you are going to have to deal with me in pajamas. I will give you an hour and then it is bedtime for the both of us."

"Deal! There will be a cup of coffee ready for you."

The sugar had just dissolved into the creamy color of the coffee, steam rising and swirling around, making a long tendril to tickle my nose and offer the scent of promised yumminess, when Zeke barges into the office, stomps over to me and grabs the cup from my hands.

"Oh, no, you don't, that is my coffee, and I am not sharing! The cost of waking me up."

Zeke laughs at the downhearted look on my face from the loss of the fresh cup of coffee. Nodding my defeat, I turn around and make my own cup.

Once finished we head over to the map table.

"The system you put in place is great, Zeke, the pattern is evading me. There is something there, but I cannot see it," I explain, letting out a fatigued sigh.

"You are in luck, my future Queen. This Beta figured there would be questions brought up, difficult to answer from just the human/wolf perspective; therefore, yours truly designed a program to input all this. An upgrade was done to the table and every time you put a piece in place it loads into my system. We can go now and get the data."

"What a genius you are!" Laughing, I wrap my arms around Zeke's waist and snuggle into him.

Zeke wraps his arms around me, returning the hug. "Well, it is time you see my secret." He smiles down.

Taking my hands from around his waist, he continues to hold on to one of them, leading me out of the office, ignoring the inquisitive look on my face. Trust is not an issue between us, and I willingly follow him out of the room.

Within minutes we stop outside his bedroom door.

"Zeke, there is no computer system in here, why are we here?"

"Like I said, My Moon, time to see my secret."

With that he opens his door ushering me inside, makes his way to his bookshelves, pushing aside a few novels, he punches in a code. Another shelf swings outward, exposing a door, once the door opens, there is a media center of which I never imagined visible. A small gasp leaves my lips at the view in front of me.

Chapter 91:

Secrets on the Table

(Ezekiel's POV)

So, this is actually happening, I knew there would come a day Jasmine would know about my secret room and the different programs I have developed for our pack. My stomach is a ball of activity as we make our way to my room and my secret that will soon be exposed.

We come to my door and enter my room, thankfully Jasmine has no concerns about entering, she knows she is safe here with me. I make my way directly to the bookcase that holds the panel to access my computer chamber. Once my code is entered the mechanisms click into place and a set of bookshelves move, revealing my hidden door. The look on Jasmine's face is priceless, a laugh builds its way up from my stomach and out my mouth.

"Welcome to my hidden chamber, My Moon," I gasp out as I enter my inner sanctum.

Jasmine follows behind, a look of bewilderment etched on her face. She takes in the entire room a couple times before deciding to speak.

"Zeke, when did you do all this? I don't even know what half this equipment is. You aren't doing anything illegal, are you?"

She turns to me, a look of concern mixed with hesitation crosses her face. "The only times I have done any slightly illegal hacks is at the request of our former Alpha, specifically for the safety of the pack. Other than that, all is on the up-and-up. I have been designing computer programs that will benefit the pack, no one knows about them except for me...and now you."

Pride at my work is evident in my voice as we carry on our conversation.

"However, we are here for a specific reason, and I will show you the rest later. Let me boot up a couple of my machines and then I will run the data you are requesting. Just let me know any variables you would like to enter in the system to pull out the data. We can run multiple scenarios if you want."

My excitement is growing as I take my seat at my computer, the buzz and whir of my equipment is music to my ears, here I am in my element.

"This room is amazing, Zeke. We will need to revisit this space and what you have been working on as soon as possible. At the moment, the safety and welfare of our allies takes precedence."

Jasmine gets quiet and gently clears her voice, a wave of uncertainty passes over her. Choosing to remain silent, I give her time to come to terms with whatever is bothering her.

Jasmine slips into the space between my chair and the wall, she gently places her hands on my shoulders and takes in a deep breath, letting it out slowly. "One of the inquiries we need to run is why only witches have been attacking our pack, dark witches to be specific. Brooke and Nóox have felt the darkness in them, pretty sure Grace has too since she seems especially vicious when attacking them."

Nodding my head, I put in the request she has made, my machines jump to life, sending the calming sound of information gathering to my ears. "Give it a couple minutes and we will have the report. There will also be detailed information about possible next attacks and the likelihood of the occurrences happening based off the pattern so far. Until that comes through, are there any questions you have for me?" It is impossible to turn my chair around, with her standing behind me, it would be helpful to watch her face as she processes all she has been shown, but I have to trust she will continue to be open with me.

"Can your programs show an escalation of intensity in the attacks and if the species are beginning to mix or not? There have been some reports coming in, they think species are mixing such as witches and Fae. What benefit is there to mixing these species? Is there a way to find out the benefits and disadvantages of pairing different groups?" The questions flood out of Jasmine's mouth, the way her mind works amazes me.

"There is a program developed for that, it was just completed last week, and I have been entering in the data as I can. This is the perfect time to try it out. This program can run simultaneously with the one already running causing little to no delay in the results being generated." A smile breaks across my face as Jasmine continues to discover all my lab can do.

We maintain a comfortable silence as my programs are put to the test. Finally, results begin to print out, the anticipation rolling off Jasmine is almost suffocating, she is ready for any knowledge we can gain and possibly give up an advantage. Pulling the first report off, I look over it quickly before handing it to Jasmine.

"This report breaks down which ally will be attacked next, with a percentage of the possibility of attack."

Jasmine takes the report being offered to her from my hand, the soft sound of pages turning hits my ears, as Jasmine thumbs through the information. She is silent for a long moment.

"This is very detailed, the work you have done developing this program is amazing, I always knew you would accomplish great things and save us all one day, Zeke. Looks like Night Fall and Blood Moon are going to need to thank you eventually for saving them. I also need to speak to Prince Jasper immediately. What time is it? I am going to have Dusk reach out to him, it is the quickest way, but I don't want to wake her too early."

"Jasmine, it is two in the morning, everyone with a sound mind is asleep right now. We should be asleep right now," I chuckle out as she gives me a small smile. "Dusk is meeting me for breakfast at six, do you want me to have her meet you before or after in your office?"

Surprise crosses Jasmine's face at my declaration, but she doesn't pursue it any further. "Ah, here is the second report. There is an escalation of violence and species are beginning to mix in the attacks. Every statistic is showing an increase, based off this information we should be getting to the main battle in two to three months if they continue on this path."

"Interesting. Has the report regarding advantages and disadvantages generated yet?"

"It is printing now. Patience, My Moon."

After another couple minutes the report she requested is complete. Grabbing the report off the printer, I give it my usual initial perusal, only as the end of the report gets closer, a scowl begins to form on my face, good thing Jasmine cannot see my expressions right now.

"Jasmine, this report says there are no disadvantages of any species working together, only that some tolerate each other more than others. As we saw when we were attacked here by Blaine, witches and Fae can work together to bind magic, very strong magic. The last three attacks on our pack have been a mixture of witches and Fae. Your aunt is strong, but not that strong, and only has control of a couple elements, you have control of all the elements, but you must choose between your wolf form and your human form. You can't do magic in your wolf form, maybe they are trying to bind your witch side so you will have to fight as a wolf."

The silence behind me is deafening, while Jasmine's fingers clench and unclench on my shoulders, indicating she is having some sort of anxiety about the information given to her. After a few more uncomfortable moments, I decide to gently speak to her.

"Jasmine, is there something I need to know that isn't in these reports?"

Again, silence looms in the air, finally the quiet is broken. "Yes, Zeke, there is information you need to know. You have shared your secrets with me, now it is time you know mine. Let me pull that chair over and we can talk."

Seated as comfortably as possible Jasmine turns towards me, the look on her face makes my heart ache for her, she looks so uncertain at this moment. Reaching out I take her hands in mine and rub my thumbs on the back trying to calm her.

"You can tell me anything, My Moon, I will not judge you."

Her eyes lift and meet mine. "For months now, I have been training with Brooke as you know. What you are not aware of is the training I do every morning prior to the group training. At first it was just me, then Nóox caught me and has been joining me since then. Zeke, Brooke can perform magic in wolf form, all the elements. She cautioned me to not tell anyone and keep it a secret. Brooke has told me it is time for you to know, that is why I am sharing now. Only you, Nóox and I know what Brooke is capable of. If this was to get out, the danger to our pack would exponentially increase, it is imperative we stay as safe as possible until the big war, that is when my true powers will be realized."

All I can do is stare at Jasmine slack-jawed, out of all the things she could have told me this did not register as one of the options. "Jasmine, are you sure no one else knows? This could be the reason we are getting hit with witches and Fae, besides the Collaborative just wanting to eradicate our pack."

"We train out near the Northwest border, up against Keith's pack. Nóox keeps eye in the air while we get there, and only comes down to train. There have not been any odd smells or any other indicators of being followed. The winds have cautioned me about a few members on our lands, and not to trust them. Brooke especially does not like Dusk. Sorry, Zeke, I know you two have been getting close."

"What is it about Dusk that they do not like?"

"I have caught Dusk sneaking into different meetings, attempting to listen through the door, following different pack members. Patrol states she comes out at all times of the day and night, roaming the pack grounds. Brooke specifically said not to trust her, but to keep her close. The winds have warned about a traitor in our midst. There is no proof to directly accuse her of anything, but all the same, she is not welcome into the inner circle and the knowledge we hold."

"What winds, Jasmine?"

"When I run through the woods, there are times the wind picks up and there are voices carried over it. Dad knows about them, he said one of my ancestors could communicate with them too and that is how our pack got its name."

"This is a lot of information, thank you for sharing and trusting me." My mind is spinning with all the possible outcomes due to this new information. First thing in the morning I am going to develop a new program, a more detailed program and run all the new criteria swarming in my mind through it.

Standing up, I gently pull on Jasmine's hands until she is standing also, then I wrap my arms around her in a hug, leaning my chin on her head. "We will figure this all out, but first we need sleep. Our minds cannot continue to function well sleep deprived. Let's have a meeting, you, me and Nóox after breakfast tomorrow."

Jasmine nods her head against my chest.

Pulling back, I place a gentle kiss on Jasmine's forehead and we leave my hidden office, making sure it is secure behind me. Knowing all I know now about Jasmine, there is no way she will be unescorted from this moment forward. Until the data is in front of me to confirm my thoughts, they will remain with me only.

"Let me escort you back to your room, this way I know for certain you did not escape back to your office and continue working." My smile is playful, and Jasmine giggles her agreement.

Within moments we are outside her door, another hug and brotherly kiss later she closes her door behind her. The noise has awoken Nóox, who has opened his door to check the hallway.

"Hello, Nóox, just making sure Jasmine returned safely to her room, she has been up this entire time still working." Walking over to the large thunderbird, who looks at me with a curious gaze, I continue, "We had a very interesting discussion and I need to meet with you and Jasmine later this morning. It is going to be very important Jasmine is not left alone from here forward."

Nóox nods his head and closes his door behind him, ending the conversation.

Chapter 92:

Zeke's Discoveries

(Ezekiel's POV)

After being silently dismissed by Nóox, I make my way back to my bed chamber, well, to the office in my bed chamber, there is no way sleep is coming to me after my talk with Jasmine. There is too much on my mind, too many questions that need immediate answers, the life of our future Queen depends on me. I have never been so scared in my entire life, Jasmine does not understand the true danger she is in.

Ensuring my main door is locked, I enter my lair, securing it behind me as well. The information about to be processed is too valuable to let any accidental eyes fall on it. My system is always on a secure network, but I develop a couple more levels of security to it anyway, if anyone is monitoring us, this should be invisible to them.

Pulling a file out of my safe, I look through for some coding specifications, finding them I refresh my memory of the program. There are a few adjustments that will need to be made, but this program can be up, debugged, and running in the next couple of hours, thankfully all my program specs are saved, so there will never be a need to reinvent the code, just tweak an existing one. Coding goes faster than I thought, the two hours are whittled down to only 45 minutes, thank goodness I am able to save so much time developing this program. If my thoughts are correct and the data supports my thoughts, Jasmine and this pack are facing more danger than originally thought. Before anything else can be done, a phone call needs to be made to Muerta.

We were able to find where Broken Moon has moved to, thanks to our vampire spy. Muerta hitched a ride on one of the trucks leaving the old pack grounds and sent the coordinates back to me to track. We now also have a detailed description of the new pack grounds, and an idea of who is in charge for the Collaborative. Muerta informed us the barrier and block around the new grounds are a combination of dark witch magic, dark Fae and vampire, she has never seen anything like it.

Muerta also gave intel on a cloaked figure that regularly goes in and out of the pack, only visits for an hour at most and departs. Always in secret, always covered; however, Muerta has not been able to scent them to know their species. Angie is scheduled to go over today and follow the cloaked figure to their place of origin and give a report. I must admit, I love the vampire spies Maverick brought with him, they have been able to do so much covert work for us.

Picking up my phone, I dial the number from memory now, after a few rings Muerta' s voice answers on the other end.

"Good morning, Zeke. Shouldn't you be asleep?" Her voice is dry and devoid of emotion as always.

"Good morning to you also. I was asleep until Jasmine woke me up, now there is no possibility of sleep coming to me tonight. Have you noticed any increase in witch or Fae activity there?"

Pleasantries are nice, but we are working against the clock now. Muerta can sense my urgency and responds in kind.

"They have brought in a few extra witches, slightly more powerful than Victoria, but not much. My main concern is the vampire leader here, who seems to be the head of the Collaborative. His name is Scion, he and Maverick have a nasty history together and are equally matched as far as powers go. Scion and the new witches have been holding many meetings the last couple of days, though I am not sure what about. I have not been able to get into the meeting rooms. The magic here is very dark and getting darker. Wish there were more to pass on, but that is it, I will continue to snoop around and update as new information is available."

"Thanks, Muerta, have fun."

Hitting the end call button, I throw the phone on my desk. New darker witches and a powerful vampire? What are they planning? Spinning my chair around I begin placing data into the new program, Jasmine and her powers with her wolf, Ashley, and her tie to the Blood Wolf, Nóox, being sent by the Goddess and being a thunderbird, Maverick, Scion, and the new witches. I upload all the attack information and the results from our earlier searches. My machines come to life and begin whirring and beeping. Music to my tired ears.

While the report is generating, I decide to access the dark web, to see if there is any information that can be useful to our situation. Unfortunately, there is nothing of interest, it appears the bad people of the world are taking a break from mischief for a moment. The silence itself is concerning...while there are down swings in activity, it is never silent...digging further in, I hack into a site that was run by Broken Moon previously. There is an invitation to a secret meeting, giving coordinates to the location. I take a screen shot of this information and email it to Muerta on her phone. Our favorite spy has yet another covert mission.

My printer begins making its irritating grunting noise, alerting me the report has finished generating. Pulling the pages off as they finish printing, I review them, my heart sinking a little more the more in depth the report goes. This information cannot wait until after breakfast, Jasmine needs to be alerted now.

In a matter of minutes, my fist is pounding on Jasmine's door, it is a little after four in the morning. There is no answer and Nóox has not bothered to come out of his room to check on the disruption. My mind goes back to Jasmine's and my conversation, taking off down the stairs, I make my way outside and begin running at full speed to the Northwest border. They are most likely training already.

Almost to the border, I put my nose up, into the air and try to find Jasmine's scent, catching it on the wind, I begin to trek in that direction. Before being able to locate her, Angie comes across my path.

"Hey, Angie, what are you doing out here?"

"Following the cloaked figure. Muerta called me, letting me know they made an unusual visit this morning. They met with Scion and the new witches.

I have followed them here so far, about a quarter-mile back, they took to the trees and have been traveling that way, attempting to remain undetected. It is confusing why they are being so covert in the forest."

"The most likely reason is they are spying on Jasmine and Nóox training. Show me where they are headed, we need to identify this person. It may be best both of us are together."

Angie nods in agreement and begins moving forward, her tracking ability is phenomenal, she notices every single minute detail of her surroundings. Soon we pause next to a tree, Angie points to another tree in front, we can barely make out the figure through the limbs and they still have the cloak hood in place. A hand reaches up and pushes the hood aside, this cannot be, this cannot be the traitor. My heart falls as my eyes land on the irrevocable facts before me.

"Angie, you can go, I will deal with this from here. Thank you for all the work. Meet me in my office around ten, please, there may be another job for you to do."

Again, I only receive a nod from her, and she shimmers out of the forest. I move forward, carrying on with my original plan to find Jasmine and Nóox.

Chapter 93:

Traitor Identified

(Jasmine's POV)

Brooke is getting ready to attempt to shoot fire from her mouth, like a dragon, we are a little apprehensive about it, but we will never know our abilities to their fullest if we don't try. Closing my eyes, taking in a deep breath, I center on my magic and pull it forward, Brook opens our eyes and focuses on our target, opening our mouth....

"Jasmine, I am coming up to the training area. Don't respond as if you knew I was coming up. You have a visitor in the trees observing your actions. Please don't react, I have a plan formulating and them thinking they haven't been caught is part of it," a link comes in unexpectedly from Zeke.

Brooke jumps and the fire is swallowed down, causing the worst case of heartburn ever experienced, a puff of smoke leaves our nose, and our tongue hangs out to the side, trying to cool down.

"Dammit, Zeke!" I link back. "You just caused me to swallow a fireball! Why are you here? Never mind, processing what you said. Come on already," I finish.

Turning my eyes to Nóox, my irritation is shining brightly in them. Brooke places her nose in the air and sniffs, then turns in a circle. Nóox begins to look around also trying to locate what I am smelling. Brooke hunches down, hackles rising and lets out a low growl, through the tree line steps Zeke. I allow Brooke to run forward and tackle him to the ground, pinning him by the shoulders and nipping his ears.

"Next time, don't scare me, Zeke," I laugh through the link.

"Get off, you oversized puppy!!" Zeke laughs out. "Thank Goddess, Brooke realized it was me and just wanted to cuddle; otherwise, life could be bad for me right now."

"What are you doing here?" Nóox asks, a suspicious look on his face as he glances between the two of us.

"I told you Jasmine and I had a talk early this morning. Anyway, there is more information that came through and it is imperative Jasmine take a look. It couldn't wait until our meeting after breakfast." With this information coming out, Zeke turns and winks at me, letting me know he meant to let it slip.

Brooke walks up to Zeke, licks his cheek, and nuzzles his side then turns control back to me so we can shift. Back in human form, I give him a hug.

"What new information? You were supposed to go to bed after escorting me back to my room. Don't tell me you lectured me, then went against your own lecture material, Ezekiel." Squinting my eyes into a glare and pursing my lips in disapproval, I give Zeke my best angry face.

He just laughs and pats my head.

"Don't pat our Queen!" Nóox growls out to him.

"Oh, hush, big bird. She may be our Queen, but she will always be my little sister and therefore head pats will never end."

Nóox does not look happy with his flippant response.

"What is this new information you have; I assume the papers in your hand are for me to review." Hopefully changing the subject will calm Nóox, as of now we have not seen him upset, but I have no desire to either after seeing him rain down havoc in our battles. He is a force to be reckoned with and we are lucky enough to be allies, versus enemies.

"I coded a new database last night with all the new information you shared with me, uploaded all the other information we already had and did a bunch of cross-references and other computer-genius stuff to get the information in front of you."

Jasmine's eyes are moving rapidly side to side as she views the report, Nóox is standing behind her looking over her shoulder, but his eyes give away nothing. There is no clue if he is also viewing the information on the report or not.

"Thanks, Zeke, you are correct, this needed to be viewed now. Let's change the meeting between the three of us to an entire core group meeting. Keith will need to come in from Midnight Moon, he went home to take care of a few things with Andrew. Make sure to invite Andrew also, there is information here he needs to be briefed on." Knowing we have a visitor observing us, I do not want to give them an opportunity to grab this information, a fire orb appears in my hand, and I burn the report.

"Let's head back, shall we? Zeke, you have a breakfast date this morning, don't you? You should really clean up, you smell like dust and sweat, so not romantic." Laughing, Brooke takes over, shifting us back to our beautiful blue wolf and we run at top speed back to the packhouse.

Half an hour later I make my way to the packhouse dining room for breakfast, from the corner of my eye I see Zeke sitting with Dusk. She has squeezed impossibly close to his side and is sending him big doe eyes. The girl is pretty, but everything about her screams fake to me, warns me to not let her close to my pack or allies. Brooke bristles just catching her scent. This elf is hiding a secret and it is up to me to find out what it is. Grabbing my coffee, I make my way over to interrupt Zeke's date.

"Hey, you two, looking pretty cozy over here. Hope you don't mind me invading your space, hate eating alone and all."

Not waiting for a response from them, I take a seat across the table, Ashley is soon plopped down next to me eyeing her brother and the elf with obvious disdain.

"Look here, girl, you are a great trainer, you have knowledge that has been valuable, but this is the only warning you will get about putting your hands on my brother. You are not his Goddess-given mate so back off."

Since finding her wolf, Grace, Ashley does not hold anything back, she is becoming more and more abrasive as time goes. We are going to need to find someone to help her adjust to being the Blood Wolf without losing herself.

Dusk sits up a little straighter and moves away from Zeke, allowing a little light to shine between their bodies. "Okay, ladies, do not mess this up for me. Jasmine, remember how I told you I had a plan for the traitor? Well, Dusk is needed for that plan to work; she needs to feel accepted. I will explain more at the meeting," Zeke links, while keeping his eyes down.

"Ash, don't be so hard on Dusk, she is just trying to fit in to a new place and our brother is very single. Who better to show her around than the pack Beta?"

Ash chokes on her juice as the words depart my mouth, glaring at me she slams her cup to the table and growls.

"Dusk, I need to speak with Prince Jasper, could you please summon him and request his presence here? It is very important; we have discovered information on the Collaborative, and I greatly need his input and guidance on a few pieces of the information," I request using my nicest voice but maintaining a no-nonsense manner.

"I would be happy to do that for you, Jasmine. If you like, I may be able to figure out what the information means, Prince Jasper has trained me, and my knowledge is almost parallel to his."

"I appreciate your offer, but almost parallel is not the same, we need a definitive answer on this, and we cannot accept anything less than certainty. The wellness and safety of my pack, allies and the supernatural world depend on it. Please understand, I am not attempting to undermine you, but the risks of inaccurate information are too great." Sending a soft smile her way, I hope she doesn't see the doubts I have about her.

Receiving only a nod in response, Dusk excuses herself from the table and leaves the dining area, watching her walk through the door my attention turns back to Zeke. "That girl cannot be trusted; every fiber of my being is screaming out to me. Why is she so important to this plan?"

"She is the visitor in the tree this morning."

My eyes almost pop from my head at this disclosure.

"We can pass along some disinformation for her to share with the Collaborative. Did you by chance see the new amulet she is wearing today? She didn't have it on yesterday and Muerta said she didn't have it on when visiting the Collaborative early this morning. Seems we should have Maverick make it a point to interact with her today. Can we pair them at a training this afternoon?"

A smile spreads across my face, my Beta is sneaky, sneaky. "Absolutely they can, our wolves need to know how to fight if a vampire and elf team up together. As you told me last night, there are no negative aspects of supernatural species being paired together."

Zeke just nods and finishes off his coffee.

"Hurry up, My Queen, Ash and I will escort you to the meeting room, we don't want to be late for our own meeting, now do we? Also, I think your bird is anxious to have eyes on you again."

Zeke motions towards the dining room door, where Nóox is standing, watching our table and the room around us. He is definitely protective, must be why the Goddess sent him to us.

Chapter 94:

Disinformation

(Jasmine's POV)

Once again, the core group has come together in my office. Zeke let me know he has installed cameras on the outside of the office door that send the feed directly to a tablet he has with him. Since there should not be anyone on this floor, while we are in our meeting there is a movement detector activated.

Zeke also informed me, while "cuddling" at breakfast this morning, he was able to slip a tracking device onto Dusk. He told me I missed the best part, where he was running his hands up her neck and into her hair, while whispering in her ear. The device is invisible and located near the top of her ear, on the scalp. It also will not be picked up in a scan, yet another marvelous invention of my Beta. Personally, I don't believe I missed anything, not something on my list of things to watch, Zeke feeling up a girl. I trust him completely and that is why I am allowing for him to run with this; otherwise, Ashley would have the satisfaction of ripping her throat out.

"Thank you all for coming in short notice. Zeke and I had a late night last night, but it brought about some good information. Zeke was able to run specific scenarios based off the information we have gathered so far. We think we have a decent idea where the attacks will be occurring next."

Everyone has given me their direct attention and the little teaser I put out has silenced any side talk.

"Zeke is passing around a packet for each of you. This information is highly classified and will not leave this room once the meeting is over. There is confirmation of traitors among the personnel on these grounds, some are our own, others were brought here unknowingly." Dad lets out a growl, the thought of pack members turning against their own has never sat right with him.

"Prince Jasper, we have asked you here today for a twofold reason. First, we would like to know what your knowledge base is on vampires and dark witches working together, what is their end, usually?"

All eyes turn to Prince Jasper at my question.

"Well, it would depend on the strength of the vampire in charge and the number and strength of the witches. Without this information the various reasons are too great to narrow down."

"The vampire is equal in strength to Maverick, based off reports from Muerta. There are four witches, each is strong, but not as strong as Aunt Meredith, but stronger than the witch Victoria, if you know her," Zeke fills in for the prince.

Maverick whips his head up at this information. "Well, for this pairing to be together, I would have to say, their plan is to not only bind, but kill the Midnight and Blood Wolves. Then they would search for a path to the Goddess from their blood." Maverick's eyes begin to glow bright red, his fangs elongate from his gums as he stares down the elf.

"How would you even begin to know this information, Prince?" Maverick hisses at our guest.

"My fifth cousin was a hybrid elf Queen and vampire, the same magic was used against her to try and gain access to our god. The people who killed her wanted to end our species by taking out our originator. It is only an assumption on my part, that is what is occurring now."

"Who was the vampire that led this attack?" Maverick continues to push.

"His name was Scion. He worked with four dark witches, whose souls are bound to him, they do any bidding that he desires. They are merciless and have a unique, strong power. One I do not know how to combat. If this group is anything like the five of them our hands will be full, and an attack should occur sooner than later to obliterate the threat," Jasper finishes, casting a serious glance around the room and landing lastly on Maverick.

"The group of five is exactly who we are against. Scion is the only vampire who equals my strength, his witch minions perform only the darkest magic, there is no light in them anymore. This allows for them to be defeated, the trick is killing their master to put them down for good," Maverick interjects, his voice showing his concern for the information shared. He turns his bright red eyes on me. "Jasmine, you are not safe as long as the five of them are here, neither is Ashley. I apologize to make demands and dictate to you, but from this moment forward, neither of you can be without an escort and you cannot count as each other's escorts. It will be imperative you maintain a group with you that contains a vampire, Fae or elf, and witch. This will allow time to get necessary resources to you in the event of an attack. I will send for two of my top warrior vampires to be tasked with this."

"I can task Dusk to one of you and will call back my other most trusted elven warrior for the other."

"Unfortunately, Prince Jasper, Dusk is hiding information and true alliances from you. I will allow her to be a part of my team, but an elven warrior that is not known or recognized here will also need to be added. It has been confirmed, Dusk is working with the Collaborative and has been placed here as a spy. We have decided to run a disinformation campaign against the Collaborative. We do not want Dusk to know she has been caught."

Jasper jumps from his seat, his chair tipping over backwards. "How long have you known this information, without alerting me? How long have you put yourself in danger from my people? If not for your request, I would deal with her now, her blood with stain the earth at your feet."

"I was only informed this morning and why you were invited to this meeting. Letting you know about Dusk was the second part of the reasons you were invited. It would have been preferable to get the information to you another way, so I apologize for the abruptness of it."

"No apology needed, please let me know what you need from me. The support of my kingdom is fully behind you."

"Thank you. We have no doubts about your loyalty." Turning my attention to the room again, we continue.

"Ezekiel was given additional information after the reports handed to you earlier were ran. With the new information and some inquiries added into the search engines, Zeke pulled up a more detailed background on the Collaborative. It was indeed restarted by Scion about ten years ago. Many of the battles we mistook as rogue attacks have been the Collaborative testing our borders and fighters, while also looking to see when the prophecy would begin." I pause, taking in a deep breath before continuing. The next part is going to impact many in this room.

"The Collaborative is guilty of orchestrating the deaths of many they viewed as threats. Wonderful supernaturals have lost their lives for this prophecy without knowing it. Wolves such as Andrew's parents, my grandparents and Keith's aunt and uncles; elves such as Jasper's cousin and Aunt Meredith's partner. Vampires related to Muerta and Maverick, and lastly half of Nóox' village."

Tears are dripping from every eye in the room, silence reigns over our space.

"This group was bound together before any of us knew of the prophecy, before any of us knew a fight was coming to our door. Our ancestors took the first blows of a war, un-proclaimed, to weaken us against their desired power. It is not a mistake we are together; it was not happenstance. The Goddess blessed us for a reason, they fear us and have placed spies to report on us. Let's give these spies information to report, let's continue to bring this battle to them and punish this Collaborative for all the pain, disruption, and heartache they have caused. Let us avenge all who have laid their lives down past and present. Let us build a better world, despite their best efforts."

The entire room is solemn, thinking over everything just shared. Andrew stands from his seat, looking down at his hands, then lifts his head.

"Thank you for giving me closure to the fate of my parents. I am prepared to take this battle anywhere it needs to go. Show me the direction and I will be on their doorstep, dealing out the Goddess' hand of justice. My place is beside you, My Queen and My Alpha."

Slowly the entire room stands to their feet, no words are uttered, yet the understanding amongst everyone is clear. This fight has been taken to another level and we will not fail.

"Maverick, I need you to team up with Dusk during training today, she has a new amulet after making a visit to Scion and his witches early this morning. We need any information you can bring us about it. Claire, I need you and Miles to discuss fake strategies near her, it is important we do not give the appearance of trying to include her now. We do not want her suspicious of our plans. We know Michael from the kitchen staff is working with her as well as the Kinley twins, let's drop very subtle disinformation around them as well." Sparks are beginning to take place of the pain; the fire is coming alive within my team.

"Dusk will be notified today there is a risk to my safety, and she is going to be part of a dedicated team to watch over me. Brooke has informed me now is the time to share a secret with you all, a secret that has caused all this to come to pass. You all know I hold the powers of both my parents, what you all do not know is that I am able to use my magic in wolf form. Nóox has been helping me train for a while now, and Dusk managed to find out. This is information to keep out of the general knowledge pool but should be shared with my security detail. This way, Dusk will think it is not necessarily something we are keeping as a significant secret."

Many surprised eyes turn in my direction, although Keith has not responded.

"Keith, you do not seem as shocked at my declaration as the rest of the group."

"Well, Little One, I already knew. The Goddess shared it with me when she visited me. She outed you and your wolf for knocking me on my backside that day," Keith chuckles. "Time to stretch these legs of mine, Andrew, would you like to walk with me? That is if we are dismissed?"

He raises his eyebrows in question to me. "Yes, everyone is free to go. Thank you all again for coming. Let's get to work."

The room empties, except for my dad and Nóox. I walk around the table and into the open arms of my father. At this moment I am not Alpha or future Queen, I am his little girl. Sinking into his warm and secure embrace, I feel a gentle kiss on top of my head.

"Be safe, my girl. I am so proud of you, for all you have done, the group brought together, and the fight you continue to take forward. I have no doubts you will succeed and bring peace to these lands. I love you so much." He ends with another kiss to the top of my head, pulls away gently and squeezes my hands before turning them loose to leave the room.

Nóox moves and stands beside me in his usual quiet fashion, him being by my side is becoming normal place for me. Looking up at him, I give a warm smile. "Well, I guess we should get going, we have our own duties to attend to."

He just nods and follows me from the room.

Chapter 95:

Updating the Collaborative

(Dusk's POV)

Whatever god these wolves look to must be smiling down on me, imagine my good luck to get placed on Jasmine's security detail. Personally, I quit believing in the gods years ago when my entire family was taken from me by rogue werewolves. If we had lived in our own realm, and not cohabitated with the other races, my family would still be here. I would not have the nightmares of my little brother, impaled through the chest by a claw, stuck to a tree, as the life slowly left his five-year-old body, while the hideous beast laughed, salivating the entire while. I will tolerate these creatures long enough to extract my revenge.

While I am still not part of the inner circle, my status has moved up an echelon in the trust department. Tongues have not been as guarded around me as usual, the information I am compiling from the security heads is amazing. Even that damn vampire, Maverick, has been spending more time around me. Finally, Scion is pleased with the information he is being forwarded, not only from my weekly visits, but from the video my amulet is taking.

The Collaborative now has a full layout of the Whispering Red Winds pack grounds, how they run training, the schedule and how shifts are swapped out for security and border patrol. Scion continues to want more, though; he wants the piece that will give us the edge in the final battle.

Arriving at the training ground early, there is no one else in place, I double check my watch and realize the thirty minutes is mistakenly sixty minutes too early, watch reading was never my strong suit. Nothing left to do but begin setting up the area for training while waiting. I head over to the storage shed and begin sorting through the equipment. Maverick is paired with me today and we plan on tag-teaming singular wolves in ambush-style attacks. The wolves are only allowed to have weapons they would normally carry, my mind evades me as to what to pull out for today's training, elves and wolves do not generally fight in the same style and definitely do not use the same weapons.

Hands on my hips, I let out a frustrated sigh, blowing some loose hair out of my eyes. Conversation reaches my ears as people approach the shed. Listening closer, the voices of Miles and Claire reach me. Maybe they will not notice me here and additional information can be gained for Scion.

Steadying my breathing and heartbeat, my ears strain to pick up on the conversation. Thankfully they move closer, so my ears do not have to strain as much to make out the dialog.

"Alpha Jasmine wants you to make sure the patrols are doubled up; we will go over the schedule to ensure there are enough wolves to make this happen. If needed we will pull wolves back from the ally forces, our only concern is that will leave our allies unprotected to support our homelands." The voice is Claire's.

"Alpha Jasmine knows what she is doing. There must be a valid reason for her to risk our allies being left vulnerable to attack, to bring our wolves back. Just let me know what changes are happening and I will ensure it happens on the patrols. Is there any additional equipment we should be gathering?"

"Nothing mentioned so far. It seems Alpha Jasmine may be getting ready to make a push against the Collaborative. She isn't doing well having security constantly surrounding her, her nerves are on edge. Ashley threatened to rip out the throats of her entire team yesterday. If they aren't free from this threat soon, I worry what their minds will do."

Pressing closer to the wall of the shed, I am trying to take in and remember all they are discussing. This is what I have been waiting for, Scion may finally be happy and let me leave this vile pack. My place is on the battlefield, ending these people and separating our races.

"Do you smell something? Did someone beat us to the field?" Claire inquires, her voice moving closer to my position.

Turning quickly, I pull multiple pieces of equipment down, causing it to topple on top of me. Perfect, just the excuse to get me out of training so the Collaborative can be updated. This information cannot wait.

Heavy footsteps come in the door. "Who is there? Speak so we can help you."

"Over here." My voice comes out low and weak, perfect. Time to play this happy accident up a notch or two.

Soon all the clutter is removed from the top of me, the concerned eyes of Claire and Miles view me.

"Does anything hurt? Let me carry you to the infirmary to have you checked out," Miles offers as he kneels beside me, slipping his arm firmly around me, then standing and leaving the shack.

"I will be back soon. Let Maverick know we will need to plan something else for training today."

In no time we have made it to the pack clinic, Miles sets me down in the waiting room, alerts a nurse to my arrival, getting ready to walk out the door he pauses. "Hopefully there is nothing serious happening. We need you; you are a big part of our security and training teams, without you, I am not sure where we would be." Flashing a small smile my way, he then walks through the door.

Watching until he is out of sight, I wait another ten minutes, then get up and approach the nurse's station. "Excuse me." She turns to me with a warm smile. "Thank you for working to get me in. It seems my amulet has taken care of any injuries. You all are busy, so I am just going to head back to training."

She nods her head, then turns to pick up a ringing phone, that is my cue to depart.

Forty-five minutes later the looming walls of the gate leading into Vengeance's Gate are before me, in my excitement the travel time decreased by close to ten minutes. A small door to the left of the gates opens, Maurice, Scion's assistant, meets me. Narrowing his eyes at me, he curls his lips into a sneer.

"What is it you want? The master is too busy to be bothered by your frivolous information, if you have nothing helpful then you need to leave."

Maurice has become the bane of my existence when it comes to delivering my information. For whatever reason he has decided all my information needs to pass through him, prior to me meeting with Scion. I don't trust vampires in general, but I really do not trust this vampire, he makes my skin crawl and stomach tighten in fear.

"My information is for Scion only; I do not care that you are his self-appointed guardian. Now move! Time is not on my side, and you are wasting what little I have to be here."

"We will see, Dusk; you have been nothing but a regular disappointment and regret since sending you in undercover. I hope this time your blood darkens the floors of Scion's entryway as a warning to others. Not even a vampire wants to suck your blood, it would curse us."

Pushing around Maurice I enter through the doorway and march with all the determination left in my body to Scion's coven house. Even though this will ultimately be Alpha Blaine's pack lands, until the Collaborative has taken control, they reside on the same grounds, in their own separate areas. Standing before Scion's door, I gulp down my fear and nervousness, time to enter the lion's den, my mind thinks as my fist raps against the wooden door.

Immediately the door swings open and Scion is before me. He elevates one eyebrow looking down at me in question. "Dusk, I did not expect to see you so soon after our last meeting." His voice is as cold as his eyes, I have no doubt he would end my life if he did not like what I brought to him.

Bowing my head slightly, to show respect that did not reside in my heart, I begin. "Scion, this meeting is unplanned. I overheard a conversation between the Gamma and the lead warrior today. They say Jasmine is getting fed up with having to live under heightened security measures, she and the Blood Wolf. They are planning on pulling back their traveling training instructors and warriors to begin planning a push forward. There were no dates mentioned, but the two expressed concerns about leaving the allies vulnerable to attacks." Keeping my eyes downcast, my heartrate increases waiting for Scion's response to the little news brought to him. Will he think it is valuable enough to not harm me?

"Indeed, interesting developments, it is good to see we have been able to push them into this heightened sense of security and it is having adverse reactions to their wellbeing. You are correct, Dusk; this is important information and needed to be brought to me immediately. For now, go back to the pack and resume your role, we will monitor for when the movement begins. When it does, we will bring you back here to participate in the war."

A sickening smile crosses his face and chills me to the very core. At least I live to see another day.

Scion moves his hand in a shooing movement near my general direction, his indicator I am dismissed from his presence. His thoughts have already moved on from me and our meeting. Normally this type of attitude and behavior would irritate me, but I am just happy to leave his building, still converting oxygen to carbon.

Chapter 96:

Deceiving the Collaborative

(Jasmine's POV)

A growl rips through my lips as I turn around tripping over a member of my security team, barely catching myself before slamming face first into the wall; they are always underfoot, and I am unable to do anything without them directly in my personal space. It does not matter who it was this time or why, this is beyond acceptable.

"All of you move away from me, if I can smell you, you are too close. If you fail to heed my warning your blood will paint my walls." My voice comes out as a snarl and my eyes begin to glow.

The entirety of the group, except Nóox, backs away, most likely because he was sent by our Goddess and is immune to my fits of rage. A huff passes through my grimace, and I stalk off down the hallway, at wit's end with the entire group. They may have a mission to be accountable for my safety, but they are sorely trying my sanity. This girl was not meant to be hovered over and coddled, I am the future Queen and a warrior of the Goddess!

Making it to the Alpha floor, I bang the door to my room open, my rage still boiling through my system. I failed to notice the door did not slam shut behind me, until a gentle hand grasps me by my elbow and turns me around. The deep chocolate eyes of Nóox look down at me in concern and amusement.

"I dismissed the group. Your acting skills are phenomenal, but it seems to me there was a bit of truth in your tirade out there. Do you want to talk about it?"

Shaking my head side to side, I let out a deep breath, recentering myself.

"Nóox, while I understand the dangers to me, I do not want to show weakness. Living my current life, in the middle of a security team is not the image I want to portray. I am a warrior and Queen sent by the Goddess to help my people." My gaze does not falter from his, he loosens his grip on my elbow and takes a step back. "A smaller team would be ideal, a team made up of you, Maverick, Ashley and myself. We would be able to respond to any threats. We could keep Dusk on the detail so she can continue to filter information back to the Collaborative as we want her to. By the way, has she left yet?" I ask.

"Not yet, she was seen headed back to her room. Angie is keeping track of her while she is on pack grounds and follows her to the gates of the Collaborative, where Muerta takes over. Muerta will update us as soon as she leaves."

"Let's gather the group for a meeting as soon as she is through the front gate. Make sure Miles is a part of the meeting please. It is time to begin our deception."

Nóox nods and opens the door to leave, standing before him, fist raised in the air ready to knock on my door is Keith, behind him is Zeke.

No doubt they heard about my behaviors from my wolf guard and came straight away to see if this is the start to our initial move on the Collaborative.

"Come in, Keith and Zeke. All is well, Nóox is headed up to let the group know we are planning a meeting for as soon as Dusk leaves the front gate. You all were helpful enough to mark two people off his task list."

Nóox laughs and continues through the door, set on completing his mission.

"How are you doing? Rumor has it from some in the know, your act seemed to be very realistic. How much was acting and how much was real?"

Concern shines from Keith's eyes as he looks down at me.

"Everyone knows a good actress always puts some truth into her performance; otherwise, it would come across stiff and false." I turn tossing my hair behind my shoulder in a playful, sassy way.

"On the serious side of the matter, it is time we start making our move against the Collaborative. I was going to head to my office and wait for everyone to gather there. Do the two of you want to act as my makeshift security detail and escort me to my office just a few doors down?"

My smile is dripping sweetness. Zeke chuckles and wraps me in his arms.

"Soon, My Moon, you can let down this façade. We know this is not who you are, but it is necessary to pull off our plans."

Returning Zeke's hug, I am once again thankful for the two brother figures I have in my life to help keep me centered and on track. The Goddess has blessed me more than any one wolf deserves.

Departing my room, our small group reconvenes in my office waiting for the others. I sink down into the dark brown leather of my chair. My father and I changed offices, he now has his office back and I took my mother's office. It is just as large as Dad's but has a softer feel to it. The comfort that surrounds me in this office reminds me of my mother and that is something this wolf/witch so desperately needs.

Taking in a deep breath, her scent still lingers and calms me, but also strengthens me. Her voice rings through my head: *You were blessed by the Goddess to serve and protect your people, to bring them from the darkness that looms ahead. Sweetheart, she was not wrong to trust in you, but it is up to you to find that inner strength and courage necessary to bring this prophecy to fruition. There are no guarantees on how this whole thing will play out. Never forget, we are all beside you, supporting you, fighting with you. I love you, my sweet girl, but you must turn into my strong warrior and fair leader.* I feel the first tear begin to fall from my eyes and turn my chair to look out the window behind me.

My office door swings open, Father walks in and I hear his footsteps pause for a moment. Swinging my chair back around to face him, his face is shadowed by sadness and his eyes show he is lost in a memory. Leaving my chair and making my way over to my dad, I wrap my arms around him, sharing a moment. The three other men in the room remain silent, giving us space, understanding the heartache.

Father straightens and clears his throat. "What do we need to set up before the rest arrive?"

"Zeke completed my map table yesterday and updated my system with all the necessary software. The kitchen staff has set up a coffee and snack bar by the couches and table. Everything is ready, we are just waiting on Dusk to make her departure." Dad nods, then walks to the cedar snack bar, making himself a coffee.

Maverick is next to make his way in. "Angie just passed through the front gates following Dusk. The trip to Scion's is usually about an hour, depending on how excited the girl is to pass on her information."

"Thank you, Maverick. Have you found enough trusted vampires to begin the first phase of our plan?"

"I have, Jasmine. They will be here in the next hour, we thought it best they arrive while Dusk is out. We have also set their rooms up in one of the warrior buildings. Once they have settled, I will be taking them to all the ally strongholds, this time it will be quicker than when Angie, Muerta and myself did this. I am able to shimmer them directly and then they can shimmer to and from. By nightfall, my team will be ready to implement any plan you have."

"Perfect!" As the word leaves my mouth the rest of the group arrives in my office. "Great, everyone is here. Go ahead and get refreshments if needed, we aren't going to wait to start until everyone is seated."

Nods come from the group in the room and a couple of members go to grab coffee.

"Maverick has informed me his team will be here in an hour, give or take a few minutes. In that hour we need to secure our turn coats. Our traitor in the kitchen was sent to gather additional supplies to account for the increase in pack members. Miles, what have we done with our patrol guards?"

"Alpha Jasmine, they were sent with a senior member to check on the status of our farthest trainers. It will take them a week to travel there by car." "Exactly what we needed for them, normal missions to not raise suspicion.

We need to begin quietly getting the back-up warriors gathered. Alpha Keith, have the men you are sending meet at the Crescent side of the pack with our warriors. Only a few at a time, so there is no mass exodus to cause tongues to wag. Maverick, once you have completed the initial shimmers with your team, meet the warriors there. We want them in place before we make a show of pulling our guy's home. If anyone questions the number of men missing, we will tell them we set up a border encampment to cut down on response time to the farthest borders. To help this, I will be placing a protective order on the pack to not approach within a half-mile of the borders."

"Jasmine, Andrew has requested to be sent out on this detail. He wants to go to the territory most likely to be attacked,"

Keith informs me in a quiet tone. Casting my gaze towards Keith, I notice he has carefully covered any facial expressions that would give away his preference. It is obvious to me he has some doubt about sending Andrew out on this detail.

"I will leave that call up to you." Keith nods once. "This plan is now hot. We are inviting hell into our lands, folks. Let's lure them in and snuff them out, our realm is depending on us."

A loud war cry goes up around the room, and everyone moves to take care of their tasks.

There is no doubt in my mind we will be victorious in this endeavor, our fighters and allies are strong, it is time to end this threat.

CHAPTER 97:

UNWITTING AGGRESSORS

(Scion's POV)

Word has arrived, the false Queen is finally pulling her trainers and warriors back, leaving small packs and allies without extra support. This is the gift I have been waiting to be handed to me.

Although patience is not my strong suit, it is imperative enough time is allowed for the forces to move away prior to attacks beginning. The last thing we want is the warriors turning around and coming back to reenforce the small packs. It is difficult not to smile when thinking of the devastation about to be brought against these traitors to their species.

Turning to look out the window that faces my main enemy's grounds, I clasp my hands behind my back and contemplate all that has occurred, my thoughts turn to the forces Jasmine has been able to surround herself with. Of course, Maverick and his cohorts, Angie and Muerta, are backing her, he has never been a true vampire and used his powers to his benefit, he fails to rule over all others. Maverick is the only true threat to myself and the witches working with me, he is unaware of their presence so far and this benefits me in the long run.

At least I think Maverick is the main threat; this thunderbird shifter is new to me, my experience is lacking, but their power is nothing to disregard. He did take out a good amount of the vampires sent to attack the first pack. A definite mar to my plans. The benefit is we know of his presence and can plan accordingly.

A loud knock on my office door turns my attention towards the entrance. "The door is open, come in," I call out.

The large mahogany door opens, revealing Maurice, Alpha Blaine behind him. Maurice is doing his best to hold the werewolf back. Letting out a sigh of irritation I turn my complete attention to them.

"Maurice, let Alpha Blaine in," I snap at my self-appointed aide; he will need to be dealt with soon. He has been causing too many issues with all the members vital to this plan.

Maurice lowers his head in submission and moves to the side, allowing Alpha Blaine to enter. The werewolf is shifting from foot to foot, while clenching and unclenching his fists.

"You called for me, Scion? Is there new movement?" His anticipation and excitement is evident in his voice.

The werewolves have been getting harder and harder to control, they want to move forward and take action preemptively. Their spontaneity is why there is someone else in control. We would have already lost this war if Blaine and crew were in charge.

"I called you and the rest of the heads, there are significant new updates. Everyone will be briefed at the same time, please take your seat at the conference table and await the rest of the group." Turning my back so I can look back out the window, Blaine is dismissed. This time, while the others arrive is necessary to begin formulating my plan.

When Dusk initially told me of Jasmine pulling people back, I thought the girl had gone mad from being in such close proximity to the enemy for so long, a flaring of PTSD in her fragile mind. After all, the beasts did slaughter her entire family and original tribe. It delights me to be playing this mind game with her, watching her struggle to maintain her façade. If only I had the ability to put the rest of the group through the same torment.

Soon the rest of the heads of the Collaborative arrive and take their seats at the table. The buzzing of their side conversations is like nails on a chalkboard to my ears. The fact they are in my mere presence irritates me to no end. I can feel the ire and disgust rise in me. It is best to get this meeting over with before my office is painted red and new heads must be found.

Turning from the window, I walk to my place at the head of the table. Looking at the assembled party, my pawns, still conversing, paying no attention to my presence at the table, glaring around me I clear my throat. Soon silence looms in the air, all eyes are where they belong, but hold undertones of irritation at being interrupted, their insubordination is displeasing.

"Welcome, everyone," I drone out in a bored tone, "we have gathered here to go over new information provided by Dusk. It is time to lay out our plan of attack and begin taking what is ours."

Looking around the table, malevolent smiles begin to grace the faces of those amassed. A dark smirk graces my lips, my plot is finally coming to fruition, my pawns are playing as needed. When victory is mine, they will all get their just desserts, those in this room included.

"It seems Jasmine is pulling all her troops and trainers back to prepare for a large-scale battle against the Collaborative. She is going to bring them back in increments starting with those farthest away. This is our opportunity to go in and decrease her ally population prior to the battle. We can also decrease her warrior count by attacking those traveling back to their pack lands." Relaying this information brings me the closest I have ever been to joy. Such a silly emotion.

"Excuse me, Scion," Murick calls out from his seat at the table, "didn't we try this once before and were handed our backsides? I seem to remember Jasmine had forces hidden away in the ally lands. Why would now be any different?"

"This is true, but last time we did not have insiders. This time we not only have reports, but we have video confirmation. Jasmine is unstable at the moment; the Midnight Wolf is being confined and she is wanting to break out. She is making rash and rushed decisions so she can have her freedom. This is all to our advantage and we must strike now." Just enough urgency comes out in my voice to encourage these imbeciles to my point of view.

"The werewolves are with Scion on this, it is time to move. We have been idle for way to long; it is time to have blood in our fur and flesh hanging from our claws. It is time to take out the mixed-bloods and segregate. Now is the time, while packs and groups are weak, down on manpower and separated from larger forces, multiple attacks occurring simultaneously." Blaine agrees with me for the first time, his support on this is not surprising, he has not been able to commit genocide for a while now, and the beast in him is fighting to get out.

"Have we had anyone scouting these groups making the pilgrimage home? Are we certain there are no allies or enforcements lying in wait for us? What if they are using simple spells to mask the additional warriors? That has happened before, Red Crescent, I believe." Victoria snips out.

My lips pull back slightly, wanting to bare my fangs and push my power on her to bow before me. This can't be done now, though; they need to continue to believe we are all on equal footing.

"Patrol groups have been sent out, didn't your subordinates, Elise, specifically let you know they were sent out to unmask any magic?" My anger is beginning to creep into my voice.

Victoria looks down at her hands momentarily and then focuses blazing eyes on me. "They did not, but neither did you. Since when do you think it is acceptable to command my witches? We are to meet and then I direct them from there. Have you commanded any other groups without the heads being knowledgeable of your actions?" She looks around the room for reactions before landing her gaze back on me.

Chuckling out loud, I take a moment prior to responding. "Oh, Victoria, you forget this group voted me to be the ultimate head, in charge, until we can separate for good. There was no time to inform you, no one could locate you and there was no information on where you had gone. Naturally, speaking to the second-in-command was my next move. Please explain to us how I commanded your people?"

Victoria looks down at the table, playing with her fingers, as if she wants to conjure a spell against me. "It appears no wrong was done with the explanation just given," she finally concedes, her eyes sending daggers my way. This is one I will have to watch, she has too much fight in her.

"If that is all settled, let's put the squabbling aside and set a plan. Blaine's idea for a simultaneous multi-attack is a good place to start. Once we hit the lands and troops, we will have to assume Jasmine's pulling back of warriors will stop. Once that occurs, we will regroup and look at bringing the main battle to her before she can finish establishing her forces and formulating an attack plan."

Pointing to a map on the wall, we begin pointing out the areas where warriors have already departed, their routes back to their pack, and lands that have had partial warriors pulled back.

Two hours later all plans are in place, confidence rolls off me on to the others around the table. Every head knows where they and their people should be, when to attack and how to communicate in short time. Who knew the werewolves would be beneficial for communication needs? This plan is solid and will bring the odds into our favor for the last battle. The Midnight Wolf will never see us coming.

Chapter 98:

New Assistance

(Scion's POV)

The sun begins to set, a deep red bleeding into blue, as I gaze out towards the West, soon the Collaborative will begin the attacks on the Midnight Wolf's troops and allies. It has been near impossible to control myself the last 36 hours as well as the rest of the members. As we wait to begin anxiousness invades our systems, a need to bring an end to this threat to our ideals and purity of our species.

We are spread out among the ally lands, those who have had troops withdrawn at least; a group is set to ambush the unsuspecting warriors returning home. Anticipation courses through my body, anticipation at dealing a horrendous blow to my nemesis. Most of her pack has to come right by my lands, of course we will not attack them near here. We do not want them to locate our hideaway.

One werewolf is with each group to ensure we are able to communicate with all groups at the same time. Blaine is responsible for alerting us to start the attacks. This part of the plan still does not sit well with me, but it was important I give them some responsibility, some hope they are all equal in this endeavor.

My witches and I stay back at Vengeance's Gate, not wanting to be seen as part of the group. Hopefully we will be able to keep my participation in this quiet until the last moment, until the last battle. During that battle, my witches and I will expose ourselves, we will kill the Midnight and Blood wolves, kill their Goddess and the gods of all other supernaturals, setting myself on the seat as the true ruler.

As I am deep in thoughts of my future, the office door slams open, Saul rushes forward.

"Scion, it is beginning, Blaine has given the direction and the battles are commencing. Victory will soon be ours and we can push on to the end battle, rid ourselves of this foolish prophecy, this hoax."

This time I will overlook him barging into my space, but only because of the news he bears.

"Very good, Saul. Next time, knock before you enter and await a response, regardless of the information you have." Saul nods, lowering his eyes to the ground. What a weak being he is, ruthless, but weak. "Stay here for now and give me updates as they come in. I want to know all the details as they arrive."

From what was explained to me, the wolves have the ability to leave the mind-link open, while they are in battle, this allows for easier communication and response during a fight. The way they can communicate is perfect for me to have somewhat of a play-by-play as we wait for our plan to work its way out.

"Blaine breached the gates, but there is no one on the grounds. He says it is abnormally quiet. They are going to inspect the area. Micah, Paul, and the others have the same reports. The vampires are still waiting for the warriors to arrive, but the scouts have not relayed anything back regarding movements. There seems to be a standstill...wait...wait...what...no... how...when?" Saul stammers as he continues receiving information from the mind-link.

"Stop the stammering and tell me what is happening!" My nerves are shot, and Saul's incoherent babbling is not helping matters. I am close to snapping his neck.

"As they went farther into the lands all groups ended up being surrounded. She did it again, decoys. The pullback of troops was just for show. Somehow Jasmine was able to put in replacement warriors that went unseen by us and unreported by our insiders. All the groups are reporting the same thing, and the ambush is in reverse. They have all called for retreat, returning for a regroup to save as many fighters as possible." Saul's scared eyes come up to meet mine.

Without any thought to my actions, my speed brings me behind Saul, my hands grasp each side of his head, then I pull and twist, removing his head from his shoulders. A satisfying popping sound occurring as the muscles break loose and the spine gives way. The saying is not to shoot the messenger, but nothing has ever been said about decapitating the messenger, especially when they bring nothing but bad news.

"Maurice!" My voice echoes through the empty halls. "Maurice! Get in here and attend to this mess." Maurice appears before me and fear flashes in his eyes taking in the scene before him. "He gave me bad updates. Clean him up and dispose of him before the others arrive. Apparently, they are all retreating."

With my orders given, I leave the room. My witches and I must quickly get to the individual we have been saving as our back-up, our only hope of victory is with his assistance.

My footsteps echo down the hall as I rush to gather all necessary items for the impromptu meeting we are headed to. The witches arrive in the same room and surround me, clasp hands with each other, and begin chanting in their strange tongue. Soon a mist begins to rise from the floor and before I am aware of what is happening, we are hurtling through time and space.

In what seems mere seconds we desist our hurtling and come to rest in an arid, hot, and unforgiving environment. This place is reflective of the very individual we are seeking. I follow the witches as they lead me to our host, not a word is spoken between us and never do their eyes veer away from what is directly in front of them. They are hyper-focused on getting me to this meeting and the end mission. Bringing them to my side was the wisest move I made, their unwavering devotion to me has saved me on more than one occasion.

Soon, a large house sits before us, the outside matching the scorched earth around it. Sweat is dripping down my back, into the waistband of my slacks, vampires are not supposed to sweat, but this place has made everything that is known alter. I pause, leaning up against what appears to be a rock, catching my breath. The witches all turn to me and as one beckon to me with their hands to continue. I suppose there is time for comfort after this ordeal is done and the war is won.

We arrive before the massive stone door of this monolith, slowly it opens, showing four large men in chains pushing it to allow entrance. Their backs are crisscrossed with welts and scars, appendages crooked from being broken and setting incorrectly, faces mangled, causing an overall grotesque appearance.

I swallow in fear, even though there is no saliva left in my mouth, something that is not common for me. Our steps echo down the long corridor as we make for a room located at the opposite end, no one stops the witches, or me since it is apparent I am with them.

Without knocking, the door before us opens and we enter a large throne room, I flinch back as the smell of sulfur and decay hit my nose, continuing to move forward my eyes take in the space around me. Crosses are all around the edges of the room, on those crosses are bodies in varying degrees of death and decay. I alter my eyes to focus on only what is before me and not to take in any more detail of the room we are in.

On the throne is the most fearsome creature I have ever come face to face with, the throne must be at least ten feet tall from legs to seat, and this beast before me sits in it comfortably, his feet firmly set on the ground. There are no pupils or irises in his eyes, his teeth are sharp fangs, in the grimace he is trying to pass off as a smile. This thing is built, and looks like the very stone that surrounds him, but the air of evil radiates from him.

The witches stop before him and bow, taking their lead I follow suit.

"What have you brought to me, my dears?" a voice like thunder booms out into the room.

"Our true Lord, we have brought you the vampire we have been serving. He is looking for your grace to assist him. The prophecy is here, the Midnight Wolf has assembled her army, the army of the Goddess, this vampire has failed to stop her," the lead witch hisses to her lord.

Those dark human-less eyes fall onto me, eyes that are only pools of black. Those eyes take me in, measuring me, taunting me, reading me. A pain begins to throb in my head, but I do not move, a sinister smile spreads across the beast's face.

"You will be a welcome part of my followers. I have seen all you have done, your plans have not been horrible, but lack the correct power behind them. Swear yourself to me and I will help you defeat them; let you rule over them and pass my judgments onto them."

Without meaning to, my head nods in agreement to his order. A searing pain engulfs my left shoulder blade, there is a liquid running down my back from the spot. Looking over, I see a brand, burning itself into my flesh, oozing my bodily fluids from the site. Looking forward again there is a tether, connecting me with the creature. He lets out a painfully loud laugh and fear spreads throughout my body.

"Go back to where you came from, continue to wage small battles and when the time is right you will have some of my warriors to assist you. Do not fail me." The last words I hear before all goes black.

Chapter 99:

Small Battles

(Nóox' POV)

For a little over a month, we have been engaging in small battles, all based against our allies, it started with a significant move by the Collaboration, when they attacked all allies simultaneously. We didn't think it would be that largescale of an attack, maybe one or two packs, but it was every pack we had pulled warriors from. Thankfully Queen Jasmine was wise enough to supplement all the packs and give the warriors coming home back-up as well.

Scion has had no victories in his battles, but he is depleting our warriors and resources with the regular attacks, same as his, but at greater levels than ours. Muerta reported back there has been a change in him since the failure of his integrated attack on the allies and he has become more ruthless, darker.

We need to know what has caused this change, Angie is taking me to the location of the hidden pack lands, just getting close to the grounds will allow me to sense the energy coming from the place. The hardest part will be to remain hidden, I tend to stand out because of my height and bulk, even cloaked. Our plan is to remain in the forest, with trees as cover until we must leave them.

Shrouded in rough black fabric that conceals my entire body and hides my face, I make my way to the main gate of the pack grounds. Angie and I will be walking to our destination, after my first and only experience with shimmering, I refuse to use it as a means of transportation anymore.

"Nóox, let me walk with you to the gate," Queen Jasmine's voice catches me as I descend the last step of the packhouse. "I want to place an invisibility spell on the two of you, if I was thinking better, I would have done it in the packhouse away from any prying eyes, but at least I caught the two of you before you departed," she explains in a whisper as she approaches me, her green eyes lock onto mine and a smile brightens her face as she catches up to me.

Nodding to her, I offer my arm and she takes it, we make our way to the gate in a comfortable silence.

"Angie, I would like to see you and Nóox in the holding room before you depart, please," Queen Jasmine directs.

We all walk into the room, the fewer words spoken in public the better, we do not want many people knowing what we are doing. The door closes behind us and Queen Jasmine's voice reaches my ears.

"Sorry to catch you as you are departing, but I want to spell the two of you, invisibility. Hopefully it will give added protection, especially since Nóox doesn't blend in well with a crowd."

Angie laughs at this last part and all I can do is agree. Queen Jasmine is very straightforward in her thoughts and dealings. This is one of the reasons why I continue to assist her in this battle, this prophecy. She is strong, smart, and honest; she looks out for the wellbeing of all others.

With the spell in place Angie and I depart through the gate, following behind a merchant. It would be odd for the gates to open when it appears no one is there. The merchant continues his path South, while Angie and I break away, making our trip North. In about an hour's time we are nestled in the woods looking across to a section of land that looks no different from any others, one would never guess the area was a pack land.

"They had the four dark witches place a spell around the grounds to hide it from sight. The main gate is over there, hidden from regular view, so it doesn't cause suspicion when vehicles just disappear as they enter and leave," Angie points out.

The spell the witches have used is strong, there is no aura or presence coming from this place.

"Let's move to where the main gate is. I am unable to get a feel for what is happening here. Perhaps when the gate opens, some will slip through."

We move our position and wait for a car or truck to enter, luckily, we don't have to wait long, a five-ton full of warriors comes back, looks to be a scouting party. They must have been scouting a distance away to go via vehicle prior, I will have to remember to report this to Queen Jasmine on our return.

The gate opens to allow entrance to the truck, the darkest magic I have ever felt washes over me, there is only one place and one being that can cause this sort of dark and evil magic.

"Angie, shimmer us back to the pack grounds, Queen Jasmine's office. We have no time to lose."

Angie turns startled eyes towards me, but grabs hold of my hands and does as requested.

Next thing I know I am standing in Queen Jasmine's office, she is sitting in her chair behind her desk, the sunlight falling over her face as she concentrates on the paperwork in front of her. She is truly a beautiful being in every way.

Clearing my head of these thoughts, and dizziness from shimmering, I clear my throat. "Queen Jasmine, we have returned."

She looks up, raises a hand, and chants something. Soon Angie and I are visible again.

"I apologize for having Angie shimmer us directly into your office, but I must get to the Goddess. There is an evil and darkness present that we are not prepared for, I am going to leave immediately."

"What evil and darkness, Nóox? We know Scion is not a good person, but is he really that bad?"

"He is now, he has a new alignment. It is imperative I get to the Goddess; I will explain more when I return. Please tell Maverick and your aunt to begin training for the darkest magic they know how to defeat, and we should up the patrols and training regiments, include all the pack, even the children."

Queen Jasmine looks at me in concern.

I open the doors to the balcony and transform into Wiláu, this is the quickest way to get to the Goddess, as a thunderbird we have access into her realm, we do not have to wait for her to come to us in a dream. With an earpiercing screech, Wiláu takes to the air, and we shoot straight up through the clouds, just like an arrow.

We land in an open field, the Goddess' favorite lake only thirty feet away. This time of day my bets are she will be here, and when she sees Wiláu she will make her way to us in no time. Before I can finish my thought, gentle hands are felt on my feathers, turning my massive head, the Goddess stands before me.

"Wiláu, what a surprise to see you, even though it is lovely, the reasoning must not be, especially since you are unannounced. Shift back, my friend, and speak to me." Her gentle voice and touch soothe my anxiety.

My feathers recede and I once again take the form of a man.

"My Goddess, Wúlx has taken Scion as a follower and is assisting him in this battle." The Goddess' head snaps up at this information and her eyes turn a stormy blue. "All I can smell is his scent, no other beings are present right now, except Scion and the four witches. We have been being hit with small battles, almost daily, different ally groups. Our warriors and resources are taking large hits, but not near the hits Scion's warriors are taking, this leads me to believe when the final battle comes, Wúlx will send his warriors up from the depths." My voice cracks a little under the urgency. The thought of anything happening to Queen Jasmine and the others causes a pit to form in my stomach, nausea sweeps over me and the excessive saliva in my mouth warns me of the vomit about to leave my system.

Turning away from the Goddess, I empty the contents of my stomach onto the lush green grass, the vomit is as black as the darkest night. The evil that seeped in from just a few moments of exposure clearing from my system.

The Goddess looks at me startled. "His evil has grown; I have never seen this reaction to any other evil exposure before. You will need to get your convocation together and send them to assist as well. This is no longer a battle you can do alone." The Goddess places her hand on my shoulder as she continues.

"Jasmine will need to gather her army, she will need to attack first, during the daylight. The more enemies you can take out before the dark forces appear the better. A thunderbird will need to be with each group to help protect. Are there any other convocation's that can assist?" The Goddess is all business, planning to take care of her people. She knows now the threat is not just to her werewolves and other supernatural species, but to the gods themselves.

"The dark witches have placed a strong cloaking spell around the pack grounds, strong enough I was not able to sense anything through it. Scion was also smart enough to place it close enough to a human town, that if we were to have a battle the humans would be alerted to it and suffer casualties as well." She nods her head at the new information. "My cousin, Yulúm, his convocation would be happy to assist us in this battle. He has been itching for a good fight for a while now. His is a warrior convocation, no families reside there, only those faithful to you and fighting for you."

"We can break the cloaking spell easily enough; the humans are another issue," the Goddess mumbles, while deep in thought. She has her head down, lower lip in between her teeth, pacing as she processes all the information she has been given in this short amount of time.

"Nóox, go and speak with Yulúm, if he agrees to assist both of you come back here. We will discuss how to proceed then. I must think on this and not be rash in my choices. There are too many moving parts in this to not look at all aspects, but we still need to work quickly. Go now!" she urges me, and takes multiple steps back, allowing me room to transform. "Go in safety, my friend," she finishes.

Wiláu comes forward and we take off to Yulúm's convocation. I already know his answer, so this is just a formality, a formality directed by the Goddess and intended to be carried out.

Chapter 100:

Planning with the Goddess

(Nóox' POV)

Wiláu settles in a large, open prairie, wildflowers giving bursts of color to the emerald green of the tall grass, Spring in my cousin's lands is beautiful, there is still a chill that comes down from the mountains, snow scattered about their rocky faces, the cool wind rustles my feathers and Wiláu shakes them out, before allowing me to shift back to my human form.

Shifted back, I begin the walk to Yulúm's village. Before I am able to enter into the forest lands three warriors come from the tree line, as recognition crosses their faces, a smile breaks out over my own. My cousin's convocation and my own are very close, we often celebrate special occasions together, especially since my cousin's pack does not have any of the old recipes in it. All his warriors take turns cooking their meals, so trips to my lands guarantee good eating.

The three warriors come up to me with hands extended, reaching out we shake, and have a quick embrace, this is important in our culture, it shows respect and kinship, outside our homelands we don't often do this, unless we have integrated into a society, we develop a closeness to.

"Túu pée k'uuyám. Ma paxám kayaw á xumá." (Hello, friend. You come eat food.) The oldest warrior directs me.

"Tuuwuú'k." (Thank you.)

I begin to follow the men to the village. While my presence here is not uncommon, usually there are others with me, by the way the warriors are looking at me it is apparent they are wondering why I am alone. Actually, they are probably wondering where my mother is, they can always count on a great meal when she comes with me. My mother believes all people are perpetually hungry and it is her sole mission in life to feed them all.

We arrive at my cousin's house, and he steps outside. Laying eyes on me, he smiles and rushes forward, wrapping me in a tight hug. "Cousin, it has been a long time since I have seen you. Come, eat and tell me what you have been doing with yourself," he invites, while searching behind me. "Have you come alone? Is all well?" Concern begins to creep into his voice.

"The Moon Goddess has sent me. We need to talk; the supernatural world is in danger and dire need of our assistance." I fix him with a look that lets him know how serious this situation is.

"Come inside, cousin, let's talk."

"I have spent many months with a werewolf pack, sent there by the Goddess to assist them. The Midnight Wolf prophecy is coming to fruition."

Surprise enters Yulúm's eyes, as he sets a platter of salmon, acorn mush, and vegetables on a table between us, then takes his seat, not speaking, listening intently as I continue.

"Initially the attacks were conducted by a group called the Collaborative, headed by a vampire, but with representatives of many species. Their belief is purity of all species, no mixing of bloodlines, and those that are mixed must die. Queen Jasmine, the Midnight Wolf, has been training her army in all forms of warfare and battling by their side to ensure this does not come to pass. The Collaborative made a big push about a month ago to deplete the Queen's forces, they failed and suffered significant losses to their own numbers. This caused the vampire leader, Scion, to reach out for new assistance." Here, I pause, wanting to make sure I have my cousin's complete attention.

"Scion is now bound to Wúlx, he is a follower. Even though her forces are strong and well trained, the Queen's army is no match for what hells he will unleash. The Goddess has directed my convocation to join the battle, she is requesting yours do the same. This is a matter of the fate of us all. What we thought was mere segregation has ended up being a plan to rid us of our gods."

Yulúm stops eating, his eyes widening. "The Goddess backs this wolf and her claims of being the Midnight Wolf? She is pure of soul?"

"She is cousin. I have seen her wolf, helped train her wolf, fought beside her. The Midnight Wolf is a hybrid of werewolf and witch, her mother has already passed defending the supernatural world from this threat, her father continues to fight beside her, she does not kill out of vengeance, even though she would like to, when it comes to a certain male wolf, the one responsible for her mother's death."

"Very well, my convocation will answer the call of the Goddess, we will go into battle, we will stand beside you."

"The Goddess needs us to return to her for planning as soon as possible. We do not have time to waste."

Yulúm nods, we get up from our places, the platter empty, and head for the main door. As we walk out his second-in-command is there.

"Yáakhw, I am leaving with Nóox to meet with the Moon Goddess, we are being called to war, begin preparing the warriors for battle, when I return, we will depart immediately."

A curt nod is given and he is gone, carrying out his orders. Yulúm and I change into our thunderbirds, and depart, not wasting time to walk back to the prairie.

Moments later we are landing in the same field as before, this is the place the Goddess does her best thinking, it is doubtful she would have gone back into her palace after my departure. Sure enough, I once again feel gentle hands on my feathers, Wiláu remains still as she strokes his feathers, but Lóom screeches at her.

Yulúm changes immediately and looks down to the ground ashamed. "I apologize, Goddess, I will speak with my thunderbird, Lóom, and let him know you are not a threat."

"Do not worry yourself, it is your thunderbird's first time in my presence, and he was defending his family." The Goddess giggles. "He will soon learn; I am not a threat. Come, we have grave matters to discuss."

We follow her across the meadow to a gazebo located next to the lake and take the seats she indicates to us.

"The biggest matter we need to address is the humans in close proximity to the battlegrounds. Is there any way we are able to evacuate the area, without giving notice to Scion's group something is happening?" the Goddess begins.

"The areas are so close together, if any evacuation is made, the enemy will be alerted. As you know, humans are hard-pressed to leave their homes, even in the event of natural disasters, a mass exodus would cause suspicion and action, they would have their defenses up, even if we did the evacuation while our warriors waited in the woods, losing our element of surprise."

Both nod at this observation.

"Nóox, you mentioned the Queen is a hybrid witch, I would assume there are other witches supporting our Queen. Is there a way to place protective and sound barriers around the towns, then do a mind alter of the events post-battle of the human sections? Make it impossible for them to leave a specific border?" Yulúm inquires, still thinking through the plan he just put forward.

"Goddess, do you know? I would need to speak to Queen Jasmine regarding the ability to do that. Her aunt is allied with us, along with a few other covens, all strong witches, pair them with the fae and they are almost unstoppable. It is something to consider." Hope begins to well inside me as we start to work through how to protect the humans.

"I think it is possible, especially since we do have so many species working together and combining their powers. It is time we went to Whispering Red Winds and spoke with the core group, this time I will accompany the two of you. The rest of our discussion cannot be completed without Jasmine and the others," the Goddess finishes.

"You are coming with us, wouldn't you rather continue to bring Jasmine, um, our Queen, to you while in dream? It is not safe for you to cross over to their realm with Wúlx being involved." The caution has to be vocalized, our Goddess is more than strong enough to defend herself, but someone has to try and be the voice of reason.

"Thank you for looking out for my wellbeing, Nóox, but the current situation calls for me to make an appearance. I will ride down on the back of Wiláu, that way if there are any threats, you are right there to defend me, also since I will arrive at the same time as you, I can disguise myself until in the meeting room," she replies, smiling, our Goddess is happiest when up to some sort of playful mischief.

We all stand, Yulúm and I transform back into our thunderbirds, Wiláu gets as low to the ground as is possible and stretches out his wing, allowing the Goddess to climb up onto his back. With a couple strong flaps of our wings, we are airborne, heading back to the pack lands.

Chapter 101:

Time to Prepare

(Jasmine's POV)

Nóox' departure was quick and poorly explained, even though the reasoning was not laid out for me, I trust him completely and did take his requests seriously. Miles and Claire worked together to increase our patrols, while still being able to allow for the guards to have adequate rest time, thankfully Alpha Keith was able to lend some manpower to assist with this.

Many of our guards and warriors are injured or passed away with all the small battles the Collaborative has been waging against us. My heart aches at the loss of so much life, at families being torn apart, children being displaced due to that loss. We were able to set up new housing for the children orphaned by this battle, and man it with volunteer wolves to look after them. The children are being nurtured and cared for as best we can. Once this war is over, I will do more to make sure they thrive, to make sure all thrive.

My father walks into my office, sporting a large cut and bruise on the left side of his face. He sustained it while assisting Alpha Pete's pack in a current attack, an attack we could have used Nóox' help with. Hopefully he will return soon with information regarding the Goddess' plan for moving forward, or she will come to me in a dream and explain.

Shaking my head, I turn my attention to my father. "How are you feeling today, Dad? Did you ever make your way to the clinic and have that cut looked at?" Concern drips from my voice and I try desperately to not make it sound like I am a parent admonishing their child.

Dad lets out a hearty laugh. "My dear Jasmine, I appreciate your concern, love, but your old man is more resilient than you give him credit for, kiddo. It is a simple cut and will be healed in no time. If those darn fae wouldn't have used silver, it would be healed already, but yes, I went and had it looked at, just for you. Do not worry so much, I am not going anywhere besides the table over here to get some coffee. By the way, how is your leg? Did you have it looked at?" Dad quips back, eyebrows raised before he turns to walk to the coffee bar.

I watch him for a moment as he crosses the room, he moves slightly slower since Mom passed, but he is as strong and lethal as ever. The fear that resides in me is losing both of my parents, both of my rocks, tears sting my eyes as I think about the possibility. Placing a smile on my face and blinking away the tears, I turn back to the paperwork on my desk. This is not a topic I wish to discuss, but there is no getting out of it. In the same battle an arrow laced with wolfsbane, sliced my calf open, luckily it did not lodge in the leg or bone.

"Of course I did, Dad, can't have the future Queen unable to protect her people, but back to work; Miles and Claire have done a phenomenal job of working out the schedule for patrol and training, it was a monumental task."

Dad turns around at the comment and moves towards me.

"Yes, why did Nóox request the increase? Not that you tricked me into changing the subject, mind you." Dad winks at me with a smile.

"He did not explain it in detail. Only said there was an evil and darkness we are not prepared for. Whatever it was, it was significant enough to have Angie shimmer him directly into my office. We all know how he feels about that mode of travel," I chuckle out, remembering the first time he shimmered.

"Yes, yes. So, they have Ashley training the pups today, perhaps we should go to the training grounds and see how the Blood Wolf does with training children."

My eyes widen at this news, it was not mentioned to me they were having her train the young ones.

"Let's go see how that is going and make sure no one is traumatized by a simple training task directed by their Alpha," I blurt out, walking from behind my desk, I link my hand through my dad's arm, and we exit my office, making small talk as we go to our destination.

In record time we make it to the training grounds, much to my surprise, Ashley is doing a wonderful job with the pups. She has managed to make their training seem like a form of play, so they are learning and having fun at the same time. Ashley is not my main concern, but her wolf, Grace, is a little on the scary side, as she is meant to be. Maybe that is why Ash remains in human form to train the pups. What looks like an unorganized free for all dog pile is scattered with offensive and defensive moves. The pups are attacking Ashley, and she is defending while attacking back. One big fun "wrestling match."

Dad and I are laughing at the sight before us when gusts of wind begin to sweep across the training grounds from out of the blue, blowing dust and debris everywhere. Some of the equipment on the field begins to sway and groan under the power of the wind. The skies are clear, no storm clouds, none of the witches are in the training area. Ashley gathers the pups and moves them into a sheltered space, until we know what is causing this odd weather.

A screech sounds out above us, looking up we see who can only be Wiláu and another thunderbird, there appears to be someone seated on Wiláu's back, but I am unable to determine who the person is. Shielding my face from the wind and debris, I wait until the birds have landed.

Fifteen small voices all scream out, "Wiláu!" at once and the massive bird is surrounded by the pups, hugging his legs, and petting his feathers, cooing softly to the large thunderbird they have missed. Wiláu lowers his massive head and gives each child a gentle nuzzle, the other bird looks at him quizzically as he does. Once done Wiláu spreads out his wing and a female departs from his back.

"Do you know this woman, Dad?" I inquire.

"Nope, never seen her before, but her aura is something else; calming and peaceful. Wonder who she is, guess we will be introduced soon enough, once Wiláu is done with the children and lets Nóox come back to us."

As we approach, the thunderbirds shift to their human forms, the second man is slightly shorter than Nóox, body build is a close match, ebony hair and his facial features are remarkably the same. If I had to guess I would say they are related, but I don't want to jump ahead of myself. The man looks at my father and I approaching then assumes a defensive pose. Nóox reaches out and places a hand on his forearm, causing the man to relax.

"Queen Jasmine, Alpha Alexander, so good to see the both of you. If we can, please, call together the group and have a meeting with the people joining me. We have a lot to discuss, and time is getting short." His eyes are full of concern and there appears to be a hint of fear as I gaze deep into his chocolate pools.

Nodding my head at his request I clear my throat. "Welcome to Whispering Red Winds, it is nice to meet you. Ashley, can you get one of the other warriors to finish training the pups, please, then mind-link the rest of the group you are able to. Dad, please call Alpha Keith, then get Aunt Meredith and Maverick." Turning back to Nóox and our guests, "Please come with me to my office. There are beverages and snacks, but I will reach out to the kitchen to prepare something more substantial, it is past lunchtime, and you must be hungry." Turning, I head back into the packhouse, the sound of footsteps echo behind me, alerting me our guests are following my requests.

Back in the office, I direct the newcomers to the couches, "Please have a seat, there is a coffee bar located against the far wall. The group should be assembled soon. Is there anything specific you would like me to order from the kitchens?" I look to each of the newcomers when asking this and both shake their head indicating no preferences. Not sure if any of the others will be hungry or not, I figure it is best to just request a platter of varying types of sandwiches, salad, and fruit.

"The staff should deliver sandwiches soon. I thought I would wait for formal introductions until everyone has arrived, so you are not having to repeat the process multiple times." The duo just nods to me. "Nóox, as you requested, we have increased patrols and training, as a matter of fact Ash was training the pups when you arrived. We are all curious to find out the reasoning behind it now that you are back." My eyes fall onto the man who has become one of my closest confidants over the last few months, thankful he has returned home.

"Queen Jasmine, I notice you are walking with a slight limp, and your father has some injuries to his face. What happened while I was gone?" Concern is evident in Nóox' voice and his eyes shine with worry.

"Oh, the Collaborative attacked Alpha Peter's pack again, this time with Fae and wolves, they were armed with silver weapons. One of the Fae managed to get Dad in the face with a silver dagger and I caught an arrow laced with wolfsbane to the calf. It is fine, healing as we speak."

A half-hearted smile flashes across my face. The female with Nóox sends me a look full of doubt at my statement, she doesn't know me so I am unsure how she can judge my statement.

"We lost four more warriors in that battle, good wolves." My voice quiets and my hands are very interesting as I do my best to blink back the sting of tears.

At that moment my office door opens, and the entire group enters as one. Zeke, Keith, and Dad carry the trays of food with them. Thank Goddess for the interruption.

"Well, everyone is here, and the food has arrived with them, please help yourselves and let's start this meeting. Nóox, please do the introductions and you have our undivided attention."

"Yes, as you all noticed I have brought back a couple folks with me. This is Yulúm, or Eagle, my cousin. His thunderbird is Lóom or Cedar, the lady is better known in her other form, you all know her as Moon Goddess."

Collectively we all turn our heads to the female and before our eyes she transforms back to her normal look.

"I apologize for changing my appearance, but it is important no one knows it is me who arrived with the thunderbirds. I will be leaving with Yulúm when he departs. This information and the meeting is too important for me to not be here." She sends a brilliant smile around the table and we all nod, remaining silent. Whatever is occurring is more significant than first thought, not only by me, but the rest of the group.

"When Angie took me to view the enemy lands the other day and get a sense of what power they had, I felt an evil that has not made itself known for a long time. There is a beast that lives in the underworld, a beast that answers to no one, but himself. His name is Wúlx, he is not Hades or Lucifer, but another entity; as a matter of fact, he would like to dispose of the other two and all other gods, becoming the only ruler of all, enslaving those who populate the earth and supernatural realms. He has at his disposal fighters that make hell-hounds seem like puppies."

My eyes widen as Nóox begins his explanation, my heartbeat ticking up and butterflies coming alive in my stomach.

"Scion and the witches who stand beside him are followers of him. When we go into our final battle, we will be fighting the hell he sends up from below. As a single thunderbird, I am not able to battle him, but my convocation and my cousins will join in this battle, giving us a couple hundred thunderbirds to assist in battle. Yulúm's convocation is purely warriors and trained for this type of fighting, as are my warriors." He pauses to take a breath and sip of water.

"We have been trying to think of a way to take the fight to the Collaborative, but not endanger the humans close to their lands. The main thought was to place protective and silence barriers around the human populations, with an impenetrable border from both sides, then do a mind alter of the events, post battle. Queen Jasmine, Prince Jasper or Meredith, is this something that would be able to be done?"

"Jasmine is the strongest witch out of all the covens allied to her, there is a spell, but it is difficult and has not been taught to her at that magnitude. Even if we began working on it now, my concern is it would drain her of her powers and strength, meaning she would not be able to fight in the battle, she would be exposed to the forces and unable to protect herself. The spell is meant to be defensive only, the caster is meant to be inside the shield," Aunt Meredith explains with a grim look on her face, glancing around the table.

"This is true, Meredith, but the Fae have been working on a similar shield, I am not sure exactly how they work it, but they use multiple Fae, non-warriors, elders, I seem to recall, that way, they are able to be encased in the shield and their powers are strong. We can ask Ember once she and Morg arrive," Prince Jasper speaks up.

As if on cue, there is a brilliant shimmering light in the corner of the room, as it dissipates, we can make out the figure of our Fae and troll representatives. Quickly they are brought up to detail on all that is occurring, taking their seats, Ember looks around the room.

"The Fae do have a shield that can be placed, exactly as Prince Jasper has mentioned. Our elders demanded a way to stay involved in the defense of our lands even though they could not partake in physical battle. This was our fix for them, also they will not be drained and will be able to place a charm, so the battle is unnoticed, voiding the need for mind altering. Kinder treatment to our human counterparts." Ember smiles with the last statement.

"Thank you for the information, Ember," our Goddess begins, "it looks as though the planning stage is going well. Jasmine, will you be able to house three to four hundred thunderbirds on your lands as well as all the warriors from the Fae, trolls and elves?"

"That will not be an issue. We have had a couple additional barracks built, preparing for the upcoming war. Our food stores have been well stocked, to account for additional manpower. We can easily take in all the additional troops and maintain those already here and not worry about stores for a year."

"Very good. I knew I had chosen the correct Queen. We will go to battle in no more than six weeks' time. All troops need to be in place by tomorrow noon, no later. While it would benefit us to go to battle sooner, we must train together, learn how to fight as one, with all our different styles. Our very existence depends on it. It is time Yulúm and I depart, it is best if we go alone, it will gain less attention that way."

We nod our understanding, processing the fact we will enter our final battle in such a short time.

Our Goddess morphs into her disguise once again, and she and the thunderbird depart the office. The rest of us remain behind, discussing housing, training, patrols, and how to ensure the safety of the nonfighters on all the ally lands.

Chapter 102:

Arrival of the Forces

(Jasmine's POV)

After the meeting let out last night, sleep evaded me. What else was there to do besides make sure all the accommodations for our incoming surge of forces are ready? So here I am, making sure the barracks are squared away, rooms clean, bedding in place, shower rooms have plenty of towels and soap, plus the lounge room is packed with snacks and drinks.

Daybreak is peeking through, the sky is streaked with pinks and oranges, the blazing glow of the morning orb is rising above the trees. I stand in the front yard of the last barracks building, a gentle breeze caressing my skin and rustling my hair, hints of summer teasing my nose. This is the calm before the storm.

Closing my eyes, I enjoy the breath of air swirling around me. As I stand there, I think of what else needs to be done, the safety rooms still need to be inspected, the main task is done, now it is time to ensure those who cannot fight are taken care of. There are three safe havens on the pack grounds for our members to go, everyone has been designated to a specific spot. Once the new forces arrive, we will need to find out if there is a necessity for a fourth, then have less than six weeks to build and stock it. Alpha Mason and Dad will be good points of contact for that, they will get the news at breakfast.

I make my way towards the old Red Crescent side of the pack grounds first, may as well start with the farthest one and work my way home. The sound of flapping, and a more forceful air current causes me to pause and look towards the sky, above me is Wiláu, preparing to land.

The massive bird's talons settle onto the earth, he shakes out his feathers, then sets his eyes on me, tilting his head in question. "What, Wiláu, I am checking on the bunkers for the nonfighters, making sure they are prepared and our people, my people, are safe. Don't give me that look, or I will pluck your tailfeathers!" This last part comes out with a giggle as I rub the top of Wiláu's head. Soon the feathers give way to flesh and Nóox is before me.

"Queen Jasmine, you are not supposed to be out without a guard. Did you forget in the short amount of time I was gone?" Playfulness sparkles in the dark orbs of his eyes as he gives me his half-hearted lecture.

"Oh, I remember; sleep was not my companion last night, so I thought it best to use my time wisely and prepare the barracks and bunkers. What are you doing out so early?"

"You missed our training this morning, when I checked your room and there was no response, I began to worry. Instead of waking everyone up and sounding the alarms, the best bet was you once again set out on your own and all that was needed was locating you, and look, I was correct." A warm smile is plastered to his face. "It is good to see you are safe and unharmed. I cannot stress enough this new danger." His playfulness has left him, and his eyes are serious.

"Yes, Nóox, I do not doubt the seriousness of the situation. There was no reason to rob any of you of your sleep. I let time slip away from me and forgot about training, today is going to be very hectic. Will you come with me to check the bunkers?"

"Absolutely, My Queen."

"Please call me Jasmine when we are alone. I know you will not do it when others are around, we have already had that discussion on more than one occasion, but I am not Queen yet, there is still a battle to be won."

Nóox places his hand on my shoulder comfortingly, a caring look on his face. "Yes, Jasmine, I will go with you."

By seven in the morning the bunkers have been checked and any delinquencies taken care of, my nerves are settled my people will be as prepared and taken care of as possible. Nóox and I make our way to the main dining hall for breakfast, starting today, all meals will be taken here, and I have put in place a dedicated kitchen staff. There are too many supernatural beings here to have meals occurring in multiple places. The staff will be working twelvehour shifts, and ensure there is sustenance at all times, since training and patrolling will not stop.

Stepping into the dining hall we grab plates and serve ourselves, today my plate is holding healthy servings of eggs, bacon, fruit and oatmeal with berries and cream, of course coffee on the side, lots of coffee. Nóox and I find a table to sit at and are soon joined by other members of the group. We talk shop while eating breakfast, the hours of the day seem to be decreasing and every moment has to be taken advantage of.

"Dad, Alpha Mason, do you mind taking a count of nonfighters once the additional forces are here? We need to know if an additional bunker must be built and stocked for them, or if they can be settled into one of the three, we already have." Both men nod in my direction. "The barracks are ready for the influx of forces; we have additional rooms in the two packhouses for those who are not warriors. Claire, were you able to get with Miles and figure out an around-the-clock training schedule? Let's not forget the groups arriving today will have some trainers with them to help lighten the load on our people, but I would like a good mix of all. Any disputes between any groups need to be brought to me and dealt with immediately, fighting in the ranks is not something we can afford." I push my plate to the side and rest my arms on the table, cradling my coffee as we continue to talk.

"Yes, Alpha Jasmine, everything is taken care of. Miles and I will get with the heads of training and warriors as they arrive. We will have a meeting and make your expectations known. Ashley also plans on being in that meeting, since as Blood Wolf she is general of the Goddess' army," Claire follows up, looking at me, eyebrows drawn. "Did you sleep last night, Alpha?"

"No. Let's move on, though. Zeke, please put a meeting on the books for five this evening. We will do dinner in the office. It needs to be the regular group and all key personnel from all visiting allies. Make sure all packs are linked in via conference call if they cannot make the meeting in person. I do not expect them to leave their pack lands currently, with the continuous battles occurring that is not fair to ask. Safety first."

"Jasmine, maybe you should take a moment to get a shower and rest a bit." Dad's voice cuts in as I continue to direct folks; looking at him, the nononsense parent look is plastered on his face and arguing with him will be futile at best.

"That is a good idea, Dad. If there isn't anything else, I will head to my room." No one has anything additional to add. "Please link me when Alpha Keith gets here, he plans on being present for the arrival of everyone. Also let's do some training at 10:00 to get some of this extra energy out of my system." With those last remarks, I make my departure and head to my room.

Ten o'clock comes way too soon, but my fatigued body is on the training grounds, my foggy mind fails to notice an incoming blow from Nóox, but Ash blocks him, sending me a scowl that screams at me to get my head in the game. Luckily no one has arrived yet, or this would be an awful introduction to their future Queen. Squaring up my shoulders, I shake off the tiredness, and begin engaging as I should be. Aunt Meredith sends a wind tunnel my way, I infuse it with water and send it back at her, crashing over her and those around her, while simultaneously doing a backward karate kick, into the gut of a warrior sneaking up behind me. Ash and I go back to back, while we surveille those around us.

Suddenly we break apart, landing hard thirty feet from each other, a smiling Maverick, standing where we had been just moments before. "Ladies, don't forget to use all your senses, not just your eyes, even in the heat of battle. You both should have been able to notice a change in the air around you to know something was there." These painful reminders are always good to reground us to what we need to be doing. Getting back up to our feet, we begin sparring again, all the forces of my trainers and protectors against the Blood Wolf and me.

A loud screech sounds out above us, as the sky darkens, looking up alarmed, the air above is clouded by multitudes of wings, cutting out the sun's rays. The dust is beginning to fly in our eyes; shielding ourselves, we move out of the way, allowing the thunderbirds room to land, they are spread out across the training grounds as far as I can see.

Nóox and I walk towards Yulúm, Nóox hugs his cousin, while I extend my hand out for him to shake. Surprise hits me, when a smile covers Yulúm's face, and he pulls me in for a tight embrace. I give a few awkward pats to his back, while remaining stiff in his hold. I don't mind hugging, when I know the person, but I only met this thunderbird once.

A gentle laugh reaches my ears from behind me. "Yulúm, she is not used to our customs, I think you are making her a little uncomfortable. Queen Jasmine does not tend to hug people unless she knows them well, give it time, cousin."

Finally what Nóox is saying sinks into my mind and before Yulúm can release me I genuinely return the hug; I think I like this custom of theirs.

A woman pushes her way to the front of the group, stopping once she is beside Yulúm, she turns her eyes to Nóox, and I know in an instant this is his mother. No one can look at another person with the pride and love she has shining through her deep chocolate orbs unless you have birthed them. Looking at her closer, there are bits of grey running through her black hair, she stands equal in height to me, her body is sinewy and trim. A smile lights up her face and she opens her arms.

"Khapáxa!" (Son!) Her voice is soft, smooth, and calming, running over my frayed nerves, even though I do not understand what she is saying.

Nóox walks into her open arms and hugs her tightly. While they are embracing, I take the opportunity to mind-link the kitchen we have at least 400 additional warriors on grounds, this way they will be able to make up for any short falls in the lunch plans, I also let them know we are still awaiting three other groups.

The woman runs her hands over her son's face, arms, and torso. A flash of indignations lights up her face. "Makwath páanx? (Are you hungry?) Maánii ts'ámx. (You are not healthy.) Áay wétekwath xumá kauaw a? (Do they not have food to eat?) Paxám Khapáxa, makwath xumá, makwath yúukh!" (Come, son, you have food, you have strength.) She sends me a look and then grabs Nóox' hand in a no-nonsense manner and stomps off toward the packhouse. I stare after them, my jaw hanging open, trying to understand what just happened.

"It seems his mother does not think you are feeding him enough," Yulúm states from beside me, "but then, no one can ever feed him as well as she can." He laughs. "Let's get the warriors to the barracks and settled, then I will bring the rest of the family accompanying us to the packhouse for introductions."

I nod my agreement and turn to show them the way.

Before us is a shimmering of light, from that shimmer materializes half the Fae army with Ember in front. "Alpha Jasmine," at lease someone listened when I asked not to be called Queen yet, "we are no doubt on time. Good to see you again."

"Good to see you too, Ember. I was going to show the thunderbirds to their barracks and get them settled in before lunch. If you will come with us, I will be more than happy to direct your warriors to their space as well." Ember nods and falls into step on the other side of me. "We are just waiting for Prince Jasper and his elves to arrive, then."

No sooner had the words left my mouth than loud grumbling and curses are heard behind us.

We turn to see what the commotion is about and see Prince Jasper, with a shy smile on his face, he and his warriors managed to arrive, directly in the middle of the all the other warriors.

"The Elven army has arrived!" Price Jasper declares dramatically.

Shaking my head, I turn back around, raise my arm above my shoulder and beckon the group forward with a wave of my hand.

"Once everyone is settled and has had lunch, we will have a meeting in the training grounds for everyone, afterwards Claire and Miles will meet with the head of the warriors and anyone else you see fit to go over patrol and training schedules. Please let your warriors know. I am assuming the three of you will want to stay in the packhouse?" All three nod their heads.

"Morg asked me to let you know he and his trolls will be staying in the woods instead of the barracks. They will be in for lunch and all meetings. He is worried the barracks will not be large enough for his warriors," Ember speaks up as we walk.

"That is fine. Thank you."

With all pertinent information out of the way, we make the rest of the trip in silence.

Chapter 103:

Getting in Sync

(Jasmine's POV)

Looking out before me from the podium, there are warriors as far as the eye can see and beyond. Zeke had to set up a special sound system so the meeting will be able to be heard by all. I am amazed at the number of forces that have arrived, we have filled all the additional barracks and any open rooms in the others from deceased warriors, plus all the packhouses spare rooms are taken. My heart swells with pride to know all these beings are here to fight for the benefit of the realm. To support all those who make up the supernatural world. Stepping up to the microphone I clear my voice, side chatter stops, all eyes turn to me. To be honest it is a little unnerving being the center of attention to so many.

"Welcome to Whispering Red Winds. I am Alpha Jasmine, also known as the Midnight Wolf." I quickly introduce the rest of the individuals on stage with me, to include Nóox' mother. I am unsure if this is a custom for them or not but decided not to fight it.

"From today forward we will be training together and learning each other's styles and skills in fighting, so we are a more cohesive group. Your trainers as well as Gamma Claire and our head warrior Miles will have a meeting later to discuss your rotations and hand out your schedules. If there are any issues or concerns, they will be brought to me or any of the staff here. Let me make this very clear right now. I will not tolerate any fighting in the ranks. The enemy we face is too strong to have fighting amongst ourselves;

however, in a group this large it is common for there to be some conflict so it will be resolved quickly and fairly. Understood?"

A massive echoing of "Yes, ma'am" vibrates through the air, it is a little eerie knowing there are enough bodies here to create that type of force from voice alone.

"In a few weeks' time, we will be in a battle for the fate of the supernatural world. We, here on this stage, are putting forth everything we have to ensure your training is comprehensive. If you feel there is something that needs to be addressed, please notify one of the trainers in your group. Once you have been broken into your groups, your trainers will give you a tour of the pack grounds. Thank you all for your dedication, you are the protectors of our future." Looking around me, pride shines from the eyes of those I am able to see.

"Gamma Claire, the microphone and podium are all yours."

Claire walks up beside me and gives me a respectful nod. Sending a smile to her, I step away and let her take over.

"Good afternoon. I will be the individual in charge of all training and patrols. Once we have settled the schedules, we will be having all those in the same training groups bunk together. Morg has informed me the trolls prefer to stay in the wooded areas instead of the barracks and that will be the only exception allowed. The trolls will be integrating in all other activities, so no grumblings about preferential treatment need to be started." She sends a steely gaze over the assembled pack, asserting her dominance, no sound is made, but hundreds of heads nod in unison.

"I apologize, there is one point that must be clarified, while I am in charge here, Ashley, also known as the Blood Wolf, is appointed as the general of the Goddess' army. If she directs you to do something there should be no question given, follow through with her directive. She will be making significant input on the training for us."

"We have a lot to accomplish and not much time to accomplish it. This battle coming up is not about getting Alpha Jasmine to the throne as Queen, it is about securing the future of the supernatural world, of making sure your families and kin are able to survive and live in a free world, a world without segregation. The trainers will be hard on you because this is the truth we know. We want all of you to return to your families and it is our job to prepare you for that. Are there any questions?"

Not a sound is made, quiet assaults the ears as the massive group stands in silence, not daring to question my Gamma. She has made her points and position known. Claire turns to look at me and I give her a nod of approval, she turns back to the microphone.

"You are all dismissed to go back to your barracks."

The air comes alive with activity and chatter at the dismissal.

As we step down from the stage, I take my father's arm and pull him into the throng of warriors. The rest of the group follows behind us, it is important to me to make contact with as many fighters as possible, to let them know of my appreciation at leaving their homelands. To show we are all warriors and dedicated to fighting with them. They receive us well, some with surprised looks on their faces.

Once we have made contact with as many warriors as possible, we make our way to the packhouse.

"Claire, once you get the schedules made, I need a copy, please. My plan is to circulate through the groups and train with each one. Ashley, you will need to accompany me on this as well. I will not make it a necessity for the rest of you, but if you choose to do so, I think it will only benefit you in the long run, build trust and comradery."

Nóox' melodic voice flows over me, "I will be accompanying you, My Queen."

Pausing, I turn to look at him, of course he will come with me. I also notice a look on his mother's face when he tells us this, it is difficult to tell what is on her mind and what she is thinking. She turns to me and gives a smile that doesn't quite reach her eyes but is still warm. I feel as if I am being assessed by her, but not sure why or what for.

Turning back around we continue to the packhouse, "Thank you, Nóox, that will be great. There is much you can teach the groups. Gamma Claire and Ashley, I believe there is a meeting for the two of you to get to soon. What office will you be using?"

"We will be in the main meeting room on the first floor, it is the largest and we are not positive how many will be in attendance," Ashley responds quickly.

"Very well. Dad and Alpha Mason, if you could please get with all the groups and begin on the task of getting a count on nonfighters who will need to be housed during the battle. We don't have much time to make those preparations."

"Absolutely, honey, Alpha Mason, let's get to work."

They break from the group and head out a side entrance, laughing in conversation as they go. Without the support of those two, I do not know how I would handle all this. They take on any task without complaint, they keep me grounded and logical.

"The rest of you, let's head up to my office and see what other tasks we need to accomplish."

With this directive, we begin to make the stair climb to the eighth floor, as we reach the final landing it occurs to me we could have used the elevator or at least offered it as an alternative. I will need to keep this in mind for future trips. As we enter through my office door, I motion for those with me to take a seat on the couches and chairs, a far more comfortable choice than the meeting table and chairs. "For those present who have not been to my office, there is a beverage bar with snacks located against the far wall, please help yourselves."

Waving my hand in the direction of the location, I take a seat in one of the armchairs.

"Zeke, do we have surveillance on Vengeance's Gate so we can bring Muerta back to the pack lands? I want her out of there and would prefer to have her with us for the beginning of the war, especially since Nóox has warned us about this new player siding with the Collaborative, no chances need to be taken."

"Ember and I are going after our meeting this evening, she is going to help cloak me so no one will know we are there putting surveillance in place.

You wouldn't happen to be able to do the cool bugging your mom did at Broken Moon, would you?" Zeke has his head leaned over the headrest of the chair, fingertips tapping out a beat on his chest as he gazes at the ceiling above.

"Umm…no… Aunt Meredith?"

"That is a new one for me too, dear. Really wish I could have seen it and learned it from her. Sounds like it was incredibly helpful." She sighs, taking a delicate sip of her fresh cup of tea.

"So, it is true? You are able to do magic and have all your wolf powers combined? I thought my son was teasing me," Tiiyú directs towards me, her eyes inquisitive and wise, even deeper chocolate than her son's. This is the first time she has directly spoken to me, for a moment this is what I dwell on and there is a pause in me answering her.

"It is true. For a long time Nóox was the only one who knew, he and Wiláu helped to train Brooke and myself in the finer arts of using our powers together. He has been a great teacher and friend to me." My voice is low, fatigue is beginning to creep into my body, especially sitting in this chair, maybe the table and hard chairs would have been a better idea after all.

We all sit silently for a moment after my comment.

"I would like a member of this group to assist the kitchen staff during different times of the day. Multiple can go at once if they would like, not to micromanage, but to assist in preparation and serving as well as to run interference for any disputes or suggestions. The staff should not have to shoulder that as well. We need to support them as best as possible. I am going to head there this evening."

"It would be a pleasure to assist in the kitchens, cooking comforts me and is a perfect way to allow me to be involved in the war effort. Nóox will not let me fight with the assembled masses."

Tiiyú sends a look to her son, a look of playfulness and exacerbation at his over protectiveness.

"Thank you, Tiiyú, your assistance would be greatly appreciated, and we can make sure to incorporate some of your favorite recipes and give our cooks more to work with." Her help is exactly what we need there. "Once we are done in this meeting, I am heading to the other side of the pack lands until the meeting. Even with everything going on, the children need to know, they are still important to this pack and a part of it. My mind-link will be always open, if I need to be contacted. Until we go to war, we will need to send additional warriors to watch over them, this may be good training for our junior warriors."

No one has any additional comments for me.

"We all know our jobs and what needs to be done. Let's do our best for our people, we cannot fail them, we have an entire realm depending on us to take the threat of darkness away." As I rise from my chair all the others do also. "See you all at 5, dinner will be provided in the office."

Everyone begins to file out the door. Alpha Keith hangs back as does Nóox and Tiiyú, they all receive an inquisitive look from me.

"One of you boys had better start talking and soon. The two of you waiting back from the others together tells me this is not going to be news I relish."

"Jazz, why don't we talk on the way to the pack children's home?" Keith requests.

I nod slowly in agreement, while still looking at the both of them, furrowing my brow in concern over what they could possibly have to tell me. It appears I am not the only one giving them a look, they are both receiving an all-too-famous mother look from Tiiyú.

"Alright, we will take the elevator down this time, the conversation can begin immediately."

Keith and Nóox refuse to look me in the eyes at this directive. Important, but not something they want to share or bring up. Interesting.

Walking into the elevator, the door closes behind us and Keith pushes the button for the ground floor. Silence looms as the two men share uncomfortable glances, looking as if they are mentally drawing straws to see who has to give me the news they share. Finally, Keith is the one to begin.

"Jazz, we were thinking that perhaps it would be best if you remained in the fourth phase and protected the pack lands, while we go forward and take the fight to Scion. This way, you still fight, but are also better protected."

Keith rushes his words out of his mouth as one run-on sentence. My ears cannot believe what they have just heard from his mouth.

"Who is 'we,' Keith? Obviously you and Nóox, but who else?" My gaze bores into him, driving home my displeasure and hurt at his suggestion.

"Actually Nóox, Zeke, Ashley and your father did not agree, everyone else did. We thought it was best to better protect you, allow there to be no chances on your safety so you can reign."

Keith's eyes find new interest in the elevator floor. Anger radiates off me as I maintain my silence, attempting to work through this ire to formulate a response I will not regret later.

"Everyone's concern for my safety is appreciated, there is no doubt there is a target on my back. A target put there by the Moon Goddess when she chose me for this prophecy, who are you and the rest of the group to question her? It is not an acceptable plan, and it is not a plan that will be considered. The individuals staying back to protect the pack lands will be those still recovering, those in training, half your forces, an eighth of my forces and possibly you and others in agreement with you if this is brought up again in the next few weeks. My place is at the front of this army, leading. I will not cower and refuse to stand tall, to defend those who rely on me."

"Understood, Jazz. I am sorry, I should not have doubted you," Keith mumbles out.

Even though anger still courses through my veins and Brooke is growling in my mind, I move forward and wrap Keith in a hug. This is nothing to having a falling-out over, he is still like my brother. Explains why Nóox was not willing to take any ownership in telling me this news while Keith was present. Smart man.

Chapter 104:

Battle Awaits

(Jasmine's POV)

Three weeks have passed since our lands were inundated by warriors of the realm; they are coming together as a very cohesive group, more than willing to learn the styles of their neighbors and now friends. This upcoming war has bonded us, a bond that will stay in place well after the battle is over. With that connection, the losses we suffer will be devastating. A warrior's bond as a family is special in a way that is difficult to describe unless you have been part of a group that chooses to die for each other and the greater good, lay down your life, so others will prosper. None of us want to die, but the fact is some of us will.

No warrior has voiced or shown any issue following a female into battle, Ash and I have rotated through all the training groups multiple times, taking each step with them, sparring with them. My trainers have taken these opportunities to also showcase the powers Ash and I have as the Goddess' chosen. They have done surprise attacks, even Nóox and Yulúm as a duo, I don't think Nóox told his cousin exactly how powerful we were prior to the attack, he was rather taken aback by our response to him, as he flew into a tree. Thunderbirds do not regularly get outpowered by our kind.

Besides training, we built an additional two bunkers and have them supplied, running many exercises so our people know what to do if battle finds its way to our lands. My confidence at their ability to protect and remain safe is high. The Goddess has blessed me with strong supernaturals. Dad and

Alpha Mason decided to build a bunker under the children's home, so they do not have to cross any distance, making themselves vulnerable to attack; why the idea never crossed my mind is unclear, I am so thankful for those two.

Tiiyú has been amazing assisting the kitchen staff, you can see the joy she gets watching all the warriors eat and eat well, the smile she has on her face during mealtime is broad and proud. It is funny and adorable the way she fusses over Nóox and how he turns red at the mothering he receives in front of the others. Tiiyú has rearranged the entire kitchen and made it more work friendly for the staff and she started an herb garden behind the building and some of the more frequently used vegetables are growing there too. She is amazing and actually had a tear or two in her eye when I tasked the kitchens to her solely.

I stare at the map on my office wall of the area we are going for battle, running over the plans we made and searching to see if we are missing anything. Ember and her elders came for a meeting yesterday and are solid on the plans to protect the human village from the impending battle, occurring on their doorstep. Nóox and Yulum seem a little apprehensive if their powers will be enough for the evil that will surface as we progress, so Aunt Meredith has added some of the elder witches to the cause. The combined elders are giddy in the anticipation of having a part to protect the realm, they have come alive knowing they have a place to help.

The air behind me rustles and there is an odd noise, turning around, Muerta is standing in front of me. She has cuts, scrapes and a stab wound to her abdomen. I rush to her side as she begins to fall to the floor, covered in her blood and barely holding on to consciousness, scooping her up into my arms I link all the members of the group I can, as well as the pack doctor as we run for the clinic. That is the only chance we have to save her.

Muerta's weak, raspy voice reaches my ears, she is struggling to speak. Tuning in my enhanced hearing I do my best to listen to what she says, as she lies on the brink of darkness.

"Th-they...are...coming. F-f-found...me. Barely...es-caped."

With that last effort she goes limp in my arms. There is still rise and fall to her chest, breaths are shallow and slow. She does not have much time, just then the doors of the clinic are before me, and I barge through.

The doctor has a gurney waiting for me and we settle Muerta on it, the staff rushes her to the procedure room. The door behind me bangs into the wall and I spin, seeing the rest of the group, for once Angie and Maverick have tears in their eyes.

"The doctor and nurses just took her back, she said they found her, and they are coming. She didn't get anything else out before she passed out. There were multiple injuries to her body, but I don't know the extent. Assemble the warriors and sound the alarms. War is coming to our pack."

Breaking through the packhouse doors, the sirens begin to sound behind me, all activity in the packhouse stops momentarily at the start of the blaring noise, once their minds click into place, and recognition dawns, activity begins again, this time with direction and urgency. None of the elders are in the packhouse, I run to the pack kitchen, they are frequently in there, lending their knowledge and assisting. Throwing the door open, I see the elders giving directions to the kitchen staff, and shooing others out, who need to get to safe havens, not one warrior is hanging back.

Looking around I find the fae and witch elder in charge of barrier protection, running up to them, I gently grasp their arms. "Ladies, war is coming to our pack lands. I need you to split the groups in two, one group set up a barrier around the hospital and the other group set up a barrier around the children's home."

They nod their understanding and head out of the kitchen.

Tiiyú is in front of me as I go to leave. "What can I assist with?" Her voice is full of urgency and desire to be a part of the bigger effort.

"Grab what you can in additional food and necessities. Please go to the children's home and assist with the young ones. Regardless of what happens, they will be our future and we must protect them."

She nods and gets busy in the kitchen, collecting what she deems necessary. I continue my trek, heading to the training grounds.

Walking through a stand of trees on my way to address the warriors, the wind swirls around me, moving my hair and whispering in my ears.

"The time has come, Our Queen. Move to the North, cover through to the East. Keep your Blood Wolf and Thunderbird close. Time has run out." Then it is gone as quickly as it came.

Marching up the steps of our podium, the warriors are assembled by their groups, trainers in front of them, my group stands ready for me to address the crowd. "Our inside source came back injured, but in her last moments of consciousness, she warned us the enemy is on the move. They are bringing the war to us. Only it will not be a surprise. Blood will flow today, my brothers and sisters, the battle for our families and our future has arrived. We fight together as one to battle this enemy to protect our land and our loved ones. The fate of the supernatural lies with us. You know your orders and the battle plans. ON TO VICTORY!!!" My voice rings out loud and true, a cry goes up from the warriors and we move out.

Alpha Keith, Dad and Alpha Mason, Luna Rebecca by his side, take their groups and head to the East, the rest come with me to the North. Claire and Milo spread their groups out to the Northeast remaining in the tree line. We do not want to be out in the open, easy targets for when the enemy arrives, also this allows for them to believe they still have an element of surprise left. The mood running through the air is one of anticipation and anxiousness.

It is good the warriors are on their toes, staying sharp and ready. We do not know exactly what we will encounter, but I will make sure we hold our line. We have moved as far away from the packhouse and grounds as possible, meeting the enemy at our borders.

The war cries hit us long before we see any of the opposing forces. The howls and screeches carry on the air and fill the heart with foreboding. The agonizing sounds of death and despair, heading to claim its next soul. The sounds of creatures conjured up in hell to assist the Collaborative in their final fight for segregation.

Chapter 105:

Meeting on the Battlefield

(Jasmine's POV)

We continue to hold our line, I can feel Nóox and the other thunderbirds getting antsy. Their nemesis is coming to start a war, it is ingrained in them to meet them head on and fight, the smells and sounds have them riled and ready to inflict damage to the threat, but they maintain their place as directed. Yulúm is a strong commander, just like his cousin, they have a firm hand on their convocations, I have faith in my army.

Slowly figures begin to appear, from this distance it is difficult to make out distinctive features, but they are massive, larger than our wolves, but not larger than the trolls. The odor that moves its way towards us on the wind reeks of death, decay, and sulfur, the promise of what awaits us if we do not win. As they continue to move closer into view, it appears they have no eyes, muzzles pointed into the air, scenting, their heads whip to our direction, they track purely by sound and scent, it seems.

They have large pointed ears for tunneling the sound to them better, long razor claws that cut into the earth and scorch all living things next to them, a trail of death follows where they trod the ground. Some are on two legs others on four, their tails move around them seeming to be of smoke, except for the sharp point at the end designed for piercing. One opens its mouth to let out a screech our way, its tongue is forked as a snake and it has fangs, meant for tearing away flesh, with rows of razor-sharp piranha-looking teeth behind them, saliva drips from the fangs in a murky brown color reminiscent of dried blood, as it anticipates its next kill. The saliva sizzles the grass and plants as if it is an acid when it drips from this beast's mouth.

Where is their leader? I see Alpha Blaine and his warriors behind the beasts leading the way into our territory, Dusk is there with her fighters, a smug look on her face. She managed to escape before we could capture her and Victoria, the witch who captured my mother, with her coven. I feel anger rising in me at the sight of these traitors, energy sizzling through my veins and I feel my eyes taking on the blue glow. The vampires arrive behind all the rest, but where are Scion and his witches? Is he really sending all others to war while he hides behind them, protecting his own race over the others?

Nóox already told me the under lord would not appear for this battle, but we should see Scion, as he is his messenger in this war. Their leader is a coward, who sends the others to die. Updates are coming in through the mindlink from the other heads, the beasts are closer to their points than ours.

"Get the thunderbirds ready," I link out to the groups, sending a signal to Nóox beside me. The plan is for him to cover me from the air as Ashley and Zeke fight next to me on the ground.

Movement sounds around me as Nóox and Yulúm get their fighters ready, I give the final signal and a massive push of air is felt by those around us, a loud whoosh sounding as hundreds of thunderbirds take to the air. My eyes are directed to the front, the beasts pause at the sudden sight of the thunderbirds, then they let up a raucous noise of fury, piercing our ears, our thunderbirds reply in kind with their screeches, luckily, we have been trained how to combat the immobilizing sounds.

The beasts break out into a run, heading towards us at full power, we get into our combat stance and wait. The thunderbirds begin the attack; the field is filled with blinding light as thunderbolts hit the ground below, death cries are carried our way as some of the beasts go down, turning to ash when they fall, darkening the earth beneath. The tails of the beasts let arrows fly into the air, arrows of smoke and metal. I see a thunderbird fall from the sky, unable to flap its left wing due to injury.

I cannot wait any longer, it is time to move. Linking the others, Brooke takes over as we burst through the tree line morphing into wolf form and make our presence known to the enemy. Grace is beside me ready for the feel of blood and flesh on her claws and teeth. Calling up the power of earth, I send a wave made of dirt and debris towards the oncoming beasts, knocking them from their feet. My warriors surge forward and attack as the enemy is momentarily unbalanced and unable to respond to a direct threat.

We meet body to body in the middle of the battlefield. The sounds of battle build up around me, the clang of metal on metal, squelching sounds of flesh being torn from the body, soil and vegetation being wrenched from the earth, scorching of the land, growls, war cries, and the last screams and breaths before death takes a soul. War is not a beautiful place to be, but to protect our people and our realm it is a necessary evil to endure.

Grace is out and it almost appears she has a smile on her muzzle as she moves from one enemy to another, taking their heads or hearts, the beasts do not seem to faze her and it is as if she is putting on a ballet in the middle of a fight, her movements smooth and fluid, dancing from one foe to the next dropping them to a melody playing only in her mind. One would think she is lost in her own world of bloodlust, but her eyes continue to cut back to me, ensuring I am safe.

Finding it difficult to use the magic needed for this battle in wolf form, Brooke gives me control and we shift back to human. Calling up wind, I pull two of the beasts into a mini-tornado and Nóox sends lightning directly into the middle, ending the life of the hideous creatures, flicking my wrists, the beasts fly into the trees causing the trunks to break and the tree to fall over, crushing more of the oncoming foe.

Nóox and I continue this pattern for a while, making a significant dent in the enemy forces. It seems the beasts never stop coming, though, for everyone we kill it seems two to three more replace it. Refusing to give up or show signs of defeat to my warriors I continue to battle forward. Picking up a couple more beasts in a tornado, a ball of energy slams into my torso. I lose the tornado and the beasts land back on the ground, uninjured and livid. They charge for me.

There is no time for me to do a full shift, my claws come out and my teeth elongate, Brooke pushes her strength forward for me to use. They attack simultaneously, one high and one low. I jump to meet the one that is attacking high, sinking my claws deep into where the eyes should be and around the back of the cranium; using Brooke's strength I pull as hard as I can removing the top part of the skull and brain. The foe falls to the ground, trapping the other one beneath it. Once my feet have touched the ground, I slit the throat of the other enemy and continue my forward trek.

More energy balls fly my way, fire the temperature of which I have never felt before. Looking around, Victoria is on a path straight for me, launching fireballs as she advances. Another energy ball hits my shin and I fall, the pain is severe, but to stop would mean death. Using the power of water I send a tidal wave over Victoria, then call up the branches from a nearby tree to bind her, once that is done the air forms a cocoon around her and she is held at the very top of the tree, taken out of the battle, held as a prisoner.

In order for me to heal quickly, I have to change to my wolf form, there is no option to sit to the side while the battle rages. Grace finds a place next to me, assisting me while the healing process kicks in, on my other side is Zeke in wolf form, he has some cuts and blood is staining his fur, but he appears to be alright overall. Turning my eyes back to the field Brooke and I use magic, while Grace and Zeke keep the enemy at bay. Aunt Meredith has found her way closer to us, diverting numerous threats from witch's magic.

Bodies litter the ground, the grass is either burnt or smeared red, the war has not even begun to slow. Looking over the field, Alpha Blaine and his pack are missing, they need to be accounted for along with Dusk.

"All leaders, give a report," I send out through mind-link, as I send a hurricane through some witches that have taken to the air, trapping them in the treetops, branches as bindings.

"Decrease in beasts here, but Blaine has arrived with his pack and Dusk's, Alpha Keith is going to work up and merge with us. The thunderbirds have taken out the beasts here, those that weren't killed moved towards you," Dad responds back quickly. That is why it seems like the beasts were continuously regenerating, they were moving North to our position.

"Miles and I are battling against some Fae and elves, a few witches and wolves mixed in; otherwise, the beasts moved North. We are holding our own, Maverick has joined us. The vampires are absent from our area, no sight of them," Claire adds in, slightly winded from her exertions.

"This is Simon, the trolls are having a great time battling the beasts to your West. We have nothing here, except the beasts, it seems they are trying to break the line versus engage in battle. The trolls are grabbing them by their hind legs as they try to pass and bash them into each other, then onto the ground. Grotesque, but effective." This is interesting news from Simon, why would the beasts be trying to break the line versus causing casualties?

Chapter 106:

Meeting on the Battlefield 2

(Alpha Blaine's POV)

The wood floor of my personal chamber in the packhouse is beginning to develop a worn path from my pacing back and forth. I do not understand why we continue to wait to engage this false Queen in battle, why Scion drags his feet and continues to be at the mercy of her surprise attacks and, although I am loath to admit it, superior planning.

Jasmine, if nothing else, is superb at war strategy, I doubt it is all from her hybrid brain, though. She does have plenty of purebreds, including her father, assisting her in the strategic command post. I am positive it is their influence and nothing to do with her abilities as a leader, her mixed-blood has had to have created fatal flaws in her. Flaws I will find and manipulate when we finally manage to make it into battle.

A loud knock sounds through my chamber as someone pounds on the door from the other side. Irritated, I make my way to the door and fling it open, sending a glare and a growl towards the intruder of my thoughts. How dare someone disturb me in such a manner, even though there is someone else in the leadership position of the Collaborative, my place is nothing to be ignored and I should be shown due respect.

My eyes meet with those of Maurice. He sends me a smile, dripping with malice, he bows his head to me, the respect is obviously disingenuous. Gritting my teeth together to keep from ripping his head off his body, I sink my claws into the door frame as I address him.

"What do you want, Maurice? Why are you bothering me?"

"Master Scion wants you in his meeting room now. There has been an update to the plans, and you are to be briefed with the others. You are to go back with me." His bored tone grates across my nerves.

"I will be there when I arrive, tell that to Scion. Next time you dare to order me around will be your last."

The door slams in his face behind the force of my arm closing it. Scion will not beckon me as if I am a slave to him. My appearance will occur on my terms, this is the only way I know to remind him we are equals and partners. Fifteen minutes later the others are graced with my appearance. Scion greets me with a sneer and nods curtly towards the only empty chair at the table. A smirk crosses my lips at the obvious irritation of the vampire. The door begins to swing shut behind me when I catch a glimpse of movement from the corner of my eye. Swiftly, I block the door from closing as my arm reaches to the other side grasping an uninvited guest. The gasp that reaches my ears lets me know she thought she was undetected.

The struggling figure lands on the floor at Scion's feet, his eyes narrow into slits, taking in her appearance. His features harden even more, hatred blazes from his cold orbs. Before anyone can ask questions, he moves with great speed, punching the girl, then grabbing her by her throat and slamming her against the wall, as she struggles to stand, Scion draws a knife and slices into her abdomen. Before he is able to pull the knife out of her stomach, the girl shimmers away.

"We go to war today," Scion addresses the room. "That girl is one of Maverick's minions, who are faithful to Alpha Jasmine. Prepare your people." With that Scion walks from the room.

Finally, we move on to battle, fate will be decided today. Anticipation and excitement course through my body as I take my leave to gather my warriors. There is no need to prepare them, we have been ready to go for weeks, just waiting for the word, now we get to move.

An hour later, my wolves stand in formation behind me, shifting from foot to foot, clenching and unclenching their fists, ready to lead the Collaborative and engage with those threatening our pureblood ways. Yet again, the only thing holding us back from our mission is Scion, but soon, we will part ways.

Once this battle is over, we will segregate and not be bothered by his kind anymore.

Looking at the other forces to my right and left, it is easy to tell they feel the same way my wolves do, even Scion's vampires seem restless to begin, to finally surprise Jasmine, by bringing the battle to her, on her grounds. Throw her out of her element and make her plan on the go. Victory is as good as ours. Finally, Scion appears on the podium and addresses the army we have built.

"Today we go into battle. Today we fight for the right to keep our species pure and in designated lands. No more will our blood be tainted. Victory is but a moment away. ON TO BATTLE!" He finishes with a battle cry and steps down, making his way to his coven.

Short and sweet, perfect! Jasmine's lands are not too far away from where we built Vengeance's Gate, allowing us to go by foot, no engine sounds will help to hide our arrival. The thought of ending Jasmine's life brings a smile to my face, hope springs up in me that I will be the one to have the honor of making the ground crimson with her blood, of watching her eyes go blank, while defeat is the last emotion shown in their depths.

We have been marching for close to half an hour when the air around us is permeated with the stench of death, decay, and sulfur. Stopping my men, we search the wooded area around us with our eyes. My wolf has pushed forward slightly, helping me to hear and scent better. There is no movement discernable in the tree line.

I motion for my new Beta, Bruce, to come next to me, along with a couple additional warriors. We begin to cautiously approach the area the scent is coming from. Before we are able to reach it, the most hideous beasts I could imagine begin to emerge from the darkness of the forest. Their appearance sends shivers down my spine.

My warriors and I get into defensive positions, not sure what this threat is, but we will not go without a fight. Sensing our movements, since they have no eyes, they turn to us and let out an ear-piercing shriek. It takes everything in me not to fall to my knees, but my hands fly to protect my sensitive hearing. Wetness meets my palms, alerting me to the blood that is starting to drip from them. My wolves are not faring any better than myself.

Scion comes to the front of the group and raises his hand. The screeching stops and relief floods my system, the groans of my pack can be heard as their bodies begin to relax. What are these demon animals and why are they quieting at a sign from Scion?

"These creatures have been sent to us by an ally. They will be accompanying us into the battle. A little way to ensure victory is swung to our side this time. They will be taking the lead in front of your wolves, Blaine; you will back them up and move to the Eastern border as the fight progresses." The smirk on Scion's face as he addresses me makes my blood boil.

Based on the occurrence a few moments ago, I know we cannot debate this with Scion. He will use them against us, and they appear to have few weaknesses but the ability to drop my entire pack. Giving a curt nod, my wolves fall back into formation behind the beasts, and we continue moving. The victory is what matters, not who leads the battle, but I am disappointed. Vengeance against Scion will be mine.

Time passes us by and soon we are at the borders to Whispering Red Winds, no one is here to meet us, to challenge us and our arrival. Where are Jasmine's patrols? The area is unnaturally quiet, there is no sound of the forest of the animals that make their home in it. Possibly they fled at the unknown, but evil stench of our newest members, something is not sitting right with me, though, cautiously I begin to take in the surrounding area.

The demons let out their shrieks again, turning their snouts to the tree line and begin to advance forward, while they are still a good distance from their destination the air erupts with new screeches and the sky is darkened by the presence of thunderbirds. We knew Jasmine had one in her inner group, but there are hundreds in the air, engaging with the beasts. It appears they are enemies as well, I watch, stunned as the thunderbirds rain down lightning, pick up the beasts with their talons and shred their bodies. The beasts retaliate shooting arrows from their tails into the air and using the tail as a whip and spear.

Clearing my head we move forward, as we do Jasmine and her army break through the tree line. She is leading them in this battle, Scion refused to be at the front for the Collaborative, he made excuses to remain in the back grouping.

While I want to engage with Jasmine, I know it is imperative to take my wolves to the Eastern border and clear a pathway there. We move in an arc, coming down from the North and sweeping to our desired location, leaving a trail of bodies in our wake.

After hours of battle, my eyes fall on Alpha Alexander as he battles another wolf, one can see he is tired from extended battle, but he and his wolf are still strong, not faltering or succumbing to attacks, he is an acceptable replacement to Jasmine. If I cannot kill her, I can take her last parent away from her. Now that I think of it, a life of pain is better than death; her new home can be my dungeon and torture can be her new routine. This thought pleases me much more than killing her.

Fighting my way through wolves my path finally crosses with Alexander, his eyes meet mine, and cold determination shines through him. His wife died on my lands, I kidnapped and rejected his daughter, now I have brought war to his lands. This fight will be epic and more profound when he falls. I cannot wait to hear Jasmine's wolf howl at the pain.

We circle each other in wolf form for a moment, sizing each other up. Alexander makes the first move, lunging towards my neck, I drop and roll to the right, causing him to miss. His wolf is quick to recover and is ready to attack again as I make my way to my feet. He lunges for neck again, since my retreat worked well the first time I used it again, only Alexander planned for it, pulling his wolf up short and running his claws the length of my stomach while I was mid-roll.

White-hot pain shoots through my system, the first attack was just to see how I would respond to his advance. Every warrior knows to change movements, my arrogance has made me pay, time to get my head back into this fight, Alexander will not go down easily. The wound is not too deep, we will be able to continue our fight, but my wolf will need to begin healing me quickly before blood loss begins to affect me.

Bruce has fought his way to my back and is keeping other wolves at bay while I am engaged, he has many superficial wounds to his body, his stamina is beginning to decrease, but he does not back down; Alpha Mason and Luna Rebecca are protecting Alexander in the same way. Why they allow women into battle is beyond me, they are a hindrance on the battlefield.

Alexander rushes me, catching my right shoulder in his mouth, clenching his muzzle down tightly, shaking his head back and forth to cause more tearing and ripping of the muscles and tendons there. He is deliberately not going for a kill move, they only want to detain me, it appears. I bend my head to the side and bite into Alexander's side.

Growling he lets loose of me, springing in the air and causing me to lose my hold on him. Landing Alexander sinks his claws deep into my hindquarters, pulling downward, exposing the sinew as he separates my hamstring from my bone bilaterally, my wolf hits the ground and I begin to change back into my human form. This cannot be happening; they cannot take me prisoner.

As Alexander shifts back and comes towards me, he is hit with a fireball in the left thigh, he falls to the ground growling in pain. As I watch Alexander writhe in pain, I notice I am being lifted from the ground, but no arms are holding me, moving my head around my brain processes what is occurring; a witch has saved me again. This witch is new to me, but thankfully on our side since my wolf and I are unable to move.

Before she can leave the area with me an arrow sinks deep into her chest, the shield around me collapses, we fall to the ground at the same time. Sliding a few feet on the hard earth, I look to my left; Luna Rebecca is nocking another arrow, ready to avenge the turning and death of her son as well as the lives of her friends. As she brings her bow up, a surprised look flashes over her face, crimson spreads out over her chest; Bruce is behind her, his hand deep in her back, protruding through the front, the Luna's heart grasped in his fingers.

As Rebecca falls limply to the ground, Mason's howl goes up into the air, alerting all his mate has met her end. Bruce runs up to me and pulls me into a fireman's carry, rushing us away from the main battle to allow my wolf to heal our wounds. This fight is far from over, the sooner we can reengage the better it will be.

Chapter 107:

Meeting on the Battlefield 3

(Scion's POV)

The closer we get to Jasmine's pack lands, my witches and me begin to look for a place to view the battle from. This place is not where we will be engaging in battle, we have additional plans to those we have informed the others of. They did not need to be informed of them, because they will not be around to be a part of them.

Continuing to search as we walk behind the army, we notice off to our left is a knoll, with a stand of fir trees on top, perfect for camouflage, allowing us to watch the annihilation of our enemies. The bottom of the knoll is bare allowing us to see if anyone is able to get to our position and threaten us, my four dark ladies can easily take care of any unwanted visitors from this vantage point. We make our way to the grove of trees and get settled, I choose to lean against the trunk of a sturdy fir, branches fall above and below my body, my line of sight is good. The witches with me spread out to their own areas, where to specifically that is not my concern. The beasts sent by my new ally are scenting the area below us, looking for the first area to attack, trying to pick up the smell or sound of Jasmine's border guards, they pick up something and begin to move towards a tree line, anticipation runs through my system, soon the opposing army will be here, once one of the border guards link to their Alpha, a smirk crosses my face thinking about the look of the guards, then Jasmine's army when they see my newest warriors.

Without warning there is a loud whooshing sound, then the sky is full of thunderbirds and the air carries their screeches to my ears, before I can process this lightning rains down from the heavens, turning my beasts to ash, desperation begins to spread through my body as Jasmine and her army rush forward from the cover of the trees. I bolt up from my leaned position to watch what is unfolding before my eyes.

How was she able to prepare, to get the jump on us again? There was no warning we would be attacking today, no notice, unless that vampire, Muerta, managed to make it to Jasmine before she died. Clenching my hands into fists and getting a handle on my emotions, I remind myself, while this is disappointing, it does not ruin the end game ultimately, it just speeds the process up for me. Little do any of those battling before me know, they are my sacrifice.

No one is to leave this battlefield alive, not even my own warriors and vampires, they are all meant to die here. When Whispering Red Winds and their allies are wiped out, the beasts will turn on the rest and kill them. There will be no one left more powerful to challenge me when I take over as ruler of the supernatural world, any contender is on the field before me, meeting their appointment with death, oh, the rest of the supernatural world will be segregated, in their own place, to make them weaker, no one will be able to overthrow me, they all will suffer under my rule.

We watch the progress of the battle before us for a few hours, so far it seems to be a close match, with the beasts added in, best decision I made was taking on this new ally, his support will get me to the throne I deserve. The progression and number of bodies littering the ground pleases me but there is no time left to bask in the satisfaction of my plan coming to fruition.

It is time to move on to the second part of my plan, it is time to make Jasmine feel complete loss before her demise. My witches and I leave the protection of the trees and begin our trek to the South. We have to skirt further out than anticipated due to the battle raging longer than hoped, but it is not a bother, we have time.

Arriving at the Southern border of the Whispering Red Winds pack lands more beasts emerge from the trees, this is the area of the main packhouse and functions of Jasmine's pack. Leading the small army behind me, we make our way into the heart of my enemy. We will take out her innocent and injured, crushing any chance for a future, take everything from her, while she dies in a bath of blood. The false Queen will fall, along with all those loyal to her.

As we leave the tree line and emerge into an open area, there is no activity, not uncommon, Jasmine most likely sent her people to bunkers for protection. My beasts will sniff them out, no worries, we continue forward, confident in our quest. An unknown feeling, perhaps excitement, bubbles up in my stomach at the thought of the destruction we are about to unleash and the thrill of the hunt.

We have almost made it to the packhouse without any resistance, this is not normal, there should be some guards left back to protect the pack members unable to fight, regardless of, if they are in a bunker or not, the hospital has no way of placing injured folks into a bunker, where is their protection? Something is off here, but for the life of me, it is not coming to the forefront of my mind what it could be.

"It appears Jasmine did not leave us a welcoming party, my dears, disappointing but we can destroy her home easier. Begin with the packhouse, set it ablaze, then we will move towards the hospital and see what fun is to be had there." My witches move forward at my command and send multiple fireballs into the large wooden structure, before long flames are licking up the outside walls, windows are exploding from the heat, but no screams of wolves being burned alive is heard. Interesting.

Pleased with the results on the packhouse we leave it to become nothing but embers. The hospital looms ahead of us, again there is no movement in or around the building. There is no way Jasmine was able to evacuate her pack. Off to the right of the hospital is an empty dining hall and garden.

"Burn everything here. Leave nothing behind. We will walk the entire grounds to find the rest of her people, they may have moved North into the old Red Crescent grounds, we will find them and destroy them." Displeasure is causing a sneer to mar my features, anger is burning in my stomach, where are her people?

We continue to progress farther into the pack lands than I had originally wanted to go, soon a large building is before us. Looking around it is apparent this is the school building, but it seems to house more than just the school.

There is a newer attachment near the back, this is interesting, peering in the windows of theses rooms, they are bedrooms set up for youth, an orphanage attached to the school building. Why would she house the weakest of her pack? Yet another reason she must go, eradicate the weak, survival of the fittest.

"Burn this too." My command comes out as a hiss, my anger continues to grow the longer it takes to find a victim.

Turning my back to the building in disgust, my witches send fireballs around me into the structure. The acrid smell of smoke finds its way into my nasal cavity, my witches have hit their mark again. Sending a cold smile their way, I notice their eyes go round with surprise before I can make it back to them, confusion clouds my mind at their expressions. There have been no other blasts than the sound of the initial attack on this building. What is causing their surprise?

I get my response in the form of a shadow above me followed by a screech, my beasts respond to it with cries of their own. Instantly the space around me is lit up with lightning bolts...thunderbirds. How did they get here so quickly? In no time at all myself, the witches and the beasts are involved in a battle of our own. This is not how my plan was supposed to go. People will pay, the supernatural will suffer.

Chapter 108:

Meeting on the Battlefield 4

(Tiiyú's POV)

Alpha Jasmine arrives in the kitchen, a sense of urgency and determination surrounds her, she scans the room with narrowed eyes then heads directly to Opal and Maria, the Fae and witch leaders assigned to head the protection barriers. The sirens have been going off for a little while now, so it is a fair assumption her discussion with them is regarding a looming threat. Normally, when this is a drill, it is announced as a drill then the sirens blare, which did not occur this time; I wonder what is happening, the war wasn't to start for a few more days and we were to take the battle to them. Wolves are not the only ones with super hearing and my curiosity is piqued, turning my head just slightly to hear better, their conversation reaches me.

Eyes widening at what is reaching my ears, dread begins to settle, it is clear the war is imminent, coming to our doorstep. Opal and Marie rush from the dining hall to carry out the orders of our future Queen. Pulling myself together, I make my way towards Jasmine as she prepares to depart.

"What can I do to assist you, Jasmine? The kitchens are in order, so please delegate me where it would be most beneficial." It is the least I can offer, this young woman is amazing, and she cares for all those around her.

"Please gather additional food and necessities then go to the children's bunker. They will need the extra care and assistance there, so many of them have already lost their parents to this cause and the war about to occur will possibly traumatize some of them more. It is important we protect our future;

we need you there." She squeezes my hands quickly, then departs through the door, she has an army to move forward.

Straightening my shoulders, it is time to get to work, in no time there are multiple bags lined on the island in the kitchen, each one dedicated to specific rations. Powdered beverages, fruits and vegetables, grains, water, snacks, beans and rice, protein, and baby preparations. Going through the cupboards one last time, my eyes come to rest on three books.

The spines are cracked with dark spots, where finger oils have soaked in over the years, showing they are frequently used, pulling them down I see they are from Jasmine's family line, heirlooms to the pack kitchen, without a second thought they are placed into the bag with powdered beverages. Sometimes it is easy to forget our past is as important as our future, it gives us the groundwork to build and thrive on. Food has a unique way of recalling memories of happy times.

Calling over some of my kitchen staff, not delegated to fighting, we collect the bags and head towards the children's house. As we trek across the compound to our destination a loud cry rises on the air, sending shivers down my spine. It is a cry to unite prior to leaving for battle, the cry of our brave going to face the enemy, the cry of my sons and family as they go forward to secure our future. Tears prick my eyes as I send up a prayer to the Goddess to bless them all. This entire time my feet never pause, carrying me on to our destination.

The school and children's home looms before us, we walk up the thick cement steps and push on the heavy wooden door to the school side entrance. The bunker is built under the floor of the gymnasium on the school side, it is a large area that allows room for the children to move around in, the former Alphas thought ahead and had it soundproofed as well. The children may be secured in an area, but it is designed to have as trivial effect on their lives and habits as possible, while giving them ultimate safety. I assisted Jasmine in stocking the other bunkers built recently and none of them are as spectacular, Alexander has mentioned he would like to redo all the bunkers to more closely resemble this one.

Pushing the door closed behind us, we head to the entryway leading into the depths of the bunker. Looking around the area as we make our way into the kitchen, children are cuddled up with each other, some sitting on beanbag chairs, others leaning against the walls, some assisting adults with different tasks, but all have fear radiating from them, tears looming near the surface of their eyes.

My staff and I are trying to put away the additional supplies, but there are too many to fit in the cupboards here, the decision is made to run them over to the hospital, those there can always benefit from additional nutrients as well as the children. The items left fill three bags, so this trip will be made as a solo mission, me only. I always have the ability to shift and fly away if something happens while I am out of the protected barrier area.

I have made it halfway to the hospital when a mixed scent reaches my nose, the smell of death, decay, and sulfur permeate my senses making my stomach roll with nausea and fear spike my heartrate. Dropping the bags, my thunderbird, Haayí, pushes forward and takes to the sky, if my fears are correct, we cannot stay here, the magic of the Fae and witches will not be enough. My concerns are confirmed when I reach a height that allows me to view the area.

The battle has just begun, hundreds of thunderbirds are in the air, Nóox leading them against our extreme nemesis. We have come out strong, in the blink of an eye, Jasmine and the rest of the army has joined the fray. There is no time to waste, knowing this threat is just beyond the tree line, it is time to move to plan B, which is being quickly developed in my head as we speak.

Haayí lands and we transform back to my human, leaving the bags in the middle of the area, I rush back to the school searching for Opal. She is in a nook outside the shelter area, paired with a witch unknown to me.

"Opal! We must move quickly, we need to get word to the rest of the bunkers and the hospital, we cannot stay here. The opposing side has help from the under lord, Wúlx, and he has sent his beasts to assist in this war. The magic you have to create the barriers will not stand against them; everyone is in danger." My words are rushed, urgency and concern dripping from them.

Opal's eyes widen at my revelation. Opal rushes below to the bunker and soon reappears with four wolves, two witches and two additional Fae. "Tiiyú, quickly tell them what is happening. Based off your information, we are going to make a new plan, this is the best we can do on short notice, mind-linking the Alpha is not an option while she is in battle, it is up to us."

I waste no time recanting my information to the group. "I have been thinking of a plan, but we will have to move quickly. Jasmine had all members pack a 72-hour bag, so they should have essentials for three days." The group nods their agreement to me. "There is more than enough room in our convocation to house all the members here, we can evacuate them there."

"How will we transport them? Beside you and five others, all the thunderbirds are in the battle. We have too many people for six thunderbirds to transport," Opal responds, while thinking carefully over the plan presented.

"True, if there are any witches that can create a portal, they can ride with me to the convocation, where I will get additional birds to assist with transport. We can move the children from here first, no wasted trips, everyone will count. The hospital can evacuate their patients, staff and equipment through a portal to our lands, the rest will go air thunderbird."

"There are four witches here that have the ability to create portals, myself and three others, all located in other bunkers in case we needed to make a quick escape. One of the wolves here can mind-link the others to let them know the new plan, the witches can portal here after being updated by the wolves. It will be the quickest way to get them here," the unknown witch offers. "This seems like a good plan. Is there anyone opposed to what has been suggested?" Opal puts a vote out to our newly formed committee. No one is against the alternate plan, plus there is not time for long term brainstorming. "Well, let's get started. The children from here will be moved first, how many can each thunderbird carry on their backs?" Opal is very good at getting pertinent information to get things accomplished, she has a quick mind.

"This trip we can take six each, so four witches and thirty-two children, when we come back some of the thunderbirds will be outfitted with special carrying harnesses that will allow them to carry more passengers. A few of us will need to be able to change back and forth for communication purposes. We need to start moving now, there is no guarantee how much time we have." Five minutes later the other witches are standing in the nook of the school, ready to head to my convocation, the children making this trip are assembled, backpacks in place, an undercurrent of excitement mixing with their fear.

Luckily, the children have gotten used to Nóox and Wiláu, so the size and appearance of the thunderbirds do not scare them. I think that is where the excitement is coming from, they get to ride on the back of a thunderbird.

The other members of my convocation are outside the school, shifted and ready to take on their passengers. I remain in human form, until all the children are settled then the witches and two children take my back. The providers have begun preparing their patients for immediate departure as soon as a portal is opened between them and my lands. Folks need to be moved to gurneys versus stationary beds, additional medical supplies such as dressings and bandages, IV fluids, medications, are being brought as well, to attempt to lessen the strain felt by my own people.

Finally, everyone is loaded, with one final cry, we take to the air, the giggles and wonderment of the children reach my ears, it is comforting to know, in this dire time, we can give them something positive to remember. We fly up through the clouds to allow for better coverage, just in case we were spotted leaving, those nasty beasts can shoot their arrows a great distance, none of our passengers would survive being hit by one.

Half an hour later we land in the field outside the village, members come running towards us when they see who has arrived. They assist in taking the children down, then we shift back. Moving towards the village quickly, I send other members out to grab heads of the different families, to meet me in my family home. Two of the thunderbirds who flew here with me take the children to a bunkhouse located in the center of the village, it is the most protected place here. The witches get together and follow another thunderbird to a preferred spot to portal back and forth, it is located close to our own medical facility and will make transporting easier. The witches are heading back immediately, it is not clear how long it will take to move all the patients.

Soon my parlor is filled with convocation members. "Thank you all for coming quickly. As you are aware there is a war occurring against dark forces, a war our own thunderbirds are a part of. Wúlx has sent beasts from his domain to assist in the battle, due to this there is no safe place for those who cannot fight in the battle, the children, elderly and sick or injured. It was my plan to bring them here, until the battle subsides; however, we need more thunderbirds to come and assist in the transportation. Not only are we bringing back supernaturals but supplies to assist with their stay. Those who accompany me are not meant to be part of the war itself, but there is still the danger they could be drawn in unintentionally. Please, go back to your homes and anyone who can be spared send to the field, we depart in ten minutes, others will need to be placed on a schedule to assist in the various places our guests will be staying. Currently there are thirty-two children in the bunkhouse at the center of town, it was all we could carry this trip, the witches have already created a portal and gone back to evacuate the hospital. Any questions?" Not a single question is asked, or concern raised.

"Very well, again, thank you for helping and supporting. My family and myself are so enormously proud of all you do and give in this village."

They begin to vacate my house leaving space for me to get out around them. I make a stop by one of our supply warehouses and get the workers to bring as many large carriers to the field as possible. The thunderbirds who volunteer will need to be outfitted with these, allowing us to carry more supernaturals and in a safer mode.

After checking on the children, there is still five minutes to departure when I make it to the field, the sight before me warms my heart, close to a hundred thunderbirds are awaiting my arrival, some are already shifted and have carriers in place. No one has questioned my call to serve, my sons will be proud to know how their people responded. I make my way through the crowd, showing my gratitude and appreciation to each member encountered.

Within minutes we are back in the air, making our return flight to Whispering Red Winds, hopefully the warriors have been able to hold the borders and we still have time to make our plan work, to get the innocent and nonfighters out. When the pack lands are in sight and there is no enemy activity visible to me, a sigh of relief leaves my beak.

My responsibility from here is to divide the thunderbirds up amongst bunkers, we are going to do our best to have a mass evacuation, with no return trips needed. As a bird has a full load, they will take to the sky, no unnecessary time will be spent on the ground in the warzone perimeter. We land at the farthest bunker from the schoolhouse and begin leaving thunderbirds at each location, in no time, we are back to the location from where this massive movement began.

Opal breaks through the front doors of the schoolhouse, the remaining children, staff and other members ready to depart. Every location has been well organized and calm. As the thunderbirds are being loaded, I run to the hospital to see how they are faring with their departure through the portal. Entering through their main door, I make my way to the emergency room, there is a steady line of patients, each paired with a nurse moving through the portal. My eyes make contact with one of the witches holding the portal open, she nods her head, sending a smile my way, her way of letting me know things are going smoothly.

Finding a doctor, I fall into step with her. "Is there any more assistance you need from us? The remaining members are loading onto thunderbirds as we speak, I will be the last to leave, the portals will be closed and all birds in the air prior to my departure."

As she goes the doctor is pointing out equipment and supplies that are then loaded onto a cart, it is unclear if she has heard my question.

There is a brief pause in her pointing and the loading. "Right now, everything is moving well, patients are going through the portal and equipment will follow after, we have plenty of staff to assist with the remaining needs here. I appreciate you checking with us." Then she turns back to the task at hand. Her curtness does not bother me, it is good to see in this environment, straightforward and to the point, back to task, which is what is needed to pull this maneuver off.

More thunderbirds are arriving to the school location as the bunkers are emptied and they are excess, we will have more than enough to get people and supplies out of the area, the additional birds are put as perimeter security, but remain on the ground, the risk is too great to have them in the sky for extended periods.

Opal walks up beside me, "It is amazing what we have been able to make happen here, what you have been able to make happen here. All these people are safe or will be soon. A few of us were able to get to the packhouse and a few other buildings to place small spells to help protect some of the valuables, we had to cast smaller ones, so there is no need to keep any witch or Fae in the area. While the main buildings aren't protected areas inside are. Hopefully, this will be of some assistance in the end."

I send Opal a smile as I wrap my arm around her shoulders, "I am sure our Queen will be incredibly pleased to know of all you have done to help here, of what we have all done. There is nothing left to do except see to the departure of our last group here, then check the hospital to make sure the portals are closed, once that is done, the remaining security, thunderbirds and I will be behind everyone, making sure our tails are safe." We take a moment, enjoying the connection before getting back to task.

It is unclear how much time has passed since we started this retreat, but as we near the end of it, my anxiety begins to rear its head. We have been blessed to have this much time already, we must be running out of this priceless commodity. Another half-hour passes by and the last, loaded thunderbird takes to the sky. Running to check the hospital, the portals in the emergency room are closed, no personnel or patients left, the witches have gone with the staff. My nerves are beginning to calm as I make my way back to the schoolhouse, we managed to get everyone evacuated, looking up the tailfeathers of the last thunderbird carrying people or supplies, vanish into the clouds. We have done it…and it seems just in the nick of time, the smell of Wúlx' beasts and smoke are close, they have made it to the pack lands. Rushing to the remaining wolves and thunderbirds on security, I wave them into the trees beside the schoolhouse.

Before our eyes, a small army comes into view, led by four women and one man. This must be Scion and his dark witches, he was not described to me, but he would be the only one with an ego big enough to enter pack grounds, no doubt wanting to come in behind Jasmine and her army. We watch as he looks in the windows of the orphanage, then directs his witches to burn it, this must have been the fate of the other buildings they came across, accounting for the smoke.

It is imperative we protect the army from a surprise invasion from the rear, looking at my remaining twelve thunderbirds and handful of wolves we have our work cut out for us, we nod in agreement. The smell of smoke from the school fills our noses, it is time to fight, fend off this threat, and protect our Queen. The witches have finished launching their fireballs as we soar over the trees and building, appear from the backside of the school, surprise evident in their expressions and widened eye.

Letting out a loud screech my birds and I waste no time launching lightning bolts towards the beasts and witches. We work seamlessly together, raining down punishment on this army before us without mercy. They counterattack, shooting off arrows and sending magic weapon, we have our own side battle to the greater war. Slowly the numbers of the beasts begin to decrease, pride for my birds and wolves well in my being, their fearlessness is strong, despite our age we have a place, a greater meaning.

We have been battling for a while now, Haayí swoops down shooting off lightning nonstop, picks up a beast in each claw, sending her talons deep, as we soar back into the sky to send our enemy crushing back to the ground taking out additional foes as they land, suddenly a fiery pain is growing just below my left wing on my torso.

Dropping the beasts, I do my best to get a distance away, sending out a call for assistance, letting my people know I am injured. Then my body hits the ground, piling dirt up with my head as I plow through the earth, Haayí is unable to get to her feet, we lay there for a moment, catching our breath and slowly making the shift back to human.

Footsteps sound in the distance, it seems my time has come, this thunderbird will not go down without a fight, finding my way back to my feet, I stand, looking for anything that will be of use defending myself, then stand prepared for what is destined to be my fate. My sons are grown, all good strong men who love their families and convocation, there are no regrets for this life and my mate waits for me on the other side.

Chapter 109:

Meeting on the Battlefield 5

(Nóox' POV)

The acrid, bile inducing stench in the air confirms my greatest fear for this war, Wúlx has sent his underworld beasts to wreak havoc amongst our army. While they are little match for the thunderbirds, our allies will have a significantly harder time battling them. These monstrosities are meant to cause death and destruction in their wake, every excreting orifice of their body leaks out a poison or acid. They are the ultimate killing machines, not just to the supernaturals, but to the land as well, it will take years for this area to recuperate, to have life of flora and fauna reemerge sending their roots deep.

Wiláu shakes his head bringing me back from my evasive, dark thoughts; he is restless, wanting to meet these creatures head on before they can advance closer towards our forces, he wants to protect our Queen, waiting is making it difficult to control him. Jasmine gives the signal for the thunderbirds to take to the air, with one mighty flap of his wings Wiláu has catapulted us into the clouds, air rushes over our feathers as we ascend to the heavens, letting out his cry of battle, calling the others to join him, then setting his sights on the enemy forces below us.

While the beasts send up a return cry of their own our convocations rain down lightning on the horrors of the dark, it is pleasing to watch their bodies turn to ash, as they breathe their last, soon those left begin shooting arrows from their tails in retaliation. Thankfully it is easy to maneuver to avoid them in the air, but as the mass of metal and smoke increases there is less space to move around. Eventually our first thunderbird goes down an injury to the wing, thankfully he will be ready to battle once he lands, all fighters go into war with weapons strapped to their back just in case we are brought down. We are as formidable in our human forms as we are in the air, the only downside is we do not have lightning at our disposal, and unlike the wolves we cannot do a partial shift.

The sounds of our ground army permeate the air, alerting us to the fact our allies have joined the fray. All our forces are now on the field, engaging with the threat to all supernaturals. Locating the Queen and her escorts quickly, I take my position over her in the sky, Queen Jasmine catches some of the beasts in a tornado, sending a look upward her expression clues me in on what she wants, I send my lightning into the middle of the whirl wind, my Queen then discards them into the nearest trees and we resume this cycle of battle, it is effective and we maintain it for a good while. Without warning Jasmine drops the current tornado with two of the creatures in it, unable to send down lightning due their proximity to our allies, my eyes view the area. Jasmine is injured, but holding her own against a witch, I am about to descend from the sky to assist, when the threat is expelled, at the same time Ashley and Ezekiel close in ranks around her. The best place for me is to remain in the sky.

Rage courses through my system seeing our Queen injured, I am her protector, and it occurs to me, my job is not being done. Swooping down, Wiláu grabs a beast in his talons tearing it apart, while shooting lightning down on others, he is merciless fighting to protect his Queen. Hours of fighting have passed, how many I am unsure, the monsters seem to be never ending. We have wiped out alarming numbers of them, but they continue to come, wave after wave entering the territory.

Where are they all coming from? As I continue to ponder this question while remaining engaged in battle, a howl of sorrow permeates the air, sending a shiver down my spine. Spiraling higher into the sky, I look at the battleground, Wiláu's keen eyes focusing in, below Alpha Alexander is down and wounded but recuperating, his wounds knitting together as I watch, Luna Rebecca is held in her husband's arms, a gaping hole in her chest where her heart is supposed to be located. Not far from them a witch is down, arrow through her chest, beyond that a wolf is running into the tree line, searching for cover, over his shoulder he carries a gravely injured Blaine. They cannot escape this war, if they do, this will never truly be over, the threat to our kind will continue, amazingly no beasts are fighting in this area, this must be why we have an influx.

Not wasting another moment on the scene below, Wiláu descends from our position in the sky landing next to our Queen, she turns startled eyes to me while continuing to launch her magic at the enemy, losing not another moment I begin to fill her in.

"Queen Jasmine, Luna Rebecca has perished, your father is injured but healing. Blaine is also injured but one of his men rescued him, running into the tree line between our battle and the pack lands."

It is clear from the way my Queen's eyes go back and forth between the forest and the battlefield she is caught between the difficult decision of pursuing Blaine and remaining with the fighting forces. Her brows scrunch and she chews her bottom lip, the corners of her mouth tilting down as she contemplates her choices quickly never stopping her onslaught of magic towards the battlefield. Within seconds she straightens her shoulder and yells out to her left, "Zeke, you take the battlefield; Ash, Nóox, and I along with a small group will track Blaine and any others who escaped with him. We can't give him the opportunity to create havoc on the pack lands and compromise our nonfighters. I will send a mind-link updating the others."

"Understood, Alpha, we will hold the line here."

We quickly retreat from the warzone towards the tree line where Blaine made his departure, a group of twelve warriors meet us as we progress to our point of entry.

"Nóox, remain in human form, we don't want anyone to notice a thunderbird leaving the battle, besides it could inadvertently give our position away while we are pursuing our enemy," Queen Jasmine directs.

"As you wish."

With this new direction, I reach behind me and withdraw my sword from its sheath between my scapulae. Besides my sword there are four other knives of various lengths and sizes strapped to various body parts, regardless of circumstance there is always a weapon available to me this way. Ashley and I remain close to the Queen while the warriors extend out cautiously on either side of us, hopefully the trail will be easily recognizable since they departed in haste.

Keeping our eyes open we guardedly progress forward. The lack of signs of their escape route is amazing given how they retreated in haste, one wolf carrying another. I would expect to see broken branches and limbs, deep foot imprints from added weight, overturned rocks, torn leaves, anything... something, but the woods are pristine. The only indicator things are not as they seem is the lack of noise, the forest is silent, too silent; it makes me think there may be a witch with them covering their route of egress.

Keeping my focus forward, remaining shoulder to shoulder with my Queen, my voice comes out quiet, barely disturbing the unnatural silence around us. "Queen Jasmine, they may have a witch covering their escape or hiding where Blaine is recuperating. Is it possible for you to undo any possible magic aiding them?" My Queen's response is a very slight nod of her head.

Not pausing our steps, the Queen's eyes begin to glow blue, the stillness around us begins to lessen, while there are still no sounds of animals there is the sound of wind on the plants and trees, a visible escape route is beginning to show itself, blood is tinging the air with its metallic scent, the iron heavy in my nose. We were on the correct path, without realizing it the entire time, but now there is no way for them to evade us.

Cautiously entering a denser part of the woods there is a sound of movement above me, pushing the Queen to the side, a wolf drops between us, swinging his claws into plain air, where Queen Jasmine had been. My body reacts on muscle memory and the wolf is decapitated as others begin to drop from the trees and emerge from in front of us, the darkness of the forest assisting them in hiding, but they are not all wolves, this confirms our thoughts.

In the close quarters our Queen shifts into her wolf form, choosing handto-hand combat over magic. Ashley's wolf lets out a purr at the excitement of putting down the enemy, the warriors with us all engage the threat. In this battle arena there is no way to form a tight circle to secure our backs. We will need to remain vigilant. As this thought crosses my mind, a weight drops to my shoulders. They did not all make their appearance from above at the same time, they have staggered their drops. Pulling a dagger from my thigh holster I swing my arm backward, driving my knife into what feels like an eye socket. The wolf on me screams in pain, pulling backward on my neck, at the same time a rush of wind is felt in front of me, red appears on my chest. Claws that would have originally cut my throat slice through my chest superficially thanks to my backward movement caused by the dying wolf still attached to me. Off to my right stands a livid vampire, ready to engage and finish what he started. As he barrels towards me, I flip the wolf over my shoulder onto the vampire. The vamp's claws lodge into the skull of the wolf. While the vamp is

distracted, I pull my sword, decapitating the vampire, ending both threats.

Some minutes later the group has been taken down and to our great disappointment, Blaine is nowhere to be found. We must continue his trail, we do not know how many more soldiers he has with him, and his progression is taking him towards pack lands. The concern on Queen Jasmine's face is easy to read. We continue to proceed forward, two men down after this altercation. I make a silent promise to them, to all those who have passed, their sacrifice will not have been in vain.

Nearing the edge of forest, sounds of an alternate battle fill our ears, sounds coming from Whispering Red Winds lands. Our steps quicken as we remain vigilant, we must assist those warriors left behind. We form a tight circle as we move into the open grounds, not allowing for any unseen attacks. We are nearing the pack school when a cry carries across the air.

Stopping instantly at the sound, my blood runs cold, fear grips my heart while its beat quickens, anger surges through my system. That is the cry of my mother letting others know she is injured. My vision begins to tunnel down and it becomes imperative I reach her side. A gentle hands lands on my shoulder offering comfort and support. My eyes find those of my Queen, she recognized the cry to be that of a thunderbird, she nods her head in the direction it came from and as a group, we move to find my mother.

Chapter 110:

Fighting on the Homefront

(Jasmine's POV)

This war has been waging for hours. When we were in the woods searching for Blaine the darkness upon us was due to the cover of the trees, as we emerged from the forest a blue-tinted sky met us, darkness descending to all corners of my land. This day is ending, while blood is still being spilled, we continue to search for those who desire to bring pain to my most vulnerable. These cowards have threatened our present and now they want to take our future and history; they attacked those who cannot defend themselves and injured our elders.

We continue to proceed in the direction we heard the cry come from, Nóox leading the way. Thankfully darkness is not a hinderance for us in this group, we are able to see around us, there are still shadows, but at least complete inky darkness is avoided. My mind wanders to how those on the battlefield under Zeke are doing with the change of day. My faith in him is strong and there is no doubt he will stand tall, holding our grounds.

My stomach roils, nausea threatens to turn into something more tangible, the fear of what I may find on my home grounds floods my mind, causing my shoulders to tense more, my heartrate to increase and sweat break out on my palms, forehead, and trickle down my back. Taking in a deep breath, I do my best to reset my mind, now is not the time for these thoughts. There are threats ahead of us, it is imperative I remain calm to protect my people.

There are sounds of flight above us, there should not have been any thunderbirds in this area, except the few left with Tiiyú, the lightning hitting the ground confirms the presence of thunderbirds here, though. What would have brought them out of their hiding spots? As the thought crosses my mind a familiar nauseating scent of pure evil reaches my nose. That is the only answer I need to know what is occurring on my grounds, my heart breaks for all the people left here thinking they were safe.

Through the shadows we see figures engaged in fighting, the scent of my warriors comes to me, it is difficult to make out what is beyond them, but they need assistance. Sending my ten warriors to aide them, Nóox, Ashley and I continue our route, as we proceed, I send a mindlink to Zeke. "The pack grounds are under attack. It is unclear how many aggressors are in the area, there is a small contingency of thunderbirds and wolves, we do not know how many injured. If it can be spared send additional aide."

"Yes, Alpha." Nothing else follows. Zeke will make sure to conduct my request, our homelands are not more important than the greater movement; he will send assistance when able.

The three of us skirt the outer edge of the school and orphanage, which is on fire, hopefully they were able to escape through the tunnel system put in place. Beyond the school is a patch of wooded land, then behind the woods is more open field, it is a patchwork of wooded area and open field in this section. Moving forward toward a wooded area we come up to a large mass undiscernible to the eye from this distance without light. Unable to identify what is before us, I put up a shield as we cautiously approach.

Moving forward the image becomes clearer, the mass is two bodies, one protectively covering the other, beyond them floating in the air is three witches, all with energy balls ready to be cast. Under them slowly approaching the bodies, lips pulled back over fangs are seven of the beasts, stepping on bodies littering the ground around them, foes, and allies alike, turning them to ash with the pierce of a claw; off to the side stands Scion, cold smirk gracing his features. None of them have noticed our approach yet.

"Scion is here," I send out through mind-link while there is time.

Dropping the shield, Nóox takes to the sky, instantly raining down lightning, creating a barrier between the beasts and the people huddled together. Forming my own energy balls, I rapid fire them at the witches causing them to lose concentration and drop their own, Ashley rushes forward and pulls one down by the ankle; using her large paws she secures the witch to the ground, while taking minor injuries, and rips her head from her body, once completed Ash turns to find her next victim.

I have one of the witches caught in a tangle of tree roots, she burns away the roots and frees herself, sending lines of electricity my way. Dodging to the side, my hands up in the air, a strong hurricane force wind blows through, sending the remaining two witches into the trees hard. There is the sound of snapping upon their impact, it is unclear if it is their bones or the trees. Looking around Scion is no longer around, he no doubt escaped at the first sign of danger. The beasts in the area have been taken care of thanks to team effort.

Nóox is on his knees beside the bodies, the soft sound of his voice carries to my ears, but the words are not understood. Ashley and I approach, taking in the scene before us. Tears stream down the strong thunderbird's face, he has his hands on the shoulders of the top person, gently pulling them into his arms. The body underneath is unmoving, covered in red and black, it appears they have been burnt.

Running to the unattended body I drop to my knees, placing my fingers onto their neck, while lowering my ear to their mouth, hoping for anything, a heartbeat, a breath, any sign of life. Tears begin to sting my eyes as I feel nothing, as the coldness of their form registers in my brain. Focusing now on who this lost soul is my breath is taken from me. Before me on the ground lies Miles' youngest brother, he just completed his warrior training a few weeks ago at 17. He was left back to defend the home front, not thinking the fighting would make it this far, that if needed they would evacuate the children to a safe place and remain with them. A single tear trails down my cheek, leaning forward I place a kiss on his forehead, whisper my gratitude in his ear, then close his eyelids. Ashley and Grace appear, whimpering softly and nudge his cheek, then lean forward and lick his jaw. It is their way of saying goodbye, this is the only time I have seen a tear leave the eyes of Grace.

Swallowing my hurt and a bit of my anger, my attention turns to Nóox and the individual he is cradling. Moving closer the recognizable features of

Tiiyú meet my eyes. Her eyelids flutter open and closed, there is a weak, shallow, rapid rise and fall to her chest, on her left side is a soccer ball-sized scorch mark, blood seeping from it, beyond the exposed and torn muscle is the shine of rib bones. A large laceration runs from the corner of her eye to just below her jawline, her jaw is set off to the right, the dislocation painful. Her right leg is bent at a 90-degree angle just below the knee, two bones sticking out from just beneath the skin. There are multiple burn marks and puncture wounds all over her body.

Acting quickly, I conjure sterile water, splints, dressings, and bandages from the hospital, then set about attending to Tiiyú as best as possible, the injuries could take her at any time, as I work her voice comes out soft and desperate, directed to her son.

"Phelekà'n. Háaxna." (I went to war against them. He burned it.) Tears fall from her eyes as she holds onto her son's hand.

"Tiihiliikwá'n saniyá. Eyíthe' tats' ámx. Milíispi'n wikhapayí opiì'thtíil." (I am glad to fight him. I am injured. I love you, my son, and your brothers.) Her voice rasps out, even though I cannot understand their native language, the emotions are truly clear. Tiiyú thinks she is dying and saying her goodbyes. The thought of this brave woman leaving us crushes me. Nóox sends up a mournful cry of his own, a cry I can only imagine is to his family letting them know of the circumstances.

While lost in my thoughts the menacing growl of Grace brings me back to reality. Before her floats the witches, I had cast off, a broken leg or back doesn't matter when you can be mobile without walking. We... I should have ensured they were down, instead of assuming they were. Their black eyes look on, in their hands they hold their choice of destruction. They wanted us to know they were here; they chose not to hit us with a surprise attack. My mind rushes trying to think of a spell to cast off, to immobilize them. The only thing that comes to me is a reverse forcefield, one that will keep any attack they want to throw at us in their bubble. Quickly, I mutter the words under my breath, directing the force where I need it, without moving my hands from Tiiyú, giving Nóox a look. He lowers his body protectively over his mother.

As they throw their orbs in our direction, they bounce off the wall of the shield into their bodies, scorching them where they hit, their cries of pain muffled in the protective barrier surrounding them. Two wolves and a vampire appear from the same direction as the witches, without warning Grace jumps on the closest one, tearing the heart from the chest of the wolf with her maw, while slicing at the throat of the vampire with her claws at the same time, Ashley turns her full attention to the vampire once the wolf is dead and finishes ripping his head from his body. She moves on to the third wolf, stalking him slowly as he retreats, she has no intention of letting him go.

Ashley turns back to us after shredding the last wolf, as her eyes settle on me, she pulls her lips back over her blood-stained teeth and hunkers down into a fighting position, growling and snapping. Confusion rolls over me at this response, it can't be bloodlust, she has been designed, by the Goddess, for this role. While attempting to figure out what is occurring, I feel a blade pierce my back, Ashley launches over me at the same time, taking down the attacker. The blade did not go in far, but it is made of silver, my wolf and I have no protection to silver. The burning starts at my shoulder blades and moves to encompass my entire back and front taking my breath from me.

My body writhes on the ground in pain, Nóox shoots up from where he is with his mother and pulls the blade from my body, then applies pressure against the wound, whispering his apologies to me endlessly. I swat his hands away from me, weakly getting to my feet, the silver making my system lethargic. Turning, Grace is behind me, the body of Blaine in her mouth, whipping her head from side to side beating his body into the ground with each movement of her head. As she sees me approaching, she drops him, tearing out his throat for good measure, then moves towards me, protectively taking her place next to me. I notice there is not a white patch left on Grace, she is completely red, even her mark is covered.

With Blaine dead the last thread of the mate bond left my being. It isn't painful, but a relief, knowing I am now completely free of him. Not letting myself ponder on this for long I turn my attention back to the current situation, viewing the area we see Scion just inside a tree line, watching the action take place.

Grace and I begin to stalk toward him, Nóox taking his place on my other side, our intentions are clear. As we near him there is a loud snap to our side, the witches have broken the shield. They rush to Scion, and I send roots up to stop their forward approach, one witch grasps the others belt and sends down fire, charring the roots while the other continues moving them forward. Despite my attempts to thwart them they reach his side and then disappear right before us. We look around to see if they are going to reappear, but there is no sign of them. They are just gone.

We notice silence in the area. There is no sound of fighting from the other side of the burning schoolhouse, no snarls, and screeches of the beasts. I mindlink the wolves on that side, hoping they are still with us, as we make our way back to Tiiyú. "Do you need assistance? The situation is stable here."

"No, My Queen, the beasts are gone. They just disappeared in the middle of battle, evaporated into thin air" is the stunned reply back.

"Zeke, how is the battle on your end?"

"We were getting to the last of the creatures when they all dematerialized. They just ceased to exist right before us, vanishing into thin air. We have captured the last of the opposing army and are holding them captive" comes his disbelieving reply.

"It appears when Scion left with the remaining witches, the beasts went away too. The pack grounds are on fire, we need to get to the buildings and search for any survivors. Tiiyú is gravely injured, Zeke, send her family over, please."

Falling back to my knees beside Tiiyú, I am amazed to see she is still conscious, this woman has amazing strength and fortitude. While I am using some of my healing energy on her more dire injuries; she extends her fingers towards

Nóox, who instantly wraps them into his, offering what comfort he can to his mother. Slowly she sticks out her tongue to wet her parched lips, then begins in her soft voice.

"Háapxi yap' á tíil yana emètis. Kináx má wìli-kwalá." (The children and people go away from here. They go to your village.)

Nóox looks to me, tears streaming down his eyes. "They evacuated everyone. They are all safe in my village." His voice breaks as he finishes his words.

Tears fall from my eyes knowing our kids, our elders and the others are safe, knowing this woman gave her all to protect them. "Thank you" is a whisper from my lips, as Ashley and I stand watching mother and son. The sound and feel of rushing wind around us announce the arrival of the rest of the family, they all kneel next to one of the bravest women I know.

"Háapxtekh teekwàlthkwiiph. Huulìnthe." (My children, take care of yourselves. I am tired.) With her last word she closes her eyes.

Nóox stands with her in his arms, looking to his brothers. They all share a moment, while he is not the eldest brother, the respect and love amongst them is strong. Nóox then sends a look to Yulúm, who immediately moves to my side.

Without a word the brothers change into their thunderbirds, Nóox climbs onto the eldest's back, another convocation member holding his mother, then handing her to him. Once in place they take to the skies, taking their mother home.

Chapter 111:

Is This Victory

(Jasmine's POV)

With Scion and his beasts vanished, the remaining opposition held captive, and Nóox and his brothers returning home, it is time to begin to tend our wounded, assess the damage and make plans for moving forward. First, it is imperative all the members know the good news; as Ashley, Yulúm and I make our way back to the pack grounds I send out the sweetest update via mindlink possible to the pack.

"We have blessed news this day from Nóox' mother. All pack members were evacuated prior to Scion and his army arriving. There is no recovery mission needed." Pausing a moment to let that sink in I continue. "Let's bring the wounded to pack grounds, we will care for everyone possible." Goosebumps break out across my skin and a shiver of relief runs through my system as the message is sent. Multiple replies of "Bless the Goddess" are heard in response. One small bright spot in hours of darkness.

As dawn begins to lighten our world we break through the last bit of woods, the charred schoolhouse in site, smoke mingles with early morning fog giving an ethereal appearance, even with the play of shadow and light there is something odd about it. With the fire that was raging when we first arrived, I would have thought the entire building would be embers and ash by now.

There are entire parts of the building not touched by the flames, pristine and intact. The entire housing section of the building is standing, and all the children's last mementos of their families are saved.

Continuing into the pack ground we see multiple buildings in the same state as the schoolhouse. The hospital is in shambles, but the emergency room and its supply areas are still operational, the records room is left without a mark; other members have linked in stating the same is true with the packhouse and other buildings. Hopefully, some of those evacuated will be arriving back soon, people who will be able to account for the odd happenings occurring here.

There isn't long for my mind to wander, thunderbirds begin setting down, injured warriors on their backs with escorts. It dawns on me like a ton of bricks, there are no doctors or nurses here; they were evacuated along with the other members; I have intermediate training from when medicine was my passion and goal in life, looks like it is up to me. There is no time to lose, we want to be able to save as many as possible. Quickly members in the area organize and begin offloading the injured and bringing them towards the emergency room. The thunderbirds take back to the skies to bring more home.

Directing the members where to place the injured, I form a small team to begin bringing supplies, Ashley begins to run triage, sorting the injured into specific sections based on their injuries, while Yulúm refuses to leave my side, but does assist me in treating the patients.

My first patient is a young Fae, scanning his body quickly in a rapid assessment, his left shoulder is sitting forward of his other, blood saturates the material of his uniform on his right leg, there is a jagged tear in the pants and pearl colored osseous matter protruding out. His moans of pain let me know he is not completely unconscious, but his pain is sending him closer to a black void the longer we take in treating him.

Using a makeshift weight assemblage, I reset his dislocated shoulder ensuring to stabilize it so there is decreased movement to help lessen the pain, then clean, dress, splint and bandage the open fracture to his leg. Using some of my healing powers, I do my best to ensure he will not get an infection from being exposed to bacteria with the break in skin.

All my lessons on sterile procedure have been downgraded to as clean of a technique as possible. We are truly in a combat field hospital setting and the patients outnumber the provider hundreds to one. Time is lost to me, as soon as I finish with one patient another is brought directly on their heels, there is no break, even though fatigue is letting itself known in my body I am unable to stop, I owe them this small sacrifice. I cannot fail those who are hoping their time does not come before it is their turn after all they have given.

Outside of my work area a commotion briefly catches my attention. "What is happening out there? Are Scion and the beasts back?" It is all I can link out before the emergency room doors push open and our pack doctors, nurses and technicians begin to file in, supplemented by thunderbird providers. They have brought extra supplies with them, which we have become in dire need of.

"Let me take over for you" comes a voice from behind my right side as gentle hands grasp my shoulders. Turning quickly, Michael, our lead doctor, is behind me. "You have done an amazing job caring for everyone, we are here now, go rest." His voice and eyes hold compassion and pride as he addresses me. Michael is the one I trained under from a young age, he is a mentor and role model to me, hearing his praise brings me some pleasure when I have begun to feel as if I am drowning.

Stepping back from the wound I am in the middle of cleaning Michael takes over and throws a smile my way before turning back to the patient. I have been silently but gently dismissed from the setting, relief briefly floods my system, then my body tenses back up as my mind turns to those still needing attention, our minimally or non-injured warriors and our deceased. Yulúm and I make our way to a makeshift wash station to clean our hands, Ashley appears next to me, fatigue evident in her posture. Looking over to her as I scrub residual blood from my forearms, concern sprouts in my mind.

"You look exhausted, Ash, why don't you go rest for a bit. Things are under control here."

Ashley stands, scrubbing her hands, pondering what I have said for a moment. "What will you be doing while I am resting, Jazz? If I know you, you are going to finish a walkthrough of the grounds then head to the battlefield or vice versa, who really knows the order. The point is, you are not going to be going to rest and if you are not resting than neither am I," she finishes, grabbing disposable paper towels to dry the wetness from her hands.

Stubbornness is shining brightly from her eyes directly into mine, I learned a long time ago not to argue with her when she is in this mood, especially since she is now under direct orders from the Moon Goddess to be my protector.

Giving Ash a halfhearted smile, tossing my used towel into the trash bin, I turn my tired gaze to the ground and turn towards the rest of the pack grounds, work needs to be done, our people need a place to sleep and food to eat. During my time in the emergency room, I was left out of mind-links on how those problems were being solved, so now it is time to catch up and secure necessities for those returning from battle.

"Can someone update me on where we are with lodging and food for everyone, please?" My mind-link goes out to everyone, excluding the medical staff.

"Alpha, this is Vivian, we are setting most people up in the old Red Crescent buildings, they are all intact. Scion and his army did not make it that far into the lands, it appears they started at the packhouse and worked their way north, getting stopped at the schoolhouse, everything beyond the schoolhouse is untouched, our main garden, the animals, orchards, secondary hospital, lodging and kitchen. We have gone through the bunkers to get additional resources, they all held up even under the flames."

Vivian works under our lead house steward but is also trained for combat, thank goodness we have someone with her skillsets here with us now to organize this mess and care for everyone, she is a highly capable she-wolf.

"Very good, great job, everyone. It sounds like you have everything under control, Vivian, you will remain point on this task. If there is anything you need, please let me know directly."

"Yes, Alpha."

"Claire and Miles, I need an update on what we are doing to locate Scion and his remaining witches. We must find Scion; he is our biggest threat and he managed to escape at the last moment. There is no doubt in my mind he will reappear and wreak havoc again, he must be dealt with, as quickly as possible."

"Alpha," Claire's voice comes through, "we are putting together a scouting team, we plan for it to be a long-term operation. Angie has volunteered to run the op; she has chosen a mixed team. Two of our trackers, two warriors, three witches with different skills and a Fae, who can help bind a dark witch. They are setting out immediately." Claire pauses for a moment. "The cells remained intact, the entry building has minimal damage, once the prisoners are in their cells and Meredith has charmed them so no one can escape we will begin interrogations."

"Perfect planning, Claire. I will leave these matters under your direction."

All members have done all essential tasks, while I have been treating our injured, the pride I feel for them floods my entire system, but the sobering thought of our deceased makes its way back into my mind.

"Zeke, Yulúm, Ashley and I are making our way to the battlefield, meet me where we first broke through the tree line. We need to account for every soul lost here."

"Yes, Alpha. We have begun the task of identifying those we can. There is a member of each detachment here to assist in this process...there are going to be those we cannot find. " Zeke's voice fades out, the sorrow evident.

"I understand, Zeke, we will be there shortly." Turning to my two companions, tears stinging my eyes, I take in a deep breath. "Yulúm, do you mind shifting and giving Ash and me a ride to the battlefield? I would like to do a flyover prior to a walkthrough. I need to see the entire area before walking it."

"It would be my honor to assist you, My Queen."

Yulúm changes into his massive thunderbird in a matter of seconds, his red and orange feathers catch the morning sun, appearing to be flames as the light dances over the variation of colors. He lowers to the ground, allowing easier access for Ash and me to climb aboard his back. Once settled he takes to the air with one massive push of his wings.

In no time at all we are above the battlefield. There is limited color now, no more lush green of the grass or the vibrant colors of the meadow flowers, now there is the red of many life sources covering the grounds, broken up by black, brown, and gray charred areas, the trees close to the field are all burned, looking as if they will collapse with a strong wind. Bodies litter the ground as far as the eye can see. Sorrow fills my heart and one question echoes through my mind.

Is this victory?